International acclaim for Laurell K. Hamilton's Meredith Gentry novels:

'Relentless high-paced trashiness . . . good fun'
SFX

'A gloriously erotic, funny and horrific novel . . . but it's probably not one for your granny'
Shivers

'Erotic, magical, violent, sensual and thrilling . . . an extraordinary tale of a Faerie in hiding as a private investigator in LA, and is quite simply delicious'
Bookseller

'An alternative and certainly kinky twist to the traditional whodunnit . . . a fun read'
The Times

'Her sexy, edgy, wickedly ironic style sweeps the reader into her unique world and delivers red-hot entertainment – she blends the genres of romance, horror and adventure with stunning panache'
Jayne Anne Krentz

'Wonderful . . . vastly enjoyable, good fun and highly sensual. It's a fascinating new universe with lots of potential stories waiting to be told'
alienonline

'Every bit as seductive and terrifying as the Vampires of her earlier books . . . the action, violent and sexual, comes fast and furious . . . this series is proof not only of Laurell K. Hamilton's immense storytelling abilities, but also of her continued development of contemporary dark fantasy and horror'
Enigma magazine

'A sizzling new series that blends supernatural fantasy with detective adventure . . . Memorable characters and wicked wit make it all delicious ribald fun'
Publishers Weekly

'Oozing with sensuality . . . steamy sex scenes that are wonderfully touchy-feely'
Starburst

'An edgy story of sex, violence and magic that manages to be both disturbing and entertaining'
Library Journal

'A wonderful excursion into the magic of desire'
Alice Borchardt

'Hamilton takes her world by the teeth and runs with it, devising a whipcrack adventure that moves like the wind, grips you by the throat and doesn't let go'
Locus

'I've never met a writer with a more fertile imagination'
Diana Gabaldon

'Ms Hamilton creates a fantastic, glittering world with complex characters that revel in their non-humanity. Intricate relationships highlight the other-wordly ambience and raise the heat index to high'
Romantic Times

'Infused with Hamilton's characteristic appealing blend of sex, magic, wit, and romantic dilemma'
amazon.com

Also by Laurell K. Hamilton

Narcissus in Chains
Obsidian Butterfly
Blue Moon
Burnt Offerings
The Killing Dance
Bloody Bones
The Lunatic Café
The Laughing Corpse
Circus of the Damned
Guilty Pleasures
Nightseer
A Kiss of Shadows

A CARESS

OF

TWILIGHT

Laurell K. Hamilton

BANTAM BOOKS

LONDON • NEW YORK • TORONTO • SYDNEY • AUCKLAND

A CARESS OF TWILIGHT
A BANTAM BOOK : 0 553 81384 6

First publication in Great Britain

Published by arrangement with The Ballantine Publishing Group,
a division of Random House, Inc.

PRINTING HISTORY
Bantam edition published 2003

1 3 5 7 9 10 8 6 4 2

Set in 11/12pt Times by
Falcon Oast Graphic Art Ltd.

Bantam Books are published by Transworld Publishers,
61–63 Uxbridge Road, London W5 5SA,
a division of The Random House Group Ltd,
in Australia by Random House Australia (Pty) Ltd,
20 Alfred Street, Milsons Point, Sydney, NSW 2061, Australia,
in New Zealand by Random House New Zealand Ltd,
18 Poland Road, Glenfield, Auckland 10, New Zealand
and in South Africa by Random House (Pty) Ltd,
Endulini, 5a Jubilee Road, Parktown 2193, South Africa.

Printed and bound in Great Britain by
Cox & Wyman Ltd, Reading, Berkshire.

This one's for J., who brought me endless cups of chai and, for the first time, watched the process from beginning to end. He loves me still, and for all of you married to us artistic types, you know just how much that says about both of us.

Acknowledgments

For Shauna Summers, my new editor, thanks for the professionalism. Darla Cook, who helped proof this book when there wasn't time to send it around. To my long-suffering writing group: Tom Drennan, Rhett MacPherson, Deborah Millitello, Marella Sands, Sharon Shinn, and Mark Sumner. Thanks for having patience with me while my world fell apart and remade itself.

A CARESS
OF TWILIGHT

Chapter 1

MOONLIGHT SILVERED THE ROOM, PAINTING THE bed in a hundred shades of grey, white, and black. The two men in the bed were deeply asleep. So deeply that when I'd crawled out from between them, they'd barely stirred. My skin glowed white with the kiss of moonlight. The pure bloodred of my hair looked black. I'd pulled on a silk robe, because it was chilly. People can talk about sunny California, but in the wee hours of the night, when dawn is but a distant dream, it's still chilly. The night that fell like a soft blessing through my window was a December night. If I'd been home in Illinois, there would have been the smell of snow, crisp enough, almost, to melt along the tongue. Cold enough to sear the lungs. So cold it was like breathing icy fire. That was the way air was supposed to taste in early December. The breeze crawling through the window at my back held the dry tang of eucalyptus and the distant smell of the sea. Salt, water, and something else, that indefinable scent that says ocean, not lake, nothing usable, nothing drinkable. You can die of thirst on the shores of an ocean.

For three years I'd stood on the shores of this particular ocean and died a little bit every day. Not literally – I'd have survived – but mere survival can get pretty lonely. I'd been born Princess Meredith NicEssus, a member of the high court of faerie. I was a real-life faerie princess, the only one ever born on American soil. When I vanished from sight about three years ago, the media had gone crazy. Sightings of the missing Elven American Princess had rivaled Elvis sightings. I'd been spotted all around the world. In reality I'd been in Los Angeles the entire time. I'd hidden myself, been just plain Meredith Gentry, Merry to my friends. Just another human with fey ancestry working for the Grey Detective Agency, where we specialized in supernatural problems, magical solutions.

Legend says that a fey exiled from faerie will wither and fade, die. That's both true and untrue. I have enough human blood in my background that being surrounded by metal and technology doesn't bother me. Some of the lesser fey would literally wither and die in a man-made city. But most fey can manage in a city; they may not be happy, but they can survive. But part of them does wither, that part that knows that not all the butterflies you see are actually butterflies. That part that has seen the night sky filled with a rushing of wings like a hurricane wind, wings of flesh and scale to make humans whisper of dragons and demons; that part that has seen the sidhe ride by on horses made of starlight and dreams. That part begins to die.

I hadn't been exiled; I'd fled, because I couldn't survive the assassination attempts. I just didn't have the magic or the political clout to protect myself. I'd saved my life but lost something else. I'd lost the touch of faerie. I'd lost my home.

Now, leaning on my windowsill with the smell of the Pacific Ocean on the air, I looked down at the two men and knew I was home. They were both high-court sidhe, Unseelie sidhe, part of that darkling throng that I might someday rule if I could stay ahead of the assassins. Rhys lay on his stomach, one hand hanging off the bed, the other lost under his pillow. Even in repose that one visible arm was muscled. His hair was a shining fall of white curls caressing his bare shoulders, trailing down the strong line of his back. The right side of his face was pressed to the pillow, and so I couldn't see the scars where his eye had been taken. His cupid-bow mouth was turned upward, half smiling in his sleep. He was boyishly handsome and would be forever.

Nicca lay curled on his side. Awake, his face was handsome, bordering on pretty; asleep, he had the face of an angelic child. Innocent he looked, fragile. Even his body was softer, less muscled. His hands were still rough from sword practice, and there was muscle under the velvet smoothness of his skin, but he was soft compared to the other guards, more courtier than mercenary. The face did, and did not, match the body. He was just over six feet, most of it long, long legs; his slender waist and long, graceful arms balanced all that length. Most of Nicca was shades of brown. His skin was the color of pale milk chocolate, and the hair that fell in a straight fall to his knees was a rich, dark true brown. Not brunette, but the color of fresh turned leaves that had lain a long, long

13

time on the forest floor until when stirred they were a rich, moist brown, something you could plunge your hands into and come away wet and smelling of new life.

In the moonlit dark I couldn't see his back, or even the tops of his shoulders clearly. Most of him was lost under the sheet. It was his back that held the biggest surprise. His father had been something with butterfly wings, something not sidhe but still fey. Genetics had traced his back with wings like a giant tattoo, except more vibrant, more alive than any ink or paint could make it. From his upper shoulders down his back across his buttocks flowing over his thighs to touch the backs of his knees was a play of color: buff brown, yellow tans, circles of blue and pink and black like eyespots on the wings of a moth.

He rested in the dark drained of color so that he and Rhys were like two shadows wrapped in the bed, one pale, one dark, though there were darker things to be had than Nicca, much darker.

The bedroom door opened soundlessly, and as if I'd conjured him by my thoughts, Doyle eased into the room. He shut the door behind him, as soundlessly as he'd opened it. I never understood how he did that. If I'd opened the door, it would have made noise. But when Doyle wanted to, he moved like the fall of night itself, soundless, weightless, undetectable until you realized the light was gone and you were alone in the dark with something you couldn't see. His nickname was the Queen's Darkness, or simply Darkness. The queen would say, 'Where is my Darkness? Bring me my Darkness,' and this meant that soon someone would bleed, or die. But now, strangely, he was *my* Darkness.

Nicca was brown, but Doyle was black. Not the black of human skin, but the complete blackness of a midnight sky. He didn't vanish in the darkened room, because he was darker than the moonlit shadows, a dark shape gliding toward me. His black jeans and black T-shirt fit his body like a second skin. I'd never seen him wear anything that wasn't monochromatic except jewelry and blades. Even his shoulder holster and gun were black.

I pushed away from the window to stand as he moved toward me. He had to stop gliding at the foot of the king-size bed, because there was barely room to squeeze between the bed and the closet doors. It was impressive simply to watch Doyle slide along the wall without brushing the bed. He was over a foot taller than I was and probably outweighed me by a hundred pounds, most of it muscle. I'd have bumped into the bed a half-dozen times, at least. He eased through the narrow space as if anybody should have been able to do it.

The bed took up most of the bedroom, so when Doyle finally reached me, we were forced to stand nearly touching. He managed to keep a fraction of distance so that not even our clothing brushed. It was an artificial distance. It would have been more natural to touch, and the very fact that he worked so hard not to touch me made it the more awkward. It bothered me, but I'd stopped arguing with Doyle about his distance. When questioned, he only said, 'I want to be special to you, not just one of the mob.' At first it had seemed noble; now it was just irritating. The light was stronger here by the window, and I could see some of that delicate curve of his high cheekbones, the too-sharp chin, the curved points to his ears, and the silver gleam of earrings that traced the cartilage all the way to the small hoops in the very pointed tops. Only the pointed ears betrayed that he was a mixed-blood like myself, like Nicca. He could have hidden the ears with all that hair, but he almost never did. His raven black hair was as it usually was, in a tight braid that made his hair look clipped and short from the front, but the braid's tip hung to his ankles.

He whispered, 'I heard something.' His voice was always low and dark like thick candied liqueur for the ear instead of the tongue.

I stared up at him. 'Something, or me moving around?'

His lips gave that twitch that was the closest he usually came to a smile. 'You.'

I shook my head, hands crossed over my stomach. 'I have two guards in bed with me and that's not protection enough?' I whispered back.

'They are good men, but they are not me.'

I frowned at him. 'Are you saying you don't trust anyone but you to keep me safe?' Our voices sounded quiet, peaceful almost, like the voices of parents whispering over sleeping children. It was comforting to know that Doyle was this alert. He was one of the greatest warriors of all the sidhe. It was good to have him on my side.

'Frost. . . perhaps,' he said.

I shook my head; my hair had grown out just enough to tickle the tops of my shoulders. 'The Queen's Ravens are the finest warriors that faerie has to offer, and you say no one is your equal. You arrogant . . .'

He didn't so much step closer – we were standing too close for that – he merely moved, pressing close enough that the hem of my robe brushed his legs. The moonlight glinted off the short necklace he always wore, a tiny jeweled spider hanging from the delicate silver chain. He bent his face down so that his breath pushed against my face. 'I could kill you before either of them knew what had happened.'

The threat sped my pulse faster. I knew he wouldn't harm me. I knew it, and yet . . . and yet. I'd seen Doyle kill with his hands before, empty of weapons, only his strength of flesh and magic. Standing, touching in the intimate darkness, I knew beyond certainty that if he wished me dead, he could do it, and not I or the two sleeping guards behind me would be able to stop him.

I couldn't win a fight, but there were other things to do when pressed together in the dark, things that could distract or disarm as well or better than a blade. I turned minutely toward him so that my face was pressed into the curve of his neck; my lips moved against his skin as I spoke. I felt his pulse speed pressed against my cheek. 'You don't want to hurt me, Doyle.'

His lower lip brushed the curve of my ear, almost but not quite a kiss. 'I could kill all three of you.'

There was a sharp mechanical sound from behind us, the sound of a gun being cocked. It was loud enough in the stillness that I jumped.

'I don't think you could kill all three of us,' Rhys said. His voice was clear, precise, no hint of sleep in it. He was simply awake, pointing a gun at Doyle's back, or at least I assumed that's what he was doing. I couldn't see around the bulk of Doyle's body; and Doyle, as far as I knew, didn't have eyes in the back of his head, so he had to guess what Rhys was doing, too.

'A double-action handgun doesn't need to be cocked to fire, Rhys,' Doyle said, voice calm, even amused. But I couldn't see his face to see if his expression matched his tone; we'd both frozen in our almost embrace.

'I know,' Rhys said, 'a little melodramatic, but you know what they say: One scary sound is worth a thousand threats.'

I spoke, my mouth still touching the warm skin of Doyle's neck. 'They don't say that.' Doyle hadn't moved, and I was afraid to, afraid to set something in motion that I couldn't stop. I didn't want any accidents tonight.

'They should,' Rhys said.

The bed creaked behind us. 'I have a gun pointed at your head, Doyle.' It was Nicca's voice. But not calm, no, a definite thread of anxiety wove his words together. Rhys's voice had held no fear; Nicca's held enough for both of them. But I didn't have to see Nicca to know the gun was trained nice and steady, the finger already on the trigger. After all, Doyle had trained him.

I felt the tension leave Doyle's body, and he raised his face just enough so that he was no longer speaking into my skin. 'Perhaps I couldn't slay you all, but I could kill the princess before you could kill me, and then your lives would mean nothing. The queen would hurt you much more than I ever could for allowing her heir to be slaughtered.'

I could see his face now. Even by moonlight he

18

was relaxed, his eyes distant, not really looking at me anymore. He was too intent on the lesson he was teaching his men, to care about me.

I braced my back against the wall, but he paid no attention to the small movement. I put a hand in the middle of his chest and pushed. It made him stand up straighter, but there really wasn't room for him to go anywhere but on the bed.

'Stop it, all of you,' I said, and I made sure my voice rang in the room. I glared up at Doyle. 'Get away from me.'

He gave a small bow using just his neck for there wasn't room for anything more formal, then he backed up, hands out to his sides to show himself empty-handed to the other guards. He ended between the bed and the wall with no room to maneuver. Rhys was half on his back, gun pointed one-handed as he followed Doyle's movement around the room. Nicca was standing on the far side of the bed, gun held two-handed in a standard shooter's stance. They were still treating Doyle like a threat, and I was tired of it.

'I am tired of these little games, Doyle. Either you trust your men to keep me safe, or you don't. If you don't, then find other men, or make sure you or Frost are always with me. But stop this.'

'If I had been one of our enemies, your guards would have slept through your death.'

'I was awake,' said Rhys, 'but truthfully I thought you'd finally come to your senses and were going to do her up against the wall.'

Doyle frowned at him. 'You would think something that crude.'

'If you want her, Doyle, then just say so. Tomorrow night can be your turn. I think we'd all step aside for an evening if you'd break your . . . fast.' The moonlight softened Rhys's scars like a white gauzy patch where his right eye should have been.

'Put up your guns,' I said.

They looked at Doyle for confirmation. I shouted at them. 'Put up the guns. I am the princess here, heir to the throne. He's the captain of my guard, and when I tell you to do something, you will, by Goddess, do it.'

They still looked at Doyle. He gave the smallest of nods.

'Get out,' I said. 'All of you, get out.'

Doyle shook his head. 'I don't think that would be wise, Princess.'

Usually I tried to get them all to call me Meredith, but I had invoked my status. I couldn't take it back in the next sentence. 'So my direct orders don't mean anything, is that it?'

Doyle's expression was neutral, careful. Rhys and Nicca had put up their guns, but neither one was meeting my eyes. 'Princess, you must have at least one of us with you at all times. Our enemies are. . . persistent.'

'Prince Cel will be executed if his people try to kill me while he's still being punished for the last time he tried to kill me. We have six months' reprieve.'

Doyle shook his head.

I looked at the three of them, all handsome, even beautiful in their own ways, and suddenly I wanted to be alone. Alone to think, alone to figure out exactly whose orders they were taking, mine or Queen Andais's. I'd thought it was mine, but suddenly I wasn't so sure.

I looked at them, each in turn. Rhys met my gaze, but Nicca still wouldn't. 'You won't take my orders, will you?'

'Our first duty is to keep you safe, Princess, and only second to keep you happy,' Doyle said.

'What do you want from me, Doyle? I've offered you my bed, and you've refused.'

He opened his mouth, started to speak, but I held a hand up. 'No, I don't want to hear any more of your excuses. I believed the one about wanting to be the last of my men, not the first, but if one of the others gets me with child, according to sidhe tradition that person will be my husband. I'll be monogamous after that. You'll have missed your chance to break a thousand years of forced celibacy. You haven't given me a single reason good enough for that kind of risk.' I folded my arms across my stomach, cradling my breasts. 'Speak truth to me, Doyle, or stay out of my bedroom.'

His face was almost neutral, but an edge of anger showed through. 'Fine, you want truth, then look at your window.'

I frowned at him, but turned to look at the window with its gauzy white drapes moving ever so gently in the breeze. I shrugged, arms still held tight. 'So?'

'You are a princess of the sidhe. Look with more than your eyes.'

I took a deep breath, let it out slowly, and tried not to respond to the heat in his words. Getting angry at Doyle never seemed to accomplish anything. I was a princess, but that didn't give me much clout; it never had.

I didn't so much call my magic, as drop the

21

shields I had to put in place so that I wouldn't travel through my day seeing mystical sights. Human psychics and even witches usually have to work at seeing magic, other beings, other realities. I was a part of faerie, and that meant I spent a great deal of energy not seeing magic, not noticing the passing rush of other beings, other realities that had very little to do with my world, my purpose. But magic calls to magic, and without shields in place I could have drowned in the everyday rush of the supernatural that plays over the earth every day.

I dropped the shields and looked with that part of the brain that sees visions and allows you to see dreams. Strangely, it wasn't that big a change in perception, but suddenly I could see better in the dark, and I could see the glowing power of the wards on the window, the walls. And in all that glowing power I saw something through the white drapes. Something small pressed against the window. When I moved the drapes aside, nothing was on the window but the play of pale color from the wards. I looked to one side, using the edge of my sight, my peripheral vision, to look at the glass. There, a small handprint, smaller than the palm of my hand, was etched into the wards on the window. I tried to look closer at it, and it vanished from sight. I forced myself to look sideways at it again, but closer. The handprint was clawed and humanoid, but not human.

I let the drape fall shut, and spoke without turning around. 'Something tried the wards while we slept.'

'Yes,' Doyle said.

'I didn't feel anything,' Rhys said.

Nicca said, 'Me, either.'

Rhys sighed. 'We have failed you, Princess. Doyle's right. We could have gotten you killed.'

I turned and looked at them all, then I stared at Doyle. 'When did you sense the testing of the wards?'

'I came in here to check on you.'

I shook my head. 'No, that's not what I asked. When did you sense that something had tested the wards?'

He faced me, bold. 'I've told you, Princess, only I can keep you safe.'

I shook my head again. 'No good, Doyle. The sidhe never lie, not outright, and you've avoided answering my question twice. Answer me now. For the third time, when did you sense something had tested the wards?'

He looked half-uncomfortable, half-angry. 'When I was whispering in your ear.'

'You saw it through the drapes,' I said.

'Yes.' One clipped, angry word.

Rhys said, 'You didn't know that anything tried to get in. You just came through because you heard Merry moving around.'

Doyle didn't answer, but he didn't need to. The silence was answer enough.

'These wards are my doing, Doyle. I put them up when I moved in to this apartment, and I redo them periodically. It was my magic, my power, that kept this thing out. My power that burned it so that we have its . . . fingerprints.'

'Your wards held because it was a small power,' Doyle said. 'Something large would still get through any ward you could put in place.'

'Maybe, but the point is that you didn't know

any more than we did. You were just as in the dark as we were.'

'You're not infallible,' Rhys said. 'Nice to know.'

'Is it?' Doyle said. 'Is it really? Then think on this – tonight none of us knew that some creature of faerie crept to this window and tried to get in. None of us sensed it. It may have been a small power, but it had big help to hide this completely.'

I stared at him. 'You think Cel's people risked his life tonight, by trying to take mine again.'

'Princess, don't you understand the Unseelie Court by now? Cel was the queen's darling, her only heir for centuries. Once she made you co-heir with him, he fell out of favor. Whichever one of you produces a child first will rule the court, but what happens if both of you die? What happens if you are assassinated by Cel's people and the queen is forced to execute Cel for his treachery? She's suddenly without heir.'

'The queen is immortal,' Rhys said. 'She's agreed to step down only for Merry or Cel.'

'And if someone can plot the death of both Prince Cel and Princess Meredith, do you really think they will stop at the death of a queen?'

We all stared at him. It was Nicca who spoke, voice soft. 'No one would risk the queen's anger.'

'They would if they thought they wouldn't get caught,' Doyle said.

'Who would be that arrogant?' Rhys asked.

Doyle laughed, a surprised bray of sound that startled us all. 'Who would be arrogant enough? Rhys, you are a noble of the sidhe courts. The better question would be who would not be arrogant enough?'

24

'Say what you like, Doyle,' Nicca said, 'most of the nobles fear the queen, fear her greatly, fear her much more than they fear Cel. You have been her champion for eons. You don't know what's it like to be at her mercy.'

'I do,' I said. They all turned to me. 'I agree with Nicca. I don't know anyone but Cel who would risk his mother's anger.'

'We are immortal, Princess. We have the luxury of biding our time. Who knows what tricksy serpent has been waiting centuries until the queen was weak. If she is forced to kill her only son, she will be weak.'

'I'm not immortal, Doyle, so I can't speak for that kind of patience or cunning. All we know for certain is that something tried the wards tonight, and it will bear a burn on its hand, or paw, or whatever, a mark. It can be matched just like fingerprints.'

'I've seen wards set up to harm something that tries to break them, or even mark the intruder with a scar or burn, but I've never seen anyone take imprints before,' Rhys said.

'It was clever,' Doyle said. Which from him was a great compliment.

'Thank you.' I frowned at him. 'If you've never seen anyone do something like this with a ward, how did you know what you were seeing through the drapes?'

'Rhys said that *he* had never seen anything like it. I did not say that.'

'Where else did you see it?'

'I am an assassin, a hunter, Princess. Tracks are a very good thing to have.'

'The print on its hand will match this, but it

won't leave tracks as it travels.'

Doyle gave a small shrug. 'A pity, it would have been useful.'

'You can make a creature of faerie leave magical tracks?' I asked.

'Yes.'

'But they would see them with their own magic and ruin the spell.'

He shrugged. 'I've never found the world big enough to hide quarry that I tracked.'

'You're always so. . . perfect,' I said.

He glanced past me at the window. 'No, my princess, I fear I am not perfect, and our enemies, whoever they may be, know that now.'

The breeze had become a wind, billowing out the white drapes. I could see the small-clawed print frozen in the glittering magic. I was half a continent away from the nearest faerie stronghold. I'd thought L.A. was far enough away to keep us safe, but I guess if someone really wants you dead, they'll catch a plane or something with wings. After years of exile I finally had a little slice of home with me. Home never really changed. It had always been lovely, erotic, and very, very dangerous.

Chapter 2

THE WINDOWS OF MY OFFICE SHOWED A NEARLY faultless sky, like somebody had taken a single blue cornflower petal and stretched it to fill the air above us. It was one of the most perfect skies I'd ever seen over Los Angeles. The buildings of downtown sparkled in the sunlight. Today was one of those rare days that allows people to pretend that L.A. sits in an eternal summer where the sun shines constantly, the water is always blue and warm, and everyone is beautiful and smiling. Truth is that not everyone is beautiful; some people are downright grumpy (L.A. still has one of the highest homicide rates in the country, which is pretty grumpy if you think about it); the ocean is more grey than blue; and the water is always cold. The only people who go into Southern California waters without a wetsuit in December are tourists. We actually do get rain occasionally, and the smog is worse than any cloud cover I've ever seen. In fact, this was the prettiest, most truly summery day I'd seen in over three years. It must happen more often than that for the myth to survive. Or maybe people just need some magical golden place to believe in, and Southern California seems to be that for some people. Easier to get to and less dangerous than faerie, I guess.

I actually hated to waste such a beautiful day inside. I mean, I was a princess; didn't that mean I didn't have to work? Nope. But I was a faerie princess; didn't that mean I could just wish for gold and it would magically appear? I wish. The title, like so many royal titles, came with very little in the way of money, land, or power. If I actually became queen, that would change; until then, I was on my own. Well, not exactly on my own.

Doyle sat in a chair by the windows almost directly behind me, as I sat at my desk. He was dressed as he'd been last night, except he'd added a black leather jacket over the T-shirt and a pair of black wraparound sunglasses. The brilliant sunlight sparkled in all those silver hoops and made the diamond studs in his earlobes positively dance, sending tiny rainbows across my desk. Most bodyguards would have worried more about the door than the windows. We were twenty-three stories up, after all. But the things Doyle guarded me against were as likely to fly as to walk. The creature that had left its tiny pawprint on my window had either crawled like a spider or flown.

I sat at my desk with sunlight pressing warm against my back; a rainbow from Doyle's diamond sat on my clasped hands, bringing out the green in my fingernail polish. The polish matched my jacket and the short skirt that was hidden under the desk. The sunlight and the emerald green cloth brought out the red in my hair so that it looked like spun rubies. The color also brought out the green and gold of my tricolored irises, and I'd chosen eye shadow to bring out more of the green and gold. The lipstick was red. I was all color and joyous light. One of the good things about not having to pretend to be human was I didn't have to hide the hair, the eyes, the luminous skin. I was so tired my eyes burned, and we still had no clue what, or who, had come to my window last night. So I'd dressed up for the office, just a little extra makeup, a little extra sparkle. If I died today, at least I'd look good. I'd also added a small, four-inch knife. It was strapped to my upper thigh so the metal hilt touched my bare skin. Just the touch of steel or iron could make it harder for any fey to do magic against me. After last night Doyle had thought it wise, and I hadn't argued.

I had my legs politely crossed, not because of the client sitting across from me, but because a man was under my desk, hiding in the cave that it made. Well, not man, goblin. His skin was moonlight white, as pale as my own or Rhys's, or Frost's, for that matter. The thick, softly curling black hair cut short was the perfect blackness of Doyle's hair. He was only four feet tall, a perfect male doll, except for the stripe of iridescent scales down his back, and the huge almond-shaped eyes a blue as perfect as the day's sky, but with striped elliptical pupils like a snake's. Inside his perfect cupid-bow mouth were retractable fangs and a long forked tongue that made him lisp unless he concentrated. Kitto wasn't doing well in the big city. He seemed to feel best when he could touch me, huddle at my feet, sit in my lap, curl against me while I slept. He'd been banished from my bedroom last night because Rhys wouldn't tolerate him. Goblins had taken Rhys's eye a few thousand years ago, and he'd never forgiven them for it. Rhys tolerated Kitto outside the bedroom, but that was about all.

Rhys stood in the far corner near the door where Doyle had ordered him to stand. His clothing was almost completely hidden under an expensive white trench coat just like Humphrey Bogart used to wear, except that it was made out of silk and was more for looking at than keeping off the weather. Rhys loved the fact that we were private detectives, and he usually wore either the trench coat or one of his growing collection of fedoras to work. He'd added his daywear eye patch. This one was white to match his clothes and his hair, with a pattern of tiny seed pearls sewn into it.

Kitto smoothed a hand over my hose-clad ankle. He wasn't trying to be overly friendly; he just needed the comfort of touching me. My first client of the day sat across from me, from us. Jeffery Maison was just under six feet tall, broad shouldered, narrow waisted, and designer suited, with blunt-fingered hands manicured and brown hair perfectly coifed. His smile was that bright perfect whiteness that only expensive dental work can create. He was handsome, but in an unremarkable bland sort of way. If he'd paid for surgery, he'd wasted his money, because it was the kind of face you recognized as attractive but you'd never remember it. Two minutes after he walked out the door you'd have a hard time remembering any one feature. If he'd been wearing less-expensive clothing, I'd have said he was a wanna-be actor, but wanna-bes couldn't afford perfectly tailored designer-name suits.

The perfect smile never faltered, but his eyes flicked behind me, and the eyes weren't smiling. The eyes were worried. His gaze kept flicking to Doyle, and it seemed an effort not to look behind him at Rhys. Jeffery Maison was very unhappy about the two guards being in the room. It wasn't just the feeling that most men got around my guards, the feeling that if it came to a fight, they'd lose badly. No, Mr Maison talked about privacy; after all I was a private detective, not a public one. He'd been so unhappy that it was tempting to have Kitto bounce out from beneath the desk and yell 'Boo.' I didn't do it. It wouldn't have been professional. But I amused myself with the thought while I tried to get Jeffery Maison to stop harping on the guards and actually mention something that might be job related.

Only when Doyle had said in his deep rolling voice that it was an interview with either all of us or none of us had Maison gone quiet. Too quiet, he'd sat and smiled but told me nothing.

Oh, he'd talked. 'I've never seen anyone whose true hair color was Sidhe Scarlet. It's like your hair is made of rubies.'

I'd smiled, nodded, tried to get down to business. 'Thank you, Mr Maison, but what brings you to the Grey Detective Agency?'

He opened that perfectly detailed mouth and tried one last time. 'I was instructed to speak with you in private, Ms NicEssus.'

'I prefer Ms Gentry. NicEssus means daughter of Essus. It's more a title than a name.'

The smile was nervous, and the eyes looked self-deprecating, golly shucks ma'am. It had the feel of

31

a look he practiced in the mirror. 'Sorry, I'm not accustomed to dealing with faerie princesses.' He flashed me the full smile, the one that filled his eyes with good, clean humor, and a deeper flash of something else, something I could pursue or ignore. That one look was enough. I was pretty sure how Jeffery was paying for the designer suits.

'Princesses are rather rare these days,' I said, smiling, trying to be pleasant. But truth was, I hadn't gotten much sleep and I was tired. If we could just get Jeffery to go away, maybe we could have a coffee break.

'The green of your jacket brings out the green and gold in your eyes. I've never seen anyone with tricolored irises before,' he said, and the smile warmed.

Rhys laughed from his corner, not even bothering to try to turn it into a cough. Rhys was as versed in surviving at court as I was. 'I've got a tricolored iris, but you haven't told me how pretty I am.' Rhys was right; it was time to stop being polite.

'I didn't know I was supposed to.' He looked confused, a genuine, unpracticed look at last.

I uncrossed my legs and leaned forward, hands clasped on my desk. Kitto's hand slid up my calf, but he stopped at my knee. We'd had a talk about what the limits were if he hid under the desk, and the limits were my knees. Above that line and he had to go home. 'Mr Maison, we've delayed our day and rearranged a number of appointments to accommodate you. We have been polite and professional, and complimenting me on my beauty is neither polite nor professional.'

He looked uncertain, but his eyes were probably

the most sincere they'd been since he stepped through the door. 'I thought it was considered polite to compliment the fey on their appearance. I was told that it was a deadly insult to ignore a fey when they are obviously trying to be attractive.'

I stared at him. He'd finally done something truly interesting. 'Most people don't know that much about fey culture, Mr Maison. How is it that you know?'

'My employer wanted to be sure that I would give no offense. Was I supposed to compliment the men, as well? She didn't tell me I was supposed to do that.'

She. I knew his employer was female. It was the most information I'd gotten from him the entire time he'd been sitting across from me. 'Who is she?' I asked.

He looked at Rhys, at me, eyes flicking to Doyle, and then finally back to me. 'I am under express orders to tell only you, Ms Gentry. I . . . I don't know what to do.'

Well, that was honest. I felt a little sorry for him; Jeffery was obviously not good at thinking on his feet. And that was being charitable.

'Why don't you call your employer,' Doyle said. Jeffery jumped at the sound of that deep, rich voice. I didn't jump; I shivered. His voice was tremblingly low, a sound that made my insides quiver. I let out a low breath, as Doyle said, 'Tell your employer what's happened, and maybe she can come up with a solution.'

Rhys laughed again. Doyle gave him a less-than-friendly look, and Rhys stopped laughing, though he had to cover his face with his hand and cough. I didn't care. I had the feeling that if we made fun of Jeffery, we'd be here all damn day.

I turned the desk phone around to face him. I pressed the code to get him an outside line and handed the buzzing receiver to him. 'Call your boss, Jeffery. We all want to get on with our day, right?' I'd used his first name deliberately. Some people respond to the respect of titles, Mr and Ms, but some people need bullying to get them moving, and one way to bully is to use their first name.

He took the receiver and punched buttons. He said, 'Hi, Marie, yes, I need to talk to her.' A few seconds of silence, then he sat a little straighter, and said, 'I'm sitting across from her right now. She has two bodyguards with her, and they refuse to leave. Do I talk in front of them or just leave?'

We all waited as he made small *hmm* noises, *yes*, *no*; finally he hung the phone back up. He sat back in his chair, hands folded in his lap, a slightly worried look on his handsome face. 'My employer says I may tell you her request but not her name, not yet anyway.'

I raised eyebrows and made a helpful face. 'Tell us.'

He gave one last nervous glance at Doyle, then let out a long breath. 'My employer is in a rather delicate situation. She wishes to talk with you but says that your . . .' He frowned, groping for an appropriate word. It looked like it might take a while so I helped him.

'My guards.'

He smiled, obviously relieved. 'Yes, yes, your guards would have to know sooner or later, so sooner it is.' He seemed inordinately pleased with

34

himself for that one small sentence. No, thinking wasn't Jeffery's forte.

'Why doesn't she just come into the office and speak with us?'

The happy smile faded, and he looked perplexed again. Puzzling Jeffery slowed things down; I wanted to speed things up. The trouble was, he was so easily puzzled, I couldn't figure out how to avoid it.

'My employer is afraid of the publicity surrounding you, Ms Gentry.'

I didn't have to ask him what he meant. At that very moment a pack of reporters, both print and film, was camped out in front of the office building. We kept the drapes closed at the apartment for fear of telephoto lenses.

How could the media resist a royal prodigal daughter coming home after being given up for dead? That alone would have earned some uncomfortable scrutiny, but add a huge dose of romance, and the media couldn't get enough of me, or should I say, us? The public story was I'd come out of hiding to find a husband among the royal court. The traditional way for a royal of the high court to find a spouse was to sleep with them. Then if she became pregnant, she married; if not, she didn't. The fey don't have many children; the royals have even fewer, so a pairing, even a love match, that doesn't produce children isn't good enough. If you don't breed, you don't get to marry.

Andais had ruled the Unseelie Court for over a thousand years. My father had once said that being queen meant more to her than anything else in the world. Yet, she'd promised to step down if either Cel or I would just produce an heir. Like I said, children are very important to the sidhe.

That was the public story. It hid a lot, like the fact that Cel had tried to kill me and was even now being punished for it. There was lots the media didn't know, and the queen wanted it kept that way, so we kept it that way.

My aunt told me that she wanted an heir of her own bloodline, even if that blood was tainted like mine. She once tried to drown me as a child because I wasn't magic enough and thus, to her, I wasn't really sidhe, though I wasn't really human either. It was good to keep my aunt happy; her happy meant fewer people died.

'I can understand your employer not wanting to get caught up in the media circus outside,' I said.

Jeffery gave me that brilliant smile again, but his eyes were relieved not lustful. 'Then you'll agree to meet with my employer someplace more private.'

'The princess will not meet your employer alone anywhere,' Doyle said.

Jeffery shook his head. 'No, I understand that now. My employer simply wants to avoid the media.'

'Short of using spells that are illegal against the media,' I said, 'I don't see how we could possibly avoid them all.'

Jeffery was back to frowning again. I sighed. I just wanted Jeffery to go away at this point. Surely the next client of the day would be less confusing, Goddess willing. My boss Jeremy Grey had a non-refundable retainer. We had more business than we knew what to do with. Maybe I could just tell Jeffery Maison to go home.

'I'm not allowed to say my employer's name out loud. She said that would mean something to you.'

I shrugged. 'I'm sorry, Mr Maison, but it doesn't.'

His frown deepened. 'She was very sure that it would.'

I shook my head. 'I am sorry, Mr Maison.' I stood up. Kitto's hand slid down my leg so that he could hide himself completely in the little cave that my desk made. He didn't melt in sunlight, contrary to folklore, but he was agoraphobic.

'Please,' Jeffrey said. 'Please, I'm sure it's because I'm not saying it right.'

I crossed my arms under my breasts and did not sit back down. 'I'm sorry, Mr Maison, but we've all had a long morning, too long a morning to play twenty questions. Either tell us something concrete about your employer's problem, or find another private detective firm.'

He put his hand out, almost touching the desk, then let his hand fall back to his well-tailored lap. 'My employer wishes to see people of her own kind again.' He stared at me as if willing me to finally catch on.

I frowned at him. 'What do you mean, people of her own kind?'

He frowned, clearly out of his depth, but doggedly trying. 'My employer isn't human, Ms Gentry, she's . . . very aware of what high-court fey are capable of.' His voice was hushed but sort of pleading, as if he'd given me the biggest hint he was allowed to give me, and he hoped I'd figure it out.

Fortunately, or unfortunately, I had figured it out. There were other fey in Los Angeles, but other than myself and my guards, there was only one high royal – Maeve Reed, the golden goddess of Hollywood. She'd been the golden goddess of Hollywood for fifty years now, and since she was immortal and would never age, she might be the golden goddess of Hollywood a hundred years from now.

Once upon a time she'd been the goddess Conchenn, until King Taranis, the King of Light and Illusion, had exiled her from the Seelie Court, exiled her from faerie, and forbidden any other fey to speak with her ever again. She was to be shunned, treated as if she had died. King Taranis was my great-uncle, and technically I was fifth in line to his throne. In reality I wasn't welcome among the glittering throng. They'd made it clear at an early age that my pedigree was a little less than ideal and that no amount of royal Seelie blood could overcome being half Unseelie.

So be it. I had a court to call home now. I didn't need them anymore. There'd been a time when I was younger that it had meant something to me, but I'd had to put away that particular pain years ago. My mother was a part of the Seelie Court, and she had abandoned me to the Unseelie to further her own political ambitions. I had no mother.

Don't misunderstand, Queen Andais didn't like me much either. Even now, I wasn't completely sure why she'd chosen me as heir. Perhaps she was just running out of blood relatives. That tends to happen if enough of them die.

I opened my mouth to say Maeve Reed's name, but stopped myself. My aunt was the Queen of Air and Darkness; anything said in the dark would eventually travel back to her. I didn't think King Taranis had an equivalent power, but I wasn't 100 percent sure. Caution was better. The queen didn't care about Maeve Reed, but she did care about having things to negotiate with, or hold against, King Taranis. No one knew why Maeve had been exiled, but Taranis had taken it personally. It might be worth something to him to know that Maeve had done the forbidden. She'd contacted a member of the courts. There's an unspoken rule that if one court banishes someone from faerie, the other court respects the punishment. I should have sent Jeffery Maison running back to Maeve Reed. I should have said no. But I didn't. Once, when I was young, I asked one of the royals about Conchenn's fate. Taranis overheard. He beat me nearly to death; beat me the way you'd strike a dog that got in your way. And that beautiful, glittering throng had all stood and watched him do it, and no one, not even my mother, had tried to help me. I agreed to meet with Maeve Reed later that day because for the first time I had enough clout to defy Taranis. To harm me now would mean war between the courts. Taranis might be an ego-maniac, but even his pride wasn't worth all-out war.

Of course, knowing my aunt, it might not be war, at first. I was under the queen's protection, which meant that anyone who harmed me had to answer to her personally. Taranis might prefer a war to the queen's personal vengeance. After all, he'd be a king in the war, and kings rarely see frontline action. If he pissed off Queen Andais enough, Taranis would be the front line all by his little lonesome. I was trying to stay alive, and they don't say knowledge is power for nothing.

Chapter 3

WHEN THE DOOR CLOSED BEHIND JEFFERY MAISON, I expected the two guards to argue with me. I was half-right.

'Far be it from me to question the princess,' Rhys said, 'but what if the king objects to you breaking Maeve Reed's exile?'

I winced at the mention of the name out loud. 'Does the king have the ability to hear everything said in daylight, the way the queen hears after dark?'

Rhys looked puzzled at me. 'I don't . . . know.'

'Then let's not help him find out what we're doing by saying her name out loud.'

'I have never heard that Taranis has such a power,' Doyle said.

I turned in my chair to stare at him. 'Well, let's hope not when you've just said his name out loud.'

'I have plotted against the King of Light and Illusion for millennia, Princess, and much of that plotting was done in broad daylight. Many of our human allies over the centuries have flatly refused to meet with the Unseelie after dark. They seemed to think that agreeing to meet during the day was a sign we trusted them, and that they could trust us. Taranis never seemed to know what we were doing, day or night,' Doyle said, head to one side, sending rainbows dancing through the room from the diamonds in his ears. 'I believe that he does not have our queen's gift. Andais may hear everything spoken in the dark, but I believe that the king is as deaf as any human.'

Anyone else I would have asked if he was sure, but Doyle never spoke unless he was certain. If he didn't know something, he'd say so. There was no false pride in him.

'So the king can't hear us talking thousands of miles away,' Rhys said. 'Fine, but please tell Merry what a bad idea this is.'

'What is a bad idea?' Doyle asked.

'Helping Maeve—' Rhys glanced at me, then finished with, 'the actress.'

Doyle frowned. 'I don't remember anyone by that name ever being exiled from either court.'

I turned around in my chair and stared at him. His face was dark and unreadable against the bright sunlight. The glasses hid a great deal of his expression, but I was betting, glasses or no, he would have looked puzzled.

I heard Rhys's silk coat whispering as he walked across the floor toward us. I glanced at him. He raised his eyebrows at me. We both looked at Doyle.

'You don't know who she is, do you?' I asked.

'The name you mentioned, Maeve something – should I recognize it?'

'She's been the reigning queen of Hollywood for over fifty years,' Rhys said.

Doyle just looked at us. 'People from this Hollywood have approached the queen and the court over the years to come and make movies, or allow them to film movies of their lives.'

'Have you ever actually seen a movie?' I asked.

'I have seen movies at your apartment,' he said.

I glanced at Rhys. 'We have got to get all of them out to a movie.'

Rhys half leaned, half sat on my desk. 'We could all use a night out.'

Kitto plucked at the hem of my short skirt, and I moved my chair so I could look down into his face. A bar of sunlight fell full across his face. For a second the light filled his almond-shaped eyes, turning the solid sapphire blue orbs paler as if they were water and I could see down, down into the sparkling blue depths to a place where white light danced. Then he closed his eyes, wincing against the brightness. He buried his face against my thigh, one small hand wrapped around my calf. He spoke without looking up. 'I don't want to sss-ee a movie.' He was slurring his Ss badly, which meant he was upset. Kitto worked very hard to talk normally. When you have a forked tongue, that's not easy.

I touched his head; his black curls were so soft, soft the way that a sidhe's hair is soft, not the roughness of goblin hair. 'It's dark in the theater,' I said, stroking his hair. 'You could curl up on the floor beside me and never look at the screen.'

He rubbed his head against my thigh like some giant cat. 'Truly?' he asked.

'Truly,' I said.

'You'll like it,' Rhys said. 'It's dark and

sometimes the floor is so dirty that it sticks to your feet when you walk on it.'

'I'll get my clothessss dirty,' Kitto said.

'I wouldn't think a goblin would worry about staying clean. The goblin mound is full of bones and rotting meat.'

'He's only half goblin, Rhys,' I said.

'Yeah, his father raped one of our women.' He was staring down at Kitto, though all he could have seen was perhaps a pale hand or arm.

'His mother was Seelie, not Unseelie,' I said.

'What does it matter? His father forced himself on a sidhe woman.' His voice held heat enough to scald.

'And how many of our sidhe warriors took their pleasure on unwilling women, even goblins, during the wars?' Doyle asked.

I glanced at Doyle and could see nothing through the dark glasses. I looked quickly at Rhys and saw a pale blush chase up his cheeks. He glared at Doyle. 'I have never touched a woman who did not invite my attentions.'

'Of course not, you are a member of the Queen's Guard, her Ravens, and it is death by torture for one of her Ravens to touch any woman except for the queen herself. But what of the warriors who are not members of the personal guards?'

Rhys looked away, his blush darkening to a bright, deep red.

'Yes, look away, as we've all had to look away over the centuries,' Doyle said.

Rhys's neck turned slowly, as if every muscle had gone suddenly tight with anger. Last night he'd had a gun in his hands and he hadn't been frightening. Now, just sitting on the edge of my desk, he was frightening.

He did nothing; even his hands were loose in his lap, just that terrible tension in his back, the set of his shoulders, the way he held himself as if he were a blink away from some terrible physical action – something that would rip the room apart and paint the sparkling glass with blood and thicker things. Rhys had done nothing, nothing, yet violence rode the air like a kiss just above the skin, something to make you shiver with anticipation, even though nothing had happened. Not yet, not yet.

I wanted to look behind me at Doyle, but I couldn't turn away from Rhys. It was as if only my gaze kept him in check. I knew that wasn't true, but I felt that if I looked away, even for a moment, something very, very bad would happen.

Kitto was pressed so close to my legs that I could feel a fine trembling all along his body. My hand was still on his curls, but I don't think it was a comforting touch anymore, because I could feel the tension in my arm, my hand.

Rhys's face turned milky as if something white and luminous moved under his skin, like soft, glowing clouds – moved not across his face but underneath the skin of his face. The brilliant corn-flower blue around his pupil glowed like neon; the sky blue that circled it was a match for the sunny sky outside; and the last circle of winter sky shimmered like blue heat. The eye only glowed. The colors didn't swirl, and I knew they could. His hair was still just white curls; the glow hadn't spread to them. I'd seen Rhys when his power was full upon him, and this wasn't one of those times,

45

but it was close, too close for the bright office and the man behind me.

I both wanted to turn and see Doyle's face, and didn't. I really didn't want a full-out duel here and now, especially over something this stupid. 'Rhys,' I said softly. He didn't look at me. That one glowing orb was set on the man behind me, as if nothing else existed.

'Rhys!' I said again, voice more urgent.

He blinked, looked down at me. Having the full weight of all that anger directed at me made me scoot the chair back. The moment I realized what I'd done, I stopped myself. I couldn't take the movement back, but I could pretend I'd meant to do it. I stood up, and that was my biggest mistake. Standing up made Kitto scoot out from under the desk, trying to keep himself huddled around my legs. The moment the little goblin was visible, Rhys's angry gaze dropped down to that pale figure, dropped down and hardened.

Kitto seemed to feel that gaze, because he wrapped his arms around my legs so tightly that I almost fell. I had to recover my balance, a hand on the desktop, and Rhys threw himself across the desk, glowing hands scrambling for Kitto. I felt Doyle stand behind me, but there was no time. I'd seen Rhys kill with a touch. I grabbed the front and back of his coat and used his own momentum to slide him off the desk and into the wall past Doyle's legs. The wall shuddered with the impact, and I had a second to wonder what would have happened if he'd hit the windows instead. I saw from the corner of my eye that Doyle's gun was out, but I was still moving, still carried along on my own momentum.

I drew the knife at my thigh, and as Rhys came up on his hands and knees, shaking his head, I pressed the tip of the blade against the side of his neck. It would have been better if I could have pinned him, or done anything to make sure he couldn't simply turn and take my legs out from under me, but it was the best I could do in the time I had. I knew how quickly the guards recovered, and I'd had only seconds to do anything.

Rhys froze, head down, breathing ragged. I could feel the line of his body tense against my legs. I was too close, *so* too close, but the blade was firm against the side of his neck. I could feel the skin give a little under the blade tip and knew I'd bloodied him. I hadn't meant to; I was just too rushed to be careful. But he didn't know it was an accident, and nothing convinces people you mean business like their own blood.

'I'd hoped you would grow more tolerant of Kitto as time ran on, but you seem to be getting worse.' My voice was soft, almost a whisper, each word spoken very carefully, as though I didn't trust what I might do if I yelled. In truth I could barely speak past the pulse in my throat.

Rhys shifted his head, and I kept the point where it was, letting him put a little more flesh on the blade. If he thought I'd move back, he was wrong. He stopped moving. 'Understand this, Rhys, Kitto is mine, as you are all mine. I won't let your prejudices endanger him.'

His voice squeezed out, as if he was finally aware that I might use the blade as it was meant to be used. 'You'd kill me over a goblin.'

'I'd kill you for harming what is mine to protect. By attacking him like this, you've shown

47

me no respect, none. Last night Doyle showed me no respect. If I've learned anything from my aunt and my father, it's that a leader who is not respected by her people is just a figurehead. I will not be something you fuck and cuddle. I will be queen or I will be nothing to you.' My voice had dropped down even lower, so that the last words were said in a hoarse whisper. And I knew in that moment that I meant it, that if spilling Rhys's blood would gain me the power I needed, I'd kill him. I'd known Rhys my entire life. He was my lover, and on some level, my friend. Yet I could kill him. I'd miss him, and I'd regret the necessity of having to do it, but I knew now that I had to make the guards respect me. I lusted after the guards; I liked the ones I was sleeping with; I even half loved one or two, but there were precious few I'd want to see on the throne. Absolute power, true life and death – who would you trust with that kind of power? Which of the guards was incorruptible? Answer, none. Everyone has their blind spots, the place where they are so sure of themselves that they see only their own rightness. I trusted myself, yet there were days when I doubted me. I was hoping that doubt would keep me honest. Maybe I was fooling myself. Maybe no one can be given that kind of power and stay fair and just. Maybe that old saying is true; power corrupts and absolute power corrupts absolutely. I'd do my best, but I knew one thing for certain: if I didn't get a handle on the situation now, the guards would ride over me. I might gain the throne, but I'd lose everything else. I didn't even really want the throne; but I wanted to rule, to rule and try to make things better. And, of course, that very desire was probably my blind spot, and the beginnings of corruption. To think I knew what would be better for all the Unseelie. How terribly arrogant.

I started to laugh. I laughed so hard, I had to sit down on the floor. I held the bloody knife and watched the two guards gaze down at me, worried looks on their faces. Rhys wasn't glowing anymore. Kitto touched my arm, gently, as if afraid of what I'd do. I wrapped my arms around him, hugged him to me, and the tears streaming down my face stopped behind laughter, and I simply cried. I held Kitto and the bloody knife and cried.

I was no better than the others. Power corrupts – of course it does. That's what it's for. I huddled on the floor and let Kitto rock me, and I didn't fight when Doyle took the knife, very gently, from my hand.

Chapter 4

I ENDED UP HUDDLED IN ONE OF MY OWN CLIENT chairs with a mug of hot mint tea and my boss, Jeremy Grey. I don't know what had alerted him to the trouble, but he'd come through the door like a small, neat storm. He'd ordered everyone out, and Doyle, of course, had argued that Jeremy couldn't guarantee my safety. Jeremy had countered with, 'Neither can any of you.' The silence in the room had been profound, and Doyle had gone without another word. Rhys had followed with a handkerchief pressed to his neck, trying to keep any more blood spots off his white coat.

Kitto had stayed because I was clinging to him, but I was calmer now. Kitto merely sat at my feet, one arm across my knees, the other running up and down the front of my leg. It was a sign of nervousness when a fey touched someone too intimately and too often, but I was stroking Kitto's hair in endless circles with my free hand, so it was all right. We were even.

Jeremy leaned against my desk watching me. He was dressed, as always, in a designer suit, perfectly tailored to his four-feet, eleven-inch frame. He was an inch shorter than me, strong and slender, with a masculine swell of shoulders. The suit was charcoal grey, about five shades darker than his own skin. His short, immaculate barbered hair was lighter grey than his skin, but not by much. Even his eyes were grey. His smile was a brilliant white, the best caps money could buy, and matched the white dress shirt he'd chosen for the day. The only thing that truly ruined his perfect modern profile was the nose. He'd spent loads on his teeth, but left the rather long and beaky nose alone. I'd never questioned it, but Teresa had. She was only human, after all, and didn't understand that among the fey a personal question is the worst insult. To imply in the same breath that something about their physique is not appealing . . . well, it just wasn't done. Jeremy had explained that a large nose among the trow was like large feet among humans. Teresa had blushed and not asked any more questions. I'd gone over and rubbed his nose with my fingertips and said *ooh*. It had made him laugh.

He crossed his arms over his chest, flashing the gold of his Rolex, and looked at me. Among the fey it was impolite to ask why a person was having hysterics. Hell, sometimes it was considered impolite to notice they were having hysterics at all. Usually that was for ruling royalty, though. Everyone had to pretend that the king or queen wasn't bug nuts. Mustn't admit that centuries of inbreeding had done any damage.

He took a deep breath, let it out, and then sighed. 'As your boss, I need to know if you're up to the rest of your appointments today.' It was a nicely circular way of asking what was wrong, without actually asking.

I nodded, raising the tea up to my face, not to drink, but just to breathe in the sweet scent of peppermint and spearmint intermingled. 'I'll be okay, Jeremy.'

He raised eyebrows that I happened to know he had plucked and shaped. Apparently trow have that bushy-eyebrow-across-the-entire-head thing going. The beetle-browed Neanderthal look just doesn't go with Armani suits and Gucci loafers.

I could have just left it at that, and by our culture he'd have had to accept my word and let it go. But Jeremy had been my boss and friend for years, long before he knew I was Princess anything. He'd given me a job on my own merits, not because the publicity of having a real live faerie princess on staff brought in business galore. In fact, the massive media coverage had made me useless for undercover work unless I used major personal glamour to change my appearance. Most of the reporters who specialized in tracking the fey had some magical ability. If they spotted the glamour, then it dissolved. Sometimes just for that reporter, but sometimes, if they were psychically talented enough, the glamour failed for everyone in sight. That was a very, very bad thing in the middle of an undercover operation.

I'd been out among the humans long enough to think I owed Jeremy an explanation. 'I don't exactly know what happened, Jeremy. Rhys started ranting about goblins, then he made a grab for Kitto, and I threw him into the wall.'

Jeremy looked surprised, which wasn't very flattering, or polite.

I frowned at him. 'I may not be in the same weight class as they are, Jeremy, but I can put my fist through a car door and not break a bone.'

'Your guards could probably lift the car up and drop it on somebody.'

I took a sip of tea. 'Yeah, they're stronger than they look.'

He gave a small laugh. 'You, my dainty beauty, do not look anywhere near as tough as you are.'

'I return the compliment,' I said, toasting him with the mug.

He smiled, flashing that expensive smile. 'Yes, I have surprised a few humans in my day.' The smile faded around the edges. 'If you had just told me to mind my own business, I'd have done it, but you volunteered information, so I'm going to ask some questions. Just tell me if you don't want to answer.'

I nodded. 'I started it, Jeremy. Go ahead.'

'Rhys didn't get blood on his coat from you throwing him into a wall.'

'That's not a question,' I said.

He shrugged. 'How did he get bloodied?'

'A knifc.'

'Doyle?'

I shook my head. 'I cut Rhys.'

'Because he tried to hurt Kitto?'

I nodded, but I met Jeremy's direct gaze with one of my own. 'They wouldn't obey my orders last night. If I don't gain their respect, Jeremy, I may gain the throne, but I will be queen in name only. I don't want to risk my life and the lives of people I care about just to be some sort of figurehead.'

'So you cut Rhys up to prove a point?'

53

'Partly. And partly, I just reacted, didn't think. He was trying to hurt Kitto over some stupid thing that happened centuries ago. Kitto has never given Rhys any reason to hate him like this.'

'Our fair-haired guard hates goblins, Merry.'

'Kitto is a goblin, Jeremy. He can't change that.'

Jeremy nodded. 'No, he can't.'

We looked at each other. 'What am I going to do?'

'You don't mean just with Rhys, do you?'

We exchanged another long look, and I had to look down, but that meant staring into Kitto's searching blue gaze. Everywhere I looked, people were expecting something of me. Kitto wanted me to take care of him. Jeremy, well, he just wanted me to be happy, I think.

'I thought I had their respect back in Illinois, but it's as if something's changed over the last three months.'

'What?' he asked.

I shook my head. 'I don't know.'

Kitto raised his head, which slid my hand to the warm curve of his neck. 'Doyle,' he said softly.

I looked down at him. 'What about Doyle?'

He half lowered his eyes, as if afraid to look directly at me. He wasn't being coy; it was a habitual gesture, a subservient gesture. 'Doyle says you made a good start, but you have made no use of your treaty with the goblins.' He raised his eyes a little. 'You have the goblins as your allies for only three more months, Merry. For three more months if the Unseelie go to battle, it is you who the queen must come to for the goblin's aid, not our King Kurag. Doyle fears you are simply going

54

to fuck everyone and make no move on your enemies.'

'What's he want me to do, declare war on someone?'

Kitto hid his face against my knee. 'I do not know, mistress, but I do know that the others follow Doyle's lead. It is he who you must win over, not the others.'

Jeremy pushed away from my desk, came closer to the two of us. 'I find it a little strange that sidhe warriors would speak so freely in front of you. No offense, Kitto, but you are a goblin. Why would they confide in you?'

'They did not, as you say, confide in me. But sometimes they talk over me like I am not there. Like you just did.'

Jeremy frowned. 'I am talking to you, not over you, Kitto.'

He looked up at both of us. 'But before, you were talking as if I were something that couldn't understand you, like a dog or a chair. All of you do it.'

I blinked down at him, staring into that innocent face. I wanted to deny it, but I held my tongue and thought about what he'd said. Was he right? The conversation that I'd just had with Jeremy had been private, sort of. Kitto had just been there. I hadn't wanted his opinion, or his help. Truthfully, I hadn't thought he could be of any help. I saw him as someone to be taken care of, a duty, not a friend, not, truthfully, a person.

I sighed and let my hand fall away from him, so that he was touching me, but I wasn't touching him. His eyes widened frantically, and he grabbed my hand, put it back on his head. 'Please, don't be angry with me. Please!'

'I'm not angry, Kitto, but I think you're right. I treat you like you're a pet, not a person. I would never just sit and pet one of the other men. I've been taking liberties. I'm sorry.'

He rose to his knees. 'No, no, that's not what I meant. I love that you touch me. It makes me feel safe. It's the only thing that makes me feel safe here in this ... place.' The look on his face was distant, lost.

I offered the tea mug to Jeremy, who took it and put it on the edge of my desk. I cupped Kitto's face in my hands, moved his gaze back to mine. 'You tell me I treat you like a dog, a chair, and I try to treat you like a person, and you don't want that either. I don't understand what you want of me, Kitto.'

He put his warm hands against mine, pressed my flesh firm against his face. His hands were so small; he was the only man I'd ever met with hands smaller than mine. 'I always want you to touch me, Merry. Don't stop. I don't mind that people talk over me. It lets me hear things, know things.'

'Kitto,' I said softly.

He clambered into my lap like a child, forcing my hands to encircle him to keep him from falling. My right hand slid over the slickness of the scales on his back; my left cupped the smooth, hairless curve of his thigh. The sidhe didn't have much body hair, and snake goblins had none. The mixed heritage had left Kitto smooth and perfect like he'd been waxed from neck to toe. It added to the doll-like image and made him seem perpetually childlike. He'd been a product of the last sidhe-goblin war, which meant Kitto was a little over two thousand years old. I knew my history, I knew the date, but holding him in my arms like an oversize doll, it was hard to really believe it. Almost impossible to grasp that the man curled in my lap had been born not long before the death of Christ.

Doyle was even older, and Frost, too. Rhys, under a different name, which he would never tell me, had been worshipped as a death deity. Nicca was only a few hundred years old, young by comparison. Galen was only seventy years older than me; in the courts it was almost the same thing as being raised together.

I'd grown up seeing them all remain the same. They were immortal; I wasn't. I was aging a little slower than a pure human, but not by much. I was about a decade or two behind where I should have been. Twenty extra years was great, but it wasn't forever.

I looked up at Jeremy for a hint of what to do with the goblin. He spread his hands wide. 'Don't look at me. I've never had an employee crawl into my lap and want to be petted.'

'He doesn't exactly want to be petted,' I said. 'He wants to be reassured.'

'If you have all the answers, Merry, then why don't you reassure him?' Jeremy said.

'A little privacy, maybe,' I said. The moment I asked for privacy I felt Kitto's body begin to relax against me. He slid his arm underneath my suit jacket, to curve at the small of my back. His knees unclenched enough so that he tucked them underneath my arm, sending my hand on his thigh sliding downward to the very edge of his shorts. Since Kitto never saw clients, he got to dress like it was casual day every day.

Jeremy straightened his tie, smoothed the edges of his jacket. Nervous gestures, all. 'I'll leave you two alone, though I think that once Doyle finds out you're alone except for Kitto, he'll be in here.'

'We don't need much time,' I said.

'My condolences,' Jeremy said. He opened his mouth like he was going to add to that, then shook his head, tugged on the sleeves of his suit jacket, and went, very firmly, for the door.

The door shut behind him, and I looked down at the goblin. We weren't going to do what Jeremy obviously thought we were going to do. I'd never had intercourse with Kitto, and didn't plan to start now. I'd had to share flesh with one of the goblins to cement the treaty between them and me, but sharing flesh can mean a lot of things to a goblin. Technically, once I'd let Kitto leave a perfect imprint of his teeth in my shoulder, we'd shared flesh, and it was done. But what should have been a scar had faded, then vanished from my skin. I'd shown King Kurag the bite mark when it was fresh, and neither Kitto nor I had mentioned that it had faded. Without the scar there was no proof that I *belonged* to Kitto.

The pain of Kitto's bite had been lost somewhere in the middle of sex with someone else, lost when my body had gone forward into that place where pleasure and pain are blurred. From a dead start, with no foreplay, getting a piece bitten out of you just hurts.

Kitto was within his rights, by goblin culture, to expect reassurance in the form of sharing flesh, whatever that meant for us. I was very lucky with my little goblin; he was subservient to me and liked it that way. My father had made sure I understood all the cultures of the Unseelie Court, and I knew what was true reassurance and what wasn't for Kitto's world. I had to play him fair, not cheat. I suspected, strongly, that Kurag would be upset that I had no visible mark of goblin on my body; and insult to injury, Kitto wasn't getting intercourse either. So I was trying to be very careful about all the other cultural rules and taboos.

I needed to reassure Kitto and continue the day's business. There were two other clients to see before we could go off to visit Maeve Reed. Ms Reed, through Jeffery Maison, had been most insistent that we see her this afternoon, not this evening. If we couldn't make it this afternoon, then tomorrow morning would be next best.

Kitto cuddled against me, his small hands kneading along my back and waist. It was a gentle reminder that he was still there, waiting.

The door opened. Rhys hesitated just inside the door, staring at us. A spurt of anger flashed through me. 'Come in, Rhys, join us.' My voice was cold, distant, angry.

He shook his head. 'I'll get Doyle for you.'

'No,' I said.

He stopped in the doorway, and finally looked at me, met my eyes. 'You know I don't share you with the—' He caught himself before he could say *goblin*, and finished awkwardly. '—him.'

'And what if I say you will share me with him?'

'I came in here to apologize, Merry. If I had injured Kitto, it could have jeopardized your treaty with the goblins. I'm sorry I lost my

59

temper.'

'If this had been the first incident, I'd accept the apology. But it's not the first. It's not even the fifteenth. Words aren't enough anymore.'

'What do you want from me, Merry?' He was looking angry and sullen again.

'Distract me while I reassure Kitto.'

He shook his head hard enough to send his white curls flying. He winced, and put a hand up to his neck. There was a bandage on it, but apparently it still hurt. The wound wouldn't last long; a couple of hours and he'd be healed.

'I vowed never again to let goblin flesh touch mine, Merry. You know that.'

'He's going to be touching me, Rhys, not you.'

'No, Merry, no.'

'Then pack your bags and go.'

His eye widened. 'What do you mean?'

'I mean that I can't risk you hurting Kitto and screwing up the treaty with the goblins.'

'I said I was sorry about that.'

'But not sorry enough to make friends with Kitto. Not sorry enough to behave like a body-guard instead of a spoiled, bigoted child.'

He stood in the half-open doorway, staring at me. 'You can't mean that you'd kick me out in preference to this . . . goblin.'

I shook my head. 'My enemies are the goblin's enemies for three more months. That has kept me safer than any of you have managed to do. No one wants to risk facing the entire goblin army. The fact that you can't see past your own prejudices to how important this is means you're too flawed to be my guard.' I ran my hand down Kitto's arm, pressed his head more firmly into my shoulder, forced Rhys to look at him.

The rage in his face was raw. 'They' – he pointed at Kitto – 'made me flawed.' He tore his eye patch off and stalked into the room. 'They did this to me.' He kept his finger pointed at Kitto as he advanced toward us. 'He did this!'

Kitto raised his face enough to say, 'I have never harmed you.'

Rhys's hands trembled as he balled them into fists. He stood above us, looming, trembling with rage, with the need to strike out at something, at someone.

'Don't, Rhys,' I said, my voice low, calm. I was afraid if I raised my voice, it would set him off. I really didn't want to lose him, but I didn't want Kitto hurt either.

I heard a sound behind us, though I couldn't see the doorway through Rhys. Doyle's voice came clear and deep. 'Is there a problem?'

'Thanks to Rhys, I need to renew my vows with Kitto, so I told him he needed to distract me while we did it.'

'I would be happy to distract you, Princess,' Doyle said.

'Oh, yeah, you're great at foreplay as long as there's no follow-through, and let me just say that that's really beginning to get on my nerves, too,' I said.

'Frost should be back from his assignment very soon. He's told the starlet that she'll have to find someone else to guard her from her would-be fans.'

We were still speaking around Rhys's body. 'I thought Frost's bodyguarding gig lasted until the end of the week, at least.'

'I thought it prudent after last night's attempt

that we have him with us. I've sent him on ahead to scout Ms Reed's home.'

'Scout?' I made it a question.

'She is, after all, full Seelie Court sidhe, once a goddess, but yet no longer of either court. She might feel she is beyond the limits of our laws. I would be a poor guard indeed to simply allow you to walk into her home without some preparation.'

'So you just pulled Frost off a job for our agency and reassigned him, without asking Jeremy, or me.'

Silence.

'I'll take that as a yes.' I frowned up at Rhys. 'Move to one side, Rhys. The threat display is getting a little old.'

Rhys looked a little surprised, as if I was supposed to be quaking in my boots. Of course, maybe the show wasn't for me. Kitto looked pale and very frightened.

'Move!' I said.

'Do as the princess bids,' Doyle said.

Only then did Rhys move, reluctantly, to one side. I stared past him at Doyle, who was just inside the door. 'Either Rhys helps distract me while Kitto gets reassured, or he packs his bags and goes back to Illinois.'

Doyle looked completely surprised. You didn't see that response too often in the Queen's Darkness. It made me just a little happy. 'I thought you enjoyed Rhys's attentions.'

'I love having Rhys in my bed, but that doesn't matter. If he can't control himself around Kitto, then eventually he's going to blow up and hurt him. You know Kurag didn't want to join a treaty with me, Doyle. He tried to weasel out of it from the beginning. I forced an alliance on him, but if Kitto is injured, or worse, killed, then Kurag could use it as an excuse to break the alliance.' I stroked the side of Kitto's face, turning him from staring at Rhys. 'And do you really think that if Kurag has to send us a second goblin, it will be anyone as pleasant as Kitto? It's my flesh and blood being offered up, not Rhys's, not yours.'

'That is true enough, Princess,' Doyle said. 'But if you send Rhys home, our queen will also send a new guard to replace him, and there are many less pleasant guards she could send than Rhys.'

'It doesn't matter. Either Rhys does this, or he's out. I'm tired of the histrionics.'

Doyle took a deep enough breath that I could see the rise and fall of his chest from across the room. 'Then I will stay and guard everyone's safety.'

Rhys turned toward him. 'You don't mean that I have to do this.'

'Princess Meredith NicEssus, wielder of the hand of flesh, has given you a direct order. If you do not obey it, then the princess has already told you the penalty.'

Rhys walked toward Doyle, the anger fading. 'You would cast me aside for this? I am one of your best guards.'

'I would hate to lose you in this fight,' Doyle said, 'but I cannot go against the princess's wishes.'

'That's not what you said last night,' Rhys said.

'She is right, Rhys, you have endangered our alliance with the goblins. If you cannot control your rage at Kitto, then you are a hazard to us all.

She is right to make you face this fear.'

'I am not afraid of him,' Rhys said, pointing again.

Kitto cowered back against me at Rhys's anger.

'All mindless hatred comes from a root of fear,' Doyle said. 'The goblins hurt you long ago, and you fear ending up in their hands again. You can hate them if you like, and you can fear them, if you must, but they are our allies, and you must treat them as such.'

'I will not help that . . . thing sink its fangs into an Unseelie princess.'

'If you had behaved yourself,' I said, 'I wouldn't be forced to do this again so soon. You're about to cause me pain, Rhys, and if I'm willing to endure it, then the least you can do is make it not completely unpleasant.'

Rhys went to the window, gazing out. He spoke without turning around. 'I don't know if I can do this.'

'Just try,' I said, 'but really try. You can't just put a toe in, declare the water cold, and run home. You have to stay with it. If you truly can't bear it, we'll talk, but first you have to try.'

He leaned his head against the window glass. He finally raised his head, squared his shoulders, and turned to face the room. 'I'll do my best. Just make sure he doesn't touch me.'

I looked down at the little goblin's pale face and frightened eyes. 'Rhys, I hate to break it to you, but I don't think Kitto wants to touch you any more than you want to touch him.'

Rhys gave a small nod. 'All right then, let's do this. We've got clients waiting.' He managed a faint smile. 'Mysteries to solve, bad guys to catch.'

I smiled at him. 'That's the spirit.'

Doyle closed the door behind him and leaned against it. 'I will not interfere unless there is danger.'

For the first time Doyle was protecting me not from any outside force, but from one of my own guards. I watched Rhys as he walked toward Kitto and me. The bandage on his neck was almost as big as my palm. Maybe Doyle wasn't around just to keep Kitto and me safe from Rhys; maybe, just maybe, he was also here to keep Rhys safe from me.

Chapter 5

RHYS LAID HIS SILK TRENCH COAT ACROSS MY DESK and came to stand in front of us. Kitto curled into a tight ball in my lap, eyes staring up at Rhys the way small mammals watch cats. As though the cat won't see them, if they stay still enough.

The shoulder holster was stylishly white against Rhys's button-down shirt. The butt of the gun was like a black imperfection among all that cream and white. 'Give your gun to Doyle, Rhys, please.'

He glanced at Doyle, who had gone back to his chair against the windows. 'I believe you are making the little one nervous, Rhys.'

'Well, isn't that just a pity,' he said, and his voice was cruel.

I glared up at him and felt the first stirrings of power. I didn't fight the anger or the magic. I let it fill my eyes, knew there was a glimmer in my eyes of colors and light nowhere in the room but in my eyes.

'Be careful, Rhys, or you can leave now, without your second chance.' My voice was low and careful again. I was holding on to my magic the way you hold your breath, controlled or you start yelling.

I must have looked like I meant it, because he turned without another word and walked to Doyle. He handed the gun butt first to the dark man, then he stood there for a few seconds, shoulders squared, hands in fists at his sides. It was almost as if he felt more insecure without the gun. If he'd been facing true mortal danger, I could have understood it, but Kitto wasn't that kind of threat to Rhys. He didn't need the gun.

He turned toward us with a shaky breath, which I heard clearly from feet away. Some of the anger had been stripped away, and what was left was barely disguised fear. Doyle was right; Rhys feared Kitto, or rather, goblins. It was like a phobia for him. A phobia with a basis in reality; those are the kind that are almost impossible to cure.

He stopped just in front of us again, staring down at me, face diffident, but underneath was a vulnerability that made me want to say, no, you don't have to do this. But I would have been lying. He did have to do this. If something wasn't done, Rhys would lose his temper once too often and Kitto would get hurt, or worse. We couldn't risk the treaty. And Kitto was mine to take care of. I wasn't sure where my duties would lie if Rhys killed him in a fit of panic. I didn't want to have to order an execution of someone I'd known all my life.

I wanted to reassure Rhys, tell him it was all right, but I didn't want to appear weak, either. So I sat there with a very tense Kitto curled tight in my lap, and said nothing.

'I've always left the room when you deal with . . . it, him,' Rhys said, 'What happens now?'

I'd had enough, and I suddenly didn't feel sorry

for Rhys. I looked down at Kitto. 'I offer you small flesh or weak blood.' *Small flesh* was goblin slang for light foreplay. *Weak blood* meant barely breaking the skin, or even just raising welts. There was every possibility that Kitto would choose something I wouldn't need any distraction for. I'd slowly been teaching Kitto new definitions of petting and foreplay, definitions that were a lot less stressful to all concerned.

He looked down, not meeting anyone's eyes, and whispered, 'Small flesh.'

'Done,' I said.

Rhys frowned. 'What just happened?'

I looked up at him. 'You always negotiate with goblins before sex, Rhys. If you don't, you end up hurt.'

He frowned down at me. 'I was a prisoner for a night. I had no ability to negotiate.'

I sighed, and shook my head. Most sidhe, Seelie or Unseelie, knew very little about cultures outside their own. It was a type of prejudice that believed nothing but sidhe culture was worth knowing. 'Actually, according to goblin law, you did. If they'd tortured you, then, no, you'd have simply had to endure what they did to you, though truthfully there is some room for negotiation even in torture. For sex, though, you always have room to negotiate. It's custom among them.'

The frown deepened. That single eye was so confused, so pain-filled. I spilled the small goblin to his feet and stood in front of Rhys, putting Kitto almost between us. For once Rhys didn't seem to notice how close the goblin was to him.

'The goblins will rape, and there's no saving yourself from it, but you can dictate terms, things

68

that can be done and cannot be done.'

His hand rose slowly toward his scars, then stopped before he touched them, his hand just hanging in midair. 'You mean . . .' And he left the rest of the sentence unfinished.

'That you could have forbidden them from permanently disfiguring you, yes.' My voice was very, very soft, as I said it. I'd been half wanting to tell Rhys, and half dreading, since I found out a few months ago how he'd lost his eye.

He turned to me with such horror in his face. I touched his cheeks, rose on tiptoe, and leaned his face down toward me. I laid a gentle kiss on his lips, a bare touch from my mouth to his, then stretched until my body leaned full against his, stretching as tall as I could, my hands still on his face, bringing him closer to me. I laid the same gentle kiss on his scar.

He jerked back, making me stumble. Only Kitto's arm around my waist kept me from falling. 'No,' Rhys said, 'no.'

I held my hands out to him. 'Come to me, Rhys.'

He just kept backing away. Doyle had moved up behind him without either of us noticing. Rhys stopped backing away when he smacked into his captain's body. 'If you fail her here, Rhys, then you must go back to faerie.'

He glanced at Doyle, then at me. 'I haven't failed, I just . . . I didn't know.'

'Most sidhe don't know anything about goblin culture,' I said. 'It's one of the reasons that the goblins are such feared warriors, because no one understands them. We might have won the goblin wars centuries sooner if anyone had taken time to study them. And I don't mean torture them. You don't learn a person's culture by torture.'

Doyle put a hand on either of Rhys's shoulders and began walking him back toward us. Rhys didn't look afraid anymore, more shell-shocked, as if a piece of his world had broken away and left him hanging with his feet on thin air.

Doyle walked him back to us, and I touched his face gently. Rhys blinked, startled, as if he'd forgotten I was there. 'You're not ruined, Rhys. You're beautiful.' I lowered his face toward me, but the six inches of difference hampered my intentions. I could kiss his mouth, but not his eye. I went back on tiptoe, which stretched my body along the length of Rhys's. Kitto's arm had still been around my waist, and now his arm was pressed between our bodies, trapped with the pressure of our flesh. Rhys didn't scream about it, so I let it go. I would finish what I'd started.

I kissed slowly up the edge of his face, until I touched the edge of the scar. He jerked, and I think only Doyle's hands on his shoulders kept him from running again. He closed his eye tight like a condemned man who didn't want to see the bullet coming. I kissed my way across the scars, until I felt the rough, slickened skin under my lips. I laid a gentle kiss over the empty socket, where the other beautiful eye should have been.

He was so tense under my hands, almost shaking. I kissed more firmly over the thickened skin, letting my lips open and close loosely over the spot. Rhys made a small sound. I licked, very gently, over the scar. Another small sound came from his throat, and it wasn't a pain sound.

I licked, slowly, carefully, over the slick skin.

His breath came in short, sharp gasps. The fists at his side were shaking, but not with anger. I ran tongue and lips over the scar until his knees buckled, and it was Kitto who caught him around the waist. The small man held him as if he weighed nothing.

I kissed Rhys on the mouth, and he kissed me back like he was drowning and would find the breath of life in my mouth. We ended on our knees on the floor with Doyle standing above us, and Kitto still wound around Rhys's waist.

Rhys put his arms behind my back and pressed me against him, hard enough that even with Kitto's arm between us I knew Rhys was hard and firm. Some buckle or strap must have bruised into Kitto's skin, because he made a small sound.

That one tiny sound brought Rhys up for air, made him look around, and when he saw the little goblin's arms around his waist, he gave something very like a scream and scrambled away from both of us.

I was about to open my mouth and say that Rhys had done enough to satisfy me, but Kitto spoke first. 'I declare myself satisfied.'

I stared at him. 'You've had nothing for yourself yet.'

He shook his head, blinking those drowning blue eyes. 'I am satisfied.' He seemed about to add more, appeared to think better of it, and just shook his head again.

It was Rhys who said, 'You haven't had your bit of flesh, yet.'

'No,' the goblin said, 'but I am within my rights to forgo it.'

'Why would you do that?' Rhys asked. He was

71

still crouched on the floor, face wild, panicked.

'Merry needs all her guards to be safe. I would not have her lose one of them over me.'

Rhys stared at him. 'You would give up your bit of flesh and blood so that I can stay?'

Kitto blinked, then looked at the floor. 'Yes.'

Rhys frowned. 'Are you feeling sorry for me?' and a tiny edge of anger crept into his voice.

Kitto looked up, clearly surprised. 'Sorry for you, why? You are beautiful and share Merry's body as well as her bed. You have a chance to be king. The scars that you think ruin you are a mark of great beauty among the goblins, and a mark of great valor, showing you have survived great pain.' He shook his head. 'You are a sidhe warrior. No one bullies you but the queen herself. Look at me, warrior, look at me.' He held out his small hands. 'I have no claws, precious little fang. I am like a human among the goblins.' For the first time there was a bitterness in Kitto's voice. A bitterness of years of abuse, of being in a culture where violence and physical prowess is prized, of being trapped in a body that was soft by their standards. He'd been born a victim among the goblins. He held those tiny hands out to Rhys, and there was anger in that small, delicate face. Anger, and a helplessness born of truth. Kitto knew very well what he was, and what he wasn't. Among the goblins he was anyone's meat. No wonder he wanted to stay at my side, even in the big bad city.

Chapter 6

ASK MOST PEOPLE, ESPECIALLY TOURISTS, WHERE the rich and famous live in Southern California and they'll say Beverly Hills. But Holmby Hills is full of money and fame, and land – land with high fences that block the view of the peons driving by, straining for a look at the rich and famous. Holmby Hills is not the fashionable address it once was, not the place for the young rising stars to make their home, but one thing hasn't changed: you need money for those walls and gates, lots of money. Come to think of it, maybe that's why the newly famous don't move to Holmby Hills much; they can't afford it.

Maeve Reed could afford it. She was a major star, but lucky for us, not in the top 2 percent. If she'd been, say, Julia Roberts, we'd have had to evade her media hounds as well as mine. One set of rabid reporters was more than enough for one day.

There were ways around the media that didn't need magic – for instance, a white van with rust spots that sat unused in the parking garage most of the time. The Grey Detective Agency used it for surveillance when the usual van would stand out too much. If it was a nice neighborhood, we used the nice van. If it was a bad neighborhood, we used this van. The media had started following the nice van every time it went out, on the theory that it could be hiding the princess and her entourage. That left us with the old van, even though it stood out like a sore thumb in Holmby Hills.

One of the back windows was covered with cardboard and tape. Rust decorated the white paint like wounds. Both the cardboard and the rust held places to hide cameras and other equipment. The hidey-holes could even be used as gunsights in an emergency.

Rhys drove. The rest of us hid in the back. He'd piled all that white hair under a billed cap. A high-quality fake beard and mustache hid all those boyish good looks. The cap and the facial hair even covered most of the scars. The guards had become almost as camera recognizable as I was, so it had to be a good disguise. And Rhys loved playing detective. He'd dressed up as if the day was any day and all the emotional turmoil had been a dream.

Kitto was literally hiding under my legs in the floorboard. Doyle sat on the far side of the seats away from me. Frost took up the center seat.

Sitting beside each other, the two men were almost exactly the same height. Standing, Frost was the taller by a couple of inches. His shoulders were a little wider and his body slightly bulkier. It wasn't a large difference, and not one you usually noticed when they had clothes on, but it was a difference all the same. Queen Andais treated them almost as if they were just two sides of the same coin. Her Darkness and her Killing Frost. Doyle had a name aside from the queen's nickname; Frost did not. He was simply Frost or Killing Frost, and that was all.

Frost was dressed in charcoal grey dress slacks cut long enough that they covered the tops of his charcoal gray loafers. The shoes were polished to a mirror sheen. His shirt was white with a ribbed front and a banded collar that encircled the smooth firm line of his neck. A pale grey jacket hid his shoulder holster and shiny nickel-plated .44. The gun was so big that I could barely hold it one-handed, let alone shoot it.

His silver, Christmas-tinsel hair was pulled back in a firm ponytail that left his face strong, clean, and almost too handsome to look at. The tail of silver hair had spilled mostly over the backseat and half across his shoulder. A few strands trailed over my shoulder and arm as he gave his report to Doyle. I touched those shining strands, feeling the spiderweb softness of them. The hair looked metallic, like it should feel harsh, but it was wonderfully soft. I'd had all this silken grace spill over my naked body. There was a part of me that thought that a man's hair should be at least to his knees. High-court sidhe took great pride in their hair, among other things.

Frost's hip pressed against mine, hard to avoid in the close confines of the seat. But his thigh pressed the length of mine, and that he could have avoided.

I had raised a lock of his hair in front of my face, letting the strands fall down, while I watched the world through a lace of his hair, when Doyle said, 'Are you listening to us, Princess Meredith?'

I startled and let Frost's hair fall away. 'Yes, I was listening.'

The look on his face said, clearly, he didn't believe me. 'Then repeat it back to us, if you can.'

I could have told him I was a princess and I didn't have to repeat anything, but that would have been childish, and besides, I really had been listening, to some of it.

'Frost saw some of Kane and Hart's people behind the walls. Which means that they are doing some sort of job for her, either bodyguarding or something that needs psychic talent.' The Kane and Hart Agency was the only real competition that the Grey Detective Agency had in L.A. Kane was a psychic and a martial-arts expert. The Hart brothers were two of the most powerful human magicians that I'd ever met. The agency did more bodyguard work than we did, or had, until my guards showed up.

Doyle looked at me. 'And?'

'And what?' I asked.

Frost laughed, a purely masculine sound that said more than words that he was pleased.

I knew what had pleased him without having to ask. He was pleased that I'd been so distracted by just having him near me. I found Frost the most distracting of the guards that I was sleeping with.

He turned to me with his storm grey eyes, laughter still shining in them. The laughter softened the perfection of his face, made him seem more human.

I touched my fingertips to his cheek, the lightest of touches. The laughter melted slowly from his face, leaving his eyes serious and full of a tender weight of words unspoken, things not yet done.

I stared up into his eyes. They were just grey, not tricolored like mine or Rhys's, but, of course, they weren't just grey. They were the color of clouds on a rainy day, and like clouds the colors changed and swirled not with the wind but with his moods. They were a soft grey like the breast of a dove as he lowered his head to kiss me.

My pulse filled my throat so that I couldn't breathe. His lips brushed mine, laying a gentle kiss that trembled against my flesh. He raised back from that one tender movement, and we looked into each other's eyes from inches away, and there was a moment of knowing. We'd shared a bed for three months. He'd guarded my safety. I'd introduced him to the twenty-first century. I'd watched the solemn Frost relearn how to smile and laugh. We'd shared a hundred intimacies, dozens of jokes, a thousand new discoveries about the world in general, and none of it had been enough to push either one of us over the edge. Then suddenly a look in his eyes and a gentle kiss, and it was as if my feelings for him reached critical mass, as if it had only been waiting for one last touch, one last lingering glance, before I knew. I loved Frost, and from the startled look on his face as he stared down at me, I think he felt it, too.

Doyle's voice cut across the moment, making us both jump. 'What you didn't hear, Meredith, is that Maeve Reed's land is warded. Warded as only a goddess, who has lived on the same piece of land for over forty years, could bespell.'

I blinked up at Frost's face, trying to shift the gears in my head to listen to Doyle, and to care about what he was saying. I had heard him, but I wasn't sure I cared, not yet.

If Frost and I had been alone, we would have talked about it, but we weren't alone, and really being in love with each other didn't change much. I mean, it changed everything, and nothing. Loving anyone changes you, but royalty seldom marries for love. We marry to cement treaties, to stop or prevent wars, or to forge new alliances. In the case of the sidhe, we marry to breed. I'd been sleeping with Rhys, Nicca, and Frost for over three months and I wasn't pregnant. Unless one of them could get me with child, I wouldn't be permitted to marry any of them. It had been only three months, and it typically took a year or more for a sidhe to conceive. I hadn't been worried, until now. And I wasn't worried that I wasn't pregnant; I was worried that I wasn't pregnant and that it might mean I lost Frost. In the moment I finished the thought, I knew I couldn't afford to think that way.

I would have to give my body to the man whose seed made me pregnant. My heart could go wherever it wanted, but my body was spoken for. If Cel became king, he'd have the power of life and death over the court. He'd have to kill me, and anyone he saw as a threat to his power. Frost and Doyle would never survive. I wasn't sure about Rhys or Nicca. Cel didn't seem as afraid of their power; he might let them live. He might not.

I drew back from Frost, shaking my head.

'What's wrong, Meredith?' he asked. He grabbed my hand as I moved it away from his face. He held my hand in his, pressing it, almost painfully, as if he'd seen some of my thoughts on my face.

If I couldn't talk about love in front of the others, I certainly couldn't talk about the price of being a princess in front of them. I had to get pregnant. I had to be the next queen of the Unseelie Court, or we were all dead.

'Princess,' Doyle said softly. I looked past Frost's shoulder to meet Doyle's dark eyes. And something in those eyes said that he, at least, had followed my thinking. Which meant he'd also realized how I felt about Frost. I didn't like that it was so apparent to others. Love, like pain, should be private until you want to share it.

'Yes, Doyle,' I said, and my voice sounded hoarse, like I needed to clear my throat.

'Wards of such power prevent another fey from seeing all the magic inside a place. Frost scouted it as best he could, but the strength of the wards means we do not know what mystical surprises might await us inside the walls of Ms Reed's estate.' He talked of normal things, but his voice still held that edge of softness. In anyone else I would have said it was pity.

'Are you saying we shouldn't go in?' I asked. I drew my hand back from Frost's grip.

'No, I agree that I find her desire to meet with you, with all of us, intriguing.'

The van pulled to a stop outside a tall gate. Rhys turned in the seat as much as his seat belt would allow. 'I vote we go home. If King Taranis finds out we've talked to her, he'll be pissed. What could we possibly learn that would be worth the risk?'

'Her banishment was a great mystery when it happened,' Doyle said.

'Yes,' Frost said. He slid back in his seat, eyes distant, as if he was shutting himself away from me. I'd pulled away, and Frost didn't react well to that. 'The rumor was that she would be the Seelie's next queen, then suddenly she was exiled.'

He moved his leg away from mine, putting physical distance between us. I watched his face grow cold and hard and arrogant, the old mask he'd worn in the court for all those years, and I couldn't bear it. I took his hand in mine. He frowned at me, clearly puzzled. I raised his knuckles to my lips and kissed them, one by one, until his breath caught in his throat. For the second time today I had tears in my eyes. I kept my eyes very wide and very still, and managed not to cry.

Frost was smiling again, visibly relieved. I was glad he was happy. You should always want the people you love to be happy. Rhys just looked at us, his face neutral. He'd had his turn last night, tonight was Frost's turn, and Rhys had no problem with that.

Doyle caught my gaze, and his face was not neutral, but worried. Kitto stared up from the floorboard, and there was nothing I could understand on his face. For all that he looked so sidhe, he was other, and there were times when I had no idea what he was thinking or feeling. Frost held my hand and was happy with that. Happy that I hadn't turned away. Of all of them, only Doyle seemed to understand exactly what I was feeling and thinking.

'What does it matter why she was exiled?' Rhys said.

'Perhaps it doesn't matter,' Doyle said, 'or

perhaps it matters very much. We won't know until we ask.'

I blinked at him. 'Ask, ask outright, without an invitation to ask something so personal?'

He nodded. 'You are sidhe, but you are also part human. You can ask where we cannot, Meredith.'

'I have better manners than to ask such a personal question right out of the bag,' I said.

'We know you have better manners than that, but Maeve Reed does not.'

I stared at him. Frost's fingers rubbed along my knuckles, over and over. 'Are you saying I should pretend to not know any better?'

'I am saying we should use all the weapons in our arsenal. Your mixed heritage could be a decided advantage today.'

'It would be almost the same thing as lying, Doyle,' I said.

'Almost,' he agreed, then that small smile of his curled his lips. 'The sidhe never lie, Meredith, but shading the truth is a long-honored pastime among us.'

'I'm very well aware of that,' I said. My voice held enough sarcasm to fill the van.

His smile flashed suddenly white in the darkness of his face. 'As are we all, Princess, as are we all.'

'I don't think it's worth the risk,' Rhys said.

I shook my head. 'We had this conversation once, Rhys, I do think it's worth the risk.' I looked up at Frost. 'How about you?'

He turned to Doyle. 'What do you think? I would not risk Meredith's safety for anything, but we are badly in need of allies, and a sidhe that has been exiled from faerie for a century might be willing to risk much to come back.'

'You're suggesting that Maeve wants to help Meredith to be queen,' Doyle made it half question, half statement.

'If Meredith is queen, then she could offer Maeve a return to faerie. I do not think that Taranis would risk all-out war for one returned exile.'

'You really think a royal of the Seelie Court would be willing to come to the Unseelie Court?' I asked.

Frost looked down at me. 'Whatever prejudices Maeve Reed might once have had against the Unseelie, she has been without the touch of fey hands for a century.' He raised my hand to his mouth, kissed my finger-tips, blowing his breath along each of them before he touched me. It brought shivers up and down my skin. He spoke with his mouth just above my skin. 'I know what it is to want the touch of another sidhe and be denied. I at least had the court and the rest of faerie to comfort me. I cannot imagine her loneliness all these years.' The last was said in a whisper. His eyes had gone solid rain-cloud grey.

It took effort, but I drew my attention away from Frost to look at Doyle. 'Do you think he's right? Do you think she's looking for a way back into faerie?'

He shrugged, making the leather of his jacket creak with the movement. 'Who can say, but I know that after a century of isolation, I certainly would be.'

I nodded. 'All right then, we're agreed. We go in.'

'We are not agreed,' Rhys said. 'I'm going in under protest.'

'Fine, protest all you want, but you're outvoted.'

'If something really awful happens to us in there, I get to say I told you so.'

I nodded. 'If we're alive long enough for you to say it, knock yourself out.'

'Sweet Goddess, if we die that quickly, I'll just have to come back and haunt you.'

'If there's anything in there that can kill you, Rhys, I'll have died long before you.'

He frowned at me; even through the beard I could see it. 'That isn't comforting, Merry, that isn't comforting at all.' But he turned around to face the big gates and leaned out his open window to press the intercom and announce our presence. Though I was betting that she knew we were there. She'd had forty years to bespell this land. Conchenn, goddess of beauty and charisma, knew we were here.

Chapter 7

ETHAN KANE WASN'T AS TALL AS HE SEEMED. HE actually was about Rhys's height, but always seemed bigger, as if he took up more room in some way that had nothing to do with physical size. His short hair was a dark brunette, almost but not quite black. He wore glasses with no frames, so they were almost invisible on his face. Ethan should have been handsome. He was broad shouldered, athletically built, square jawed, with a deep dimple in his chin. The eyes behind the glasses were long-lashed and hazel. His clothes were tailored to his body so he'd fit in with the stars he usually ran with. He had everything going for him but personality. He always seemed to be disapproving of something; a perpetual sour expression stole all his charm.

He stood with one hand gripping the other wrist, feet wide apart, balanced. He frowned down at us from just outside Maeve Reed's large double doors. We were all standing at the foot of the marble steps that led up to those doors. Ethan's men were ranged among the graceful sweep of white pillars that supported the roof of Maeve

Reed's narrow porch. It was huge and imposing, but there was no room to put out chairs and have iced tea on hot summer nights. It was a porch for looking at, not for enjoying.

Four men, obviously hired muscle, ranged on the steps between us and Ethan, and the door. I recognized one of them. Max Corbin was nearing fifty. He'd been a bodyguard in Hollywood most of his adult life. He was an inch shy of six feet and built like a box, all angles, squares, including huge knuckled hands. His grey hair was cut in a long butch cut, which made it look stylish and cutting edge, but Max had had the same haircut for forty years. His nose had been badly broken enough times that it was crooked and just a little squashed. He probably could have traded his designer suit for a nose job and fixed it, but Max thought it made him look tough. It did.

'Hi, Max,' I said.

He nodded at me. 'Ms Gentry, or should I say, Princess Meredith?'

'Ms Gentry is just fine.'

He smiled, a quick flash of humor, before Ethan's voice cut across us both, and Max's face went back to blank bodyguard stare. That stare says we see nothing and will remember nothing, and we see everything and will react at the blink of an eye. Your secrets are safe with us, and so is your body. Bodyguards do not work in Hollywood if they get a reputation for tattling to the press, or anyone else.

'What are you doing here, Meredith?'

Ethan and I didn't know each other well enough to use first names, but that was okay, because I was going to do the same to him. 'We're here at

Ms Reed's invitation, Ethan. Why are you here?'

He blinked at me, the slightest flexing of shoulders letting me know that something was bothering him, or his shoulder holster didn't fit quite right. 'We're Ms Reed's bodyguards.'

I nodded, smiled. 'I figured that. You must not have been on the job long.'

'What makes you say that?'

I felt the smile widen. 'You've got most of your muscle here. If Kane and Hart were all booked up, we'd be getting more referrals.'

His frown deepened. 'I've got a lot more than just four employees, Meredith, and you know it.' He said my name like it was a bad word.

I nodded. I did know it. 'Is there a reason you're keeping us out here, Ethan? Ms Reed was very concerned that we see her today, not tonight, but today.' I glanced up at the sun sinking behind a stand of eucalyptus trees near the distant sweep of wall. 'It's late afternoon, Ethan. If you keep us out here much longer, it'll be night.' It was an exaggeration; we had hours of daylight left, but I was tired of standing around.

'State your business and maybe we'll let you in,' Ethan said.

I sighed. I was about to be blunt even for a human being; it was beyond blunt for a fey, but I just didn't care. I wanted to go away someplace quiet and think. Frost was standing a little back and to one side, and Doyle mirrored him, but they both stood so that they were somehow clearly facing off with the bodyguards on the steps. Rhys was standing nearly in front of Max, grinning at him. Max was almost as big a Humphrey Bogart fan as Rhys. They'd spent one long afternoon trapped together on a long bodyguard job, different clients, trading film noir trivia. They'd been friends ever since.

Kitto did not face off with the last bodyguard. He stood just a little behind me, almost but not quite hiding. He looked oddly out of place in his short-shorts, tank top, and child-size Nikes. He'd put on black wrap-around sunglasses, but aside from that he could have passed for someone's nephew, the kind that usually isn't a nephew at all but a boy toy. Kitto always managed to give off the vibe that he was subservient, someone's toy, or victim. I had no idea how he'd survived among the goblins.

I looked at everyone facing off, Ethan standing on the steps like some slightly taller version of Napoleon, and shook my head. 'Ethan, you want to know why Ms Reed called us, when she's already hired you. You're wondering if you're all about to be replaced.'

He started to protest.

I said, 'Ethan, please, save it for someone who cares. I'll save you all the power plays. Ms Reed hasn't told us exactly why she wants us here, but she wanted to talk to me, not my guards, so I think we're all safe in assuming she doesn't want us for bodyguard duty.'

If his frown deepened any more, it looked like it might actually hurt his forehead. 'We don't do just bodyguard work, Meredith. We're detectives, too. Why does she need you?'

The unsaid part, *when she has us*, hung in the air between us. I shrugged. 'I don't know, Ethan, truly, I don't. But if you let us inside, we can all find out together.'

The frown smoothed slowly away, leaving his face younger, and puzzled. 'That's almost . . . nice of you, Meredith.' Then he looked suspicious, as if wondering what I was up to.

'I can be very nice if people give me the chance, Ethan.'

Max spoke low so that Ethan couldn't hear him. 'And how nice can you be?'

Rhys answered, voice low, 'Very, very nice.'

The two of them shared one of those masculine laughs that women never seem to be able to participate in, but are always the subject of.

'Is something funny?' Ethan asked, the sour look back in place, his voice whip sharp.

Max shook his head, as if he didn't trust himself to speak. Rhys actually answered, 'Just passing the time of day, Mr Kane.'

'We're not paid to pass the time of day, we're paid to keep our clients safe.' He gave a look that somehow took all of us in one big sweep. 'We'd be piss-poor bodyguards if we let all of you inside the house, especially armed.'

I shook my head. 'You know that Doyle won't let me go anywhere without bodyguards, and you also know that they won't give up their guns.'

He smiled, an unpleasant smile. 'Then you don't get in.'

Standing on the hard driveway in my three-inch heels, under the sun that was beginning to make sweat bead on my skin, I just didn't want to mess with it. I did probably the most unprofessional thing I've ever done. I started yelling at the top of my voice, 'Maeve Reed, Maeve Reed, come out to play. It's Princess Meredith and her entourage.' I kept yelling the first part. 'Maeve Reed, Maeve Reed, come out to play.'

Ethan tried to yell me down a few times, but I'd had voice training, years of public speaking – I was louder. None of Ethan's people knew what to do. I wasn't hurting anyone, I was just yelling. Five minutes of confusion and a young woman opened the door. She was Marie, Ms Reed's personal assistant. Would we like to come inside? Yes, we would. It took another ten minutes to get us through the door because Ethan wanted to take our weapons. It took Marie hinting that Ms Reed would fire them all, before he backed down.

Max and Rhys were laughing so hard that we had to leave them outside, hanging on to each other like a couple of drunks. At least someone was enjoying themselves.

Chapter 8

MAEVE REED'S LIVING ROOM WAS LARGER THAN my entire apartment. Off-white carpet stretched like a vanilla sea down the steps to the sunken living room and a fireplace big enough to roast small elephants. The mantel alone took up most of one white stuccoed wall, with red and tan bricks punctuating the rough whiteness of the wall. A white sectional sofa big enough to seat twenty curved in front of the fireplace. Tan, gold, and white pillows were thrown around artfully. There was a grouping of white chairs with a small pale wood table between them. A chessboard with oversize pieces sat between the two chairs, and a curving Tiffany floor lamp provided a splash of color in the otherwise monochrome room.

A painting to one side of the fireplace echoed the lamp's colors, and a second conversational group of white chairs and cushions was set on the raised edge of the room opposite the entrance. A large white Christmas tree stood in the center of the chairs. The tree was covered in white lights with gold and silver ornaments that should have livened the room but didn't. The tree was just another decoration without life or feeling to it. A table was pushed to one side to make room for the Christmas tree, with what looked like lemonade and iced tea in tall pitchers. A few more paintings were scattered throughout the room, most of them matching the color scheme of the lamp. The room screamed interior decorator and probably said nothing about Maeve Reed except that she had money and let other people decorate her home. When a person doesn't have a single mismatched thing in a room, down to the last light on the Christmas tree, then it's not real. It's just for show.

Marie was tall, slender, dressed in a sleek oyster-white pantsuit that did not flatter her olive complexion or her short brunette hair. In her high-heeled boots she was a touch over six feet, a tall, smiling, twenty-something. 'Ms Reed will be joining us presently. Would anyone like refreshments?' She motioned toward the table set with tea and lemonade.

Actually, it would have been nice, but it was a rule that you never took any food or drink from a fellow fey until you were sure they meant you no harm. It wasn't poison you had to worry about, but spells, a little potion mixed in with the lemons.

'Thank you . . . Marie, is it? We're fine,' I said.

She smiled, nodded. 'Then please sit down. Make yourselves comfortable while I tell Ms Reed you're here.' She moved at a graceful stride down the steps and across to the far opening that led into a white hallway that vanished somewhere deep within the house.

I glanced at Ethan and his two muscle men. He'd left one of his people outside with Max and

Rhys. Marie hadn't offered them refreshments, since I guess you didn't have to entertain the hired help. Which begged the question, if we weren't going to be hired help, then what were we going to be? Did Maeve Reed really just want to visit with other high-court sidhe? Would she risk breaking a century of taboo to have small talk? I didn't think so, but I'd seen royals of the high courts do sillier things for less reason.

I went down the steps to the large sectional sofa. Kitto followed me like a shadow. I glanced back at the men. 'Come on, boys, let's all sit down and pretend that we like each other.' I moved about seven feet from the end of the couch and sat down, adjusting the tan and gold pillows, smoothing my skirt in place.

Kitto curled at my feet, though Goddess knew there were enough couches for everyone. I didn't make him get up, because even through the dark glasses I could see his nervousness. The big white living room seemed to have triggered his agoraphobia. He sat pressed up against my legs, one small arm encircling them like I was his teddy bear.

The men were still standing in the large open archway, eyeing one another.

'Gentlemen,' I said, 'let's all sit down.'

'A good bodyguard doesn't relax on the job,' Ethan said.

'You know we aren't a threat to Ms Reed, Ethan. I don't know who you're supposed to be protecting her from, but it isn't us.'

'They may clean up for the press, but I know what they are, Meredith,' Ethan said.

'And what would that be?' Doyle's deep voice

rumbled through the room, causing echoes in the archway.

Ethan actually jumped.

I had to turn my face away to hide the smile.

'You're Unseelie.' Ethan stretched that last word out, made it hiss.

I looked back at them. Doyle stood facing him, his back to me. I couldn't tell what he was thinking; and I probably couldn't have told even if I'd seen his face. Doyle did better blank face than anyone I'd ever met. Frost was standing closer to the unknown muscle man, his face the arrogant mask he wore in court. Even the new muscle was keeping pretty blank, except for a certain nervous flicker around the eyes. But Ethan, Ethan had a fine angry tremble to his hands. He was staring at Doyle as if he hated him.

'You're just jealous, Ethan, jealous that most of the major stars prefer a sidhe warrior at their back instead of you.'

'You've bewitched them,' he said.

I raised an eyebrow at that. 'Me personally?'

He made a small angry gesture toward the two warriors. I think it would have been a large angry gesture but he was worried about how Doyle would take it. '*They* have.'

'Ethan, Ethan,' another male voice called from across the room. 'I've told you before that that is simply not true.' I knew at a glance that it was one of the Hart brothers. He was walking down the steps toward me before I was certain it was Julian Hart. Jordon and Julian were identical twins, both with medium brown hair cut very short on the sides and left just a little long on top so that they could gel it into short spikes; very hip, very now.

They were both six feet, both handsome enough to model, which they had done briefly in their early twenties to raise start-up money for their detective agency. Julian's jacket was a deep burgundy satin over a pair of ordinary, but designer, burgundy-brown, pinstriped pants. He wore shiny black loafers with no socks, so that you got flashes of his tanned feet as he moved gracefully through the room. His eyes were hidden behind yellow tinted glasses that on anyone else would have clashed with the clothes; but on Julian they looked just right.

I started to rise to greet him, but he said, 'No, no, my fair Merry, stay seated, I'll come to you.' He walked around the couch, eyes flicking to the four men still standing in the archway. 'Ethan, darling, I've told you time and again that the sidhe warriors are not doing a thing to attract our business away from us. They are merely more exotic, more beautiful than anything we have on staff.' He took my hand and gave it a negligent kiss, before flopping gracefully down beside me, one arm flung across my shoulders so that we sat like a couple.

He spoke back over his shoulder, 'You know what Hollywood is like, Ethan. Any star guarded by a warrior is guaranteed publicity. I think some people are making things up just so they can be escorted.'

'That has been my experience,' Frost said. The unnamed muscle standing closest to him flinched. What stories had Ethan been telling the others about the Unseelie?

'And who wouldn't wish to be accompanied by you, Frost?' Julian said.

Frost just looked at him, grey eyes very still.

Julian laughed and hugged me. 'You are the luckiest girl I know, Merry. Are you sure you won't share?'

'How's Adam?'

Julian laughed. 'Adam is purrrfectly wonderful.' And he laughed again. Adam Kane was Ethan's older brother and Julian's lover. They'd been a couple for at least five years now. When they were in private where they didn't get hostile comments from strangers, they still acted like newlyweds.

Julian fluttered his hand in the air. 'Come, gentlemen, come and sit down.'

I glanced back. No one had moved. 'Doyle and Frost won't move until Ethan and the new man do.'

Julian turned around to look at them all. 'Frank,' Julian said, 'our newest recruit.' The man was tall, lanky, and looked young – fresh-faced, wet-behind-the-ears young. He did not look like a Frank. A Cody maybe, or a Josh.

'Nice to meet you, Frank,' I said.

Frank looked from me to the still-scowling Ethan; finally he gave a small nod. He looked as if he wasn't sure that being friendly to us would help his chances of staying employed.

'Ethan,' Julian said, 'all the senior partners discussed your views on the sidhe warriors. You were outvoted.' His voice had lost all of that teasing quality and was now low and serious and full of something very like a threat.

I wondered what the threat was. Ethan Kane was one of the founding partners of their firm. Could you fire a founding partner?

'Ethan,' Julian said, 'sit down.' His voice held a

note of command I'd never heard before. For just a second I wondered if I'd gotten the wrong twin. Jordon was more likely to turn to force, while Julian was more the joking diplomat. I studied his profile, and, no, the dimple was just a touch deeper at the corner of his mouth, the cheeks a fraction less sculpted. It was Julian. What had been happening behind the scenes of Kane and Hart to put such hardness in his voice?

Whatever it was, it was enough, because Ethan started moving down the steps. Frank followed him. Doyle and Frost watched them for a moment, then slowly followed them around the room. Ethan sat on the section opposite me. Frank sat down like he wasn't sure he was allowed. He placed himself far enough away from Ethan not to crowd him.

Doyle sat on the other side of me opposite Julian. He'd made a point of sitting there and forcing Frost one seat over. He'd murmured, 'Meredith needs to concentrate.' It hit me suddenly that he'd been calling me Meredith for a little while. I was usually 'the princess' or 'Princess Meredith,' although he'd called me Meredith at the beginning when he first got to L.A. He'd distanced himself with language about the time he distanced himself physically.

Frost was clearly not happy about the seating arrangements, but I doubted that anyone but one of us noticed. The slight stiffness to his shoulders spoke volumes if you knew what book you were reading. I'd spent a lot of time learning to read this book. Doyle knew all his men's moods like any good leader. Kitto might have been oblivious, but it was hard to know what the little goblin noticed and what he didn't.

Julian stayed pressed to my side, a lot closer to me than Doyle was sitting, though he moved his hand to let Doyle's shoulder touch mine. It also put Julian's hand on the back of the couch, touching Doyle's back.

Julian was in love with Adam, I knew that, but I also knew that he wasn't entirely kidding about me sharing my men. Maybe he and Adam had a special arrangement, or maybe no one could be around the sidhe and not wonder. Maybe.

Julian was stiffer, quieter beside me now, as if he were concentrating on not moving his hand too much. Doyle would tolerate the touch, but not if it was too much. Doyle had the same rules for uninvited men as for uninvited women. A thousand years of forced celibacy had made Doyle, and many of the guards, make very unfey-like rules about casual touching. If you couldn't complete the act, then teasing was too much like torture. Rhys had always had different rules, as had Galen: they preferred something to nothing.

Ethan looked at the two guards, his scowl deepening. His eyes flicked to Kitto, and disgust showed on his face.

'What's your problem, Ethan?' I asked.

He blinked and glared at me. 'I just don't like monsters, no matter how pretty they are.'

Julian took his arm off the couch and sat forward, leaning toward the other man. 'Am I going to have to send you home?'

'You're not my father . . . or my brother.' That last was said with a lot of heat. Did Ethan have a problem with Julian dating his brother?

Julian leaned back a little, his head to one side

as though he'd just thought of something new. 'We're not going to air our private business in front of anyone, no matter how charming. But if you can't deal with this assignment, then I'll call Adam and the two of you can change jobs. He won't have a problem with Meredith being here.'

'He doesn't have a problem with a lot of things,' Ethan said, and the heat was very clearly directed toward Julian

'I'll call Adam and tell him you'll be heading his way.' Julian took a small cell phone from an inner jacket pocket.

'I'm in charge of this operation, Julian You're just here in case we need magical backup.'

Julian sighed, gazing at the phone in his hand. 'If you're in charge, Ethan, then act like it. Because right now you're embarrassing yourself in front of these good people.'

'People?' Ethan stood, doing his best to tower over us. 'These aren't people; they're non-humans.'

A clear ringing voice came from behind Ethan. 'Well, if that's how you feel, Mr Kane, perhaps I was in error when I employed your agency.'

Maeve Reed was standing in the hallway on the edge of the vanilla carpet sea. She didn't look happy.

Chapter 9

MAEVE REED WAS USING MAGIC TO APPEAR MORE human. She was tall, slender with a bare swell of hips to ruin the line of her tan slacks. Her long-sleeved blouse was pale harvest gold unbuttoned to midchest, giving tantalizing glimpses of tanned flesh and the edge of small firm breasts. If I'd tried wearing something like that, I'd have fallen out all over the place. She was built like most of the top fashion models, except she didn't have to starve or exercise to look like this. It was just the way she looked.

A thin brown headband kept her long blond hair in place. The hair hung straight and fine to her waist. Her skin was a nice medium tan. After all, the immortal don't have to sweat skin cancer. Her makeup was so light and so artful that at first I thought she wasn't wearing any. The bones of her face were sculpted and lovely, and the eyes were a startling, drowning blue.

She was beautiful as she came toward us, but it was a human beauty. She was hiding herself from us. Maybe it was habit by now, or maybe she had her reasons.

Julian was on his feet meeting her before she got to the couch. He murmured to her, probably apologizing for Ethan and his unfortunate 'non-human' comment.

She shook her head, making her tiny gold earrings shiver. 'If this is how he really feels about the fey, then I think he would be more comfortable working elsewhere.'

Ethan walked around the couch, too. 'I have no problem with you, Ms Reed. You're Seelie Court, the Bringers of Beauty and Wishes.' He pointed at us a little dramatically, I thought. 'They are the stuff of nightmares and should not be allowed in this house. They are a danger to you and to everyone around them.'

'How much business are you losing to us?' I asked, and for some reason my voice carried into the sudden silence.

Ethan turned on me, probably to say something else unfortunate. Julian grabbed his arm; it looked like a firm grip from where I was sitting. Ethan's body reacted as if he'd been hit, and for a second, I thought we'd get to see a fight.

'Just go, Ethan,' Julian said, voice low.

Ethan yanked free of Julian. He gave a stiff little bow to Ms Reed. 'I'll go. But I just want you to understand that I know the Seelie are different from what the Unseelie are.'

'I have not set foot in the Seelie Court for over a century, Mr Kane. I will never be a member of it again.'

Ethan frowned; I think he'd thought Ms Reed would agree with him. Normally, he was sullen and unpleasant, but not to this degree. We must have really been cutting into their business.

Ethan fumbled over some more apologies, then stomped out. After the door slammed behind us, I said, 'Is he like that often?'

Julian shrugged. 'Ethan isn't fond of a lot of people.'

'I'm feeling terribly neglected here, Julian, with Ethan gone and all,' Maeve said.

I blinked at her smiling, carefully beautiful face. She looked so sincere, even her blue-blue eyes sparkled with the force of it. She was working just a little hard at being charming, and human. It would have been a whole lot easier to be charming if she'd dropped the glamour she was wasting in order to appear humanly – rather than inhumanly – beautiful.

Julian glanced at me, then turned his full smiling self on Maeve Reed. In his own way Julian was turning on the charm, too. I realized with a start that he had his own personal glamour. It might have been actual conscious magic, but I doubted it. Most personal glamour that bolsters charisma is accidental for humans. Most of the time.

I watched them doing a minor job of shining at each other, and realized that the charm wasn't for our benefit. I glanced behind me at Frank. He was staring at her as if he'd never really seen a woman before, or at least not one like this. Maeve Reed was trying to be inhumanly charming, but still humanly beautiful, for the benefit of her human bodyguards, not us. She would have used more special effects if the show had been for us.

'Ms Reed,' Julian gushed, moving in to take her elbow, steering her away from us, 'we would never neglect you. You're not only our client, but one of the most precious objects we've ever been asked to guard. We would lay our lives down for you. What more can men do when they worship a woman?'

I thought he was laying it on a bit thick, but I hadn't spent any time around Maeve Reed. Maybe she liked the compliments thick.

She managed a delicate blush that I knew was magic and not real. I could feel it in the air. Sometimes the most simple physical changes take the most magic. She slid her arm through his and lowered her voice enough that we couldn't hear what was said. Oh, we could have eavesdropped, but that would have been rude and she would probably have sensed the spell. We didn't want to antagonize the goddess; not yet, anyway.

They turned back to face us, both smiling, both charming, her grip on his arm very firm. Something in Julian's eyes was trying to give me a message, but I couldn't quite read it behind his hip yellow tinted glasses.

'Ms Reed has persuaded me to remain at her side for the duration of your visit.' He raised an eyebrow as he spoke.

And finally I got the message. Ms Reed had hired Kane and Hart to protect her from *us*. She was afraid of the Unseelie Court, enough that she wouldn't be alone with us without backup, both magical and physical. Although her magic thrummed through this house, this land, these walls, she still feared us. You'd think the fey wouldn't be so superstitious, especially about other fey, but they often are. My father said it came from knowing almost nothing about any other fey culture but the one we were born into. Ignorance breeds fear.

There'd been so much magic inside Maeve's walls that almost from the moment we'd driven through the gates I'd begun to not 'hear' it. It was a skill you learned if you spent too much time in and around major-brouhaha magic. You had to deaden its touch, or you spent all your time sensing the constant magic around you, and it deadened you to newer spells, more immediate dangers. It was like being bombarded by a hundred radio stations at once. If you tried to listen to all of them, you heard nothing.

I looked into Maeve Reed's smiling, unreadable face and shook my head. I turned to look at Doyle. I tried to ask with my eyes and face how rude and how human I was allowed to be today.

He seemed to understand, because he gave a tiny nod. I took it to mean I could be as rude and human as I wanted. I hoped that was what it meant, because I was just about to pay several mortal insults to the golden goddess of Hollywood.

Chapter 10

I WALKED AROUND THE COUCH TO GREET THE Goddess. Kitto followed me, and I had to make him stay by the couch. Left to his own devices, he'd have stayed glued to my side like an overly devoted puppy.

I smiled toward Maeve and Julian 'I can't tell you what an honor it is to meet you, Ms Reed.' I held out my hand, and she took one hand off Julian's arm long enough to shake.

She gave me just the tips of her fingers; it wasn't so much a handshake as a touch. I'd seen a lot of women who didn't know how to shake hands, but Maeve hadn't even really tried. Maybe I was supposed to take her hand and kneel, but if she was waiting for genuflecting, she was in for a long wait. I had one queen and one queen only. Maeve Reed may have been a queen of Hollywood, but that just wasn't the same thing.

I knew my face looked puzzled, but I couldn't decide what was going on behind that lovely face of hers. We needed to know.

'You really did hire Kane and Hart to protect you from us, didn't you?'

Maeve turned a perfect look on me, pleasant, bemused, incredulous: eyes wide, beautifully lip-sticked mouth open in a small *o*. It was a look for a camera, for a screen that would make her face twenty feet tall. It was a face to win over audiences and the heads of studios.

It was a great face, but it wasn't that great. 'A simple yes or no will suffice, Ms Reed.'

'I'm sorry,' she said, voice apologetic, face soft, eyes a little confused. Her grip on Julian's arm was too tight; it gave a lie to that casual confused act.

'Did you hire Kane and Hart to protect you from us?'

She gave the laugh that *People* magazine had once called the five-million-dollar laugh, the one where her eyes crinkled and her face shone and her mouth was just a little open. 'What a strange idea. I assure you, Ms Gentry I am not afraid of you.'

She'd avoided a direct answer. She wasn't afraid of me; that much had to be true, because it is taboo among us to truly lie. If Doyle hadn't suggested in the van that I be rude, I'd have let it go, because pursuing it relentlessly would have been more than rude; it would have been insulting, and duels had started over less. But only among highborn sidhe could one be expected to know the rules. We were counting on Maeve assuming I'd been raised by savages – Unseelies and humans.

'Are you afraid of my guards, then?' I asked.

The laughter was still making her face shine, her eyes sparkle as she looked at me. 'Whatever gave you such an absurd idea?'

'You did.'

She shook her head, sending that long yellow sheet of hair sliding around her body. The glow of the laughter still shone in her face, and her eyes were just a little more blue. I realized suddenly that it wasn't the glow of laughter, which should have faded, but a very subtle type of glamour. She was purposefully making herself glow, just a little. And if she was glowing, she was using magic to try to persuade me to believe her.

I frowned, because I couldn't feel magic being used against me. Usually when another sidhe uses magic, you know it.

I glanced behind me at the guards. Doyle and Frost were standing, but they were unreadable now, imperious even. Kitto was still standing beside the couch where I'd left him. One small hand had a death grip on the white back, as if touching anything was better than standing untouched.

I wondered if he was feeling things I couldn't. I was only part fey; I was always willing to believe that I'd missed parts by that mixed heritage. I'd gained things, too – being able to do major magic surrounded by metal, for instance – but with every gain there can be a loss.

'Ms Reed, I'll ask you one more time, did you hire Kane and Hart to protect you from my guards?'

'What I told Julian and his men was that I had some overzealous fans.'

I didn't bother to look at Julian for confirmation. 'I believe that's what you told Julian, Ms Reed. Now, what's the real reason that you hired them?'

She stared at me with mock horror, or maybe it was real. She glanced at Frost and Doyle, and said, 'Have you taught her no manners?'

'She has what manners she needs,' Doyle said.

A look flickered through Maeve's eyes, fear, I think. She looked back to me, and down in those softly glowing blue eyes, that flicker remained. She was afraid. Very, very afraid. But of what?

'Did you really hire Julian and his people because of some overzealous fan?'

'Stop this,' she whispered.

'Do you really believe that we will harm you?' I asked.

'No,' she said, and she said it too quickly, as if she was relieved to finally be able to give a straightforward answer.

'Then why are you afraid of us?'

'Why are you doing this to me?' she asked, and her voice held all the sorrow of every maiden who had ever asked that question of a lover gone astray.

It tightened my throat to hear it. Julian looked stricken. 'I think you've asked enough questions, Meredith.'

I shook my head. 'No, I haven't.' I met those pain-filled blue eyes, and said, 'Ms Reed, you don't have to hide yourself from us.'

'I don't know what you mean.'

'That is entirely too close to a lie,' I said softly.

Her eyes suddenly looked like blue crystal, and I realized I was seeing those blue-blue eyes through the shine of unshed tears. Then the tears slid slowly down her golden cheeks, and as they fell, the blue of her eyes blurred, changed, still blue, but tricolored like my own.

There was a wide outer edge of rich deep blue like a bright sapphire, then a much thinner ring of melted copper, and an equally thin circle of liquid gold around the dark point of her pupil. But what set her eyes apart even among the sidhe was that the gold and copper trailed out across her iris like streaks of color in a good piece of lapis lazuli, so that metallic glints shone out from that ring of faultless deep blue.

Her eyes were like a stormy blue sky shattered by colored lightning.

In the forty years she'd been a movie star, no camera had ever seen these eyes. Her real eyes. I'm sure some agent or studio head had long ago convinced her to hide the least human of her features. I'd hidden what I was and what I looked like for only three years, and it had killed parts of me to do it. Maeve Reed had done it for decades.

She kept her eyes averted from Julian, as if she didn't want him to see them. I took her hand from Julian's arm; she tried to fight me, and I didn't tug on her. I just kept a light pressure on her wrist until she raised the hand of her own accord. Then I took her hand full in mine, cradling it. I knelt in front of her and brought her hand to my lips. I laid the lightest of touches on that golden hand, and said, 'You have the most beautiful eyes I have ever seen, Maeve Reed.'

She took her other hand from Julian's grip and just stood there staring down at me, tears streaming like crystal drops down her cheeks. Slowly, she let the rest of the glamour go. The tan began to fade, or change, until she was no longer honey brown but an overall soft gold. Her hair grew paler, blond and blonder, until it was almost a white blond. I could not imagine why she'd changed her hair to the more standard yellow blond. Either color was well within human standards.

I held both her hands in mine while she stripped away a century of lies and stood before me a shining thing. Suddenly there seemed to be more colors in the room, a breath of sweet scented flowers that grew thousands of miles away from this desert place. She gripped my hands as if they were her only anchor, as if she might vanish into the light and sweetness if I let her go.

She threw back her head, eyes closed, and her golden glow filled the room as if a small sun had suddenly risen before me. She glowed, and she cried, and she held my hands so hard it hurt. Somewhere during all of it, I found I was crying, too, and her glow had called my own, so that my skin looked as if it were filled with moonlight.

She came to her knees beside me, looking wonderingly at my hands and hers, one glow pressed against the other. She began to laugh joyously, a little hysterically.

Somewhere in all the laughter, I could make out her words, 'And I . . . thought the men . . . were the danger.'

She leaned into me suddenly and pressed her lips to mine. I was so startled by the kiss that I simply froze for a second. What I would have done if she'd given me time to think, I don't know, because she jerked away from me and ran back out the way she'd come.

Chapter 11

JULIAN HAD GONE AFTER MAEVE. IT LEFT YOUNG Frank standing by the exit looking lost. His eyes were too large in his pale, startled face. I doubted Frank had ever seen a sidhe in her full power.

I was still kneeling, the glow beginning to fade from my skin, when Doyle came to stand beside me. 'Princess, are you well?'

I looked up at him and realized I must have looked a little startled myself. I could feel the heat on my mouth where her lips had touched mine. It was like I'd taken a sip of spring sunshine.

'Princess?'

I nodded. 'I'm all right.' But my voice came out hoarse, and I had to clear my throat before I said, 'I've just never . . .' I tried to put it into words. 'She tasted like sunshine. And until this second I didn't know that sunshine tasted like anything.'

Doyle knelt beside me and spoke softly. 'It is always difficult to be touched by those who hold such elemental powers.'

I frowned at him. 'She said she thought it was the men she needed to be afraid of. What did she mean by that?'

'Think how you were after just a few years alone out here .. and magnify that by a human century.'

I felt my eyes widen. 'You mean she's attracted to me.' I shook my head before he could say anything. 'She's attracted to the first sidhe she's touched in a hundred years.'

'Do not underestimate yourself, Meredith, but I have never heard it said that Conchenn was a lover of women, so, yes, it is the touch of sidhe flesh that she craves.'

I sighed. 'I cannot blame her.' And then another thought occurred to me. 'You don't think she's invited us here to ask if I'll share one of you with her?'

Doyle's dark eyebrows raised over the top of his sunglasses. 'I had not thought of such a thing.' He seemed to be thinking about what I'd said. 'I suppose it is possible.' He frowned. 'But it would be the height of rudeness to ask such a thing. We are not merely your lovers but potential husbands. It is not casual.'

'You said it yourself, Doyle, she's been alone for a century. A hundred years might wear down anyone's sense of politeness.'

There was movement behind us; we turned to find Frost already on his feet facing the entrance. It was Rhys. 'What have you guys been doing in here?'

'What do you mean?' I asked.

He gestured at Doyle and me kneeling on the floor. There was still the faintest of glows to my skin like a memory of moonlight.

I let Doyle help me to my feet; I was strangely unsteady. Maeve had caught me off guard, true,

111

but I'd been touched a great deal more by other sidhe and not been this shaken.

I spoke. 'Maeve Reed dropped her glamour.'

Rhys's eye widened. 'I felt it outside. You're telling me that all she did was drop her glamour?'

I nodded.

He gave a low whistle. 'Sweet Goddess.'

'And that is the point,' Doyle said.

Rhys looked at him. 'What do you mean?'

'We have all been worshipped in the past, but for most of us it is in the long past. For Conchenn it has been less than three hundred years. She was still being worshipped in Europe when we were asked to . . . leave.'

'So you're saying that she's got more power because she was being worshipped?' Rhys asked.

'Not more power,' Doyle said, 'but more . . .'

'Oomph,' I suggested.

'I am unfamiliar with the word,' he said.

'More . . . jazz, more bite, more crack to the whip.' I waved my hands in the air. 'I don't know. Rhys knows what I mean.'

He came down the three steps to the living room. 'Yeah, I know what you mean. She's got more of a charge to her magic.'

Doyle finally nodded. 'I will accept that.'

Frost came to stand with us. Doyle looked at him from behind dark glasses, and the bigger man hesitated, frowning. 'I have an insight to add, my captain.'

The two men carefully measured each other. I interrupted. 'What's wrong with you two? If Frost has something to add, then let him say it.'

Frost continued to look at Doyle, as if waiting. Finally, Doyle gave one quick nod. Frost gave a small bow. 'I have watched movies on Meredith's television set. I have seen how humans react to these movie stars. Their adoration of the actors is a type of worship.'

We all looked at him. It was Rhys who whispered, 'Lord and Lady, if anyone could prove that she's been worshipped . . .' He let his voice trail off.

Doyle finished the thought for him. 'Then there would be grounds to exile us all from this country. The one thing we were forbidden to do was set ourselves up to be worshipped as gods.'

I shook my head. 'She did not set herself up to be worshipped as a deity. She was just trying to earn a living.'

The men thought about that for a few seconds, then finally Doyle nodded. 'The princess is correct by law.'

'I don't think Maeve intended to get around the law,' I said.

He shook his head. 'I do not mean to imply otherwise, but whatever her intent, she has the added benefit of having been worshipped by humans for the last forty years. A human movie star cannot take advantage of that kind of energy exchange, but Maeve is sidhe, and she will know exactly how to use such energy.'

'What does that say about the models and actors in Europe that have sidhe blood in them?' I asked. 'Or even the royal families of Europe? Sidhe had to marry into all the royal houses of Europe to cement the last great treaty. Are they all taking extra benefit from their human admirers?'

'It is not something I can speak to,' Doyle said.

'I'll take a guess at it,' Rhys said.

113

Doyle frowned at him, and the look was clear even through the dark glasses. 'We are not paid to guess.'

Rhys grinned through his fake beard. 'Think of it as an extra plus when you hire me.'

Doyle lowered the glasses enough for Rhys to see his eyes.

'Ooh,' Rhys said. Then, laughing, he said, 'I'll bet that anyone with enough sidhe blood in them can gain power from all that human adoration. They may not be aware of it, but how else do you explain the successful reigns of the royal houses with the highest percentage of sidhe blood? All are still active, while the houses that took the sidhe only once treated it like a plague and stopped, and they have died out.'

Julian came back into the room. 'Ms Reed has requested that this meeting continue out by the pool, unless there is some strong objection against it.'

'I don't see a problem with taking this outside on such a beautiful day,' I said.

'Nor I,' Doyle said.

The others agreed – everyone but Kitto. He was still huddled by the couch. I finally had to go to him and take his hand. He whispered, 'It will be very open and very bright out there.'

Kitto had spent centuries inside the dark cramped tunnels of the goblin mound. I'd always wondered why in the old stories the goblins always fought under a dark sky, as if they brought the darkness of the ground with them. If they were all as bothered by openness and light as Kitto, maybe they couldn't have fought without their darkness. Or maybe it was just Kitto. I shouldn't

114

make such a wide assumption based on only one goblin.

I took his hand in mine and led him like a child. 'You can stay by me. If it gets to be too much, Frost can take you back to the van.'

'Is there some problem?' Julian asked.

'He's agoraphobic.'

'Oh, my,' Julian said.

'If he wishes to remain here in L.A., he's got to work on it,' I said.

Julian gave a small nod of his head, almost a bow. 'As you like, he is your . . . employee.'

Kitto was one of the few guards who did not work for the agency. He just wasn't suited for that kind of work. I wasn't sure what kind of work he was suited for, but it wasn't bodyguard work, and it wasn't detecting. But I didn't correct Julian about Kitto's status.

'If you're sure?' Julian made it a question.

I gripped Kitto's hand more firmly. 'I'm sure.'

'Then follow me, Princess, gentlemen.' He started down the hallway that Maeve had fled down, and we followed. Doyle insisted on walking first and insisted that Frost go last. I ended up in the middle with Rhys on one side and Kitto on the other. Rhys took my other hand and tried to get me to skip down the hallway, while he hummed 'We're off to See the Wizard' under his breath.

Chapter 12

JULIAN LED US THROUGH ONE EXPENSIVE ROOM
after another until we ended up at the pool. It was
blue and flashed light, like a broken mirror. Maeve
sat in the shadow of a big umbrella. She was
wrapped tightly in a white silk robe. She'd given us
the briefest glimpse of a gold and white bathing
suit before tying the robe tightly in place, so that
only her perfectly pedicured feet showed. She was
smoking, taking furious puffs and grinding out the
cigarette before it was halfway done. Julian had
been granted the unenviable task of lighting the
cigarettes for her with a gold lighter from the small
tray that held the cigarette box. Lighting the cigs
wasn't the unenviable part of the job – trying to
calm Maeve down was the hard part.

She had put her glamour back on like a well-
worn shirt. She was still beautiful, but she looked
like Maeve Reed the movie star again, though a
very stressed version. Anxiety flowed off her in
waves.

The other bodyguards, including young Frank
and Max, had come back to stand around the
pool and look menacing. Some of the menacing

seemed to be directed at us, but we didn't take it personally, or at least I didn't. I wasn't 100 percent sure about my men. Whatever they felt, they were keeping it to themselves.

Maeve insisted on all of us sitting in full sun. I wasn't sure why, but I could guess. Superstition said that the Unseelie Court couldn't abide sunlight. In truth, some could not, but no one with me had that problem. Kitto's eyes were light sensitive but nothing he couldn't handle with dark glasses.

I didn't burst Maeve's bubble. She was still obviously shaken, making sure all that lovely body was covered by the silk robe, and she'd moved from smoking to drinking while we got arranged in chairs. At least the alcohol didn't invade my stomach without my consent. So, personally, I found it a step up. If Maeve got drunk, I might change my mind.

Julian sat on a much smaller chair, pulled up beside her lounge chair. She'd insisted on him being close enough that his shoulder touched the back of her chair. The rest of the Kane and Hart bodyguards stood at her back like three ladies-in-waiting, albeit muscular, well-armed ladies-in-waiting.

Maeve had also insisted that I have my own lounge chair. I was a little too short, and so was my skirt, for a lounge chair; but I took it graciously. I just had to pay attention that I didn't flash too much leg and underwear. If it had just been other fey, I wouldn't have cared so much, but with more humans than fey standing around, we'd try to stay polite by human standards. Besides, I'd found years ago that if I let a bunch

117

of strange human men see my underwear, they tended to get the wrong idea. Fey males would have enjoyed the show and never remarked on it.

Doyle and Frost stood at my back like good bodyguards. Rhys had gone with the personal assistant, Marie, to take off his disguise. Maeve had seemed fascinated by the fact that he'd used a human disguise instead of glamour to escape the press's attention.

Either her glamour was better than ours, or reporters simply didn't see her as anything but Maeve Reed, movie star. The word *glamorous* comes from the idea of faerie glamour; maybe seeing the truth behind a movie star's facade just wasn't what the press wanted to see.

Kitto sat beside me in his own little chair, but he did everything but perch on the arm of my lounge chair. Julian tried to keep a distance between himself and Maeve; Kitto made sure that he touched some part of my body continuously.

A human woman in her sixties came out of a nearby pool house. She wore a maid's outfit, complete with apron, though the skirt was suitably long and the shoes suitably sensible. She offered us all drinks, which we refused. Only Maeve kept drinking wine-dark Scotch. She'd started with ice, but when it melted she didn't replace it. Although she finished off a fifth of Scotch while we watched, there was no change in her. She was fey and we could drink a lot without getting even the least bit tipsy, but a fifth of Scotch is a fifth of Scotch, and I hoped she'd drunk enough to quiet her nerves and would stop there. She didn't.

'I'm going to have rum and coke. Would anyone else care for anything?'

'No, thank you,' I said.

'I know that the men are working, yours and mine, so they shouldn't drink. It might spoil their reflexes.' She put a little bit of the old Maeve Reed purr into her voice, a pale imitation of her usual suggestiveness. Apparently, I hadn't broken her completely. 'But you and I can indulge.'

'I'm fine, but thank you for offering.'

A small frown appeared between those perfect brows. 'I really do hate to drink alone.'

'I'm not much for Scotch or rum.'

'We have an extensive wine cellar. I'm sure we could find you something to suit your tastes.' She smiled, not the dazzling smile she'd started the visit with but a smile nonetheless. It was an encouraging sign, but I shook my head.

'I'm sorry, Maeve, but I really don't drink this early in the day.'

'Early,' she said, perfectly plucked eyebrow arching. 'Honey, this isn't early by L.A. standards. If it's after lunch, it's perfectly acceptable to be drinking.'

I smiled, gave a small shrug. 'Thanks, but really, I'm fine.'

She frowned at that, but nodded at the maid, who went off toward the house, to fetch Maeve's drink, I assumed.

'I really do hate to drink alone,' she said again.

'I'm sure you've got a husband around here somewhere.'

'You'll be meeting Gordon later after we've finished our business.' There was no teasing now.

'And what business would that be?' I asked.

'It's private.'

I shook my head. 'We went over this with your

flunky earlier in our office. Where I go, my body-guards go.' I glanced at her own personal wall of muscle. 'I'm sure you understand that.'

She nodded impatiently. 'Of course I understand, but could they all sit just a little farther back so we could have some .. girl talk?'

I raised my eyebrows at the *girl talk*, but let it go. I glanced at Doyle and Frost. 'What do you guys think?'

'I suppose we could sit at the table in the shade while you and Ms Reed have your . . . girl talk.' Doyle managed to put a lot of disbelief in that last phrase.

I hid my smile by turning my head and looking at Kitto. He wasn't going to want to be in the shade of the umbrella. I didn't even bother to ask.

'Doyle and Frost will sit at the table, but Kitto has to stay with me.'

Maeve shook her head. 'That is not acceptable.'

I shrugged. 'It's the best you're going to get if you insist on being outside in the open like this.'

She cocked her head to one side. 'That is awfully blunt for a princess of the sidhe. In fact, you've been very blunt, nay rude, for a princess of the blood.'

I fought an urge to look back at Doyle. 'I could say I was raised out among the humans.'

'You could, but I don't think I'll believe you.' Her voice was very quiet, almost angry. 'No one that human would be so favored by the Lady and the Lord as you were just moments ago.' She shivered, pulling her robe tighter around her shoulders. It was eighty and the sun was warm and soft. If she was cold, it wasn't the kind of cold that a robe could help.

I did the best bow I could, sitting in the lounge chair. 'Thank you.'

She shook her head, sending her long yellow hair sliding around her body. 'Do not thank me, for I shall not thank you for what you have done to me.'

I started to tell her that it had been an accident, but stopped. Maeve had deliberately used magic to try to persuade me. It was a grave insult between one sidhe noble to another. We never used wiles to that degree against another noble. It showed clearly that she considered me a lesser fey, so the rules of sidhe chivalry didn't apply to me.

She was looking at me curiously, and I realized I'd been quiet for too long. I managed a smile. 'The sidhe have been speculating for centuries about why you left us.'

'I did not leave, Meredith. I was cast out.'

Here at last was something I wanted to know. 'Your exile was the bogeyman for all the younger sidhe in the Seelie Court. "If you don't please the king, you'll end as Conchenn did." '

'Is that what they believed? That I was exiled for not pleasing the king?'

'When pressed, that is what the king says. That you did not please him.'

She laughed, and it held derision so thick that it was almost painful to hear. 'I suppose I didn't please him, but didn't anyone question that such strict exile was a harsh punishment for merely not pleasing the king?'

I nodded. 'I'm told that some did question the severity of the punishment. You had many friends at court.'

'I had allies at court. No one truly has friends there.'

I gave her credit for that. 'As you like, you had many allies at court. I am told they did question your fate.'

'And?' There was a little too much eagerness to that one word.

She seemed to really want to know. I wanted to say, *you answer my questions and I'll answer yours*, but that was a little too crass. Subtlety, that was what was needed. Subtle had never been my natural bent, but I had learned. Eventually.

'I was beaten for asking about your fate,' I said.

She blinked at me. 'What?'

'As a child I asked why you were exiled, and the king himself beat me for asking.'

She looked puzzled. 'Had no one asked before?'

'They asked,' I said.

The expression on her face was enough to urge me on, but I didn't finish the thought. I avoided letting her turn around the conversation, because I wanted to know why she'd been exiled. If she'd kept her silence for a hundred years, then I couldn't trust that she'd easily break it now.

'By the time I came along, people had stopped asking.'

'What happened to my allies at court?' It was a very direct question, and I couldn't pretend not to understand anymore.

'The king killed Emrys,' I said. 'After that, everyone was afraid to ask after your fate.'

It was hard to tell, but I think she paled under that golden tan. Her eyes went wide before she dropped her gaze to her lap. She started to take a drink and found the tumbler empty.

122

She yelled, 'Nancy!'

The maid appeared, almost but not quite as if by magic. She had a tray with a tall dark glass of rum, a pair of white-rimmed sunglasses folded beside the drink. She'd also brought three swimsuits draped on her arm. They were all expensive, lovely, and tiny. Most of the underwear I owned covered more than those suits, and I owned a lot of lingerie.

They looked like ordinary, if elegant swimsuits, but appearance could be deceiving. Things can be done to clothes so the spell takes over only when the garment is worn. Nasty spells, some of them. For the first time I wondered, not if Maeve wanted to join our court, but if there were people at the Seelie Court who wanted me dead. Would my death be enough to undo her exile? Only if the king himself wanted my death. To my knowledge, Taranis didn't like me, but he didn't fear me, so my death should mean nothing to him.

Maeve had stopped talking. She was staring out at the pool, but I don't think she truly saw it. She was quiet for so long that I filled the silence. 'Why the swimsuits, Ms Reed?'

'I said to call me Maeve.' But she never looked at me, and the phrase had a rehearsed quality, as if she wasn't truly listening to her own words.

I smiled. 'Fine, why the swimsuits, Maeve?'

'I thought you might want to get more comfortable, that's all.' Her voice still sounded flat, like dialogue that she'd planned to say but no longer cared about.

'Thank you, but I'm fine as I am.'

'I'm sure I can find suits for your gentlemen,

too.' She finally looked at me while she spoke, but her voice was still muted.

'No, thank you.' And I put enough force into the *thank you* that I thought she'd take the hint.

Maeve set the empty glass on the tray, slipped the sunglasses on, and only then took the new drink in hand. She drained a quarter of it in one long swallow, then looked at me. The glasses were large and round with fat white rims, and they were mirrored so that I could see a distorted reflection of myself as she moved her head. Her eyes and a large part of her face were completely hidden. She didn't need glamour now; she had something else to hide behind.

She pulled the robe closer to her neck and sipped the black rum. 'Even Taranis would not dare to have Emrys executed.' Her voice was low, but clear. I think she was working on not believing me. She'd given herself enough time with her rehearsed bit about the swimsuits that she'd thought about what I'd said. She didn't like it, so she was going to try to make it not true.

'He wasn't executed,' I said, and again I watched her, waited for her to ask for more. You often learned more by saying less.

She looked up from her drink, making those mirrored glasses glint in the sun. 'But you said Taranis had had him killed.'

'No, I said he killed Emrys.'

It was hard to tell behind the large sunglasses, but I think she frowned. 'You are playing word games with me, Meredith. Emrys was one of the few among the courts that I might truly have called friend. If he was not executed, then what? Are you hinting at assassination?'

124

I shook my head. 'Not at all. The king chal-lenged him to a personal duel.'

She jumped as if I'd struck her, sloshing some of the rum over the white of the robe. The maid offered her a linen napkin. Maeve handed the drink to the woman and began to wipe at her hand, but not like she was paying attention to what she was doing.

'The king does not take personal challenges. He is too valuable to the court to risk on a duel.'

I shrugged, watching my image imitate me in her glasses. 'I just report the news, I don't explain it.'

She put the napkin on the tray, but refused the return of her drink. She leaned forward, still hold-ing the robe closed at neck and thigh. 'Swear to me, your solemn oath, that the king slew Emrys in a duel.'

'I give you my oath that this is true.'

She leaned back suddenly, as if all the energy had drained from her. Her hands were still feebly clutching at the robe, but she looked half-swooned.

The maid asked, 'Are you all right? Is there any-thing you need?'

Maeve gave a weak wave. 'No. I'm fine.' She'd answered the questions in reverse order, a bit of a slip, because she was obviously not all right.

'So, I was right.' Her voice was very soft as she said the last.

'You were right about what?' I asked, voice equally soft. I eased down to the foot of my own lounge chair so she would be sure to hear me.

She smiled then, but it was weak and not at all humorous. 'No, you won't get my secret that easily.'

I frowned, and it was genuine. 'I don't know what you mean.'

Her voice was more solid, more certain of itself as she spoke. 'Why did you come here today, Meredith?'

I sat back a little. 'I came because you asked me.'

She sighed loud and long, not for effect this time, but I think just because she needed to. 'You risked Taranis's anger simply to visit with another sidhe? I think not.'

'I am heir to the Unseelie throne. Do you really think Taranis would risk harming me?'

'He challenged Emrys to a personal duel for merely asking why I had been exiled. You yourself were beaten as a child for asking about my fate. Now, here you sit speaking with me. He will never believe that I have not told you the reason for my exile.'

'But you've told me nothing,' I said, and I tried to keep the eagerness out of my body language, though I think I failed.

She gave another slight smile. 'He will never believe that I have not shared my secret with you.'

'He can think what he likes. To harm me would mean war between the courts. I don't believe that any secret you have is worth that.'

She laughed, derisive again. 'I think the king would risk war between the courts for this.'

'Fine, the king might risk a war where he could sit safely behind the front lines, but Queen Andais would be within her rights to challenge him to one-on-one combat. I don't believe Taranis would risk that.'

'You are the heir to the dark throne, Meredith.

You have no idea what power resides in the light.'

'I've seen the Seelie Court, Maeve, and I agree that once you've fallen afoul of it, you're afraid of the light; but everyone fears the dark, Maeve, everyone.'

'Are you saying that the high king of the Seelie Court is afraid of the Unseelie Court?' Her voice held an amazing amount of outraged disbelief.

'I know everyone at the Seelie Court fears the sluagh.'

Maeve sat back in her chair. 'Everyone fears them, Meredith, at both courts.'

She was right. If the Unseelie Court was all that was dark and frightening, then the sluagh was worse. The sluagh was home even to the things that the Unseelie feared. It was a dumping ground for nightmares too terrible to contemplate.

'And who holds the reins of the sluagh?' I asked.

She looked uncertain, but said, at last, 'The queen.'

'The sluagh can be sent to punish certain crimes without a trial or a warning. One of those crimes is kin slaying.'

'That is not often enforced,' she said.

'But if Taranis killed the queen's heir, don't you think she'd remember that little law?'

'Even Andais would not dare send the sluagh after the king.'

'And I say again, that even the king would not dare slay Andais's heir.'

'I think you are wrong on that, Meredith, for this he might dare.'

'And for that crime, Andais might loose the sluagh on him. Even the King of Light and Illusion would have no choice but to run from them.'

She took the drink off the tray that the maid still held near at hand. She took a deep drink before saying, 'I do not believe that the king would think that clearly about this. I . . . I would not be the cause of war between the courts.' She took another drink. 'I have wished for Taranis's arrogance to be punished over the years, but not by the sluagh. I would not wish that on anyone, not even him.'

Having been chased by the sluagh myself, I could agree that they were terrible. But they weren't as bad as all that. At least the sluagh would simply kill you – maybe eat you alive – but you'd be dead. There would be no torture, no long, slow death. There were worse deaths than to fall to the sluagh.

And I knew something that Maeve could not know. The sluagh's king, Sholto, Lord of That Which Passes Between, called Shadowspawn, but never to his face, had no great loyalty to Andais, or to anyone else for that matter. He kept his word, but Andais had let her politics slide for a few years, and now she depended heavily, too heavily, on the threat of the sluagh. They'd been meant to be the threat of last resort. I'd learned in talking with Doyle and Frost that the sluagh had become a much-used weapon. That was not what they were meant for, and it showed great weakness on Andais's part that she used them too often.

But Maeve did not know this. No one at the Seelie Court knew, unless there were spies, which, come to think upon it, there probably were; but Maeve didn't know it.

'Do you really think that the king will learn that we spoke together?' I asked.

'I don't know for certain, but he is a god, or was once. I fear he will discover us.'

'Fine, I want to know why you were exiled – but you want something from me, as well. You want something that you would risk your very life for. What could that be, Maeve? What could be that important to you?'

She leaned forward, robe still closed tight. She leaned forward until I could smell the cocoa butter from her skin and the harsh rum on her breath. She whispered against my ear, 'I want a child.'

Chapter 13

I STAYED LEANING IN, SHOULDERS ALMOST touching with Maeve, because I didn't want her to see my face. A child? She wanted a child? Why tell me? I'd thought of a lot of things Maeve Reed could want; a baby had not been on the list.

I finally looked at her. 'What would you have of me, Maeve?' That was the question.

She sat back in her chair, settling with a small wriggling movement that reminded me of her old teasing. 'I have told you what I would have of you, Meredith.'

I stared at her, frowning. 'I know what you said, Maeve, but I don't see . . .' I tried again. 'I don't know how *I* can help you.' I put a little emphasis on the *I* because I had thought of one thing I had that she might need. I had the men.

She looked around at the men, all the men, her bodyguards included. 'You can understand now why I would want privacy for this discussion, can't you?' There was a small thread of pleading in her voice.

I sighed. I wanted to be politically savvy. I wanted to be cautious. But I did understand why she desired privacy. Some things supersede politics, your side, my side, and one of those is the plea of woman-to-woman. Maeve had given that plea, silently, but it was still there. Mother help me, but I couldn't pretend ignorance.

'All right,' I said.

Maeve put her head to one side. 'All right to what?'

'Privacy.'

I felt both Doyle and Frost move behind me. They didn't truly move, not a step, but they tensed so hard it was almost a jump.

'Princess,' Doyle began.

'It's all right, Doyle. You and the rest of the men can sit under the umbrella while we have our girl talk.'

Maeve frowned, her pale pink lipsticked mouth pouting prettily. She was definitely regaining her composure. Or maybe she'd spent so many years as Maeve Reed, sex goddess, that she didn't know how else to behave.

'I was hoping for a little more privacy than a few yards.'

I smiled at her, no pouting, no pretense. 'You've shown that you're willing to persuade me with magic. It would be stupid of me to trust you completely.'

The pout vanished, replaced by thin, almost angry lips. 'You've proven you can best me at magic, Meredith. I am not so stupid as to try my luck for a second time.'

Again, I was pretty certain that I had not bested Maeve at magic. It was more that she'd thrown her magic in my metaphysical face and my natural abilities had been awakened. It hadn't been

131

deliberate on my part; in fact, I wasn't 100 percent certain that I could have duplicated it if I'd tried. But Maeve believed that I could do it at will, and I wasn't going to dissuade her. Let her believe that I was wonderfully powerful, and paranoid. Because I wasn't going anywhere completely out of sight of the men. Powerful and paranoid – it was a recipe for royalty.

'My guards can sit in the shade while we talk out here. That is as much privacy as I'm willing to give you, even for girl talk.'

'You don't trust me,' she said.

'Why should I?'

She smiled. 'You shouldn't. You most certainly shouldn't.' She shook her head and sipped her rum, then gazed at me over the rim of her glass. 'You've refused all refreshment. You fear poison or magic.'

I nodded.

She laughed, a delighted burst of sound. I'd heard that selfsame laugh on the movie screen more than once. 'I give you my most solemn oath nothing here shall harm you a-purpose.'

Adding that last bit was nicely tricky. It meant that if I did come to harm, it wouldn't be her fault, but it also meant that I could come to harm. I had to smile. Such double-talk was so much a part of the court, where your word of honor was something you'd fight to the death to defend.

'I want your word of honor that no thing, no person, no animal, no being of any kind will harm me while I am here.'

The pout was back. 'Now, Meredith. Such a solemn oath? I will give my word to protect your safety to the best of my ability.'

I shook my head. 'Your word that no thing, no person, no animal, no being of any kind will harm me.'

'While you are here,' she added.

I nodded. 'While I am here.'

'If you had left that last little bit off, I'd have been responsible for you always, everywhere you go.' She shivered, and I don't think it was pretense. 'You go to the Unseelie Court, and that is not a place I would wish to have to guarantee your safety.'

'Everyone seems to feel that way, Maeve. Don't feel bad.'

She frowned, and again I think it was real. 'I do not feel bad, Meredith. It is not within my purview to guard your safety within those dark, shadowed corridors.'

I shrugged. 'There is light and laughter within the darkling throng, just as there is darkness and sorrow among the glittering throng.'

'I will not believe that the Unseelie Court holds the joyous wonders that await one at the Seelie Court.'

I looked over my shoulder at Doyle and Frost. I made it a long look, then turned slowly back to Maeve, allowing their beauty to fill my eyes. 'Oh, I don't know, Maeve, there are joys to be had at the dark court.'

'I have heard tales of the debauchery that exists at Queen Andais's court.'

That made me laugh. 'You have lived too long among the humans if you say debauchery with such distaste. The joys of the flesh are a blessing to be shared, not a curse to be guarded against.'

'As your wayward guard and my sweet Marie

should know.' She looked past me, smiling. Rhys and Marie were walking toward us. Rhys's white curls fell free to his waist again. His boyishly handsome face was its usual clean-shaven self. The pearl-studded eye patch was back in place. He was smiling, pleased with himself to the point of nearly laughing, as if he knew some new joke.

Marie trailed behind him. Her hair was a little less than perfect, and her white shirt was untucked. But she didn't look happy.

If Maeve's hint was true, then Marie would be smiling. Rhys had his faults, but not putting a smile on a girl's face was not one of them. You couldn't really take him as seriously in, or out of, bed as some of the other guards, but he was a lot of fun in bed.

I found myself frowning again. If he had done something sexual with Marie, how did I feel about that? He was, after all, mine. Exclusively mine, according to the queen.

I tried to be hurt, jealous, or even miffed that he might have been playing slap and tickle with Marie, and I just wasn't. Maybe it was because I was sleeping with the other men. Maybe to be truly jealous you have to have some pretense of monogamy. I didn't know why, but it simply didn't bother me. If he'd had intercourse with her, that would bother me, because I was the one that we needed pregnant, not some assistant to some star. Other than that, I didn't seem to care.

Rhys dropped to one knee in front of me, which crowded Kitto a little; but the fact that he was willing to touch the little goblin was actually a very good sign. He raised my hand to his lips, grinning.

'The lovely Marie offered me her favors.'

I raised my eyebrows. 'And?'

'And it would have been rude to have ignored such an offer.' By fey standards, he was right.

'She's human, not fey,' I said.

'Jealous?' he asked.

I shook my head, smiling. 'No.'

He came to his feet in one smooth movement, planting a quick kiss on my cheek. 'I knew you were more fey than human.'

Marie was kneeling by Maeve. She kept her face turned away from us but shook her head, and Maeve turned a very frowny face to us. 'Marie said you refused her advances, guard.'

'I made it clear that I found her lovely,' Rhys said.

'But you did not take advantage of her.'

'I am Princess Meredith's lover. Why should I look elsewhere? I showed your assistant the amount of attention she deserved, no more, no less.' The humor was gone from his face now, and he seemed almost angry.

Maeve petted the woman's hand and sent her into the house. Marie very carefully avoided looking at Rhys. I think she was embarrassed. Maybe she didn't get turned down often, or maybe Maeve told her it was a sure thing.

I stood. 'I've had enough games, Maeve.'

She reached toward me, but I was out of reach. 'Please, Meredith, I meant no offense.'

'You sent your servant to seduce my lover. You tried to seduce me, not out of plain desire, but out of a desire to gain control over me.'

She stood in one swift motion. 'That last is not true.'

'But you do not deny sending your servant to seduce my lover.'

She took off the big sunglasses so I could see how confused she was. I was betting it was an act. 'You are Unseelie Court, and all manner of temptations are open to you.'

It was my turn to be confused. 'What does my court have to do with anything? You have insulted me and mine.'

'You are Unseelie Court,' she said again.

I shook my head. 'What does that have to do with anything?'

'You would not try on the swimsuits,' she said, voice soft, eyes downcast.

'What?' I asked.

'If Marie had seen him nude, then she would have known his body was pure, except for the scars.'

I frowned harder. 'What in the name of the Lord and Lady are you babbling about?'

'You are all Unseelie Court, Meredith. I have to be sure you are not . . . unclean.'

'You mean deformed,' I said, and I didn't even try to keep the anger out of my voice.

She gave a small nod.

'Why should our bodies, whatever they look like, make any difference to you?'

'I told you what I want, Meredith.'

I nodded, and I was nice enough not to blurt out her secret in front of everyone, though heaven knows she hadn't earned the courtesy.

'If anyone who aids me in such an endeavor is impure, then . . .' She sort of nodded at me, trying to get me to finish the sentence in my head.

I leaned into her and hissed, more than

whispered, 'The child will be deformed.'

No amount of glamour could hide the smell of cocoa butter, liquor, and cigarette smoke in her hair and skin. A sudden wave of nausea rushed over me.

I backed away from her and would have fallen if Rhys hadn't caught me, steadied me. 'What's wrong?' he whispered.

I shook my head. 'I'm tired of being here with this woman.'

'Then we leave,' Doyle said.

I shook my head again. 'Not yet.' I half clutched Rhys's arm and turned back to Maeve. 'You tell me why you were exiled. You tell me the whole truth here and now or we walk away from you forever.'

'If he knew I told anyone, he would kill me.'

'If he finds out I was here, talking to you, do you really believe he'll wait to find out if you told me?'

She looked frightened now. But I didn't care.

'Tell me, Maeve, tell me or we walk, and you'll never find anyone else outside of faerie who can help you.'

'Meredith, please . . .'

'No,' I said. 'The great pure Seelie Court, how they look down on us. If a child is born deformed, then it is killed, or was, until you all stopped having children. Then even the monsters were precious. Do you know what happened to the babies after a while, Maeve? Do you know what happened in the last four hundred years or so to deformed Seelie children? Because, make no mistake, inbreeding catches up, even with the immortal.'

'I don't . . . know.'

'Yes, you do. All that bright, shining throng know. My own cousin was kept because she was part brownie. You didn't throw her out, because brownies are Seelie – not court, but creatures of light. But when the sidhe themselves breed monsters, the pure, shining, Seelie sidhe, breed deformities, monstrosities, then what happens, where do they go?'

She was crying now, soft, silver tears. 'I don't know.'

'Yes, you do. The babies go to the Unseelie Court. We take in the monsters, those pure Seelie monsters. We take them in, because we welcome everyone. No one, no one is turned away from the Unseelie Court, especially not tiny, newborn babies whose only crime was to be born to parents who can't study a genealogical chart well enough to avoid marrying their own fucking siblings.' I was crying, too, now, but it was anger, not sorrow.

'I give you my oath that I and Frost and Rhys are pure of body. Does that make it easier? Does that help? If you just wanted to sleep with the men, you wouldn't have cared if you saw me in a swimsuit, but you did care. You want a fertility rite, Maeve. You need me, and at least one man.'

I was too angry to know if anyone besides Maeve had heard what I said, or understood what I'd said. I just didn't care.

I pushed away from Rhys, my anger carrying me forward to spit the words in her face. 'Tell me why you were exiled, Maeve, tell me now, or we leave you as we found you. Alone.'

She nodded, still crying. 'All right, all right, Lady guard me, but all right. I'll tell you what you

138

want to know, if you swear to me that you'll help me have a child.'

'You swear first,' I said.

'I swear that I will tell you the truth about why I was exiled from the Seelie Court.'

'And I swear that after you have told me why you were exiled from the Seelie Court, I and my men will do our best to see that you have a child.'

She rubbed at her eyes with the heels of her hands. It was a child's gesture. She seemed thoroughly shaken, and I wondered, had one of those poor, unfortunate babies belonged to Conchenn, goddess of beauty and spring? And had the thought of giving up the only child she might ever have haunted her? I hoped so.

Chapter 14

'A HUNDRED YEARS AGO, THE HIGH KING OF FAERIE, Taranis, was ready to put aside his wife, Conan of Cuala. They'd been a couple for a hundred years and had no children.' Her voice had fallen automatically into the singsong of the storyteller. 'So he was putting her aside.'

I loved a good story told in the old ways, but I wanted out of the sun, and I wanted not to be here forever. So I interrupted. 'He did put her away,' I said.

Maeve smiled, but not like it made her happy. 'He asked me to take her place as his bride. I refused him.' She was just talking to me now, the singsong lost. It might not have been as pretty, but straight conversation would be quicker.

'That's not a reason to be exiled, Maeve. At least one other has turned down Taranis's offer before, and she's still a part of the glittering throng.' I sipped my lemonade and watched her.

'But Edain was in love with another. My reason was different.'

She wasn't looking at me, or Kitto, or anyone, I think. She seemed to be staring off into space, maybe looking at the memories in her own head.

'And that reason was?' I asked.

'Conan was the king's second wife. He had been a hundred years with this new wife, yet there was no child.'

'And?' I took another long drink of lemonade.

She took a long swallow of rum and looked back at me. 'I told Taranis no because I believe he is sterile. It isn't the women but the king who is incapable of making an heir.'

I spit lemonade all over myself and Kitto. He seemed frozen with the lemonade running down his arm and sunglasses.

The maid appeared with napkins. I took a handful, then waved her off. We were talking about something that no one should hear. When I could talk without sputtering, and Kitto and I were both relatively dry, I said, 'You told Taranis this to his face?'

'Yes,' she said.

'You're braver than you seem.' Or stupider, I added in my head.

'He demanded I tell him why I would not have him as husband. I said I wished to have a child and I didn't believe that he could give me one.'

I just stared at her, trying to think about the implications of what she'd said. 'If what you say is true, then the royals could demand the king make the ultimate sacrifice. They could demand he allow himself to be killed as part of one of the great holy days.'

'Yes,' Maeve said. 'He forced me out that same night.'

'For fear that you would tell someone,' I said.

'Surely I am not the only one to have suspicions,' she said. 'Adaria went on to have children with two others, but she was barren for centuries with our king.'

I understood now why I'd been beaten for asking about Maeve. My uncle's very life hung in the balance. 'He could just step down from the throne,' I said.

Maeve lowered her glasses enough to give me a withering look. 'Do not be naive, Meredith. It does not become you.'

I nodded. 'Sorry, you're right. Taranis would never believe it. He would have to be forced to accept that he was sterile, and the only way to do so would be to bring him up before the nobles. Which means you'd have to find a way to convince enough of them to vote your way.'

She shook her head. 'No, Meredith, I cannot be the only one who suspects. His death would restore fertility to our people. All our power descends from our king or queen. I believe that Taranis's inability to father children has doomed the rest of us to be childless.'

'There are still children at court,' I said.

'But how many of them are pure Seelie blood?'

I thought for a second. 'I'm not sure. Most of them were born long before I came along.'

'I am sure,' she said. She leaned forward, her entire body language suddenly very serious, no flirting involved. 'None. All the children born to us in the last six hundred years have been mixed blood. Either rapes during the wars of Unseelie warriors, or ones like yourself that are very mixed indeed. Mixed blood, stronger blood, Meredith. Our king has doomed us to die as a people

142

because he is too proud to step down from the throne.'

'If he stepped down because he was infertile, the other royals could still demand he be killed to ensure the fertility of the rest.'

'And they would,' Maeve said, 'if they discovered that I told him of his little problem a century ago.'

She was right. If Taranis had simply not known, then they might have forgiven him and allowed him to step down. But to have known for a century and have done nothing ... They would see his blood sprinkled over the fields for that.

The murmur of voices made me turn around. A new man was speaking pleasantries to the men around the umbrella table. He turned toward us smiling, flashing very white teeth. The rest of him was so unhealthy that the artificially bright smile seemed to emphasize the sallowness of his skin, the sunken eyes. He was so eaten away by illness that it took me a few seconds to recognize Gordon Reed. He'd been the director who took Maeve from small parts to stardom. I had a sudden image of his body rotted away and those teeth the only thing left untouched in his grave. I knew in that instant that the macabre vision was a true seeing, and he was dying.

The question was, did they know?

Maeve held out her hand to him. He took her smooth golden hand in his withered one, laying a kiss on the back of that perfect skin. How must he feel to watch his own youth fade, to feel his body die, while she remained untouched?

He turned to me, still holding her hand.

'Princess Meredith, so good of you to join us today.' The words were very civil, very ordinary, as if this were just another afternoon by the pool.

Maeve patted his hand. 'Sit down, Gordon.' She moved to give him the lounge chair, while she knelt on the pool edge, much like Kitto had earlier. He sat down heavily, and a momentary flinching around his eyes was the only outward sign that he hurt.

Maeve took off her sunglasses and kept looking at him. She studied what was left of the tall, handsome man that she'd married. She studied him as if every line of bone under that sallow skin was precious.

That one look was enough. She loved him. She really loved him, and they both knew that he was dying.

She laid her face on that withered hand and looked at me with wide blue eyes that shimmered just a little too much in the light. It wasn't glamour; it was unshed tears.

Her voice was low, but clear. 'Gordon and I want a child, Meredith.'

'How—' I stopped; I couldn't ask it, not in front of both of them.

'How long does Gordon have?' Maeve asked for me.

I nodded.

'Six . . .' Maeve's voice broke. She tried to regain herself but finally Gordon answered, 'Six weeks, maybe three months at the outside.' His voice was calm, accepting. He stroked Maeve's silky hair.

Maeve rolled her face to stare at me. The look

in her eyes wasn't accepting, or calm. It was frantic.

I knew now why, after a hundred years, Maeve had been willing to risk Taranis's anger to seek help from another sidhe. Conchenn, goddess of beauty and spring, was running out of time.

Chapter 15

IT WAS DARK BY THE TIME WE ARRIVED BACK AT my apartment. I would have said home, but it wasn't that. It had never been *home*. It was a one-bedroom apartment originally intended for only one person. I wasn't even supposed to have a roommate in it. I was trying to share it with five people. To say we were a little cramped for space was a terrifying understatement.

Strangely, we hadn't talked much on the drive back to work to exchange the van for my car, or afterwards during the drive to the apartment. I don't know what was bothering everyone else, but seeing Gordon Reed dying, practically before my eyes, had dampened my enthusiasm. Truth was, it wasn't really Gordon's dying, but the way Maeve had looked at him. An immortal in true love with a mortal. It always ended badly.

I'd threaded my way through the traffic almost automatically, the trip livened only by Doyle's soft gasps. He was not a good passenger, but since he'd never had a license, he didn't have much choice. Usually I enjoyed Doyle's little panic attacks. It was one of the few times that I saw him completely unglued. It was strangely comforting, usually.

Today when we stepped into the pale pink walls of my living room, I didn't think anything could comfort me. I was, as usual lately, wrong.

First, there was the rich smell of stew and fresh baked bread. The kind of stew that simmers all day and just gets better. And there is no such thing as bad homemade bread. Second, Galen walked around the only corner in the main room from my tiny kitchen to the even tinier dining area. Usually, I notice Galen's smile first. He has a great smile. Or maybe the pale green hair that curls just below his ears. Tonight I noticed his clothes. He was not wearing a shirt. He was wearing a white lacy apron that was sheer enough that I could see the darker skin of his nipples, the curl of darker green hair that decorated his upper chest, the thin line of hair that traced the edge of his belly button and vanished inside his jeans.

He turned his back to finish setting the table, and his skin was flawless, pearlescent white with the faintest tinge of green. The see-through straps of the apron did nothing to hide his strong back and broad shoulders, the perfect length of arm. The one thin braid of hair that still fell past his waist curved over his skin like a caress.

I hadn't realized that I had stopped dead just past the door until Rhys said, 'If you move a little bit farther into the room, the rest of us can get past.'

I felt my skin burn as I blushed. But I moved and let the others come past me.

Galen continued coming and going out of the kitchen, as if he hadn't noticed my reaction, and maybe he hadn't. It was sometimes hard to tell with Galen. He never seemed to understand how beautiful he was. Which, come to think of it, might have been part of his appeal. Humility was a very rare commodity in a sidhe nobleman.

'Stew's ready, but the bread needs to cool a bit before we cut it.' He went back into the kitchen without really looking at any of us.

There had been a time when I would have given and gotten a hello kiss from him. But there was a little problem. Galen had been injured during one of the court punishments just before Samhain, Halloween. I could still see the scene in my mind's eye: Galen chained to the rock, his body almost lost to sight under the slowly fanning butterfly wings of the demi-fey. They looked like true butterflies on the edge of a puddle, sipping liquid, wings moving slowly to the rhythm of their feeding. But they weren't sipping water; they were drinking his blood. They had taken bites of his flesh with the blood, and for reasons that only Prince Cel knew, he'd ordered them to pay particular attention to Galen's groin.

Cel had made certain that I would not be able to take Galen to my bed until he healed. But he was sidhe, and sidhe healed while you watched, their bodies absorbing the wounds like flowers blooming in reverse. Every dainty bite had vanished into that flawless skin, except the wounds on his groin. He was, for all intents and purposes, unmanned.

We'd been to every healer we could find, both medical and metaphysical. The medical doctors had been baffled; the witches had only been able to say it was something magical. Twenty-first-century witches hesitate to use the word *curse*.

No one did curses; they were too bad for your karma. You do a curse and it comes back on you, always. You can never do truly evil magic, the kind that has no intent but to harm, without paying a price. No one is exempt from that rule, not even the immortal. It's one of the reasons that a true curse is so rare.

I watched Galen bustling about the kitchen in his peekaboo apron, careful not to look at me, and my heart hurt.

I went to him, wrapping my arms around his waist, pressing my body against the warmth of his back. He went very still under my touch, then slowly his hands came up to slide along my arms. He hugged my arms against his body. I cuddled my cheek against the smooth warmth of his back. It was the closest to a hug that I'd gotten from him in weeks. He'd found any interaction painful, in more than one way.

He began to pull away and I tightened my grip. He could have forced me away from him, but he didn't. He just stood there and dropped his hands from mine. 'Merry, please.' His voice was so soft.

'No,' I said, holding him tight, tight against me. 'Let me contact Queen Niceven.'

He shook his head, sending his braid spilling against my face. The scent of his hair was sweet and clean. I remembered when his hair had draped to his knees like most of the high-court sidhe. I'd mourned when he cut it.

'I will not let you put yourself in that creature's debt,' he said, and his voice held a solemnity that was so unlike him.

'Please, Galen, please.'

'No, Merry, no.' He tried to push me away again, but I wouldn't let go.

'And what if there is no cure without Niceven's help?'

He put his hands on my arms, not to caress this time but to pry them apart so he could move away. Galen was a sidhe warrior; he could punch holes through the sides of buildings. I could not hold him if he would not be held.

He moved into the mouth of the narrow kitchen, out of my reach. He would not look at me with his pale green eyes. He studied the painting on the dining room wall: a picture of butterflies in a grassy meadow. Did the butterflies remind him of the demi-fey, or did he even see the painting? Or was it simply better to look anywhere than at me?

I'd been begging Galen's permission to go to Queen Niceven and find out what she'd done to him. He'd forbidden it. He didn't want me to put myself in her debt just to help him. I'd tried pleading, crying, which I think on anyone else would have worked, but he had held firm. He would not be responsible for me owing Niceven and her demi-fey a debt.

I stood there staring at him – that beautiful body that I had loved since I was a child. Galen had been my first crush. If he was healed, we could cool the heat that had been between us since I hit puberty.

I realized suddenly that I'd been going about this all wrong. Kitto had told me that Doyle thought I was just going to fuck everyone and not use the power I'd gained. He wasn't just referring to the goblins. Was I the future queen of the

Unseelie or not? If I was to be queen, what was I doing asking anyone's permission for anything? Who I put myself in debt to was none of Galen's business. Not really.

I turned away from Galen, back into the room. The rest of the men were watching us. If they'd been human, they would have pretended not to watch, been reading magazines, or pretending to, but they were fey. If you did something in front of the fey, they watched. If you wanted privacy, you wouldn't be doing it where they could see you; that was our culture.

Only Kitto was missing, and I knew where he was, in his oversize, fully covered cloth dog bed. It was like a small, snug tent. It sat in the far corner of the living room positioned so he could watch the television, which was one of the few technological wonders that Kitto seemed to appreciate.

'Doyle,' I said.

'Yes, Princess.' His voice was neutral.

'Contact Queen Niceven for me.'

He simply bowed and went for the bedroom. It was the largest mirror in the apartment. He would try to contact the demi-fey first through the mirror as you would contact another sidhe. It might work, it might not. The demi-fey didn't stay inside the faerie mounds very much. They liked the open air. If they weren't near a reflective surface, the mirror spell wouldn't work. There were other spells to try, but he would start with the mirror. We might get lucky and catch the little queen flying by a still pool of water.

'No,' Galen said. He took two quick strides, not to me, but to Doyle. He caught the other guard's arm. 'No, I won't let her do this.'

Doyle met Galen's eyes for a second, and Galen didn't flinch. I'd seen gods flinch from that look on Doyle's face. Either Galen was braver than I'd thought, or stupider. I was betting on the latter. Galen simply didn't understand politics, personal or otherwise. He would grab Doyle's arm, prevent him from leaving the room, even though that might mean a duel between the two of them. I'd seen Doyle fight, and I'd seen Galen fight. I knew who would win, but Galen wasn't thinking. He was reacting, and that, of course, was Galen's great weakness, and why my father had given me to another. Galen didn't have it in him to survive court intrigue; he just didn't.

But Doyle didn't take offense. His gaze slid from Galen to me. He arched an eyebrow, as if asking what to do.

'You act as if you are already king, Galen,' I said, and it sounded harsh even to me, because I knew he was thinking no such thing. But I had to get him under control before Doyle stepped in. I had to lead here, not Doyle.

The look of astonishment on Galen's face as he turned to me was so genuine, so Galen. Almost any other of the Queen's Ravens would have been able to guard their expression better than that. His emotions had always been painted on his face.

'I don't know what you mean.' And he probably didn't.

I sighed. 'I gave one of my guards an order, and you have stopped him from carrying out that order. Who but a king would supercede the orders of a princess?'

Confusion chased across his face, and his hand

fell slowly away from Doyle's arm. 'I didn't mean it that way.' His voice sounded young and unsure of itself He was seventy years older than me, yet politically he was still a child, and always would be. Part of Galen's charm was his innocence. It was also one of his most dangerous flaws.

'Do as I bid, Doyle.'

Doyle gave me the lowest and most courtly bow he'd ever given me. Then he went for the bedroom door and the mirror beyond.

Galen watched him go, then turned back to me. 'Merry, please don't put yourself in that creature's power because of me.'

I shook my head. 'Galen, I love you, but not everyone is as inept politically as you are.'

He frowned. 'What's that supposed to mean?'

'It means, my sweet, that I'll negotiate with Niceven. If what she asks is too great a price, I won't pay it. But trust me to take care of things. I won't do anything stupid, Galen.'

He shook his head. 'I don't like this. You don't know what Niceven's become since Queen Andais has been losing some of her hold on the court.'

'If Andais lets her power slip, then others will hurry to grab it up. I know that, Galen.'

'How? How do you know that, when you've been away while it's all been happening?'

I sighed again. 'If Andais's power has slipped so that her own son, Cel, would plot around her, if her power has deteriorated to the point where the sluagh are being used to police her court instead of being the ultimate threat that they should be, then everyone must be scrambling to pick up the pieces. And they will do their best to keep the pieces they grab.'

Galen looked at me, uncomprehending. 'That's exactly what's been happening for three years, but you haven't been there. How did you . . .' A look of astonishment showed, and then, 'You had a spy.'

'No, Galen, I had no spy. I don't have to be there to know what the court will do if the queen is weak. Nature abhors a vacuum, Galen.'

He frowned at me. He had no desire for power, no political ambitions. It was as if that part of him was missing; and because it was totally lacking in him, he did not understand it in others. I'd always known this about him, but I'd never realized just how profound his lack of understanding was. He couldn't conceive of me seeing all the puzzle without having seen all the pieces first. Because he couldn't have done it, he couldn't understand someone else doing it.

I smiled, and it felt sad. I went to him, touched his face with my fingertips. I needed to touch him to see if he was real. It was as if I'd finally realized just how profound his problem was, and knowing it, it seemed as if I'd never really known him at all.

His cheek was just as warm, as real, as ever. 'Galen, I will negotiate with Niceven. I will do it because to leave one of my guards so crippled is an insult to me and all of us. The demi-fey should not be able to unman a sidhe warrior.'

He flinched at that, gaze sliding away from me. I touched his chin, moved him back to look at me. 'And I want you, Galen. I want you as a woman wants a man. I won't mortgage my kingdom to cure you, but I will do my best to see you whole.'

A faint flush climbed up his face, darkening the green cast to his skin so that it was almost orange, instead of red. 'Merry, I don't—'

I touched my fingertips to his lips. 'No, Galen, I will do this, and you will not stop me, because I am the princess. I am the heir to the throne, not you. You are my guard, not the other way around. I think I forgot that for a while, but I won't forget again.'

His eyes looked so worried. He took my hand from his lips and moved it palm up. He laid a slow, gentle kiss upon my palm, and that one touch made me shiver.

He was so hopeless at the politics that to make him king would be almost a death sentence. It would be disastrous not just for Galen personally, but for the court, and for me. No, I could not have Galen as my king, but I could have Galen. For a brief time before I found my true king, I could have Galen in my bed. I could quench the fire that had been burning between us, quench it with the flesh of our bodies. As he lowered my hand from his mouth, the look in those pale green eyes was enough to make me want for a moment to mortgage my kingdom. I wouldn't do that; but I would do much to have those eyes looking down at me while I lay underneath him.

I gave his knuckles a quick kiss, because I didn't trust myself to do anything more. 'Go, finish setting the table. I think the bread should be cool enough by now.'

He smiled suddenly, a flash of his old grin. 'I don't know . . . it feels pretty hot from here.'

I shook my head and pushed him half-laughing toward the kitchen. Maybe I could just keep

Galen as the royal mistress, or whatever the male equivalent was. The sidhe had been around for several millennia, and surely there was court precedent for a royal lover somewhere in all that history.

Chapter 16

OVER DINNER WE DISCUSSED WHAT TO DO WHEN Niceven called back. Doyle had left a message that would let her know who had called. He was sure she'd be intrigued enough to call back, and he was also sure she'd know what we wanted. 'Niceven has been anticipating this call. She has a plan. I don't know what that plan will be, but she will have one.' Doyle was sitting on my right so that his body blocked me from the window. He'd made me draw the drapes, but allowed the window to be opened for the breeze.

It was December in California, and the wind through the window was delightfully cool, like late spring or very early summer in Illinois. By no stretch of imagination did it feel cold or wintry in the least.

'She is an animal,' Galen said, pushing back his chair. He took his empty bowl to the sink and began to run water into it, his back to us.

'Do not underestimate the demi-fey because of what they did to you, Galen. They used teeth because they enjoyed it, not because they don't have swords,' Doyle said.

'A sword the size of a straight pin,' Rhys said, 'not much of a threat.'

'Give me a blade no bigger than a pin and I could slay a man,' Doyle said, deep voice soft.

'Yes, but you're the Queen's Darkness,' Rhys said. 'You've studied every weapon known to man or immortal. I doubt Niceven's crew has been as thorough.'

Doyle stared at the pale-haired man across the table from him. 'And if it were your only weapon, Rhys, wouldn't you study how it could be used on your enemy?'

'The sidhe are not the enemies of the demi-fey,' he said.

'The demi-fey, like the goblins, are tolerated, and barely that in the courts. And the wee-fey do not have the goblins' fierce reputation to protect them from the slings and arrows of mischance.'

For some reason mention of the goblins made it hard not to look at Kitto. He hadn't sat at the table but had crouched underneath. He'd eaten his stew, then crawled to his oversize doggie bed. He seemed shaken by the afternoon at Maeve Reed's pool. Too much sun and fresh air for a goblin.

'No one harms the demi-fey,' Frost said. 'They are the queen's spies. A butterfly, a moth, a tiny bird can all be demi-fey. Their glamour is almost undetectable even by the best of us.'

Doyle nodded around a mouth full of stew. He sipped a little of his red wine, then said, 'All that you say is true, but the demi-fey were once much more respected in the courts. They were not merely spying eyes, but truly allies.'

'With the wee-ones,' Rhys said. 'Why?'

I answered, 'If the demi-fey leave the Unseelie

Court, then what remains of faerie will begin to fade.'

'That is an old wives' tale,' Rhys said. 'Like if the ravens leave the Tower of London, Britain will fall. The British Empire has already fallen, and yet they still clip the poor ravens' wings and stuff them full of food. The damn things are as big as small turkeys.'

'It is said that where the demi-fey travel, faerie follows,' Doyle said.

'What does that mean?' Rhys asked.

'My father said that the demi-fey are the most closely allied with the rawness that is faerie, the very stuff that makes us different from the humans. The demi-fey are their magic more than any of the rest of us. They cannot be exiled from faerie because it travels with them wherever they go.'

Galen leaned against the counter at the end of the kitchen, arms crossed over his now bare chest. He'd put the apron away, I think to save me embarrassment. I don't know why his bare chest wasn't as eye-catching as his chest peeking through all that sheer cloth, but I couldn't eat and sit across from him while he wore the apron. The second time I missed my mouth with the stew, Doyle asked him to take the apron off.

'That doesn't work for most of the rest of the smaller fey. The rule is, the smaller you are, the more dependent you are on faerie, and the more likely you are to die when away from it. My father was a pixie. I know what I'm talking about,' Galen said.

'How big a pixie?' Rhys asked.

Galen actually smiled. 'Big enough.'

'There are many different kinds of pixies,' Frost said, either missing the humor or ignoring it. I loved Frost, but his sense of humor wasn't his best feature. Of course, a girl doesn't always need to laugh.

'I've never known another pixie who wasn't a member of the Seelie Court,' Rhys said. 'Did you ever learn what your father did to earn exile from Taranis and his gang?'

'Only you would refer to the glittering throng as Taranis and his gang,' Doyle said.

Rhys shrugged, grinned, and said, 'What'd your daddy do?'

The smile faded, then grew, on Galen's face. 'My uncles tell me that my father seduced one of the king's mistresses.' His smile faded. Galen had never met his father, because Andais had had him executed for the audacity of seducing one of her ladies-in-waiting. She never would have done it if she'd known there was going to be a child. In fact, the pixie would have been elevated to noble rank and there would have been a marriage. It had happened with stranger mixes. But Andais's temper made her a little too quick on the death sentence, and thus Galen never met his father.

If any humans had been in the room, they would have apologized for bringing up such a painful subject, but there weren't any and we didn't bother. If Galen was in pain, he'd have said something, and we'd have taken care of it. He didn't ask and we didn't pry.

'Treat Niceven as a queen, an equal. It will please her and catch her off guard,' Doyle said.

'She is a demi-fey. She can never be the equal of a sidhe princess.' This from Frost, who sat on the other side of Galen's empty chair. His handsome face was as severe and haughty as I'd ever seen it.

'My great-grandmother was a brownie, Frost,' I said. My voice was soft, so he wouldn't think I was chiding him. He didn't take well to that. Frost seemed impervious to so much, but I'd learned that he was really one of the most easily wounded of the guards.

'A brownie is a useful member of faerie. They have a long and respected history. The demi-fey are parasites. I agree with Galen: they are animals.'

I wondered what else Frost would say that about. What other members of faerie would he dismiss out of hand?

'Nothing is redundant in faerie,' Doyle said. 'Everything has its purpose and its place.'

'And what purpose do the demi-fey serve?' Frost asked.

'I believe that they are the essence of faerie. If they were to leave, the Unseelie Court would begin to fade even faster than it already is.'

I nodded, getting up to put my own bowl in the sink. 'My father believed it was so, and I haven't found much that my father believed turn out to be false.'

'Essus was a very wise man,' Doyle said.

'Yes,' I said, 'he was.'

Galen took the bowl from my hands. 'I'll clean up.'

'You made dinner. You shouldn't have to clean up, too.'

'I'm not much good for anything else right now.' He smiled when he said it, but it didn't quite reach his eyes.

I let him take the bowl so I could touch his face. 'I'll do what I can, Galen.'

'That's what I'm afraid of,' he said softly. 'I don't want you to put yourself in debt to Niceven, not for me. It's not a good enough reason to owe that creature anything.'

I frowned and turned to the room at large. 'Why call her creature? I don't remember the demi-fey's reputation being this bad before I left the court.'

'Niceven's court has become little more than the queen's errand runners, or Cel's. You cannot retain respect if you have been regulated to a threat and nothing more.

'I don't understand. What threat? You've all been saying that the demi-fey are no threat.'

'I have not said that,' Doyle said, 'but what the demi-fey did to Galen was not the first time it has been done, though this time was more . . . severe. More flesh was taken than I'd seen before.'

Galen turned away at that and began to busy himself at the sink, rinsing out the bowls, placing them in the dishwasher. He seemed to be making more noise than was necessary, as if he didn't want to hear the conversation anymore.

'You know that crossing the queen can get you sent to the Hallway of Mortality to be tortured by Ezekiel and his redcaps.'

'Yes.'

'Now she will sometimes threaten us with being given to the demi-fey. In effect, Niceven's court, once a court of faerie with all the respect and ceremonies of any court, has been reduced to nothing more than another boggle to be dragged out of the dark and sent to torment others.'

'The sluagh are not merely boggles,' I said, 'and they have a court with their own customs. They have been one of the greatest threats in the Unseelie arsenal for a thousand years.'

'Much longer than a mere thousand years,' Doyle said.

'But they have retained their threat, their customs, their power.'

'The sluagh are what remain of the original Unseelie Court. They were Unseelie before there was such a term. It was not they who joined us, but we who joined them. Though there are very few among us now who remember that, or who will admit to remembering it.'

Frost spoke. 'I hold with those who say that the sluagh are the essence of the Unseelie Court, and if they leave, we will fade. It is they, and not the demi-fey, who hold our most primitive power.'

'No one knows for certain,' Doyle said.

'I don't think the queen would chance finding out,' Rhys said.

'No,' Doyle said.

'Which means that the demi-fey are in a position similar to the sluagh,' I said.

Doyle looked at me. 'Explain.' The sudden full weight of that dark gaze made me want to squirm, but I resisted. I wasn't a child anymore to be frightened of the tall dark man at my aunt's side.

'The queen would do almost anything to keep the sluagh on her side, and at her beck and call, but wouldn't the same be said for the demi-fey? If she truly fears that their leaving would make the Unseelie decline even faster than they are already, then wouldn't she do almost anything to keep them at her court?'

Doyle stared at me for what seemed a long time, then finally he gave one long blink. 'Perhaps.' He leaned toward me, clasping his hands on the nearly empty table. 'Galen and Frost are correct about one thing. Niceven does not react like another sidhe. She is accustomed to following the commands of another queen, to have, in effect, given her royal authority over to another monarch. We must make her think of you in that way, Meredith.'

'What do you mean?' I asked.

'We need to remind her in every way that you are Andais's heir.'

'I still don't understand.'

'When Cel contacts the demi-fey, he is his mother's son. His requests are usually as bloody, or more so than his mother's. But you are asking for healing, for help. That automatically puts us into a position of weakness, for we ask a boon of Niceven and have little power to offer her in return.'

'Okay, I understand that, but what can we do about it?'

'Lounge upon the bed with your men. Drape us around you for effect just as the queen would do. It is a way of looking powerful, for Niceven envies the queen her bevy of men.'

'Doesn't Niceven get her pick of the demi-fey?'

'No, she had three children by one male, and he is her king. She cannot be freed of him.'

'I didn't know Niceven had a king,' Rhys said.

'Few do. He is king in name only.'

The thought wasn't the idle gossip it should have been. Sleeping with all the guards was lovely. But being forced to marry one of them, simply because we made a child ... What if the father was someone I didn't respect? The thought of gentle Nicca tied to me forever was a frightening one. He was lovely to look at, but he wasn't powerful enough or strong enough to help me much as king. In fact, he was more likely to end up a victim instead of a help. Which reminded me.

'Is Nicca still working on that bodyguard case?'

'Yes,' Doyle said, 'he took over from Frost.'

'How did the client feel about trading guards in midstream?'

Doyle looked at Frost, who shrugged. 'She is in no real danger. She merely wants a sidhe warrior on her arm to show how much a star she is. One sidhe warrior is much like another for her purposes.'

'How much of a show do we need to put on for Niceven?' I asked.

'As much as you are comfortable with,' he said.

I raised my eyebrows at that and tried to think.

'Don't include me in the show,' Galen said. 'I don't want to see any of those things, not even from a distance.' He'd loaded the dishwasher and turned it on, so that the quiet *chug-chug* of the machine followed him as he returned to his chair. Apparently, he'd help us plan, as long as he wasn't included in the event.

'That makes it tough. You and Rhys are the only two of this group who really don't mind major flirting in public. Both Frost and Doyle are usually pretty circumspect in public.'

'For tonight, I am willing to help,' Doyle said.

Frost looked at him. 'You would pander in front of the wee ones?' He made it a question.

Doyle shrugged. 'I think it is necessary.'

'I will be on the bed, as I have been for some of the queen's calls, but I will not pander, not for Niceven.'

'That is your choice. But if you will not play the part of Meredith's lover, something you actually are, then do not ruin the show that the rest of us put together. Perhaps you should wait in the living room while we talk to the wee-fey.'

Frost narrowed those grey eyes of his. 'You held me back today when I would have aided Meredith. Twice you held me back. Now you suggest that I not be in her bed while you play her lover. What's next, Darkness? Will you finally break your fast, and take my night in her bed for truth and not just playacting?'

'I am within my rights to do so.'

That made me stare at Doyle. His face was blank, neutral. Had he just said he would share my bed tonight, or was he just arguing with Frost?

Frost stood up, looming over the table. Doyle stayed seated, calmly looking up at the other man. 'I think we should let Meredith decide who shares her bed tonight.'

'We are not here to make Meredith choose,' Doyle said. 'We are here to see her with child. The three of you have had three months and her womb is empty. Would you truly deny her a chance to have a child, to be queen, knowing that if Cel succeeds and Meredith fails, he will see her dead?'

Emotions chased over Frost's face too quickly for me to follow them all. Finally, he hung his head. 'I would never wish Meredith ill.'

I stepped forward and touched his arm. The touch made him look at me. His eyes were filled with such pain, and I realized that Frost was jealous of me. As much as I cared for him, he hadn't earned the right to be jealous of me in that way. Not yet. Though I realized with a start that the thought of never having him in my arms again was a painful one. I couldn't afford the sinking sense of loss any more than he could afford the jealousy.

'Frost . . .' I began, I don't know what I would have said, because there was a sound of sharp bells from the bedroom. It was as if someone had taken the delicate sound of silver bells and turned them into alarm bells. The sound sent my pulse racing, and not in a good way. I'd let go of Frost's arm when the sound came. We stood there looking at each other while everyone but Galen and Kitto moved toward the bedroom.

'I have to go, Frost.' I started to apologize but didn't. He hadn't earned it, and I didn't owe it.

'I will come with you,' he said.

I gave him wide eyes.

'I will do for my queen what I would do for no one else.' And I knew in that moment that he didn't mean Andais.

Chapter 17

DOYLE WAS KNEELING ON THE BURGUNDY bedspread, speaking to the mirror, when Frost and I entered the room. 'I will allow shared sight as soon as our princess is with us, Queen Niceven.'

The mirror was a swirl of mist as I crawled across the bed. It put Doyle kneeling at my back, slightly to one side. Rhys was sitting behind both of us, against the headboard, propped up among the pile of burgundy, purple, mauve, pink, and black pillows. I couldn't tell for certain, but he seemed to be nude, except for a few well-placed pillows. I had no idea how he'd stripped that quickly.

Frost crawled onto the bed to half sit, half recline a little behind me and to one side, so that I was framed by Doyle and him.

Doyle made a sideways movement with his hand and the mist cleared. Niceven sat in a delicate wooden chair, carved so that her wings slipped through the slotted back without damaging them. Her face was a near perfect triangle of white skin. But her whiteness was not the same as mine, or Frost's, or Rhys's. Her white skin held a greyish tinge. Her white-grey curls had been done in elaborate ringlets like those of some old-time doll. A tiny tiara held those curls back from her face, and the tiara sparkled with the cold warmth that only diamonds can manage. Her gown was white and flowing. The looseness of the cloth would have hidden her body, except that it was absolutely sheer and you could see the small pointed breasts, the almost skeletal thinness of her ribs, the dainty crossed legs. She wore slippers that seemed to be made of flower petals. A white mouse, as large to her as a German shepherd to me, sat beside her chair. She stroked the fur between its ears.

A trio of ladies-in-waiting stood behind her, each in a different color dress that matched the brilliance of their wings, rose-red, daffodil-yellow, and iris-purple. Their hair was black, yellow, and brown, respectively.

Niceven had gone to a great deal more trouble than we had to stage her little scene.

I felt positively ordinary in my green skirt outfit. But I didn't mind too much. It was a business call, after all.

'Queen Niceven, it is good of you to return our call.'

'In truth, Princess Meredith, I have been awaiting your call these three months. Your affection for the green knight is well known among the court. I am most surprised that it has taken thee so long to contact me.'

She was being very formal. I realized it wasn't just the speech that was formal. She wore her crown; I had no crown, not yet. She sat upon her throne, while I was sitting in the middle of a slightly rumpled bed. She had ladies-in-waiting like a silent Greek chorus behind her. And a mouse, mustn't forget the mouse. I had only Doyle and Frost on either side of me and Rhys in the pillows behind. Niceven was trying to put me at a disadvantage. We'd see about that.

'In truth, we have sought the aid of healers out here in the world of mortals. It is only recently that we had to admit that a call to you was necessary.'

'Sheer stubbornness on your part then, Princess.'

'Perhaps, but you know why I have called, and what I wish.'

'I am not some fairy godmother to be granting wishes, Meredith.' She'd dropped my title, a deliberate insult.

Fine, we could both be rude. 'As you like, Niceven. Then you know what I want.'

'You want a cure for your green knight,' she said, one hand tracing the pink edge of the mouse's ear.

'Yes.'

'Prince Cel was most insistent that Galen remain injured.'

'You told me once that Prince Cel does not yet rule the Unseelie Court.'

'That is true, but it is not at all certain you will ever live to be queen, Meredith.' She'd dropped the title again.

Doyle moved from beside me to put his back to Rhys. He made sure he was still at the edge of the bed, at the limit of my peripheral vision and well within the queen's. As if they'd arranged it, Rhys rose from the pillows to his knees and showed clearly that he was nude. He rolled Doyle's long braid in his arms until he came to the end and began to undo the ribbon that bound it.

Niceven's eyes flicked behind me to the movement, then back to my face. 'What are they doing?'

'Preparing for bed,' I said. Though I wasn't 100 percent sure of that.

Delicate grey brows furrowed. 'It is, what ... nine o'clock where you are. The night is young to waste in sleeping.'

'I did not say we would sleep.' I kept my voice even.

She drew a deep enough breath that I could see the rise and fall of her dainty chest. She tried to keep her attention on me, but her gaze kept flicking to the men. Rhys was working Doyle's thick hair free of the braid. I'd seen Doyle with his hair free of that braid only once. Only once had it been like some dark living cloak to shroud his body.

Niceven watched them furtively, giving me very little eye contact. I wasn't sure if it was Doyle's hair or Rhys's nudity. I doubted the nudity, because being nude just wasn't that unusual among the court. Of course, maybe she was gazing at Rhys's washboard abs, or what lay just below them.

Frost sat up, took off his suit jacket, and began to slip out of his shoulder holster. Her eyes flicked to him.

'Niceven,' I said softly. I had to repeat her name twice more before she looked at me. 'How do I cure Galen?'

'It is not certain that you will be queen, and if

Prince Cel becomes king, then he will hold it ill that I helped you.'

'And if I am queen, I will hold it ill that you did not.'

She smiled. 'So I must find a way between the two snarling dogs. I will help you here, because I have already helped Cel. It will even things up.'

I remembered Galen's screams, and the pain in his eyes these last months, and I didn't think it evened things up. I didn't think fixing what she'd ruined came close to evening things up. But we were doing faerie politics here, not therapy, so I said nothing. Silence is not a lie. A sin of omission, but not a lie. Our cultures allow you to omit as much as you can get away with.

'How is Galen to be cured?' I asked.

She shook her head, making her curls bounce and her diamond tiara glitter. 'No, we talk price first. What would you give me to make your green knight whole?'

Frost and Doyle moved up beside me almost simultaneously. 'You will have the goodwill of the Queen of the Unseelie, and that should be enough,' Frost said, his voice as cold as his name.

'She is not queen yet, Killing Frost.' Niceven's voice was full of a cold, cold anger. It had the taste of an old grudge. Was it personal to Frost?

I saw Doyle begin to reach toward the other man, and I stopped him with a look. There was a tension between them tonight. It wouldn't make us look strong to argue amongst ourselves. Doyle stayed at my side, only his eyes looking at Frost. The look was not friendly.

I touched Frost's arm, squeezing slightly. He startled, muscles tightening, looked first to Doyle, then realized it was my touch. He'd expected it to be Doyle. He relaxed, slowly. He let out a deep, quiet breath and moved a fraction behind me.

I turned back to the mirror and found Niceven's face shrewd, watchful. I half expected her to say something, but she did not. She merely sat and waited for me to commit myself.

'What would Queen Niceven of the Diminutive Fey want from Princess Meredith of the Unseelie Court in return for curing her knight?' I'd purposefully put both our titles in the same sentence, emphasizing that I knew she was queen and I was not. I was hoping to make up for Frost's outburst.

She looked at me for a few heartbeats, then gave a very small nod. 'What would Princess Meredith of the Unseelie Court offer us?'

'You said once that you would give much for a longer drink of my blood.'

She looked startled before she could school her face to courtly blankness. When she could control herself, she said, 'Blood is blood, Princess. Why should I care for yours?'

Now she was just being difficult. 'You said that I tasted of high magic and sex. Or have you forgotten me so quickly, Queen Niceven?' I made my face fall, my eyes downcast. 'Did it mean so little to you?' I shrugged, and let my newly shoulder-length hair fall across my face. I spoke behind a curtain of hair that sparkled like spun rubies. 'If the blood of the heir to the throne means nothing to you, then I have nothing to offer.' I turned my eyes toward her, knew the effect that those tri-colored green and gold eyes could have through a frame of blood auburn hair, coupled with glimpses of skin like polished alabaster. I'd grown up among women, and men, who used their beauty like a weapon. I would never have dreamed of doing it with another sidhe, because they were all more beautiful than I, but with Niceven and her hungry eyes that followed my men, with her, I could use my own otherworldliness as she'd tried to use hers.

She slapped her tiny hand on the arm of her chair hard enough to startle the white mouse. 'By Flora, you are your aunt's blood. Prince Cel has never mastered his beauty as Andais has, and as you have.'

I gave a small bow, because it's always hard to bow from a sitting position. 'A pretty compliment from a lovely queen.'

She preened, smiling, petting the mouse, leaning back in her chair so that her sheer dress showed off more of her body. Her body had gone past slender into cadaverous, so that it was like looking at a little starved thing. But she thought her body was beautiful, and I could show nothing less in my face.

Frost stayed unmoving a little behind me. He'd removed his belt, his shoulder holster, his suit jacket, but nothing else. Even his shoes were still on. He was not going to strip for Niceven.

Doyle on the other hand had removed his shoulder holster, his belt, and his shirt. The silver ring in his left nipple glinted so that Niceven could see it, even in profile. Rhys continued to work at all that thick black hair as if he were smoothing out the train of a dress.

The men moved about me like ladies-in-waiting preparing themselves for bed. They left me alone to deal with Niceven. Which meant I was doing all right on my own. Good to know.

I flashed her a curve of lips as red as the red, red rose, no lipstick needed. 'A drink of my blood to cure my knight, you agree?'

'You give your own life's fluid away very freely, Princess.' She was being cautious.

'I only give that which I own.'

'The Prince thinks he owns all the court.'

'I know that I own only the body I inhabit. Anything else is hubris.'

The queen laughed. 'Will you come home so that I may feed?'

'Do you agree that another feeding is worth my knight's cure?'

She nodded. 'I agree.'

'Then what would a feeding once a week be worth?'

I felt the men behind me tense. The atmosphere of the room was suddenly thicker. I was careful not to look at them. I was princess, and I didn't need the permission of my guards to do anything. I either ruled, or I did not.

Niceven's eyes narrowed into pale little flames. 'What's that supposed to mean, a feeding once a week?'

'It means exactly what I said.'

'Why would you offer to make a weekly blood offering to me?'

'For an alliance between us.'

Frost pushed toward me over the bed. 'Meredith, no . . .'

He was going to say something unfortunate and ruin everything. I had the beginnings of an idea and it was a good one. 'No, Frost,' I said, 'you do

175

not tell me no. I tell *you* no or yes. Don't forget that.' I gave him a look that I hoped he understood, which was *shut the fuck up, and don't ruin this*.

He closed his mouth into a tight, thin line, so obviously unhappy, but he sat there, sulking. At least he was quiet about it.

I heard Doyle take in a breath, and I just looked at him. The look was enough. He gave a small nod of his head and let Rhys begin to brush out his long hair. There was a wave to all that blackness, because of the braid, I think; I remembered Doyle's hair as straight. I was distracted for a moment watching Rhys kneeling so pale and perfect against all that darkness. It was Doyle clearing his throat who made me jump and turn back to the mirror.

Niceven laughed, the sound of just slightly off-key bells, as if it were something lovely that had been just a bit malformed.

'My apologies for my inattention, Queen Niceven.'

'If I had such a bounty awaiting me, I would make this a short conversation.'

'And what if you had the bounty of my blood awaiting you? What then?'

Her face sobered. 'You are persistent. It is most unfeylike.'

'I am part brownie, and we are a more persistent people than the sidhe.'

'You are part human, as well.'

I smiled. 'Humans are like the sidhe; some are more persistent than others.'

She didn't smile back at me. 'For another drink of your blood, I will cure your green knight, but that is all. One drink, one cure, and we are done.'

'For one drink of my blood, King Kurag of the goblins became my ally for six months.'

Her delicate eyebrows raised. 'That is goblin and sidhe business, and none of ours. We are the demi-fey. No one cares who we ally ourselves with. We fight no battles. We challenge no duels. We mind our business and everyone else minds theirs.'

'So you refuse an alliance?'

'I think caution is the better part of valor here, Princess, no matter how tasty you may be.'

In negotiations, always try to be nice first, but if nice doesn't work, there are other options. 'Everyone leaves you alone, Queen Niceven. Because they consider you too small to worry about.'

'Prince Cel thought us big enough to spoil your plans with the green knight.' Her voice held the first hint of anger.

'Yes, and what did he offer you for that bit of work?'

'The taste of sidhe flesh, knight's flesh, and blood. We feasted that night, Princess.'

'He paid you in someone else's blood, when his body was full of blood only one step down from the queen herself. Have you ever tasted the queen?'

Niceven looked nervous, almost frightened. 'The queen shares only with her lovers, or her prisoners.'

'How that must irk you, to see such a precious gift wasted.'

Niceven pouted tiny ghost silver lips. 'If only she would take some of my people to her bed, but we are . . .'

177

'Too small,' I finished for her.

'Yes,' she hissed, 'yesss, always too small. Too small a power for an alliance. Too small a power to be used except as her sneak spies.' Tiny, pale hands balled into fists. The white mouse cowered away from her as if he knew what was coming. Even the trio of ladies behind her throne shuddered as if from the brush of an icy wind.

'And now you do dirty work for her son,' I said. My voice was carefully neutral, almost pleasant.

'At least he sought us to do his work.' The anger in that small, delicate figure was frightening. Her rage made her take up more space than mere physicality could explain. She was truly regal in her rage.

'I offer you what the queen will not. I offer what the prince will not.'

'And what is that?'

'Royal blood, blood of the very throne of the Unseelie Court. Ally with me, Queen Niceven, and you will have such blood. Not only once, but many times more.'

Her eyes became narrow little slits again, glittering with a fire colder than the diamonds on her crown. 'What would either of us gain from such an alliance?'

'You would gain the ear and the aid of my allies.'

'The goblins have little to do with us.'

'And what of the sidhe?'

'What of them?'

'As ally to one of the heirs, you would gain status. They would no longer be able to dismiss you, for fear that you might bear a grudge and whisper it back to me.'

She kept those glowing eyes on me. 'And what would you gain from this alliance?'

'You would spy for me, as well as for the queen.'

'And Cel?'

'You would cease to spy for him.'

'He won't like that.'

'He doesn't have to like it. If you are my ally, then to injure you is to insult me. The queen has decreed that I am under her protection. To harm me now is a death sentence.'

'So he insults me, then you step in. Then what?'

'Threaten to bring your entire court out here to Los Angeles, out here to me.'

She shivered. 'I would not wish to take my people out into the city of men.' She spoke as if there were only one city of men, *the* city.

'You could live in the botanical gardens, acres of open land. There's room for you here, Niceven, I swear it.'

'But I do not want to leave the court.'

'Wherever the demi-fey travel, faerie follows.'

'Most sidhe do not remember that.'

'My father made sure I knew the history of all the fey. The demi-fey are the most closely allied with the rawness that is faerie, the very stuff that makes us different from the humans. You are not leprechaun, or pixie, to pine and die away from faerie. You *are* faerie. Is it not said that when the last demi-fey fades, there will be no more faerie upon the earth?'

'A superstition,' she said.

'Maybe, but if you leave the Unseelie Court and the Seelie Court retains its own demi-fey, the Unseelie will be weakened. Cel may not remember

179

that bit of our lore, but the queen will. If Cel insults you enough for you to pack your belongings, the queen will intercede.'

'She will order us to stay.'

'She cannot order another monarch to do anything. That is our law.'

Niceven looked nervous. She feared Andais. Everyone did. 'I do not wish to anger the queen.'

'Neither do I.'

'Do you really believe that the queen would punish her own son if he drove us away, rather than take out her anger on us?' She had crossed her legs again, arms folded over her chest, forgetting to flirt, forgetting to be regal in her fear.

'Where is Cel now?' I asked.

Niceven giggled, a most unpleasant little giggle. 'Being punished for six months. There are bets going round that his sanity will not survive six months of isolation and torment.'

I shrugged. 'He should have thought of that before he was such a bad, bad boy.'

'You are flippant, but if Cel comes out insane, it will be your name that he screams. Your face that he wants to smash.'

'I'll cross that bridge when I come to it.'

'What?'

'It's a human saying. It means that I'll deal with the problem when and if it comes to pass.'

She seemed to be thinking very hard, then said, 'How would you offer this blood to me? I do not think either of us would relish a weekly trip between faerie and the Western Sea.'

'I could put it upon a piece of bread, and the essence could be sent to you via magic.'

She shook her head, ghostly curls bouncing

around narrow shoulders. 'The essence is never the same.'

'What do you suggest?'

'If I send one of my people to you, they could act as my surrogate.'

I thought about it for a moment, feeling Frost's stillness, hearing the heavy, almost tearing sound of Rhys pulling the brush through Doyle's hair. 'Agreed. Tell me the cure for my knight and send your surrogate.'

She laughed, off-key bells ringing. 'No, Princess, you will gain the cure from the lips of my surrogate. If I give it to you now before I have been paid, you may think better of it.'

'I have given you my word. I cannot go back upon it now.'

'I have dealt with the great of faerie for too long to believe that everyone keeps their word.'

'It is one of our most stringent laws,' I said. 'To be forsworn is to be outcast.'

'Unless you have friends in very high places who make sure such tales are never spread.'

'What are you saying, Queen Niceven?'

'I say only this, that the queen doth love her son much, and has broken more than one taboo to keep him safe.'

We stared at each other, and I knew without asking that Cel had made promises and broken them. That alone should have made him outcast and certainly denied him the right to any throne. Andais had always spoiled Cel, but I never realized just how much.

'When can we expect your surrogate?' I asked.

She seemed to consider this, reaching an idle hand out toward where the mouse was crouched.

It crept close to her, its long whiskers twitching, ears alert, as if it still wasn't sure of its welcome. She stroked it gently. 'A few days,' she said.

'We are not always at home to welcome visitors. I would be loath to have your envoy receive less than our best hospitality.'

'Leave a pot of flowers by your door and that will sustain him.'

'Him?'

'I believe a him would please you more, would it not?'

I gave a small nod, because I wasn't sure I cared. I was sharing blood, not sex, so I didn't have a preference; or at least I didn't think I did. 'I am sure the queen is wise in her choosing.'

'Pretty words, Princess. It remains to be seen whether you have pretty actions to back up all those words.' Her eyes flicked back to the men and settled on Doyle and Rhys. 'Pleasant dreams, Princess.'

'And to you, Queen Niceven.'

Something harsh crossed her face, made it look even thinner and sharper, as if her face were a mask. If she reached up and ripped her face off, I was not going to be able to hold my business face in place. But she didn't. She merely spoke in a voice that was like the whisper of scales on stone. 'My dreams are my own business, Princess, and I will keep them as I like them.'

I gave her another half bow. 'I meant no insult.'

'None taken, Princess, merely envy rearing its ugly head.' With those words, the mirror went blank and smooth.

I sat gazing into my own reflection. Movement caught my gaze, and I watched Rhys and Doyle still on their knees. Muscles worked in Rhys's arms as he brushed Doyle's hair. Frost didn't so much move as just look at me in the mirror so hard that it turned me to look at him.

Frost glared back. The other two seemed unaware of my attention. 'Niceven is gone. You can stop pretending,' I said.

'I haven't finished brushing out all of this hair,' Rhys said. 'This is why I stopped growing mine down to my ankles. It's almost impossible to take care of it by yourself.' He separated out another section of hair, hefted it in one hand, and began to brush with the other.

Doyle was silent as Rhys worked on his hair with the serious-faced concentration of a child. There was absolutely nothing else childish about him as he knelt nude, surrounded by a sea of black hair and multi-colored pillows. His body was, as always, tightly muscled, pale, gleaming. He was lovely to look at, but he wasn't excited. Nude didn't mean sex to the sidhe, not always.

Frost made a small movement that turned me to him. His eyes were the dark grey of the sky just before a storm. He was angry; it showed in every line of his face, the tension of his shoulders, the way he sat, so careful, immobile, and shimmering with energy at the same time.

'I'm sorry if it upset you, but I knew what I was doing with Niceven.'

'You have made it abundantly clear that you rule here and I merely obey.' His voice was harsh with anger.

I sighed. It was early, but it had been a long day. I was too tired for Frost's hurt feelings. Especially since he was in the wrong.

'Frost, I cannot afford to appear weak to anyone right now. Even Doyle holds his opinion in public, no matter how unfavorable it is in private.'

'I have approved of everything you've done today,' Doyle said.

'I am so happy to hear that,' I said.

He gave me a very level gaze, ruined only a little by the tugging of his hair from the brush. It's hard to look menacing when you're being fussed with. He stared at me, until most people would have looked away or flinched. I met his gaze with my own empty one. I was tired of games. Just because I could play them, and play them fairly well, didn't mean I enjoyed them.

'I've had enough power plays for one day, Doyle. I don't need any more, especially not from my own guards.'

He blinked those dark, dark eyes at me. 'Hold off, Rhys. Meredith and I need to talk.'

Rhys stopped obediently, sitting back among the pillows, the brush still in his hand.

'In private,' Doyle said.

Frost jumped as if he'd been struck. It was his reaction more than Doyle's words that made me suspect we were talking about more than just a few secrets.

'It is my night with Meredith,' Frost said. His anger seemed to have vanished on the wings of possibilities he hadn't foreseen.

'If it was Rhys, then he would have to wait his turn again, but I have not had a turn, so I am within my rights to ask for this evening.'

Frost stood, almost stumbling in his haste and the lack of space at the foot of the bed. 'First you hold me back from helping her today, now you take my night in her bed. I would accuse you of jealousy, if I did not know you better.'

'You can accuse me of anything you wish, Frost, but you know I am not jealous.'

'Perhaps, perhaps not, but you are something, and that something has to do with our Merry.'

Doyle sighed, a deep, almost wounded sound. 'Perhaps I thought that by making the princess wait for my attentions I would intrigue her. Today I saw that there is more than one way to lose a woman's favor.'

'Speak plainly, Darkness.'

Doyle stayed kneeling, half-naked, his hands limp and empty resting against his thighs, surrounded by a sea of his own hair. He should have looked helpless, or feminine, or something, but he didn't. He looked like something carved out of the elemental darkness, as if he'd risen as one of the first things to ever draw breath, before the light came. The silver ring in his nipple caught the light as he breathed. His hair had covered all the earrings, so that this one silver spark was the only color on him. It was hard to look away from that shining silver light.

'I am not blind, Frost,' Doyle said. 'I saw the way she looked at you in the van, and you saw it, too.'

'You are jealous.'

He shook his head. 'No, but you have had three months and there is no child. She is a princess and will be a queen. She cannot afford to give her heart away where there is no marriage.'

'So you'll step in and win her heart instead?' Frost's voice held more heat than I'd ever heard in it, outside of the bed.

185

'No, but I will see that she has choices. If I had paid closer attention, I would have stepped in sooner.'

'Oh, you in her arms will make her forget all about me, is that it?'

'I am not so arrogant as that, Frost. I told you, today I realized there was more than one way to lose a woman's heart, and waiting too long is one of them. If there is to be any chance that Meredith will not turn to you, or Galen, then something must change now. Not later, but now.'

'What does Galen have to do with any of this?' Frost asked.

'If you have to ask that, then it is not I who am blind,' Doyle said.

Confusion chased over Frost's face. Finally he frowned and shook his head. 'I don't like this.'

'You don't have to like it,' Doyle said.

As interesting as the conversation was, I'd had enough of it. 'You are all talking as if I'm not here, or as if I have no choice in the matter.'

Doyle turned his so serious face to me. 'Do you object to me sharing your bed tonight?' He asked it in the same neutral voice that he would have used to order at a restaurant or talk to a client, as if my answer meant nothing to him.

But I knew he sometimes used that neutral voice when he felt anything but neutral. It was a way of shielding himself from the emotion; act as if it doesn't matter, and maybe it won't.

I looked at him, the sweep of shoulders, the swell of his chest and that sparkling glint of silver, the flat plains of his stomach, the line where his jeans cut across his body. I had never seen Doyle nude, ever. He did not participate in the casual nudity of the court; neither did Frost.

I looked at Frost. His silver hair was still back in the loose ponytail, so his face was clean and unadorned, if anything that beautiful could ever be called unadorned. He had his jacket and shoulder holster, complete with gun, hung over one arm. He was wearing his arrogant mask again, the one he hid behind so often at court. That he felt he had to wear his mask here and now in front of me hurt my heart.

I wanted to go to him, wrap my arms around him, lay my cheek against his chest, and tell him *don't leave*. I wanted to feel his body against mine. I wanted to wake in a cloud of his silver hair.

I did go to him then, but not the way I wanted to go. I got close, but didn't trust myself to touch him. I was afraid if I did, I wouldn't let him go. 'I have the chance to satisfy mine and many a court ladies' curiosity tonight, Frost.'

He turned away so he couldn't see my face. 'I wish you joy in it,' but he didn't sound like he meant it.

'I want you tonight, Frost.'

That turned him to me, with a startled look.

'With Doyle in my bed looking like that, and all the waiting, I still want you. My body begins to ache when you're not with me. I hadn't realized until today what that meant.' I couldn't keep the pain out of my eyes, and finally stopped trying.

He stared down at me, raised a hand to touch my face, but stopped himself just short of my skin. 'If that is true, then Doyle is right. You will be queen. And some things ... you cannot be as others. You must be queen before all else.'

I laid my face against his open hand, and even that small touch made me shiver.

He drew his hand away, rubbing it against his pants as if something clung to his skin. 'Tomorrow night, Princess.'

I nodded. 'Tomorrow night, my—' and I stopped there for fear of what word I might use to finish.

He turned without another word and left the room, shutting the door firmly behind him.

Some small noise turned me back to the room. Rhys slid to the other side of the bed near the window and picked up his clothes that were lying in a hasty heap on the floor. 'The first night shouldn't be a group effort.'

'Making this a threesome had not occurred to me,' Doyle said.

Rhys laughed. 'I didn't think it had.' He worked his way round the bed, holding the clothes with the brush balanced on top, all held above waist level so my view was uninterrupted. It was a nice view.

'A little help with the door, please.' The moment he asked, I knew that he was feeling left out. He was flaunting his charms and I was ignoring him. A deadly insult among the fey.

I got up to open the door for him, as if he couldn't have shifted his clothes around to do it himself. But I stopped before opening the door and raised up on tiptoe to kiss him. I balanced with one hand behind his head, lost in the curls at his neck, and the other hand trailing down the side of his body, caressing over his ribs, the sweep of his hip. I let him see in my eyes how beautiful he was to me.

188

It made him smile, and he gave me a shy glance out of his one perfect eye. The shy was pretend, but the pleasure wasn't.

I stayed on tiptoe long enough to put my forehead against his. My hands played in the curls at the back of his neck, and he shivered under my touch. I stood back on the ground flat-footed and moved out of the door so he could pass.

Rhys shook his head. 'That was her idea of a good-bye kiss, Doyle.' He glanced back at the other man, still kneeling in the bed. 'Have fun, kiddies.' But his serious face didn't match the flippant words.

Rhys offered me the hairbrush from the pile of clothing, then I let him out. I shut the door behind him, and was suddenly very aware that I was alone with Doyle. Doyle, whom I'd never seen nude. Doyle, who had frightened me when I was a child. Doyle, who had been the queen's right hand for a thousand years. He'd kept me safe, guarded my body and my life, but somehow he hadn't really been mine. Somehow he wouldn't really be mine until I'd touched that dark body, seen all of him bare before me. I wasn't sure why that was so important to me, but it was. By withholding himself from me, it was almost as if he was holding his options open. As if he believed that once he was with me, he'd have no more options. Which wasn't true. I'd been with my one-time fiancé, Griffin, for seven years, and in the end he'd found plenty of options, none of them me. Having sex with me hadn't been a life-altering experience for him. Why should it be different for Doyle?

'Meredith.' He said my name once, but for once

his voice wasn't neutral. That one word held uncertainty, a question, and a hope. He spoke my name once more, and it turned me around to face the bed and what lay waiting for me among the burgundy sheets.

Chapter 18

HE SAT ON THE EDGE OF THE BED CLOSEST TO THE mirror, closest to me. He was almost lost among the black dream of his hair. Almost all the other sidhe I knew had some contrast from hair to skin to eyes, but Doyle was all of one piece. His unbound hair cascaded around him like a black cloud, so that his ebony skin was almost lost in the folds of it. A long, long lock of hair had fallen over his face, and his black-on-black eyes were lost in that darkness. He looked like a piece of night itself come to life. He swept a hand up to draw back the hair and try to tuck it behind one pointed ear. The earrings glittered like stars against his darkness.

I walked forward until the bed bumped against my thighs. My legs pressed into the bed, but all I could feel was the thickness of his hair, trapped between my body and the firmness of the bed. He turned his head, and I felt the hair tug underneath me. I pressed in harder, trapping his hair.

He turned those dark eyes up to me, and there were colors in his eyes that shone nowhere in the room, like a swarm of brilliant fireflies – blue, white, yellow, green, red, purple, and colors I had no name for. The pinpoints danced and swirled, and for a second I could almost feel them flying around me, the tiny wind of their passing like being caught in a cloud of butterflies; then I was falling and Doyle caught me.

I came to myself in his arms, in his lap, where he'd sat me. When I could speak, I said, 'Why?'

'I am a power to be reckoned with, Meredith, and I want you to never forget that. A king should have more to offer than seed.'

I slid my hands across his skin, wrapping my arms around his neck. 'Are you auditioning?'

He smiled. 'We all are, Meredith. Some of the others may forget that in the rush of hot skin and sex, but you must never forget. You are choosing a father for your children, a king for the court, and someone you will be tied to forever.'

I hid my face in the curve of his neck. His skin was warm to the touch. His pulse beat against my face. His smell was so warm, so very warm. 'I've been thinking about that.' I spoke the words against his skin.

He rubbed his neck against my face. 'And what conclusions have you come to?'

I drew back enough to see his face. 'That Nicca would be a victim and a disaster on the throne. That Rhys is lovely in bed, but I can't see him as a king. That my father was right and Galen would be utterly disastrous. That there are more knights at court that I would rather kill than be tied to for the rest of my life.'

He laid his lips against the side of my neck, not quite kissing me. He spoke with his own mouth against my skin, so that his words made small

kissing movements against me. 'There is Frost and
. . . me.'

The feel of his lips made me shiver, writhing in
his lap. Doyle drew a sharp breath, his hands
wrapping around my waist, across my thighs. He
whispered, 'Merry,' against my skin, his breath
warm and fierce, his fingers digging into my thigh,
my waist. There was such strength in his hands,
such pressure, as if with little effort he could plunge
his fingers into my body and bring my blood and
flesh to the surface, peel me apart like something
ripe and sweet. Something that had been waiting for
his hand to open me, to bring me, to spill me in a
rush of pleasure over his hands, across his body.

He half lifted me, half threw me onto the bed. I
waited for him to press his body against mine, but
he didn't. He got up on all fours, straddling above
me like a mare with a colt, but there was nothing
motherly about the way he stared down at me.
He'd thrown all that hair over one shoulder so
that his naked upper body was exposed to the
light. His skin gleamed like polished ebony. His
breathing was deep and rapid, making the nipple
ring wink and shimmer above me.

I raised my hand to touch it, brushed my fingers
over that bit of silver, and a sound came out of
Doyle, low in his body and growing, a growl like
some great beast, echoing through that slender,
muscled body. He straddled my body, lips curving
back to flash white teeth, while that growl trickled
out of his lips, past his teeth like a warning.

It made my pulse race, but I wasn't afraid yet.
Not yet. He leaned down into my face and
snarled, 'Run!'

I just blinked at him, my pulse in my throat.

He threw back his head and howled, a sound that echoed and echoed in the small room. The hair on my body stood, and I stopped breathing for a second, because I knew that sound.

That lone, clear evil belling of the Gabriel Ratchets, the dark hounds of the wild hunt. He put his face inches from mine and growled, 'Run!'

I scrambled out from underneath him, and he watched me with those dark eyes, his body immobile but so tense it seemed to shimmer with the promise of some violent action, violence contained, constrained, restricted, but there all the same.

I had crawled off on the wrong side of the bed. I was trapped between the window and the bed. The outer door lay across the bed, past Doyle. I'd played games of hunt and catch before. A lot of things in the Unseelie Court liked to catch you first, but that was pretend, play, foreplay. The look in Doyle's eyes was hungry, but one hunger looks much like another until it's too late.

His voice fought out from his clenched teeth. 'You ... are ... not ... running!' With that last, he made a rush at me on all fours, a black blur. I threw myself over the edge of the bed, rolled, and fell to the floor in front of the outer door. I was on my feet, hand on the doorknob when his body crashed into mine. The door shook and my body bruised with the violence of it. He jerked my hand off the doorknob, and I could not withstand his strength.

I screamed.

He tore me away from the door, threw me on the bed. I tried to slide off to one side, but he was there, his lower body pressing against mine, keeping me pinned to the side of the bed. I could feel the firmness of him through his jeans, through my panties.

The door opened behind us, and Rhys looked in. Doyle growled at him. Rhys said, 'You screamed?' His face was serious. There was a gun in his hand, held next to his leg, not pointed but there.

Doyle growled, 'Get out!'

'I leave at the princess's order, not yours, sire.' He shrugged. 'Sorry. You having a good time, Merry, or . . .' He made a vague motion with the gun.

'I'm . . . I'm not sure.' My voice came out breathy. The feel of Doyle pressed tight and firm against me was exciting, even the promise of violence was exciting, but only if it was the *promise* of it, a game.

His hands on my thighs were shaking, his entire body quivering with the effort not to finish what he'd started. I touched his face gently. He startled as if I'd hurt him, then turned, looked at me. The look in his eyes was barely human. It was like looking into the eyes of a tiger, beautiful, neutral, hungry.

'Are we having fun here, Doyle, or are you going to eat me?' My voice was a little steadier, firmer.

'This first time I would not trust myself to put my mouth to such tender places.'

It took me a second to realize that he had misunderstood me. 'I don't mean eat me in the euphemistic sense, Doyle. I mean, am I food?' My voice sounded utterly calm now, ordinary. Pinned to the bed by his body, his eyes still animalistic and wild, and I sounded like I was in the office, talking business.

He blinked and I saw the confusion in his eyes. I realized that I was asking him to think too deeply. He'd given himself over to a piece of himself that he rarely let out. That part didn't think like a person.

He did something with his legs that pressed him tighter against me. It made me cry out, but not in pain. 'Do you want this?' His voice was almost normal, breathy, but almost normal.

I searched his face, tried to read something there that would comfort me. There was a glimpse of him in the eyes, a sliver of Doyle left behind. I took a deep breath, and said, 'Yes.'

'You heard her. Get out.' His voice began to fall into the growl again, every word lower and lower.

'You sure, Merry?' Rhys asked.

I'd almost forgotten him standing there. I nodded. 'I'm sure.'

'So we just close the door and ignore the noise and trust that you'll be all right?'

I stared into Doyle's eyes and found nothing but need, a need like nothing I'd ever seen in any man. It went beyond desire and became a true need, like food, or water. For him, tonight, this was need; if I turned from him now, we might come together as lovers, but he'd never let himself go this far again. He might close this part of himself away forever, and it would be a little death.

I'd endured that little death for years, dying by inches on the shores of the human sea. Doyle had found me and brought me back to faerie. He'd brought back all those parts of myself I'd had to leave behind to pass for human, to pass for lesser

196

fey. If I turned from him now, would he ever find this piece of himself again?

'I'll be all right, Rhys,' I said, but I wasn't looking at him, I was looking at Doyle.

'You sure?'

Doyle turned and spoke in a voice that was almost too low and animal to understand. 'You heard her. Now get out.'

Rhys gave a small bow and shut the door behind him. Doyle turned those eyes back to me. He growled more than spoke, 'You want this?' He was giving me one last chance to say no. But his body ground against mine, his fingers digging into my thighs, as he said it. His mind and mouth were trying to give me a way out, although his body didn't want to.

I had to close my eyes as I shuddered under the press of him. He growled against my face, and the sound traveled through his body, vibrating along mine, as if the sound could travel places that his body hadn't touched yet.

Even as his body ground into mine, forced small noises from my throat, he growled, 'Do you want this?'

'I want this.'

One of his hands slid from my thigh to the side of my panties. The silk tore with a wet sound like skin being cut. My body jerked as he stripped the silk away and pressed the rough material of his jeans against my naked body. He ground himself against me until I cried out, half in pleasure, half in pain.

He scooted me onto the bed just enough so that he could tear at his pants. The belt opened, the button, the zipper, everything slid down until I saw him nude for the first time. He was long and thick, and perfect. He slid a finger inside of me. It made me cry out, but that wasn't why he'd done it. When he found me wet and open, he pushed himself inside me, and even wet, he had to work himself in. I was screaming underneath him before he'd managed to get himself all inside me. He seemed to fill me up, every inch, and I writhed underneath, just from the feel of him stiff and large inside me.

Then he began to drag himself out of me, and push himself into me, and the small waves of pleasure began. I watched the dark length of him sliding in and out of my white, white flesh, and the sight alone made me cry out.

My skin began to glow like I'd swallowed the moon, and his dark skin gleamed in answer, filled with all the colors that had been in his eyes. It was as if he were still black water reflecting the glow of the moon, and I was the moon. The bright dancing colors flowed under his skin, and the room brightened, brightened, flickering as if we both burned with colored flame. We cast shadows on the wall, the ceiling, as if we lay at the center of some great light, some great flame, and we became that light, that fire, that heat.

It was as if our skins melted into each other and I felt those dancing lights flow across my skin. I sank into his dark glow as he was swallowed by my white shine, and somewhere in all of that, he brought me screaming, screaming, screaming, drowning in pleasure that was so intense it was like pain. I heard him cry out, heard that bell-like howl, but in that one moment I didn't care. He could have ripped my throat out and I'd have gone with a smile.

I came to myself with Doyle collapsed on top of me, his breathing labored, his back covered in a sheen of sweat and blood. I raised my hands and found blood on my white skin, glowing like neon against the fading glow. In that last moment when I hadn't been aware, I'd bloodied his back. I felt the first stinging trickle of blood and found his teeth marks in my shoulder, bleeding, hurting a little, but not too much, not yet. Nothing could hurt too much with Doyle's body still on top of mine, him still inside me, as we both relearned how to breathe, how to be in our own bodies again.

His first panting words were, 'Did I hurt you?'

I touched my bloody fingers into the bite on my shoulder, mixed the neon glows together like mixing paint, and held up my fingers before his face. 'I think I should be asking you the same question.'

He put a hand back to touch the blood on his back, as if he hadn't felt it until that moment. He propped himself up on one elbow and stared at the blood on his hands. Then he threw back his head and laughed, laughed until he collapsed on top of me again, and when he finished laughing, he cried.

Chapter 19

WE LAY ENTWINED TOGETHER ON A BED OF Doyle's hair. It was like having fur rubbing the length of my bare body. My head was cradled in the curve of his shoulder. His body was like warm muscled silk. I traced my fingers along his waist, over the curve of his hip, an idle gesture, not exactly sexual. More to know that I could touch him. We'd been quietly touching each other for several minutes. His one hand was trapped underneath my body, curved up around my back, holding me close, but not too close. He wanted room to run his free hand down my body, and he wanted to give me room to touch him. He wanted the feel of hands on his body. It was as if he wasn't merely starved for sex, but starved for touch. I knew that humans could become touch-starved. Infants will die from lack of enough touch, even if every other need is met. But I hadn't known it of the sidhe, especially the unmovable object known as the Queen's Darkness.

But he lay beside me, smiling, his fingers running over my stomach and tracing the edge of my belly button.

I caught a glimpse of the mirrored bureau behind his head. My blouse hung across the middle of the mirror, as if flung there.

He caught me looking behind him. He brought his hand up to my face, tracing the edge of my cheek. 'What do you see?'

I smiled at him. 'I was just wondering how we managed to get my blouse on the mirror.'

He turned his head as much as he could with both his own weight and mine on his hair. He had a very wide smile when he turned back. 'Have you looked for your bra?'

I gave him wide eyes and started to prop myself up to see the rest of the bureau over his body. He held me down with one gentle hand on my shoulder. 'Behind you.'

I fell back, still in the circle of his arm. My green lace bra, which had matched both my blouse and my panties, was hanging forlornly from the philodendron plant that sat on the black lacquered armoire in the corner. It hung like a badly chosen Christmas decoration.

I shook my head, half laughing. 'I don't remember being in that much of a hurry.'

He curved his free hand over my waist, down my hip, drawing closer to me as he pulled me in against his body. 'I was in a hurry. I wanted to see you naked. I wanted to feel the touch of you on my bare skin.' He pressed that bare skin along the length of my body. Just the strength in his arms made me shiver, but the feel of him growing larger against my body was almost an overwhelming thing.

I slid my hands over the smooth tightness of his buttocks and drew him in tighter against me. He moved his own hands down my body to cup my buttocks and pressed our bodies together until I had to wonder if it hurt him to be shoved so hard against the unyielding front of my body. As he grew, the length of him pressed into my stomach, and it was softer, more yielding. He drove himself against my flesh, and I cried out.

I felt the prickling rush of magic a second before the voice filled the room. 'Well, isn't this a pretty sight?'

We both rolled over to see the Queen of Air and Darkness, Andais, my aunt, Doyle's keeper, sitting on the foot of her own bed watching us.

Chapter 20

THE QUEEN WORE AN ELBORATE BLACK BALL gown, with black satin gleaming in the candlelight, black ribbons to hold back the flounces, black satin gloves to cover her white arms, black straps over pale shoulders. Her black hair was piled atop her head with trails of curls artfully framing her face and slender neck. Her lips were the color of fresh blood, her tricolored grey eyes had been kohl-lined so that they seemed enormous in her slender face.

Seeing her dressed to the nines was nothing new. Andais was fond of parties, and any excuse would do. What was new was the fact that the bed behind her was empty. The queen never slept alone.

We stayed half-frozen, staring back at those eyes. Doyle squeezed my arm, and I spoke without really thinking. 'Your Majesty, how good of you to call, though unexpected.' My voice was neutral, or as neutral as I could get it. It was considered polite to make some sign first before popping in like this. You never knew what people might be doing.

'Are you criticizing me, niece?' Her voice was very cold, almost angry. I hadn't done anything to anger her, not that I knew of at least.

I settled myself a little more comfortably against Doyle's body. I wished for a robe, but knew that covering up when she'd been nothing but polite would imply that I didn't like, or trust, the queen. The fact that it was true was a matter for my own worries, not hers.

'I meant no criticism, Aunt Andais. I was merely stating a fact. We did not expect your call tonight.'

'It is not night, niece, it is morning, just not yet dawn. I see you have slept no more than I.'

'I, like you, aunt, have had better things to do than sleep.'

She touched the full skirt of her ball dress. 'Yes, another party.' She didn't look happy about it.

I wanted to ask if the party had not gone to her liking, but didn't dare. It was too personal a question to ask the queen, and she was too easily offended.

She took a deep breath that made the front of her gown shift, almost as if it wasn't tight enough around her body, a bustier without a boost. If you weren't too well endowed, you could wear those gowns that seemed to just float around your body. For me, it would have been an embarrassment waiting to happen. Nudity on purpose is very different from falling out of your dress by accident.

She turned those dramatic eyes to us. The unhappy look changed, narrowed, to one I knew all too well. Malice.

'You're bleeding, my Darkness.'

I glanced down at Doyle and realized he was still mostly on his side, turned toward me, which gave her a view of his back and the fingernail marks on his dark skin.

'Yes, my queen,' he said in his perfectly neutral, perfectly careful voice.

'Who has harmed my Darkness?' But her eyes were already on me, and it was a very unfriendly gaze.

'I do not see it as harm, my queen,' Doyle said.

Her eyes flicked down to him, then back to me. 'You've been a busy girl, Meredith.'

I pushed up from Doyle, so that I was more or less sitting upright. 'I thought you wished me to be a very busy girl, Aunt Andais.'

'I don't know if I've seen your bare breasts before, Meredith. They are a little large for a sidhe, but very nice.' Her eyes didn't hold lust, or kindness, only a dangerous light. All that she'd said so far could be mistaken for politeness. She'd never seen my breasts bare, so she should compliment them; but only if I was trying to be attractive, which I was not. I just happened to have no clothes on. I did not feel the least bit luscious around my aunt, and there was more to it than just being heterosexual, much more.

'And you, my Darkness, it's been so many centuries since I saw you nude that I can't remember. Is there some reason you have your back to me? Is there some reason you hide yourself from my sight? Is there some . . . aberration that I don't remember that spoils all that darkness?'

She was within her rights to compliment him, but asking if he was deformed, demanding he flaunt himself to her, that was impolite. If it had been almost anyone else, I'd have told her to go to hell.

'There is nothing spoiled here, Aunt Andais,' I said, and I knew my tone wasn't neutral enough. I'd lost the knack of keeping my voice in line over the years I'd been away from the court. I was going to have to relearn, and quickly.

She gave me very cold eyes. 'I was not talking to you, Princess Meredith. I was speaking to my Darkness.'

She'd used my title; not niece, or just my name, but my title. It was not a good sign.

Doyle squeezed my arm again, tighter this time, as if telling me to behave. He answered Andais, but not in words. He rolled onto his back with his knees bent so his thigh hid him from her view, then he lowered the leg closest to her, slowly, like a curtain coming down.

There was heat in her eyes now, real heat, real need. 'My, my, Darkness, you have been keeping secrets.'

He turned and looked at her. 'Nothing you couldn't have discovered at any time in the last thousand years.' Now it was his voice that was not neutral. It was just a slight change in tone, a mild inflection of reproof, but I'd never heard him lose even that much control in front ofAndais.

It was my turn to lay a warning hand on his stomach, just a touch to remind him who we were speaking to. I don't think my face showed the fear that was curling along my spine.

King Taranis might not hurt me for fear of Andais, but Andais might hurt me in a fit. She might regret it later, but dead is dead.

The look she gave Doyle was enough to tighten

my hand against his skin, just a light digging of nails. It made his body react, and I hoped I'd done enough to remind him to tread lightly.

'Have a care, Darkness, or I will grow distracted and forget why I called.'

'We await your news, Queen Andais,' I said.

She looked at me then, some of the heat going from her eyes, replaced by puzzlement and, underneath, tiredness. Andais wasn't usually this easy to read, I think because she didn't have to be careful around anyone. 'The Nameless is free.'

Doyle spilled his legs to the floor and sat up. Suddenly it didn't matter that he was nude, nobody cared. The Nameless was the worst of both courts, Seelie and Unseelie. It was the last great spell that the two courts had cooperated on. They had stripped themselves of everything too awful, too hungry, to allow us to live in this new country. Nobody had demanded it of the sidhe, but we didn't want to be forced out of the last country that would have us, so we'd sacrificed some of what we were in order to become more . . . human. Some said that the Nameless was what caused us to begin to fade, but that wasn't true. The sidhe had been fading for centuries. The Nameless was just a necessary evil. So we didn't turn America into another battlefield.

'Did you set it free, my queen?' Doyle asked.

'Of course not,' she said.

'Then who?' he asked.

'I could tell you a pretty story, but in the end, the answer is, simply, I don't know.' It was obvious she didn't like saying it, and equally obvious that she was speaking the truth. She stripped off one of the black gloves in an abrupt

207

movement and began to run it over and over through her hands.

'There are very few beings in faerie who could do such a thing,' Doyle said.

'Don't you think I know that?' she snapped.

'What would you have us do here, my queen?'

'I don't know, but the last hint we had of it, it was traveling west.'

'Do you believe it will come here?' he asked.

'It is unlikely,' she said, slapping the glove against her arm. 'But the Nameless is nearly unstoppable. It is everything we have given up, and that was a great deal of wielding power. If it was sent for Meredith, then you would need all the preparation time you could manage.'

'Do you truly think it was loosed to hunt the princess?'

'If it had merely been set free, it would have ravaged the countryside by now. But it has not.' She stood, giving us a view of the nearly naked back of the dress. She turned back to us with an abrupt gesture. 'It vanished from our sight, all of our sights, very quickly. We cannot track it, which means that the thing is getting some very highly placed help.'

'But the Nameless is a part of the courts, a part of who you were. You should be able to track it as you would track your own shadow.' The moment I finished, I knew I should have kept quiet.

All the anger flowed into her face, her posture, her hands where they gripped her elbows. She shivered with rage. I think for a second she was too angry to speak.

Doyle stood, putting himself in front of me. 'Have you told the Seelie Court?'

'You do not need to hide her away, Darkness. I am working too hard to keep her alive to kill her myself. And, yes, the Seelie know what has happened.'

'Will the two courts come together to hunt the Nameless?' he asked. He hadn't moved from in front of me, which left me peeking around his body like a child. That wasn't exactly the way to be a strong presence. I moved so I could see the mirror, but they both ignored me.

'No.'

'But it is to each one's benefit, surely.'

'Taranis is being difficult. He's acting as if the Nameless is made up of only Unseelie energy. Pretending that all his light has no taint.' She looked like she'd tasted something sour. 'He will not claim its parentage, so he will give no aid, for to give aid is to admit his part in its making.'

'That is foolishness.'

She nodded. 'He was always one more interested in the illusion of purity than in purity itself.'

'What can stand against the Nameless?' he asked, voice soft, almost as if he were thinking aloud.

'We do not know, for we bound it without testing it. But it is full of old, old magicks, things we no longer tolerate among even the Unseelie.' She sat down on the end of the bed, almost jerkily. 'Whoever released it, and hid it from our sight . . . if they can truly control it, it is a powerful weapon.'

'What do you need of me, my queen?'

She looked up at that, and the look was not unfriendly. 'What if I said come home, come home and protect me? What if I said I don't feel safe without you and Frost at my side?'

He dropped to one knee. His face was lost in a wave of his own hair. 'I am still captain of the Queen's Ravens.'

'You would come?' she asked, voice soft.

'If you commanded it.'

I sat on the bed and tried to keep my face neutral. I hugged my knees to my chest and tried to not look anything, nothing. If I could just not think, it wouldn't show on my face.

'You say you are still the captain of my Ravens, but are you still my Darkness, or do you belong to another now?'

He kept his head down and stayed silent. I kept trying to think of nothing. She gave me a very unfriendly look. 'You have stolen my Darkness from me, Meredith.'

'What do you want me to say, Aunt Andais?'

'It's good to remind me that you are my blood. Seeing his back sliced up makes me hope you are more mine than I knew.'

Nothing, nothing, I would think nothing. I imagined emptiness like looking through a pane of glass into another pane and another and another. Clear, nothing.

'The Nameless was loosed for a reason, Darkness. Until I know what that reason is, I'm covering my assets. The fair Meredith is one of those assets. I still hope to get a child out of her.'

She looked at me, and it was not a friendly look. 'Is he as magnificent as he looks?'

I fought for a neutral voice to match the face. 'Yes.'

210

The queen sighed. 'A pity, but I didn't want to give birth to puppies, now did I?'

'Puppies?' I said.

'Didn't he tell you? Doyle has two aunts whose true forms are dogs. His grandmother was one of the hounds of the great hunt. Hellhounds, humans call them now, though you know we have nothing to do with hell. A different religious system altogether.'

I remembered the baying and the look of hunger in Doyle's eyes. 'I was aware that Doyle wasn't pure sidhe.'

'His grandfather was a phouka so evil that he bred in dog form with the wild hunt itself and lived to tell the tale.' She smiled, and it was sweetly malicious.

'Doyle's as mixed a bag of genetics as I am then.' The voice was still neutral; yeah for me.

'But did you know he was part dog before you took him to your bed?'

Doyle stayed kneeling through all this, his hair hiding his face.

'I knew he owed his bloodline in part to the wild hunt before he came inside me.'

'Really?' She made it sound like she didn't believe me.

'I've heard the belling of the hounds come out of his mouth.' I moved my hair so she could see the bite mark on my shoulder, very near my neck. 'I knew that he dreamed of my flesh in more than one way before I allowed him to satisfy either hunger.'

Her eyes grew hard again. 'You surprise me, Meredith. I never thought you had the stomach for violence.'

'I do not enjoy hurting people. Violence in the bedroom when all agree is different.'

'I've never found it different,' she said.

'I know,' I said.

'How do you do that?' she asked.

'How do I do what, my queen?'

'How do you sound so neutral, utterly neutral, yet somehow you manage to say "go to hell" with a smile and a neutral word.'

'It's not deliberate, Aunt Andais, believe me.'

'At least you didn't try to deny it.'

'We do not lie to each other,' I said, and this time my voice was tired.

'Arise, Darkness, and show your queen your ravaged back.'

He stood without a word, gave his back to the mirror, and swept his hair to one side.

Andais came close to the mirror, reaching out with one gloved hand, so that for a second I thought her hand would keep traveling and come out like a 3-D image. 'I had taken you for a dominant, Doyle, and I don't enjoy being dominated.'

'You never asked what I enjoyed, my queen.' He was still facing away from the mirror, his back to it.

'I also never thought you'd be so blessed down below.' She sounded wistful now, like a child who hadn't gotten what she wanted for her birthday. 'I mean, you are descended from dogs and phoukas, and they are not much in that way.'

'Most phoukas have more than one shape, my queen.'

'Dog and horse, sometimes eagle, yes, I know all about that. What does that have to do ...' She stopped in midsentence, and a smile crooked at the edges of her lipsticked mouth. 'Are you saying that your grandfather could turn into a horse as well as a dog?'

He spoke softly. 'Yes, my queen.'

'You're hung like a horse.' She started to laugh. He said nothing, only shrugged his broad shoulders. I was too startled at her laughter to join in. It wasn't always a good thing to amuse the queen.

'My Darkness, it is wondrous, but a horse you are not.'

'The phoukas are shape-shifters, my queen.'

The laughter faded around the edges, then she said in a voice still light with it, 'Are you implying that you can change the size?'

'Would I imply something like that?' he asked in his neutral voice.

I watched emotions flow across her face too fast to catch: disbelief, curiosity, and finally a hard-edged wanting. She stared at him the way misers stare at gold, a covetous, clinging, selfish want.

'When all this is over, Darkness, if you have not fathered a child with the princess, we will make you live up to this boast.'

I think I failed at the neutral face, but I tried to hang on to it.

'I do not boast, my queen,' Doyle said, almost in a whisper.

'I don't know what to wish for now, my Darkness. If you make babies with Meredith, I will never know the joy of you. And I still believe what I have always believed, and what has truly kept you out of my bed.'

'Dare I ask what that is?' he said.

213

'You may dare. I may even answer.'

Silence stretched for a second or two, then Doyle said, 'What do you believe that has kept me out of your bed all these years?' He turned his head enough to see her face when he asked.

'That you would be king in truth, not merely in name. And I will not share my power.' She looked past him to me. I fought to keep a blank face, and knew I was losing. 'What of you, Meredith? How do you feel about having a true king, one who will demand a share of your power, and a share of more than your bed?'

I thought of several answers, discarded them all, and tried, very carefully to tell the truth. 'I share better than you do, Aunt Andais.'

She stared at me, a look in her eyes that I couldn't read. I met that gaze with one of my own, letting the sincerity of what I'd said show in my eyes.

'You share better than me, you share better than me. What does that mean, when I do not share at all?'

'It is the truth, Aunt Andais. It means exactly what it says, nothing more, nothing less.'

She stared at me for a long, long moment. 'Taranis does not share his power either.'

'I know,' I said.

'You cannot be a dictator if you do not dictate.'

'I am learning that a queen must rule those around her, truly rule them, but I am not learning that a queen must dictate to all around her. I am finding that the counsel of my guards, who you so wisely sent with me, is worth listening to.'

'I have counselors,' she said, and it sounded almost defensive.

'So does Taranis,' I said.

Andais sat back against one of the bedposts. She seemed almost to slump, the one bare hand playing along the black ribbons on her dress. 'But neither of us listens to anyone. The emperor has no clothes.'

The last comment caught me off guard. It must have showed, because she said, 'You look surprised, niece of mine.'

'I didn't expect you to know the story.'

'I had a human lover some time ago who was fond of children's stories. He read to me when I could not sleep.' There was a dreamy wistfulness to her voice now, a true note of regret.

She continued in a more normal tone. 'The Nameless has been freed. It was last seen headed west. I doubt it will get as far as the Western Sea, but I thought you should know, all the same.' With that, she made a gesture and the mirror went blank.

My eyes were very wide in the glass. 'Can you make the mirror so that no one can get through without signaling to us first?'

'Yes,' he said.

'Do it.'

'The queen may take that ill.'

I nodded, looking at my scared face in the mirror, because now that I didn't have to pretend, I could look as scared as I felt. 'Just do it, Doyle, just do it. I don't want any more surprises tonight.'

He went to the mirror and made small gestures at its edges. I felt the spell prickle along my skin as I climbed back into the bed.

Doyle turned from the mirror and hesitated by

the edge of the bed. 'Do you still want company?'

I held out my arms to him. 'Come to bed, and hold me while we sleep.'

He smiled and slipped under the sheet. He spooned his body against mine until I lay cupped in his arms, his chest, his stomach, his groin, his thighs. He encircled me and I pulled the warm silken hardness of him around me.

He spoke softly as I began to drift off to sleep. 'You do not mind that my grandmother was a hound of the wild hunt and my grandfather a phouka?'

'No.' My voice was thick with sleep. Then I asked, 'Could I really end up having puppies?'

'It is unlikely.'

'Okay.' I was almost asleep, when I felt him hold me tighter, as if I was his security blanket instead of the other way around.

Chapter 21

THE GREY DETECTIVE AGENCY DIDN'T USUALLY get called to murder scenes. We had helped the police in the past when something mystical was doing something bad, but that was usually as decoys or advisers. I could count on both hands the number of murder scenes I'd seen and still have a couple of fingers left over.

I had one less finger to count today. The woman's body was already on a gurney. Her yellow hair trailed across her face, darker gold where the ocean had touched it. Her very short evening dress was pale blue on the edges but dark blue where the water had soaked into it. A broad ribbon, probably white, sat just under her breasts, tightening the dress enough to show cleavage. Her long legs were bare and tanned. Her toenails were painted a funky blue to match the fingernails. Her lips were an odd blue color, too; but it was lipstick, not some sign of her death.

'The lipstick color is called asphyxiation.'

I turned to the tall woman just behind me. Detective Lucinda Tate walked up with her hands plunged inside the pockets of her slacks. She tried to give me her usual smile, but it didn't work. Her eyes stayed worried and the smile vanished before it had really gotten started. Her eyes were always cynical under the humor, but today the cynicism had spilled out and swallowed the humor.

'I'm sorry, Lucy, what did you say about the lipstick?'

'It's called asphyxiation. It's supposed to mimic the lip color of a corpse who died from suffocation. Nicely ironic,' she said.

I looked down at the woman again. There were bluish and white tints around the eyes, the nose, the edges of the lips. I had a strange urge to wipe off the lipstick and see if the lips really were the same color. I didn't do it, but the urge was like a great itch across my palms.

'So, she suffocated,' I said.

Lucy nodded. 'Yeah.'

I frowned. 'She didn't drown?'

'I doubt it. None of the others did.'

I stared up at her. 'Others?'

'Jeremy's had to go with Teresa to the hospital.'

'What happened?' I asked.

'Teresa touched a lipstick that one of the women had been about to put on before she died. Teresa started hyperventilating, then she couldn't breathe. If we hadn't had paramedics on the scene, she might have died. I should have known better than to invite one of the most powerful clairvoyants in the country into this mess.'

She glanced at Frost, who was standing a little out of the way, one hand on the other wrist, very bodyguardish. The effect was somewhat ruined by his silver hair spilling around him in the wind, as if it was trying to pull loose from the ponytail. A pale pink shirt matched the show hankie in the white suit jacket that matched the slacks. The slender silver belt matched his hair. His shiny loafers were creamy tan. He looked more like a fashion plate than a guard, though the wind gave occasional glimpses of the black shoulder holster underneath all that white and pink.

'Jeremy said you were running late today,' Detective Lucy said. 'You getting much sleep lately, Merry?'

'Not much.' I didn't bother to explain it wasn't Frost who had kept me up last night. We were doing friendly banter, empty, meaningless, something to say to fill the windy silence while we stood over the dead woman.

I looked down at her face, lovely even in death. The body looked thin, not exactly strong, more like she'd dieted her way to a size whatever. If she'd known she would die last night, would she have gone off her diet the day before?

'How old was she?'

'Her ID says twenty-three.'

'She looks older,' I said.

'Dieting and too much sun will do that to you.' Any flash of humor had gone now. She was somber as she looked up on the cliff above us. 'You ready to see the rest?'

'Sure, but I'm a little puzzled about why you called Jeremy and all of us in. It's sad, but she got herself killed, or choked to death, or something. She suffocated, it's horrible, but why call us in?'

'I didn't call in your two bodyguards.' For the first time there was true hostility on her face. She pointed down the beach at Rhys. Frost might have been uncomfortable, but Rhys was having a very good time.

He watched everything with an eager eye, smiling, humming the theme song to *Hawaii Five-O* under his breath. Or at least that's what he'd been humming when he went farther down the beach to watch some of the uniforms wade in the surf. Rhys had already done *Magnum, P.I.*, until Frost told him to stop. Rhys preferred film noir and would always be a Bogart fan at heart, but Bogie wasn't making movies anymore. In the last few months Rhys discovered reruns in color that he actually enjoyed.

He turned toward us and waved, smiling. His white trench coat billowed out around him like wings as he began to trudge his way back up the beach. He had had to take off his tan fedora to keep it from blowing into the sea.

'Rhys is creepy around murder scenes,' Detective Lucy said. 'He always has such a good time, like he's happy someone's dead.'

I didn't know how to explain that Rhys had once been worshipped as a god of death, so death didn't bother him all that much. But that part was best not shared with the police. I said, 'You know how much he loves film noir.'

'This isn't a movie,' she said.

'What's got you all upset, Lucy? I've seen you at worse murder scenes than this. Why are you so . . . bothered?'

'You just wait. You won't need to ask once you've seen it.'

'Can you just tell me, Lucy, please?'

Rhys came up to us, face all shiny like a kid on Yule morning. 'Hi, Detective Tate. There's no burst blood vessels in the girl's eyes, no bruising anywhere that I could find. Does anyone know how she suffocated?'

'You looked at the body?' Her voice was cold.

He nodded, still smiling. 'I thought that's what we were here to do.'

She pointed a finger at his chest. 'You weren't invited to this show. Merry was, and Jeremy was, and Teresa was, but you—' She poked the finger into his chest. '—were not.'

The smile faded and left his tricolored blue eye cold. 'Merry has to have two bodyguards with her at all times. You know that.'

'Yeah, I know that.' She poked again, hard enough that he was shoved backwards just a little. 'But I don't like you around my murder scenes.'

'I know the rules, Detective. I haven't messed with your evidence. I've stayed out of the way of everyone from the EMTs to the video photographer.'

The wind gusted, blowing her dark hair across her face, so she was forced to take a hand out of her pocket to smooth it back. 'Then stay out of my way, too, Rhys.'

'Why, what did I do wrong?'

'You enjoy this.' The last was almost spit in his face. 'You're not supposed to enjoy it.' She stalked back up the beach toward the stairs that led up to the road, the parking lot, and the club on its little promontory.

'Who licked her fur the wrong way?' he asked.

'She's creeped out by whatever's up the stairs, and she needs someone to take it out on. You're it.'

'Why me?'

Frost had joined us. 'Because she is human and humans mourn death. They don't enjoy poking at it like you do.'

'That's a lie,' Rhys said. 'A lot of the detectives enjoy their work, and I know the medical examiner does.'

'But they don't go around humming at the crime scene,' I said.

'Sometimes they do,' Rhys said.

I frowned at him, trying to figure out how to make it more clear. 'Humans hum, or sing, or tell bad jokes over the bodies so they won't be scared. You hum because you're happy. This doesn't bother you.'

He glanced down at the dead woman. 'She doesn't care anymore. She's dead. We could stage a Wagnerian opera on top of her and she wouldn't care.'

I touched his arm. 'Rhys, it's not the dead you should try to placate; it's the living.'

He frowned at me.

'Be less happy in front of the humans when you are looking at their dead,' Frost said.

'Very well, but I don't understand why I should pretend.'

'Pretend that Detective Tate is Queen Andais,' I said, 'and it bothers her that you go around chortling over the dead.'

I watched some thought slip over his face, then he shrugged. 'I can seem less happy around the detective, but I still don't understand why.'

I sighed, and looked at Frost. 'Do you understand why?'

'If it were my kinswoman on the gurney, I would feel something for her death.'

I turned back to Rhys. 'See.'

He shrugged. 'I'll be sad around Detective Tate.'

'Just somber will do, Rhys.' I'd had this sudden image of him falling on the next corpse with weeping and wailing. 'Don't overdo it.'

He grinned at me, and I knew that he'd been thinking of exactly what I'd feared. 'I mean it, Rhys. If you don't behave yourself, Tate could get you barred from crime scenes.'

He suddenly looked somber; that mattered to him. 'Okay, okay, I'll be good. Sheesh.'

Detective Tate yelled back at us, her voice riding the wind like seagulls overhead. She was halfway up the stairs, and it was impressive that her voice carried back to us so clearly. 'Hurry it up. We don't have all day here.'

'Actually, we do,' Rhys said.

I was already walking through the soft sand toward the stairs. I was very sorry that I'd worn high heels today, and I didn't protest when Frost offered me his arm. 'Actually we do what?' I asked.

'We have all day. We have all eternity. The dead aren't going anywhere.'

I glanced at him. He was watching the tall detective with a sort of faraway, almost dreamy look on his face. 'You know what, Rhys?'

He looked at me, raising one eyebrow.

'Lucy's right. You're creepy at a murder scene.'

He grinned again. 'Not nearly as creepy as I could be.'

'What's that supposed to mean?'

Rhys wouldn't answer. He just started walking ahead of us in his lower-heeled shoes. I looked up at Frost. 'What did he mean by that?'

'Rhys was once called the Lord of Relics.'

'And that means what?' I asked, nearly stumbling in the heels, holding tighter to his arm.

'*Relics* is an old poetic word. It means corpse.'

I stopped him with my hands on his arm and stared up at him. I tried to see his eyes through a tangle of his silver hair and my own red fluttering across my face. 'When a sidhe is called a lord of anything, it means they have power over it. So you're saying what? That Rhys can cause death? I knew that.'

'No, Meredith, I am saying that he could at one point raise the old dead, those that had grown stiff and cold, to rise and fight on our side in battle.'

I just stared at him. 'I didn't know Rhys had that kind of power.'

'He no longer does. When the Nameless was created, Rhys lost the power to raise armies of the dead. We had no more use for armies among ourselves, and to fight the humans in such a way would have meant our expulsion from this country.' Frost hesitated, then said, 'Many of us lost our most otherworldly powers when the Nameless was cast. But I do not know of any who lost so much as Rhys.'

I watched Rhys walking ahead of us, his white curls blowing in the wind to mingle with the white of his coat. He had gone from being a god who could raise armies at his will, to being . . . Rhys. 'Is that why he won't tell me his real name, the name he was worshipped under?'

'When he lost his powers, he took the name Rhys and said that the other was dead along with his magic. Everyone, including the queen, has always respected that. It could so easily have been any one of us who gave the most of ourselves to the spell.'

I balanced on one foot while I slipped off the heels. My stocking feet would do for the sand. 'How did you get everyone to agree to the Nameless?'

'Those in power decreed death for any who opposed it.'

I should have guessed. I transferred my shoes to one hand and slipped my other hand back on Frost's arm. 'I mean, how did Andais get Taranis to agree?'

'That is a secret only the queen and Taranis know.' He touched my hair, smoothing it back from my face. 'Unlike Rhys, I do not like being around so much death and sadness. I look forward to tonight.'

I turned my face and kissed his palm. 'Me, too.'

'Merry!' Lucy Tate screamed at me from the top of the steps. Rhys was almost even with her. Lucy walked out of sight, with Rhys almost but not quite chasing her. If you could call it chasing at a casual walk.

I tugged on Frost's arm. 'We had better hurry.'

'Yes,' Frost said. 'I do not trust Rhys's sense of humor alone with the detective.'

We exchanged a glance on the windy beach, then we began to hurry toward the steps. I think we were both hoping to get there before Rhys did something cute and unfortunate. I, for one, didn't believe we'd make it in time.

Chapter 22

SOME OF THE BODIES WERE IN BODY BAGS, PLASTIC cocoons from which nothing would wake. But they'd run out of body bags and just started laying the uncovered bodies out. I could not count at a glance how many there were. More than fifty. Maybe a hundred, maybe more. I couldn't bring myself to start counting, to make them just things in a row, so I stopped trying to estimate. I tried to stop thinking at all.

I tried to pretend that I was back at court and this was one of the queen's 'entertainments.' You never dared show distaste, disgust, horror, or least of all fear at one of her little shows. If you did, she'd often make you join in on the fun. Her shows ran more to sex and torture than true death, and suffocation wasn't one of Andais's kinks, so this little disaster wouldn't have pleased her. She'd probably see it as a waste. So many people who could have admired her, so many people she could have terrorized.

I pretended that my life depended on keeping a blank face and feeling nothing. It was the only way I knew to walk among the bodies and not have hysterics. My life depended on not going into hysterics. I repeated it in my head like a mantra – *my life depends on not having hysterics; my life depends on not having hysterics* – and it kept me moving down the rows, kept me able to look down at all this horror and not scream.

The bodies that weren't covered all had lips almost the same shade of blue as the girl on the beach, except this obviously wasn't lipstick. They'd all suffocated, but not instantly. They hadn't dropped magically and mercifully in their tracks. There were nail marks on some of the bodies where they'd clawed at their throats, their chests, as if trying to get air into lungs that no longer worked.

Nine bodies seemed different from the others. I couldn't figure out what it was, but I kept pacing in front of the nine, scattered in a row among the others. Frost had paced beside me at first, but he was back at the edge of the floor, trying to stay out of the way of the hurrying uniforms, plain-clothes, paramedics, and all the extra people who seem to accumulate at any murder scene. I remembered being surprised the first time I saw how very many people tracked through a murder scene.

Behind Frost was something covered with a tablecloth but it wasn't a body. It took me a few seconds to realize that it was a Christmas tree. Someone had covered the artificial greenery, covered the entire Christmas display. It was as if someone hadn't wanted the tree to see the bodies, like hiding the eyes of the innocent so they won't be tarnished. It should have seemed ridiculous, but it didn't. Somehow, it seemed appropriate to cover the decorations in this room. To hide them away so they wouldn't be spoiled.

Frost seemed unaware of the covered tree, or much of anything else. Rhys, on the other hand, seemed aware of everything.

He stayed right at my side. He wasn't humming or even smiling now. He'd been subdued since we walked in on the carnage. Though *carnage* seemed the wrong word for it. Carnage seemed to imply blood and flesh ripped and torn. This was strangely clean, almost impersonal. No, not impersonal – cold. I'd seen people who enjoyed slaughter, and they literally enjoyed the act of cutting someone up, the feel of the blade in flesh. There was no savage joy in this scene. It was just death, cold death, as if the Grim Reaper had been brought to life to ride through this place.

'What is it about these nine that's different?' I hadn't realized I'd spoken aloud until Rhys answered me.

'They went quictly, no nail marks, no signs of struggle. These, and only these nine, just ... dropped where they were dancing.'

'What in Goddess's name happened here, Rhys?'

'What the fuck are you doing here, Princess Meredith?' We both turned to the far side of the room. The man stalking toward us through the bodies was medium build, balding, obviously muscular, and even more obviously pissed.

'Lieutenant Peterson, isn't it?' I said. The first and last time I'd met Peterson I'd been trying to convince the police to investigate the possibility that a fey aphrodisiac had gotten out into the human population. They'd informed me that aphrodisiacs didn't work, and neither did love spells. I'd proven that it did work, and nearly caused a riot in the Los Angeles Police Department. The lieutenant had been one of the men I'd used to prove my point. They'd had to handcuff him before they could drag him off me.

'Don't be pleasant, Princess. What the fuck are you doing here?'

I smiled. 'It's lovely to see you, too, Lieutenant.'

He didn't smile. 'Get out, now, before I have you thrown out.'

Rhys moved an inch closer to my side. Peterson's eyes flicked to him, then back to me. 'I see your two gorillas. If they try anything, diplomatic immunity or no diplomatic immunity, they're going to jail.'

I glanced back just enough to see that Frost was drifting closer. I shook my head, and he stopped. He frowned, clearly not happy; but he didn't have to be happy, he just had to give me room.

'Have you ever seen this many dead before?' I asked. My voice was quiet.

'What?' Peterson asked.

I repeated my question.

He shook his head. 'What does that have to do with anything?'

'It's horrible,' I said.

'Yeah, it's horrible, and what the fuck does that have to do with anything?'

'You'd be friendlier if it wasn't such a horrible crime scene.'

He made a sound that was almost a laugh, but too harsh to be one. 'Well, hell, Princess, this is friendly. This is exactly how friendly I am to murderers like you who hide behind diplomatic immunity.' He smiled, but it was a baring of teeth, like a snarl.

I'd once been suspected of killing a man who'd attempted to rape me. I hadn't done it, but without diplomatic immunity I might have gone to jail anyway. I'd have at least seen a trial. I didn't try to deny it again. Peterson wouldn't believe me now any more than he had before.

'Why are these nine bodies the only ones that went quietly?' I asked.

He frowned at me. 'What?'

'Why are these nine bodies the only ones without signs of struggle on them?'

'This is a police investigation, and I am the senior officer on-site. This is my investigation, and I don't care if you are one of our civilian advisers on metaphysical shit. I don't even care if you've helped us out in the past. You've never done shit for me, and I don't need help from any god-damned faerie. So, for the last time, get the fuck out of here.'

I'd tried being sympathetic. I'd tried being businesslike. When being good doesn't help, you can always be bad. I reached out toward him, as if to touch his face. He did what I knew he'd do. He backed up.

'What's wrong, Lieutenant?' I made sure to look puzzled.

'Don't ever touch me.' His voice was quieter now. And, I realized, much more dangerous than the yelling.

'It wasn't the touch of my skin that drove you mad last time, Lieutenant. It was the Branwyn's Tears.'

His voice dropped even lower. 'Don't . . . ever

230

... touch me ... again.' There was something in his eyes that was frightening. He was afraid of me, really afraid, and that made him hate me.

Rhys stepped a little ahead of me, not quite putting himself between me and the lieutenant but almost. I didn't fight him. It's never comforting to have anyone look at you with such hatred.

'We've met only once, Lieutenant. Why do you hate me?' It was a question so direct that even a human wouldn't have asked it. But I didn't understand, couldn't understand; so I had to ask.

He looked down, hiding his eyes as if he hadn't expected me to see so far into his soul. His voice was very low when he said, 'You forget, I saw what you left on that bed – just a pile of raw meat, cut to ribbons. Without dental records we couldn't have recognized him. And you wonder why I don't want you to touch me?' He shook his head and looked at me, eyes blank and unreadable, cop eyes. 'Now, get out, Princess. Take your two goons and get out. I am senior officer in charge, and I won't have you here.' His voice was calm now, very calm, too calm for standing in the middle of all this.

'Lieutenant, I called the Grey Detective Agency.' Lucy Tate came in from the deck.

'And who authorized that?' Peterson asked.

'I've never needed special authorization to bring them in before.' She picked her way through the lines of bodies, and when she got close enough, Lucy was over a head taller than the lieutenant.

'The clairvoyant I understand. Even Mr Grey, because he's a well-known magician. But why her?' He jerked a thumb at me.

'The sidhe are well known for magic use,

231

Lieutenant. I thought the more heads we have on this one, the better.'

'You thought, you thought ... Well, don't think, Detective. Just follow procedure. And procedure is that you check with the head of the task force, and that's me. And I say she's not welcome.'

'Lieutenant, I—'

'Detective Tate, if you want to stay on this task force, you'll follow my lead, my orders, and you won't argue with me. Is that clear?'

I watched Lucy struggle with his sharp words, then finally she said, 'Yes, sir, that's clear.'

'Good,' he said, 'because the upper brass can think anything they want, but it's my ass on the line here, in the cameras, and I say it's some kind of toxic gas or poison. When they finish the toxicology work on the other bodies, they'll know what it is, and it'll be our job to find out who did it. Look first for whodunit, not whatdunit. You don't have to go to fairy-tale land to solve this murder. It's just another crazy son of a bitch that's as mortal as everyone else in this room.'

He turned his head to one side in an odd gesture, then looked at me, at Rhys, and at Frost beyond. 'Sorry, my mistake. Mortal as all the rest of us humans in this room. Now, you take your immortal asses and get out of here. And if I hear that anyone on my watch has been talking to you, they'll be up on disciplinary charges. Is that clear to everyone?'

'Yes, sir,' Lucy said.

I smiled charmingly at him. 'Thanks so much, Lieutenant. I hated being here among all this death. It's been one of the worst things I've ever seen in my life, so thank you for letting me leave, when it was taking everything I had not to run out.' I kept smiling as I pulled off the one surgical glove I'd put on. I hadn't touched anything, or any body, because I hadn't wanted to take the feel of their dead flesh back with me.

Rhys stripped off his gloves, too, and he had touched things. We worked our way to the bag set out for glove disposal, and I couldn't help saying just before we stepped out the door, 'Thanks again, Lieutenant, for letting me go. I agree with you, I don't know what the hell I'm doing here.' With that I left, Rhys and Frost trailing behind me like pale shadows.

Chapter 23

I WAS BEHIND THE WHEEL OF THE ACURA BEFORE I realized I couldn't remember where we were supposed to be going. I stared at the keys in my hands and couldn't think. 'Where are we going?'

The men exchanged a look, then Rhys said from the backseat, 'Let me drive, Merry.' He reached between the seats and took the keys gently from my hand. I didn't argue. The day seemed to be full of a high buzzing sound like some invisible mosquito humming in my ear.

Rhys held the door open for me, and I walked around to the passenger-side door. Frost held the door for me and got me settled in before getting into the back. I was lucky that Rhys was with me. Frost didn't know how to drive a car.

'Buckle up,' Rhys said.

It wasn't like me to forget my seat belt. It took me two tries to get the belt fastened. 'What's wrong with me?'

'Shock,' Rhys said, as he put the car in gear.

'Shock? Why?'

Frost answered, leaning forward over my seat. Most of the guards never buckled up; they could be decapitated and not die, so I guess a little trip through a windshield didn't worry them. 'You said it yourself to the policeman. You have never seen anything as awful as what you have just seen.'

'Have you seen worse?'

He was quiet for a second, then said, 'Yes.'

I glanced at Rhys, who had moved us onto the Pacific Highway with its beautiful views of the ocean. 'How about you?'

'How about me, what?' he asked, flashing me a grin.

I frowned at him. 'Have you seen worse?'

'Yes. And, no, I'm not going to tell you about it.'

'Not even if I ask nicely?'

'Especially if you ask nicely. If I was angry enough, I might try to shock you with the horrors I've seen. But I'm not angry with you, and I don't want to hurt you.'

'Frost?'

'I am sure Rhys has seen worse than I. I was not alive during the very first battles when our people fought the Firbolgs.'

I knew the Firbolgs were the first semidivine inhabitants of the British Isles and Ireland. I knew that my ancestors had defeated them and won the right to be the new rulers of the lands. It was several thousand years of history away; that I knew. What I hadn't known was that Rhys was older than Frost, older than most of the sidhe. That Rhys was one of the first of us to come to the isles now thought to be the original home of all sidhe. 'Rhys is older than you are?'

'Yes.'

I looked at Rhys.

He suddenly seemed very interested in driving. 'Rhys?'

'Yes,' he said, looking straight ahead. He maneuvered a curve a little too fast, so he'd have to play with the wheel.

'How much older are you than Frost?'

'I don't remember.' His voice held a plaintive note.

'Yes, you do.'

He glanced at me. 'No, I don't. It's been too long, Merry. I don't remember what year Frost was born.' He sounded grumpy now.

'Do you remember what year you were born?' I asked Frost.

He seemed to think about it, then shook his head. 'Not really. Rhys is right on one thing. After a time it simply is too long to think about.'

'Are you saying you all begin to lose parts of your memories?'

'No,' Frost said, 'but it no longer becomes important what year you were born. You know that we do not celebrate our birthdays.'

'Well, yes, but I never really thought about why.'

I turned back to Rhys. His face looked almost grim. 'So you've seen worse than back there at the club, restaurant, whatever?'

'Yes.' The word was very short, clipped.

'If I asked you to tell me about it, would you?'

'No,' he said.

There is *no* that can be worn down to yes, then there is NO. Rhys's no was one of those.

I left it alone. Besides, I wasn't sure I wanted stories today about awful deaths, especially if that death was worse than what we'd just walked through. It was the most dead I'd ever seen, and more than I'd ever wanted to see.

'I'll respect your wishes.'

He glanced at me almost as if he didn't trust me. 'That's big of you.'

'No need to be snide, Rhys.'

He shrugged. 'Sorry, Merry, I'm just not feeling particularly good right now.'

'I thought I was the only one having trouble handling this.'

'It's not the bodies that bothered me,' Rhys said. 'It's the fact that the lieutenant is wrong. It wasn't gas or poison, or anything like that.'

'What do you mean, Rhys? What did you see that I didn't?'

Frost leaned back away from my seat.

'Okay, what did you both see that I didn't see?'

Rhys kept staring at the road. There was silence from the backseat.

'Someone talk to me,' I said.

'You seem to be feeling better,' Frost said.

'I am. There's nothing like getting a little angry to get you through things. Now what did you two see there that I missed?'

'You were shielding too hard to see anything mystical,' Rhys said.

'You bet I was. Do you know how much metaphysical crap there is in a place where you've had a recent murder, let alone a mass execution? There are a lot of spirits that are attracted to sites like that. They flock like vultures to feed on the remaining living, feeding off their horror, their sorrow. You can go clean into a place like that and come out covered in riders.'

'We know what the spirits that fly the air can do,' Frost said.

'Probably better than I do,' I said, 'but you're sidhe and you don't get riders.'

'We don't get small ones,' Frost said, 'but I have seen others of our kind nearly possessed by incorporeal beings. It does happen, especially if someone works with dark magic.'

'Well, I'm human enough that I'll pick up things casually. I don't have to do a thing to attract them except not shield well enough.'

'You tried to sense as little as possible while you were there,' Rhys said.

'I am a private detective, not a professional psychic. I'm not even a professional magician or witch. I had no business being there today. I couldn't help.'

'You could have helped if you'd let your shields down just a little,' Rhys said.

'Fine, I'll try to be braver next time. Now what did you see?'

Frost sighed loudly enough for me to hear him. 'I could feel the remnants of a powerful spell, very powerful. It clung in stinging echoes to the place.'

'Could you sense it as soon as we got inside?'

'No, I did not wish to touch the dead, so I searched with other senses besides touch and vision. I, as you say, dropped my shields. It was then that I sensed the spell.'

'Do you know what spell it was?' I asked. I'd turned in my seat enough to see him shake his head.

'I do.' Rhys's voice turned me back around to him.

'What did you say?'

'Anyone who concentrated could have sensed the remains of magic. Merry could have seen it, if she'd wanted to.'

'It would have told her nothing, as it told me nothing,' Frost said, 'but it would have made it harder for her to endure what she saw.'

'I'm not arguing that,' Rhys said. 'What I mean is that I got down and looked at the bodies. Nine of them dropped where they stood, but the rest had time to fight, to be afraid, to try to run. But they didn't run like they'd run if, say, wild animals had attacked them. They didn't go for the doors, or break a window, not as soon as they saw what was happening. It's as if they couldn't see anything.'

'You speak in riddles,' Frost said.

'Yeah, plain English, Rhys, please.'

'What if they didn't run because they didn't realize that anything was in the room?'

'What do you mean?' I asked.

'Most humans can't see spirits of any kind.'

'Yeah, but if you're implying that spirits, noncorporeal beings killed everybody at the club, then I can't agree. Noncorporeal beings, riders, whatever, they don't have the . . . physical oomph to take out that many people like that. They might be able to do one person who was very susceptible to their influence, but even that's debatable.'

'Not noncorporeal beings, Merry, but a different kind of spirit.'

I blinked at him. 'You mean, what, ghosts?'

He nodded.

'Ghosts don't do things like this, Rhys. They might be able to scare someone into a heart attack, if the person had a weak heart, but that's it. Real ghosts don't harm people. If you get true physical damage, then you're dealing with something other than ghosts.'

'It depends on what kind of ghosts you're talking about, Merry.'

'What do you mean by that? There is only one kind of ghost.'

He glanced at me then, having to turn his head almost completely around because of the eye patch. He often glanced at me when he drove, but it was a movement without meaning because his right eye was gone; he couldn't see me. Now, he made the effort to look at me with his left eye. 'You know so much.'

I'd always assumed Rhys was one of the younger sidhe, because he never made me feel like I was in the wrong century. He was one of the few who had a house outside the faerie mound, electricity, a license. Now he looked at me as if I were a child and would never understand.

'Stop that,' I said.

He turned back to the road. 'Stop what?'

'I hate it when any of you give me that look, the look that says I'm so young and I couldn't possibly understand what you've experienced. Well, fine, I'll never be a thousand years old, but I'm over thirty, and by human standards I'm not a child. Please don't treat me like one.'

'Then stop acting like one,' he said, and his voice was full of reproach, again like a disappointed teacher. I got enough of that from Doyle. I didn't need it from Rhys.

'How did I act like a child? Because I wouldn't drop shields and see all that horror?'

'No, because you say there is only one type of

ghost, like it's the only truth. Trust me, Merry, there are more than human shades running around.'

'Like what?' I asked.

He took a deep breath, flexing his hands on the steering wheel. 'What happens to an immortal being when it dies?'

'They're reincarnated like everybody else.'

He smiled. 'No, Merry, if it can be killed, then by definition it's not immortal. The sidhe say they're immortal, but they aren't. There are things that can kill us.'

'Not without magical help there isn't,' I said.

'It doesn't matter how it's done, Merry. What matters is that it can be done. Which brings us back to the question, what happens to the immortals when they die?'

'They can't die, they're immortal,' I said.

'Exactly,' he said.

I frowned at him. 'Okay, I give up, what did that mean?'

'If something can't die, but it does, what happens to it?'

'You mean the elder ones,' Frost said.

'Yes,' Rhys said.

'But they are not ghosts,' Frost said. 'They are what remains of the first gods.'

'Come on, guys,' Rhys said. 'Think with me. A human ghost is what remains of a human after death, before it goes to the afterlife. Or in some cases, a piece gets left behind because it's too hard to let go. But it is the spiritual remains of a human being, right?'

We both agreed.

'So aren't the remnants of the first gods just ghosts of the gods themselves?'

'No,' Frost said, 'because if someone could discover their name again and give them followers, they could, theoretically, rise to "life" again. Human ghosts do not have such an option.'

'Does the fact that the humans don't have the option make the elder ones less a ghost?' Rhys asked.

I was beginning to get a headache. 'Okay, fine, say that there are ghosts of elder gods running around. What has that got to do with anything?'

'I said I knew the spell. I don't, not exactly. But I have seen the shades of the elder let loose on fey. It was as if the very air turned deadly. Their lives were just sucked out of them.'

'Fey are immortal,' I said.

'Anything that can be killed, even if it reincarnates, is mortal, Merry. Length of life doesn't change that.'

'So you're saying that these ghosts were let loose in that club?'

'Fey are harder to kill than humans. If the place had been full of fey, some might have survived, or been able to protect themselves, but, yes, I am saying that that's what did it.'

'So the ghosts of dead gods killed over a hundred people in a nightclub in California?'

'Yes,' Rhys said.

'Could it have been the Nameless?'

He seemed to think about that, then shook his head. 'No, if it had been the Nameless, the building wouldn't be standing.'

'That powerful?'

'That destructive.'

'When did you see this happen the first time?'

'Before Frost was born.'

'So a few thousand years ago.'

'Yes.'

'Who called the ghosts up then? Who did the spell?'

'A sidhe who has been dead longer than England has been ruled by the Normans and their descendants.'

I did quick history math in my head. 'So before 1066.'

'Yes.'

'Is there anyone alive today who could do the spell?'

'Probably, but it's forbidden to do it. If you're caught, it's an automatic execution, no trial, no commuting the sentence, you just get dead.'

'Who would risk such a thing to harm a crowd of humans on the edge of the Western Sea?' Frost asked.

'No one,' Rhys said.

'How sure are you that these elder ghosts did this?' I asked.

'There's always the possibility that some human magician has come up with a new spell that resembles the effects, but I'd bet a great deal that it was the elder ghosts.'

'Do the ghosts take the lives for their master?' Frost asked.

'No, they keep the lives, and they feed on them. Theoretically, if they were allowed to feed each night unchecked, they could become ... alive again, for lack of a better word. They need the aid of a mortal to do it, but some of the elder ones can be brought back to full strength if they get enough lives. Sometimes one of them will convince a cult somewhere that they're the devil and get them to sacrifice themselves, and that could work, but it would take enormous amounts of lives to do it. Taking the lives from the mouths of the victims is quicker, no wasted energy, like trying to drink blood from an offering bowl.'

'Has one of them ever been brought back to full strength?' I asked.

'No, it's always been stopped before it got that far. But to my knowledge they've never been let loose to feed directly – except for once, and that was in a controlled situation where they were contained as soon as the spell was finished. If they've gotten out without a leash on them, then . . .'

'What can stop them?' I asked.

'The spell needs to be reversed.'

'How do we do that?'

'I don't know. I'll have to talk to some of the others back at the apartment.'

'Rhys,' I said softly, because a horrible idea had just occurred to me.

'Yeah.'

'If the only person you've ever known to do this spell was a sidhe, then does that mean it's one of us again?'

Silence for a few heartbeats, then, 'That's what I'm afraid of. Because if it's a sidhe and the police find out – if they could prove it – it might be grounds to evict us all from American soil. There's an addendum to the treaty between us and Jefferson that says if we perform magic that is detrimental to the national interest, then we are considered outcast, and we'll have to move on.'

'That's why you didn't mention this in front of the police,' I said.

'One of the reasons,' he said.

'What's the other?'

'Merry, they can't do anything about this. They can't stop these things. I'm not even sure that there are sidhe alive today who can stop them.'

'There has to be at least one sidhe who could stop them,' I said.

'How do you figure?' Rhys asked.

'A sidhe let them loose. He could put them back.'

'Maybe,' Rhys said, 'or maybe the reason they slaughtered a hundred humans in a matter of minutes is that the sidhe lost control of them. They may have killed him when he couldn't control them.'

'Fine, if a sidhe raised these things, why are they in California and not in Illinois where the sidhe are?'

Rhys did another of those full-face turns. 'Merry, don't you get it? What if they wanted a way to kill you that couldn't be traced back to faerie.'

Oh. 'But we did trace it back to faerie,' I said.

'Only because I'm here. Most of the court forgets who I was, and I don't remind them, because thanks to the Nameless I don't have the power to be that anymore.' He couldn't quite keep the bitterness out of his voice. Then he laughed. 'I'm probably one of the few sidhe alive who saw what Esras did. I was there, and whoever raised the elders just forgot about me.' He laughed again, but it burned with mockery as if it hurt coming out of his throat. 'They forgot about me. Here's hoping I can make them regret that little oversight.'

I'd never heard Rhys so full of . . . anything but lust or teasing. He was never serious for long if he could help it. I looked at him as he drove us toward the apartment to pick up Kitto. There was a look to his face, a set to his shoulders. Even the grip of his hands seemed to have changed. I realized in that moment that I didn't really know him. He hid behind a veil of humor, lightness, but underneath was more, much more. He was my bodyguard and my lover, and I didn't know him at all. I wasn't sure if I owed Rhys an apology, or if he owed me one.

Chapter 24

THE DRIVE ALL THE WAY BACK TO EL SEGUNDO WAS out of the way to say the least, but when Kitto had woken up this morning he'd had circles under his eyes like purple bruises, and his pale skin had seemed tissue-paper thin, as if he'd worn thin over the night. I couldn't see him walking around on the open beach with nothing but a press of sky above him. Once I knew the location of the scene I gave Kitto a chance to decide, and he'd opted to crawl back into his covered dog bed.

I walked up the stairs from the parking area, sandwiched between Frost in front and Rhys in back. Frost spoke as we rounded the edge of the small pool. 'If the little one does not begin to thrive, you are going to have to send him back to Kurag.'

'I know,' I said. We went up the last flight of steps and were almost instantly at my door. 'I'm just worried about what Kurag will send next. He expected me to be offended when he offered Kitto in the first place. The fact that I took him and was okay with it really bothered him.'

'By goblin standards Kitto is ugly,' Rhys said.

It made me glance back at him. He still hadn't regained his usual savoir faire. He looked down-right glum. I didn't ask how Rhys, who understood almost nothing of goblin culture, knew what they considered pretty. With a sidhe warrior theirs for the evening, I was sure the goblins had given him only the most beautiful among them, by their standards. The goblins prized extra eyes and extra limbs, and Kitto didn't fit the bill. 'I know, and he's not connected to the royal house in any way. Kurag expected me to refuse, and thus he'd have gotten out of our treaty.'

We were at the door. A small potted geranium, pale pink, was sitting by the door. Galen had taken over most of the house chores, like search-ing for an apartment big enough for all of us and buying flowers for wandering fey to rest in. We'd have had a bigger apartment ages ago if price hadn't been a problem, but it was a very big prob-lem to find a place big enough for all of us that we could afford. Most places had limits on how many people they'd allow to live there, and six adults was over that limit.

I was still refusing money from the courts, because no one gives money without expecting something in return. Frost thought I was just being stubborn, but Doyle agreed that there was always a price on any favor. I was pretty sure what Andais's favor would be – not to kill her son if I got the throne – and that was one favor I could not afford to grant. I knew that Cel would never accept me as queen, not as long as he was alive. That Andais didn't understand this was simply a mother's blindness. Cel was a wretched, twisted being, but his mother loved him, which was more than I could say for my own mother.

Frost pushed the door open, entering first; he'd checked and the wards had been intact. The sweet clean smell of lavender and sage incense met us at the door. The main altar sat in the far corner of the living room so that everyone could use it. You didn't need the altar. You could stand in the middle of a meadow, or a wood, or a crowded subway and deity was always with you – if you paid attention, and if you invited it into your heart. But the altar was a nice reminder. A place to start out every day with a little communion of the spirit.

People often thought that the sidhe had no religion – I mean they were once gods themselves, right? Well, sort of. They were worshipped as gods, but most sidhe acknowledge powers greater than they are. Most of us bend knee to Goddess and Consort, or some variation thereof. Goddess is the giver of all life, and Consort is all that is male. They are the template for everything that descends from them. She, especially she, is a greater power than anything on the planet, any-thing that is flesh, no matter how spiritual that flesh may once have been.

Except for the thin trail of incense from the altar, and a small carved bowl of water that had been added to the altar, the apartment looked empty. It didn't feel empty though. There was the small skin-tingling of magic nearby – not big magic but more the everyday kind. Doyle was probably on the mirror talking to someone. He'd opted to stay behind today and try to uncover more information about the Nameless from some of our friends at court. Doyle's magic was subtle enough that he might go completely undetected as he moved around amongst them. I could not have done it.

Rhys locked the door and pulled a taped note off it. 'Galen's out apartment hunting. He hopes we like the flower.' He pulled a second note from the door. 'Nicca hopes to finish up the bodyguard job today.'

'The actress is in no danger,' Frost said, as he began to slip his jacket off. 'I believe most sincerely that her agent put her up to it, to get more attention for a ... how do they say, flagging career.'

I nodded. 'Her last two movies were pretty much flops, both financially and artistically.'

'That I did not know. But the media is there to photograph us more than her.'

'She's taking you to all the hot spots where you are bound to get seen.' I wanted to slip off the high heels, but we were going right back out to work. So instead I walked to Kitto's covered hidey-hole and knelt down, smoothing my skirt behind automatically so the buckles on my shoes wouldn't snag my hose.

I could see his back curled toward the opening. 'Kitto, you awake?'

He didn't move.

I touched his back, and the skin was cold. 'Mother help us. Frost, Rhys, something's wrong.'

Frost was at my side instantly; Rhys hung back. Frost touched the goblin's back. 'He's like ice.' He reached farther in so he could feel the pulse in the neck. He waited, waited for too long, before finally saying, 'His blood does flow but slowly.' He reached in and began pulling Kitto out from his nest. He came like one already dead, his limbs moving as if he was just dead weight.

'Kitto!' I didn't scream his name but it was close.

His eyes were closed, but it seemed I could see the vibrant blue of his pupils behind the closed lids, as if the skin was translucent. His eyes fluttered open and a slit of blue showed before his eyes rolled up into his head. He was murmuring something, and I bent close to hear. It was my name, 'Merry, Merry,' over and over.

He'd stripped down to his shorts, and I could see his veins through his skin, the muscles. A dark shape on his chest moved, and I realized that it was his heart beating. I could see it. It was as if he were melting, or . . .

I looked up at Frost. 'He's fading.'

He nodded.

Rhys had gone to the bedroom door and brought Doyle out. They gathered round us, but the looks on their faces said more than words.

'No,' I said, 'it's not hopeless. There's got to be something that we can do.'

They all exchanged looks, that flitting game of glance throwing, like the thoughts were too heavy to bear and you had to throw them to the next person and the next.

I grabbed Doyle's arm. 'There has to be something.'

'We do not know what would hold a goblin from fading.'

'His mother was sidhe. Save him the way you'd save another sidhe.'

Doyle looked a little disdainful, as if I'd insulted them all.

'Don't go all high and mighty on me, Doyle.

Don't let him die because he's less mixed than either of us.'

His expression softened. 'Meredith, Merry, a sidhe fades only if he wishes it so. Once the process is begun, it cannot be stopped.'

'No! There has to be something we can do.'

He frowned down at us all. 'Hold him, while I try to contact Kurag. If we cannot save him as sidhe, we will try to save him as goblin.'

Kitto lay still in Frost's arms. 'Merry needs to hold him,' Doyle said, as he went for the bedroom.

Frost laid Kitto in my arms, across my lap. I slumped to the floor, put a hand under his legs, and pulled him into my lap. He fit; here was a man who I could hold in my lap. I'd spent much of my life around beings smaller than Kitto, but none who had looked so sidhe. Maybe that was why he seemed so doll-like at times.

I laid my cheek against his icy forehead. 'Kitto, please, please, come back, come back from wherever you've gone. Please, Kitto, it's Merry.'

He'd stopped murmuring my name. He'd stopped making any noise, and his weight, the way his body slumped against me . . . He felt dead. Not dying, but dead. There is a weight to a dead body that the living, no matter how sick, do not have. Logically, it has to be the same, but it never feels the same.

Doyle came back out, muttering under his breath. 'Kurag is not near his mirror, or any still body of water. I cannot reach him, Merry. I am sorry.'

'If Kitto were sidhe, what would you do to save him?'

'The sidhe do not fade from lack of faerie,' Doyle said. 'The sidhe fade only when they wish to.'

I held his cold body in my arms and felt the beginnings of tears. But tears wouldn't help him, damn it. I needed to talk to Kurag, now. What was one thing all goblin warriors had on their bodies at all times? 'Give me your blade, Frost.'

'What?'

'My blade is trapped under Kitto's body. I need a blade, now.'

'Do as she says,' Doyle said.

Frost didn't like doing something he didn't understand, but he took out a knife from behind his back, one that was almost as long as my forearm, and handed it to me hilt first.

I took my hand out from under Kitto's legs, and said, 'Hold the blade steady.'

Frost dropped to one knee steadying the blade with both hands. I took a deep breath, placed my finger against the point, and jerked downward. It took a second for the blood to well.

'Merry, stop—'

'Hold the blade, Frost. That's all you have to do, so do it. I can't hold the blade and Kitto, too. Just do it.'

He frowned but stayed kneeling, holding the blade as I drew my bleeding finger down that shining surface. The blood didn't coat it, just stained it, almost beading on the immaculate surface.

I dropped the shields that kept me from seeing spirits, kept me from shedding magic like old body skin. The magic flared for a second, glad to be free, then I willed it into the blade. I pictured Kurag, his face, his voice, his rough manner.

'Kurag, I call you; Kurag Thousand-Slayer, I call you; Kurag, King of the Goblins, I call you. Thrice called, thrice named, come to me, Kurag, come answer your blade.'

The surface gleamed through the light lattice-work of blood, but it was just metal.

'No sidhe has called a goblin by blade in centuries,' Rhys said. 'He won't answer.'

'The naming of three is very powerful,' Doyle said. 'Kurag might be able to ignore it, but few others of his people could.'

'But I have something he won't ignore.' I leaned close to the blade and blew my breath warm upon it until it fogged with the heat of my body.

The blade glittered through the fog, the blood. The fog cleared and the blood soaked into the surface as if it had been drunk. I was left staring into a dim silvered surface. A blade, even the highest quality, is not like a mirror, no matter what the movies show. A blade gives an uncertain image, misty, as if you need to adjust some button or knob, but there is none. There is only a vague outline of a small portion of a person's face; their eyes are the most clear.

A blur of yellow lump-covered skin and two orange eyes appeared in the downside blade half; the upper was less clear but showed Kurag's third eye like a dim sun seen through cloud.

His voice was as clear as if he'd been standing in the room. It boomed out in a surprising rumble that made me jump. 'Meredith, Princess of the Sidhe, was that your sweet breath that blew across my skin?'

'Greetings, Kurag, Goblin King. And Twin of Kurag, Goblin King's Flesh, greetings also.'

Kurag had a parasitic twin who consisted of one violet eye, a mouth, two thin arms, two thin legs, and small, though fully functional genitalia. The mouth could breathe but not speak, and to my knowledge I was the only one who ever acknowledged his existence as separate from the king's. I still remember the horror I felt when I realized there was an entire person trapped in the side of Kurag's body.

'It has been long since a sidhe has called the goblins by blood and blade. Most of the warriors who fought beside us after the great treaty have forgotten this old trick.'

'My father taught me many tricks,' I said. Kurag and I both knew that my father had often contacted him by blade and blood. My father had been Andais's unofficial ambassador to the goblins, because no one else wanted the job. My father had taken me to the goblin hill many times as a child.

His laughter did not so much roll out of the blade as roll through the room. 'What would you have of me, Merry, daughter of Essus?'

He'd offered his help, and that was what I needed. I described the condition we'd found Kitto in. 'He's fading.'

Kurag cursed in the guttural language that was high goblin. I understood only about every other word. Something about black tits. 'The mark ties you together, you and Kitto. Your strength should sustain him.' His hand passed over his face like a yellow ghost in the blade. 'This should not be happening.'

I thought of something. 'What if the mark healed over?'

'The mark would not heal, it would scar,' he said.

'It did heal, Kurag, and it did not scar.'

His orange eyes got very close to the blade, and very wide. 'That should not happen.'

'I didn't know that it was a problem to have it heal. Kitto didn't say anything.'

'A lover's mark always scars, Merry. Always. At least among our kind.' I couldn't read his expression in that narrow piece of reflection, but suddenly he let out a great snort, and said, 'Has he been allowed to mark that white flesh only once?'

'Yes,' I said.

'And the sex?' He sounded suspicious now.

'The treaty demanded only that I share flesh. Sharing true flesh is more valuable among the goblins than sex.'

'Gabriel's Hounds take me. Yes, we value flesh, but what's a little bite without a little poke? Sinking teeth and dick into flesh, Merry girl, that's the ticket.'

'Kitto shares my bed, Kurag, and stays with me most of the time, touching me. He seems to need to touch me.'

'If the touch of your skin was all he had . . .' He dissolved into high goblin again, which goblins rarely did; it was considered rude to use a language that the other person didn't know. My father had taught me some goblin, but it had been too long, and Kurag's use was too rapid for my rusty skills.

When Kurag had ranted long enough, he paused for breath and spoke in a language we could all understand. 'The high and mighty sidhe, goblins are good enough to fight all your wars, do most of the dying, but not good enough to fuck. Sometimes I hate you all. Even you, Merry, and you're one of my favorites.'

'I love you, too, Kurag.'

'Don't sweet-talk me, Merry. If you'd have fucked Kitto regularly, the mark would have scarred. He needs a constant supply of flesh to sustain him out in the Western Lands. Either true flesh or fucking, but his tie to you is too weak without it, and he is dying because of it.'

I looked down at the still, cold figure in my arms, then realized he wasn't as cold. He was still chilled, very, but not icy. 'He's warmer.' I said it softly, I think because I couldn't quite believe it.

Doyle touched Kitto's face. 'He is warmer.'

'Is that you, Darkness?' Kurag asked.

'It is I, Goblin King.'

'Is he truly fading? I don't think Merry has ever seen anyone fade.'

'He is fading,' Doyle said.

'Then why is he warmer? If he is fading, then he should grow colder and colder.'

'Merry has been holding him in her arms for a time. I believe that is warming him.'

'Maybe it's not too late then. Is he strong enough to fuck?'

'He is barely conscious,' Doyle said.

Kurag said a sharp word that I knew meant something that no goblin ever wished on another: impotency. It was their worst insult one to the other. 'Can he tear her flesh with his teeth?'

We all stared down at the still form. He was warmer, though he still hadn't moved at all. 'I don't think so,' I said.

'Blood then, can he take blood?' Kurag asked.

'Maybe,' I said.

'If we wiped it upon his mouth, we might get some of it into him,' Doyle said. 'If it did not choke him.'

'He's a goblin, Darkness. He can't choke to death on blood.'

'Does it have to be Merry's blood?' This from Rhys.

'I know you of old ... Rhys,' and that silence held a name that no one used anymore. 'You should come visit us again, sidhe. The womenfolk still talk of you. That's high praise from a goblin female.'

Rhys had gone very pale and very quiet. He made no answer.

Kurag gave an unpleasant laugh. 'Yes, it must be Merry's blood. Later, if some of the rest of you want to share blood and flesh with Kitto, feel free. The sidhe are always good eatin'.' He glared at me with those orange eyes. 'If the blood revives him, then give him flesh, Merry, real flesh this time.' His eyes suddenly grew huge in the blade. He must have nearly pressed his nose to the blade. 'You thought you'd get the goblins as allies for six months and not have to bed one of us. You shared flesh, so I can't say you lied about the alliance. But you pixied on the spirit of it. You know it and I know it.'

I placed my still-bleeding finger against Kitto's lips, painting them crimson while I talked to his king. 'If I take him to my bed, then he has a chance to be king, king of all the Unseelie. That is worth more than a six-month alliance.'

Kitto's eyes flickered; his mouth made a small

movement. I slid my finger over his lips, between his teeth, and his body jerked, once.

'Oh, no, you won't get me that easy, Merry girl, not that easy. You give him flesh like you should have done all along, and you get only three more months out of us. After that, your battles are your own.'

Kitto began to suck on my finger like a baby, gently at first, then harder, harder, teeth beginning to graze my skin. 'He's sucking my finger, Kurag.'

'I'd take the finger out before you lose it. He's not in his right mind yet, and goblins can bite through iron.'

Kitto fought me, his mouth trying to hold on to my finger. By the time I pulled it free, his eyes were trying to open.

'Kitto,' I said.

He didn't react to his name, or anything else, but he was warmer, and he was moving.

'He's moving, and he's warmer,' I said.

'Good, very good. I've done my good deed, Merry. The rest is up to you.'

I looked directly into the blade again, instead of down at Kitto. 'You're just going to sit back and watch who wins, aren't you?'

'What matters to us who sits on the Unseelie throne? It matters to us only who sits on the goblin throne.'

Doyle's deep voice cut in. 'And what if Cel's followers were planning war with the Seelie?' Doyle knelt down, one hand squeezing gently but firmly on my shoulder. I think he was warning me not to interrupt.

'What are you babbling about, Darkness?'

'I am privy to much among the sidhe that the goblins do not know.'

'You are not at court now.'

'I am not without ears.'

'Spies, you mean.'

'I did not use such a word.'

'Fine, fine, play the word games that you are all so fond of but speak plainly to me.'

'There are those at the Unseelie Court who believe Andais is desperate to have Meredith named her heir. They believe having a mortal on the throne is the end of them. They are talking about going to war on the Seelie before they all become powerless mortals. Our strength comes from our kings and queens, as you know.'

'What you tell me is enough to make me throw in my lot with Cel's people.'

'If the goblins were Merry's allies, then no one at the Unseelie Court would risk fighting against her. They dare to challenge the Seelie only because they assume they will have the goblins' support.'

'What is it to us if the sidhe kill each other off?'

'You are bound by word, blood, earth, fire, water, and air to support the rightful heir to the Unseelie throne in all matters of strife. If Merry sits on the throne and Unseelie rebels fight against her while you sit back and do nothing, then your oath will come back upon you.'

'You can't frighten me, sidhe.'

'The Nameless walks the land again, and you think it is I whom you should be frightened of? There are terrible things far beyond me that will rise from the depths, descend from the sky, and take rightful payment from those who are forsworn by such oaths as you have taken.'

It was difficult to tell in the blurred image, but Kurag looked worried. 'I hear your words, Darkness, but Merry has fallen silent. Are you her new puppet master?'

'I tend your goblin, Kurag, and I have a better use for my tongue than telling you what you already know.'

'I remember my oaths, girl.'

'No, Kurag, that is not what I mean. The sidhe may not bear tales to the goblin mound, but you and I both know you have other means.' I did not say out loud that the lesser fey at court, some servants, some not, talked to the goblins, sometimes for a price, sometimes for the feeling of power it gave them. My father had given his word never to tell of Kurag's system of spies. I had given no such oath. I was free to reveal the goblins' secret, but did not.

'Speak freely, Princess, and do not toy with this old goblin.'

'I have spoken as freely as I intend to, Kurag, Goblin King.'

He blew out a loud breath. 'Merry girl, you are too much your father's daughter. Essus was my favorite of all the sidhe. His loss was great to all the courts of the Unseelie, for he was true friend to many.'

'That means a great deal coming from you, Kurag.' I didn't thank him, because you never thank an older fey. Some of the younger ones are cool with it now, but it's an old prohibition among us, almost a taboo.

'Do you honor all the oaths your father gave?'

'No, some I did not agree with, and some I know nothing of.'

261

'I thought he told you everything,' Kurag said.

'I am not a baby anymore, Kurag. I know that even my father kept his secrets. I was young when he died. Some things I wasn't ready to know.'

'You are wise as well as luscious; how sad. Sometimes I'd have liked you better if you'd been just a little more stupid. I like my women less bright than I am.'

'Kurag, you old charmer.'

He laughed then, a true laugh, and it was contagious. I laughed with him, and as the eyes began to fade out of the blade, he spoke. 'I will think on what your Darkness has said, and what you have said, and even what your father said. But you must give true sustenance to my goblin or in three months I will be free of you.'

'You'll never be free of me, Kurag, not until you've fucked me. Or that's what you told me when I was sixteen.'

He laughed; but at the end, he said, 'I used to think things would have been safer if you'd agreed to be my queen, but I'm beginning to think you're just too dangerous to be allowed that close to any throne.'

Chapter 25

KITTO LAY AGAINST THE DARK BURGUNDY SHEETS like a ghost. His black curls made him seem paler. His eyes kept fluttering open, flashing blue, then shutting, leaving his blue eyes like gleaming bruises behind the thin skin of his closed lids.

I touched his bare shoulder. 'He still looks . . . almost translucent,'

'The lesser fey fade in truth,' Doyle said. He stood beside me in front of the mirrored dresser.

Rhys stood at the foot of the bed and stared down at the goblin. 'He's not up to sex, no pun intended.'

I looked at him. He looked unhappy, maybe even worried, but that was all. 'You're not going to protest about me sharing my body with a goblin?'

'Would it do me any good?' he asked.

'No,' I said.

He gave a weak version of his grin. 'Then I might as well start making the best of it. Besides, I don't think we have to worry about you doing the bump and grind with him tonight. There's not enough of him left.'

'Merry must share flesh with Kitto to bring him back to himself,' Doyle said.

I sat down on the edge of the bed, and Kitto rolled toward me like the sea pulled by the moon. He cuddled against me with a sigh that was almost a whimper.

'He can't take a bite out of me if he's not conscious.'

'Put power into him as you did the sword,' Doyle said. 'Make him aware of you, as you made Kurag aware of you.'

I looked down at the tiny man. He seemed asleep, but his skin still had that awful thin quality like it was wearing away. I stroked my hand down his shoulder. He wiggled closer to me, but did not wake.

I leaned over him, putting my mouth just above the skin of his shoulder. I had raised my shields automatically when I'd finished using the magic to contact Kurag. Shielding was like breathing for me. It was dropping them that took concentration. I'd learned to shield about the same time I learned to read.

But this wasn't a spell; this was less, and more than that. The human witches call it natural magic, which means a natural ability you can perform without much training or effort.

I drew magic, energy, into my breath and blew it across his skin. I willed him to wake, to see me.

Kitto's eyes fluttered open, and this time he did see me. His voice came hoarse, 'Merry.'

I smiled at him, touching the curls on the side of his pale face. 'Yes, Kitto, it's me.'

He frowned, and grimaced as if something hurt. 'What's happening?'

'You need to take flesh from me.'

He continued to frown up at me as if he hadn't understood.

I took off my jacket and began unbuttoning my blouse. I probably could have pushed the sleeve up enough to expose my shoulder, but I didn't want to get blood on the white material. The bra underneath was white, as well, but I was pretty sure I could keep it from getting stained if I was careful.

Kitto's eyes had widened. 'Flesh?' He made it a question.

'Leave your mark on my body, Kitto.'

'We contacted Kurag,' Doyle said. 'He said that the reason you are ailing is that your mark with Meredith has healed. Her energy must sustain you away from faerie, and for that you need a new sharing of flesh.'

Kitto stared up at the tall dark man. 'I don't understand.'

I touched his face, turned his eyes back to me. 'Does it matter, does anything matter except the scent of my skin?' I put my wrist next to his face, then slid my arm slowly, just above his lips, so that our bodies touched here and there. I ended on my knees by the bed, taking my other arm behind his head to bring his face close to the upper part of my free arm, just below the shoulder. During sex, biting is great, even some bloodletting; but this was cold, and I wasn't ready for it. This was going to hurt, so I preferred it be somewhere with some cushioning, some meat.

His pupils had gone to thin black slits. There was a stillness to him, but it was not static. It was a stillness full of so many things, eagerness, need, and hunger, a terrible blind hunger. Something in that moment, as he watched the white flesh of my shoulder, reminded me his father was not just a goblin, but a snake goblin. Kitto was becoming warm and so terribly mammalian, yet something of that reptilian stillness was in him. He was still a small version of a sidhe warrior; but watching his body tense, I was reminded of a snake about to strike. For a moment, I was afraid of him, then he was moving in a blur of speed, and I fought with myself not to flinch away.

It was like being hit in the arm with a baseball bat, like being bitten by a large dog. It was the impact that startled, but it didn't exactly hurt, not right away. Blood poured from his lips down my arm. He worried at it like a dog trying to break the neck of a rat, and I cried out.

I slumped down the side of the bed, away from him, and he stayed at my shoulder, teeth dug into my flesh. Blood dripped onto my chest, staining the white bra.

I drew my breath from deep inside my body, but I didn't scream. He was a goblin; screaming and fighting back just drove them to blood lust. I blew my breath soft upon his face. He stayed locked on my arm, eyes closed, face enraptured. I blew one quick hard breath in his face the way you do on small pets when they bite. Most things don't like having you blow in their face, especially on their eyes.

It made him open his eyes. I watched Kitto flow back into those eyes, watched him fill back up, while the animal receded. He let go of my arm.

I slumped back against the dresser, and the pain was sharp and immediate. I had the urge to curse him soundly, but staring up into his face, I couldn't.

Blood covered his mouth like lipstick gone wild. It dripped down his chin, stained his throat. His eyes were focused, and he was himself again, but he still ran that narrow forked tongue across tiny bloodstained teeth. He rolled back onto the bed and basked in the afterglow.

I just sat on the floor and bled.

Doyle knelt behind me with a small towel in his hands. He raised my arm, wrapping the towel around it, not so much to stop the bleeding, but to catch the blood and keep it from getting all over everything.

The scent of flowers filled the air, pleasant but strong. Doyle glanced up at the mirror. 'Someone is asking permission to speak through the mirror.'

'Who is it?'

'I am not sure. Niceven, perhaps.'

I looked at my bloody arm. 'Is this a good enough show?'

'If you do not show pain while we bind the wound, yes.'

I sighed. 'Great. Help me sit on the edge of the bed.' He lifted me in his arms and sat me on the bed. 'I didn't need that much help.'

'My apologies. I didn't know how hurt you might be.'

'I'll live.' I took the towel and held it on the wound. Kitto curled around me, his face still bloodstained. He'd kicked off all the sheets, so that with his body pressed up against mine you couldn't see his short-shorts from the mirror. He'd look naked. He writhed against me, his forked tongue licking the blood from his lips, and further around his mouth. His hands stroked along my waist and hips.

Kurag could say what he wished, but taking flesh this way was sex for the goblins.

'Answer them, Doyle, then get me something to stop the blood.'

He smiled and gave a small bow. He motioned and the mirror sprang to life showing a hook-nosed man with skin the color of bluebells.

It was Hedwick, King Taranis's social secretary. Not only was he not Niceven, but he was so not going to appreciate the show.

Chapter 26

HEDWICK DIDN'T EVEN LOOK OUT FROM THE mirror. He was reading down a list, face half-averted. 'Greetings to Princess Meredith NicEssus from the High King Taranis Thunderer. This is to inform you of a pre-Yule ball three days hence. His majesty looks forward to seeing you there.'

During the speech, he had not looked out at the room. His hand was actually reaching out to cleanse the mirror when I spoke.

I said the one word he probably didn't expect to hear. 'No.'

His hand went down, and he looked up into the room with a cross look on his face. The look gave way to astonishment, then disgust. Maybe it was watching Kitto writhe on the bed. Maybe it was me being splattered with blood. Whatever, he didn't like the show.

'You are Princess Meredith NicEssus, are you not?' His voice dripped with disdain, as if he found it hard to believe.

'Yes.'

'Then we will see you at the ball.' Again his hand went up to cleanse the mirror.

'No,' I said again.

He lowered his hand and scowled at me. 'I have quite a few invitations to make today, Princess, so I do not have time for histrionics.'

I smiled, but could feel my eyes going hard. But underneath the anger was pleasure. Hedwick had always been an officious little bootlicker, and I knew that he gave the invitations to all the lesser fey, lesser people. Another sidhe handled all the important social contacts. That Hedwick had extended the invitation was an insult; the way he'd given it was a double insult.

'I'm not the least bit hysterical, Hedwick. I cannot accept the invitation as it stands.'

He bristled, his fingers going to his fluffy white cravat. He was dressed as if the 1700s had never passed. At least he wasn't wearing a wig. For that I was grateful.

'The high king himself commands your presence, Princess.' He sounded like he always did, as if it was the utmost honor to toady for the king.

'I am Unseelie and I have no high king,' I said.

Doyle knelt at my feet with a small basket of medical supplies. We'd started keeping them near at hand, though the bites from the other guards were usually nowhere near this bad.

Hedwick's gaze flicked down to Doyle, then up to me with a frown. 'You are a Seelie princess.'

Doyle moved around me so that he was on the side with the wound. He took the towel, applying direct pressure with it.

I took a slightly sharper breath as he pressed the cloth very firmly into the bite, but other than that my voice was normal. I sounded all business as

Doyle tended my wound and Kitto writhed against me.

'It was agreed that my title in the Unseelie Court supercedes my Seelie title. Now that I am heir to the Unseelie throne I can no longer acknowledge my uncle as high king. For me to acknowledge the title might imply that he was also high king of the Unseelie, and that is not true.'

Hedwick was clearly perplexed. He was good at following orders, flattering those above him, and playing errand boy. I was forcing him to think. He wasn't used to having to do anything that complex.

He smoothed his cravat again, and finally, looking a great deal less sure of himself, he said, 'As you like. Then King Taranis commands your presence at the ball three days hence.'

Doyle's gaze flicked up to my face at that. I smiled and gave a small shake of my head. I'd caught it.

'Hedwick, the only royal who can command my presence is the Queen of Air and Darkness.'

He shook his head stubbornly. 'The king can command the presence of anyone of lesser title than he, and you are not a queen yet—' He stressed the *yet*. '— Princess Meredith.'

Doyle opened the towel to see if my wound had stopped bleeding. Apparently it had, because he got some antiseptic to clean the wound.

'If I was King Taranis's royal heir, then he could command me, but I am not his heir. I am Queen Andais's heir. Only she can command me, because only she outranks me.'

Hedwick flinched at the mention of the queen's

true name. All the Seelie were like that, never invoking her true name, as if afraid it would call her to them.

'Are you saying that you outrank the king?' He sounded truly outraged.

Doyle began to clean the wound with soft gauze; even so, the little touches sent tiny shock waves of pain through my arm. I gritted my teeth a little and fought not to show it. 'I am saying that order of rank in the Seelie Court has no meaning for me anymore, Hedwick. When I was merely a princess of the Unseelie Court, I could also have had the same rank at the Seelie Court. But I am to be queen. I cannot have a lesser rank in any other court if I am to rule.'

'There are queens aplenty in the court who acknowledge Taranis as their high king.'

'I am aware of that, Hedwick, but they are part of the Seelie Court, and they are not sidhe. I am part of the Unseelie Court and I am sidhe.'

'You are niece to the king,' he said, still trying to think his way through the political maze I'd thrown up around him.

'So nice of someone to remember that, but it would be as if Andais had called Eluned and asked her for acknowledgment as her high queen.'

'Princess Eluned has no ties to the Unseelie Court.' Hedwick sounded terribly offended.

I sighed, and it went sharp as Doyle finished cleaning the wound. 'Hedwick, try to understand this. I will be queen of the Unseelie Court. I am royal heir. King Taranis cannot command me to do anything or to appear anywhere, because I am not his royal heir.'

'Are you refusing to appear at the king's

command?' He still looked like he didn't trust his own ears. He had to have misheard something.

'The king has no right to command me, Hedwick. It would be like him having you call the president of the United States with a command to appear.'

'You grow above your station, Meredith.'

I let the anger show on my face. 'And you no longer seem to know what yours is, Hedwick.'

'You truly are refusing the king's command?' Astonishment showed through his voice, his face, his posture.

'Yes, because he is not my king, and cannot command anyone outside his own kingdom.'

'Are you saying you renounce all titles that you hold in the Seelie Court?'

Doyle touched my arm, made me look at him. His gaze said, *careful here.*

'No, Hedwick, and for you to say such a thing is deliberately insulting. You are a minor functionary, a message carrier, nothing more.'

'I am the king's social secretary,' he said, trying to pull himself up to every inch of his small height, even though he was sitting down.

'You carry messages to lesser fey and to humans of no great account. All the important invitations go through Rosmerta, and you know it. Sending his invitation through you and not her was an insult.'

'You do not merit the attentions of the Duchess Rosmerta.'

I shook my head. 'Your message is incomplete, Hedwick. You'd best go back to your master and learn a new one. One that has a chance of being well received.'

I nodded at Doyle. He stood and blanked the mirror in the middle of Hedwick's sputtering. Doyle smiled, almost grinned at me. 'Well done.'

'You just insulted the King of Light and Illusion,' Rhys said. He looked pale.

'No, Rhys, he insulted me, and more than that. If I had accepted such a command from Taranis, it could have been interpreted that when I gain the Unseelie throne, I would acknowledge him as high king over the Unseelie as well as the Seelie.'

'Could it have been the secretary's error?' Frost asked. 'Could he simply have used the same words with you as everyone on his list?'

'Perhaps, but if so, it was still an insult.'

'Insult, maybe. But, Merry, we can swallow a few insults to stay out of the king's bad graces,' Rhys said. He sat down on the far end of the bed as if his knees were weak.

'No, we cannot,' Doyle said.

We all looked at him. 'Don't you see, Rhys? Merry will rule Taranis's rival kingdom. She must set the rules now, or he will forever treat her as less. For the sake of all of us, she must not appear weak.'

'What will the king do?' Frost asked.

Doyle looked at him, and they had one of those long looks. 'In absolute truth, I do not know.'

'Has anyone ever defied him like this?' Frost asked.

'I don't know,' Doyle said.

'No,' I said.

They looked at me.

'Just as you walk around Andais like she's a snake about to strike, you tiptoe around Taranis the same way.'

'He does not seem as frightening as the queen,' Frost said.

I shrugged, and it hurt, so I stopped. 'He's like a big spoiled child who's had his own way for far too long. If he doesn't get what he wants, he throws tantrums. The servants and lackeys live in fear of those tantrums. He's been known to accidentally kill in one of his rages. Sometimes he's sorry, sometimes he's not.'

'And you just threw a steel gauntlet into his face,' Rhys said, staring at me from the end of the bed.

'One thing I always noticed about Taranis's temper was that it never struck out at anyone powerful. If he was in this uncontrollable rage, then why was it always directed at people who were powerless to fight back? Always, his victims were either magically inferior, or politically inferior, or people with no strong allies among the sidhe.' I shook my head. 'No, Rhys, he always knows who he's lashing out at. It's not mindless. He won't hurt me, because I stood my ground. He'll respect me, and maybe begin to worry about me.'

'Worry about you?' Rhys asked.

'He fears Andais – and even Cel, because Cel's crazy and Taranis isn't sure what he'll do once he's got the throne. Taranis was probably thinking he could control me. Now he'll begin to wonder.'

'It is interesting that this invitation comes after we have spoken to Maeve Reed,' Doyle said.

I nodded. 'Yes, isn't it.'

The three of them exchanged glances. Kitto just stayed wound around me, quieter now. 'I do not think it would be wise for Meredith to attend this ball,' Frost said.

'I agree,' Doyle said.

'Unanimous,' Rhys said.

I looked at them. 'I don't intend to go. But why are you all looking so serious?'

Doyle sat down on the far side of me, forcing Kitto to scoot back a little. 'Is Taranis as good a political thinker as you are?'

I frowned. 'I don't know. Why?'

'Will he think you refused for the true reasons, or will he wonder if you refused because of something Maeve said to you?'

I still hadn't told them Maeve's secret, and they had not asked. They probably assumed that she had made me give my word not to tell them, which she hadn't. The reason I hadn't shared it was because it was the kind of knowledge that could get you killed. And now, suddenly, out of the blue, was the invitation to court. Shit.

I looked at Doyle and the others. Frost had moved over to lean against the dresser, arms crossed. Rhys was still on the bed. Kitto curled against me. I looked at each in turn.

'I wasn't going to tell you what Maeve told me, because it's dangerous information. I thought we'd just avoid the Seelie Court altogether, and it wouldn't matter. Taranis hasn't sent me an invitation to anything for years. But if we are going to have to deal with him, then you need to know.'

I told them why Maeve had been exiled. Rhys just put his head in his hands and said nothing. Frost stared. Even Doyle was speechless. It was Kitto who said it. 'Taranis has condemned his people.'

'If he is truly infertile, then, yes, he has doomed them all to death as a people,' Doyle said.

'Their magic dies because their king is sterile, dead soil,' Frost said.

'It is what I believe Andais fears for the Unseelie. But she has borne one child, and Taranis has always been childless.'

'So that's why she's so interested in Cel or me breeding,' I said.

Doyle nodded. 'I believe so, though she has kept her own counsel on her exact motives in pitting you and Cel against each other.'

'Taranis will kill us all.' Rhys's voice was quiet, but very certain.

We all looked at him. It was beginning to feel like a very confused tennis match, looking from person to person.

He raised his face from his hands. 'He has to kill everyone who knows he's sterile. If the other Seelie find out that he's condemned them, they will demand he make the great sacrifice and his blood will be spread to recover their fertility.'

Looking into Rhys's bleak face, it was hard to argue, especially since I'd thought the same thing.

'Then why is Maeve Reed alive and well?' Frost asked. 'Julian has told us there have been no attempts on her life, none whatsoever.'

'I can't explain it,' Rhys said. 'Maybe it's because she has no way to tell anyone else in faerie. We've met with her, but she can't talk to anyone else who isn't already in exile. Meredith is not in exile, and she can talk to people who would matter. People who would believe her and act on it.'

We all sort of sat there, thinking. Doyle broke the silence. 'Frost, call Julian and tell him that there may be trouble.'

277

'I cannot tell him why,' Frost said.

'No,' Doyle said.

Frost nodded and went out into the other room to call on the phone.

I looked at Doyle. 'Have you talked to anyone else about this?'

'Only Barinthus,' he said.

'The bowl of water on the altar,' I said.

Doyle nodded. 'He was once the ruler of all the seas around our islands, so contacting him by water is nearly undetectable.'

I nodded. 'My father used to talk to Barinthus that way. How is he doing?'

'As your strongest ally among the Unseelie, he's making some progress in forming alliances for you.'

I stared into Doyle's dark eyes. 'What did you just leave out?'

He closed his eyes, looked down. 'Once you could not have seen that in my face.'

'I've been practicing. What did you leave out?'

'There have been two assassination attempts on him.'

'Lord and Lady protect us, how serious?'

'Serious enough that he mentioned them, not so serious that he was truly threatened. Barinthus is one of the oldest of us all. He is a thing of the element of water. Water is not easy to kill.'

'As you said, Barinthus is my strongest ally. If they kill him, then the rest will fall away.'

'I would fear that, yes, Princess, but many fear what Cel will be like when he is released from his torment. They fear he will be completely mad, and they do not wish someone like that on the throne. Barinthus believes that is why Cel's followers are passing around the fear that you will contaminate them all with mortality.'

'They sound desperate,' I said.

'No, the desperate part is the talk about declaring war on the Seelie Court. What I did not tell Kurag is that there is talk of war no matter which of you takes the throne. They see Cel's madness, your mortality, the queen's weakness as signs that the Unseelie are slipping away, that we are fading as people. There are some who talk of going to war one last time while we still stand a chance of defeating the Seelie.'

'If we have a full-scale war on American soil, the human military will be called in. It would break part of the treaty that allowed us into this country in the first place,' Rhys said.

'I know,' Doyle said.

'And they think Cel is mad,' Rhys said.

'Did Darinthus say who's the main voice behind the idea of war with Seelie?'

'Siobhan.'

'The head of Cel's guard.'

'There is only one Siobhan,' Doyle said.

'Thank the Lord and Lady for that,' Rhys said.

Siobhan was the equivalent of Doyle. She was leprously pale with spiderweb hair and not very tall. Physically she was nothing like Doyle. But just as whenever the queen had said, 'Where is my Darkness, send me my Darkness,' and someone had bled or died, so Cel with Siobhan. But she had no nickname; she was simply Siobhan.

'I hate to be picky,' I said, 'but did she receive any punishment for following Cel's orders and trying to assassinate me?'

'Yes,' Doyle said, 'but it has been months,

279

Meredith, and the punishment is over.'

'How long was the punishment?' I asked.

'A month.'

I shook my head. 'A month, for nearly killing a royal heir. What kind of message does that send to everyone else who wants me dead?'

'Cel gave the order, Meredith, and he is experiencing one of our worst punishments for half a year. No one expects his mind to survive. They see that as the punishment.'

'And have you ever been in Ezekiel's tender care for an entire month?' Rhys asked.

Ezekiel was the court torturer, and had been for many mortal lifetimes. But he was mortal. The queen had found him plying his trade for a human city and so admired his handiwork that she'd offered him a job.

'I've never been in the Hallway of Mortality for a month, no, but I spent my share of time there. Ezekiel always said he had to be so careful of me. He'd spent so many centuries with the immortals that he was afraid he'd kill me by accident. "I 'ave to be so careful of ya, Princess, so delicate, so fragile, so human."'

Rhys shivered. 'You imitate his voice well.'

'He liked to talk while he worked.'

'I apologize, Merry, you've done your time, but that means you understand what it meant for Siobhan to be in his care for a month's time.'

'I understand, Rhys, but I'd have felt better if she'd been executed.'

'The queen is loath to lose any noble-born sidhe,' Doyle said.

'I know, there aren't enough to spare.' But I wasn't happy about it. If you tried to kill a royal heir, the punishment should have been death. Anything less and someone might try again. Come to that, Siobhan might try again.

'Why does she want war?' I asked.

'She likes death,' Rhys said.

I looked at him.

'I wasn't the only one who used to be a death deity, and I'm not the only one who lost a great deal of their weirding when the Nameless was cast. Siobhan was not always her name either.'

That reminded me. 'Tell Doyle what you discovered at the murder scene today.'

He told Doyle about the elder gods and their ghosts. Doyle looked less and less happy. 'I did not see Esras do this, but I know the queen gave the command for it. One of the agreements between us and the Seelie was that some spells were never to be performed again. That was one of them.'

'Theoretically, if we could prove that a sidhe from either court did the spell, would that negate the peace treaty between us?'

Doyle seemed to think on that. 'I don't know. In the actual agreement, yes, but neither side wishes all-out war.'

'Siobhan does,' I said, 'and she wants me dead. Could she have done it?'

They both paused to think for a few silent minutes. Kitto just lay quietly beside me.

'She wants war, so she would have no qualms about doing it,' Doyle said eventually. 'But whether she is such a power, I do not know.' He looked at Rhys.

Rhys sighed. 'Once she was. Hell, so was I, once. She might have been able to do it, but that would mean she was here in California. You don't send them out of sight and expect to be able to control them. Out of sight of their magical keeper, they'll just wander around slaughtering people. They won't hunt Merry, not specifically.'

'Arc you sure of that?' Doyle asked.

'Yes, of that much I am sure.'

'Wouldn't Barinthus have mentioned if Siobhan was missing from court?' I asked.

'He specifically said she's being a pain in his . . . ass.'

'So she's there,' I said.

'But that doesn't mean that she didn't leave for a time.'

'But it still wouldn't get Merry killed,' Rhys said.

'Good to know,' I said, then I added, 'But what if my death is only a sideline? What if the real purpose behind it all is war between the courts?'

'Then why not have the elder ones doing their horror in Illinois near the courts?' Doyle asked.

'Because whoever did it wants war, not an execution for themselves,' I said.

Doyle nodded. 'That is true. If the queen discovered anyone had performed one of the forbidden spells, she would execute them in hopes that Taranis would be appeased.'

'And he would be,' Rhys said, 'because neither ruler wants all-out war.'

'So in order to get their little war started, they have to get away with it,' I said. 'Think about it; if it's proven to the courts that it's sidhe magic at work, but can't be proven which side did it, then suspicion mounts on both sides.'

'And the Nameless,' Doyle said, 'only a sidhe

could have freed it. Only a sidhe could have hidden it from both courts.'

'Siobhan isn't capable of freeing the Nameless,' Rhys said. 'That I am sure of.'

'Wait,' I said, 'didn't the queen say that Taranis is refusing to help search for it? Refuses to admit that anything so terrible could be part of his court?'

Doyle nodded. 'Yes, she did.'

'What if it's somebody from the Seelie Court?' I said. 'Would we have more trouble tracking it?'

'Perhaps.'

'Are you saying that the traitor is Seelie?' Rhys asked.

'Maybe, or maybe we've got two traitors. Siobhan could have raised the elder gods, and someone from the other court could have freed the Nameless.'

'Why free the Nameless?' Rhys asked.

'If you could control it,' Doyle said, almost as if he was talking to himself, 'it would give someone access to all the most elder and frightening powers of faerie. If you could control it, you might become unstoppable.'

'Someone's preparing for war,' I said.

Doyle took a deep breath and let it out slowly. 'I must inform the queen about the elder ghosts. I will share some of our speculation about the Nameless, as well.' He looked at me. 'And until we are certain that the elder gods cannot be directed at you, you will stay inside the wards.'

'Can the wards hold them off?'

He frowned and looked at Rhys, who shrugged. 'I saw them let loose in open battle. I know that wards can keep out anything that means harm, but I don't know how powerful these things will become. Especially if they are allowed to feed. They may grow to be able to breach nearly any ward.'

'Thanks, that was comforting,' I said.

He turned a serious face to me. 'It wasn't meant to be comforting, Merry. Just honest.' He gave a wistful smile. 'Besides, we'll all give our lives to keep you safe, and we're pretty hard to kill.'

'You don't think you'll win,' I said. 'How do you fight something that's invisible, and untouchable, but can see you and touch you? Something that can drink the life out of your mouth, like we'd empty a soda bottle. How do you fight that?'

'For that, I will speak to the queen.' Doyle stood up and went for the bathroom, with its smaller mirror. Apparently, he wanted privacy.

He stopped at the door. 'Call Jeremy and tell him we won't be back today. Until we know if this is a direct threat to Merry, we guard her and her alone.'

'And what do we do for money?' I asked.

He sighed, rubbing his eyes as if he was tired. 'I admire your determination to owe no one. I even agree with it. But things would be simpler if we took a stipend from the court and had only court politics to worry about. There will come a time, Meredith, when we cannot work a nine-to-five job and survive the politics.'

'I don't want to take her money, Doyle.'

'I know, I know. Call Jeremy, explain that you will be sitting with Kitto. When you tell him that Kitto's fading and you've saved him, Jeremy will understand.'

284

'You don't want him to know about the elder ghosts?'

'This is sidhe business, Meredith, and he is not sidhe.'

'Sure, but if the sidhe go to war, then so do all the fey. My great-grandmother was a brownie. All she wanted to do was stay near her human's home and tend it, but she got killed in one of the last great wars. If they're going to be dragged into it, then shouldn't they know about it beforehand?'

'Jeremy is exiled from faerie, so he will not be involved.'

'You're ignoring my point,' I said.

'No, Meredith, I am not, but I don't know what to say to your point. Until I can think of what to say, I will say nothing.' With that he went around the corner. I heard the bathroom door open, then close.

Rhys patted my arm. 'Gutsy of you to suggest that fey other than sidhe should have a vote. Very democratic.'

'Don't patronize me, Rhys.'

He dropped his hand. 'I even agree with you, Meredith, but our vote doesn't count for much. Once you're on the throne, maybe that will change; but right now, there is no way in all the kingdoms of faerie that a sidhe ruler will agree to include the lesser fey in our war talks. They'll be notified when we decide to go to war, not before.'

'That's not fair,' I said.

'No, but it's the way we do things.'

'Get me on a throne and maybe that can change.'

'Oh, Merry, don't let us risk our lives to make you queen, only to have you turn around and piss off all the sidhe. We can fight off some of them, but not all of them.'

'There are a lot more lesser fey than sidhe, Rhys.'

'Numbers aren't what counts, Merry.'

'What does count?'

'Strength: strength of arms, strength of magic, strength of leadership. The sidhe have all that, and that is why, my pretty princess, we have ruled the fey for millennia.'

'He's right,' Kitto said softly.

I looked down at him, still pale, but not that frightening translucent uncolor. 'The goblins are great warriors.'

'Yes, but not great wizards. And Kurag fears the sidhe. Everyone who is not sidhe fears the sidhe,' Kitto said.

'I'm not sure that's true,' I said.

'I am,' he said, and he crept even closer, spooning his entire body around me, holding himself as tight against me as he could. 'I am.'

Chapter 27

THE UPSIDE TO KITTO'S NEAR-DEATH EXPERIENCE was that I got to go back to bed and sleep. I'd suggested that Doyle join us, but Frost had thrown a fit. So Doyle had just begged out, as long as Frost didn't get to join us either. I'd pointed out that Doyle and I had gotten the least amount of sleep last night, but Frost didn't care. I also pointed out that we were just going to sleep, so did it really matter who slept with me? Neither of them were moved by my arguments.

So, I got to go back to bed and cuddle Kitto. I made him take my usual side of the bed, though, so I could spoon around his body without lying on the shoulder that he'd bitten. I'd taken some Advil, but the shoulder still ached fiercely like it had its own pulse. It hadn't hurt nearly this much the first time he'd marked me. Maybe it was a good sign. I hoped so. I hated to have something hurt this much for no good purpose.

Jeremy had been furious that none of us were coming back to the office, until he found out that Kitto had nearly died.

He was silent for a long time, long enough for me to say his name softly.

'I'm here, Merry, just bad memories. I've seen fey fade away before. Do what you need to do to take care of him. We'll muddle through at the office. They're going to keep Teresa overnight for observation. She's sedated, so I don't know how much they're going to be observing.'

'Is she going to be all right?'

He hesitated. 'Probably. But I've never seen her like she was today. Her husband yelled at me for endangering her. He doesn't want her doing any more crime scenes. I can't blame him.'

'You think Teresa will agree with him?'

'I don't know if it matters, Merry. I've made an executive decision. The Grey Detective Agency no longer does police work. I'm a good magician, but I had no clue what did that today. I could feel the remnants of a spell, but that was all. I told Detective Tate what I'd felt, but Lieutenant Peterson didn't want to hear it. He's determined that it's something mundane. Extraordinary, but mundane.' Jeremy sounded tired.

'You sound like you need to go to bed and cuddle up to somebody, too.'

'You volunteering?' He laughed. 'Greedy ol' Merry wanting to take up all the fey men in L.A.'

'If you need to come over and be held, you'd be welcome.'

He was quiet for a moment. 'I'd almost forgotten that.'

'Forgotten what?'

'That it's okay to be held by your friends in ways that humans consider sexual. That it would be all right for me to come and cuddle close to you while we slept.'

'If you need it.'

'I've been out among the humans too long, Merry. I don't think entirely like a trow anymore. I don't know if I could go to bed with you and not have it turn sexual.'

I hadn't known what to say to that.

When I woke, the light against the drapes was fading to dusk. I was still spooned around Kitto's body, and he was still pressed against me as tight as he could get. It was as if neither of us had moved all day. I lay there for a moment feeling how stiff my body was from simply being immobile for so long. The shoulder ached distantly, ignorable. Kitto's breathing was still deep and regular. What had woken me?

Then a soft knocking sounded at the door again. It opened before I could say anything. Galen peered through. He smiled when he saw me awake.

'How's Kitto?'

I moved enough to prop myself up on one elbow and look down at the goblin. He made a small sound and cuddled in against me so that there was again no space between his body and mine.

'He looks better, and he's warm.' I combed my fingers through his curls. His head moved to cuddle in against the movement of my hand, but he never woke.

'Is anything wrong?' I asked.

Galen made a face that I couldn't quite read. 'Well, not exactly.'

I frowned at him. 'What is it?'

He came into the room, gently closing the door

behind him. We talked in low voices, so as not to disturb Kitto.

Galen came to stand at the end of the bed. He was wearing a long-sleeved shirt whose pale green color brought out the green tint in his skin, intensified the darker color of his hair. The pants were just faded blue jeans washed until they were almost white. There was a hole in the middle of his thigh where white threads gave hints of the pale green skin underneath.

I realized he'd said something and I hadn't been paying attention. 'I'm sorry, what did you say?'

He grinned, flashing white teeth. 'Queen Niceven's representative is here. He says he has strict orders to collect the first payment before he tells us the secret of how to cure me.'

My gaze went back to the hole in his pants, then traveled up his body until I met those grass green eyes. The heat in his eyes matched the tightening in my body.

Kitto stirred beside me, opened his blue, blue eyes. Talking, doors opening, and my moving hadn't stirred him; but the tightening of my body in response to Galen, that had woken him.

I explained briefly that Niceven's man was here. Kitto had no problem with the demi-fey coming into the room. I'd known he would have no problem. I'd asked for politeness' sake. The queen wouldn't have asked, but I think it was more that she didn't care what someone thought, rather than her knowing they wouldn't mind.

Galen went back to the door and opened it wide. A tiny figure fluttered in. The body was about the size of a small Barbie doll. His wings were larger than the rest of his body, and mostly rich butter yellow with lines and bars of black and spots of blue and orangey-red. He hovered over the bed, above me. His body was a slightly paler version of the rich yellow of his wings. He wore a filmy yellow skirt, or kilt, as his only clothing.

'Greetings to Princess Meredith of the Unseelie from Queen Niceven of the demi-fey. I am known as Sage, most lucky fey to be chosen as our royal majesty's ambassador to the Western Lands.' His voice was like the sound of tinkling bells, a laughing sound. It made me smile, and I knew instantly it was glamour.

I *tsk*ed at him. 'No glamour between us, Sage, for that is a kind of lie.'

He pressed tiny perfect hands to his chest, his wings beating faster, sending a breath of air against my face. 'Glamour, I? Would a humble demi-fey be able to do glamour to a sidhe of the Unseelie Court?'

He had been careful not to deny the charge; he simply skirted the issue. 'You can drop the glamour, or it can be stripped from you. You can put it all back, but for our first meeting I want to see what, or whom, I am truly dealing with.'

He flew closer, close enough that the wind from his wings played in the strands of hair around my face. 'My lovely maiden, you wound me. I am as fair as you see me here.'

'If that is true, then light upon me and let me test the truth of your words. For if you are truly as you appear, then touching my flesh will not change you, but if you play me false, then the mere touch of my skin will show your true self.' The very formality of the words was a type of spell. I had spoken truly and believed utterly what

I had said; thus it was true. When he touched my skin, he would be forced to appear as he truly was.

I sat up so I could extend a hand. The sheets slipped down, pooling at my waist. Kitto curled himself closer around me, his large eyes staring at the fluttering fey. He watched the tiny figure like a cat fascinated by a bird. I knew that the goblins were not above cannibalizing other fey. The look on Kitto's face said that, perhaps, demi-fey were a delicacy.

'Are you all right, Kitto?'

He blinked and looked up at me. His gaze slid from the fluttering fey, across my bare breasts, and the look of hunger changed but a very little. That one look frightened me. Something must have shown on my face because Kitto hid his own face against my bare hip, snuggling under the sheet.

'The taste of flesh has made our little goblin bold.' Doyle was in the doorway.

The little fey turned in midair to give a small bow. 'The Queen's Darkness, I am honored.'

Doyle gave the barest of bows, a mere nod to courtesy. 'Sage, I must say that I am surprised to see you here.'

The tiny flying man rose upward so that he could come close to seeing Doyle eye to eye; but he stayed out of reach, like the shy insect he resembled.

'Why surprised, Darkness?' His voice didn't sound so much like joyous bells now.

'I did not know that Niceven could spare her favorite lover.'

'No more that, Darkness, and well you know.'

'I know that Niceven had child and husband by

292

another, but I didn't think the demi-fey cared so very much for the niceties.'

Sage flew a little higher, a touch closer. 'You think because we are not sidhe that we do not know the law.' The anger could have sounded impotent coming from that tiny chimelike voice, but it didn't. It was the sound of chimes when storm winds strike them, a frightening music.

'So,' Doyle said, 'no longer queen's lover. Whatever have you been doing with yourself, Sage?' I had never heard Doyle so chiding before. He was deliberately baiting Sage. I'd never seen Doyle do much of anything that didn't have a purpose to it, so I let it go. But it all had a personal feel to it. What could this minute man have done to the Queen's Darkness, to earn such personal attention?

'I have had the whole of our kingdom's women to please me, Darkness.' He flew almost into Doyle's face. 'And you, one of the queen's eunuchs, what have you been doing with yourself?'

'Look at what lies in the bed, Sage. Tell me that that is not such a bounty as man or fey would sell their soul for.'

The fluttering man didn't even bother to turn around. 'I did not know that you liked goblins, Doyle. I thought that was Rhys's peculiarity.'

'You can be deliberately obtuse, Sage, but well you know the meaning of my words.'

'Rumors are swift things, Darkness. They say that you guard the princess but do not share her bed. There has been much speculation as to why you would pass by such a bounty, when the others have partaken of it.' The little man flew close enough that his wings almost brushed Doyle's face. 'Rumor whispers that perhaps there was more than one reason Queen Andais never took you to her bed. Rumor would have you eunuch in truth and not merely in lack of use.'

I couldn't see Doyle's face through the rapidly beating wings of the demi-fey. I realized that though his wings looked like butterfly wings, they beat much faster, and the physical motions weren't identical to the insect he mimicked.

'I give you my most solemn oath,' Doyle said, 'that I have taken the pleasure of Princess Meredith in the way that a man may take pleasure with a woman.'

Sage hovered for a wing beat, then his entire body dipped as if he'd almost forgotten to fly for a second. He regained himself, fluttering up to meet Doyle's eyes again. 'So, you are no longer the queen's eunuch, but now the princess's lover.' The voice sounded low and evil, a tinny hiss. Whatever was happening was definitely personal.

'As you say, Sage, rumor runs rife, and rumor whispers that Niceven took a page from Andais's book. You were her favorite lover before her one-night tryst with Pol got her with child. When she was forbidden from your bed, you were forbidden from anyone else's. If she could not have her favorite, then no one would.'

Sage hissed at him like an angry bee. 'Much pleasure must you take in our two places being switched, Darkness.'

'Whatever do you mean, Sage?' But Doyle's voice was low and held a note that said he knew exactly what the demi-fey meant.

'I taunted you and yours for centuries. The great sidhe warriors, the great ravens of old,

294

reduced to court eunuchs, oh, yes, I taunted you all. I boasted of my prowess and my queen's delights, like an evil whisper in your ears.'

Doyle just looked at him.

Sage flew a little distance from him, doing a circle in the air like one might pace on the ground. 'Now what good does my prowess do me? What good is it to see her in all her beauty but be unable to touch her?' He turned back to Doyle. 'Oh, I have thought long these many years, Darkness, on how I didst torment you. Do not think the irony of it is lost upon me, simply because I am not sidhe.' He got very close to Doyle's face, and though I knew it was a whisper, the hiss of it filled the room. 'Irony enough to choke upon, Darkness, irony enough to die of, irony enough to kill to rid myself of it.'

'Then fade, Sage, fade and be done with it.'

The little fey winged backwards. 'Fade yourself, Darkness. Fade and be done with you. I am here at Queen Niceven's command to act as her surrogate. If you wish cure for the green knight, then you must deal with me.' His voice was thick with menace.

Galen came to the still-open door from the living room. 'I wish to be cured, but not at any price.' His usual smile was gone, his face somber.

'Enough of this,' I said, voice soft, not angry.

They all turned to me. I glimpsed the rest of the men, including Nicca, crowding just outside the doorway. 'I bargained with Niceven, not Doyle. And I alone bargained for Galen's cure. The price for that cure was my blood.'

Sage fluttered over the bed, not quite over Kitto and me. 'One drink of your blue blood, one cure

for your green knight, as my queen has bid me.'
His voice wasn't the ring of bells anymore. It was
almost normal, small, thin, but a man's voice.

His dark eyes had become flat and black like
the eyes of a doll. There was nothing particularly
friendly on that pretty toy-size face.

I held up a hand, and he alit upon it. He was
heavier than he looked, more solid. I remembered
Niceven being lighter, more bone than muscle. She
felt as cadaverous as she looked. Sage was ...
meatier, or rather his slender body held more
substance than Niceven's seemed to.

His wings went still, showing them as huge
perfect butterfly wings. They fanned softly as he
stared at me. I wondered if the wings beat in time
to his heart.

His butter yellow hair was shaggy, thick,
straight, falling in careless strands around his
triangular face. The hair brushed his shoulders in
places. There was a time when Andais would have
punished him for letting his hair grow so long.
Only the sidhe men were allowed to have hair long
as a woman's. It was a mark of status, royalty,
privilege.

His hands were no bigger than the fingernail on
my smallest finger. He put one of those hands
on his slender waist, the other hanging by his side,
one foot in front of the other, a defiant pose.

'If we are given privacy, then I will take payment and give you the cure for your knight.' He
sounded petulant.

It made me smile, and the smile made his face
fill with hatred. 'I am not a child to be looked
upon with indulgence, Princess. I am a man.' He
made a sweeping gesture with both hands. 'A

296

small one by your reckoning, but I am still male. I do not appreciate being looked upon as you would smile upon a naughty child.'

It was almost exactly what I'd been thinking, that he looked cute standing there so defiant, so tiny. I had been treating him like a doll, or a toy, or a child.

'I apologize, Sage, you are correct. You are fey and you are male, size notwithstanding.'

He frowned at me. 'You are royal and you apologize to me?'

'I was taught that true royalty lies in knowing when one is wrong or right, and admitting the difference; not in false perfection.'

He turned his head to one side, an almost bird-like movement. 'I have heard from others that you deal fairly with all, like your father before you.' His thin voice sounded thoughtful.

'It is good to hear my father spoken of still.'

'We all remember Prince Essus.'

'I am always happy to share my father's good memory with others.'

Sage watched me closely, though it wasn't the same as being watched by a larger person. His idea of eye contact seemed just that. His whole face seemed to stare at only my right eye, though he'd apparently seen my smile and judged it correctly, which meant he could see all my face. I simply was not accustomed to dealing with the demi-fey. My father had always been respectful of them, but I had not been taken to Niceven's court as I had been to Kurag's and others.

'Prince Essus had our respect, Princess, but time moves on and so must we.' He sounded almost sad. He looked at me, face growing arrogant again, and I fought not to smile at this tiny figure looking so full of himself. It wasn't funny or cute; he was just as much a person as anyone else in the room. But it was hard to truly believe that.

'Let us have privacy to fulfill my queen's desires, then you will have your cure for the green knight.'

I looked at Doyle and Galen inside the room, the others just outside. Frost was already shaking his head. 'My guards do not allow me to be alone with any member of the courts.'

'Do you think I should be flattered that they see me as a potential threat?' He turned on my hand and pointed a finger at Doyle. 'Darkness knows me of old and knows what I am capable of, or thinks he does.' Sage turned back to face me, his bare feet sliding strangely against my skin. 'But I would still have privacy for this.'

'No,' Doyle said.

Sage turned back to him, fluttering inches from my hand. 'You should understand this, Darkness. Doing my queen's bidding is all that is left me. Doing exactly what she says is all that I have. What I will do tonight in this room will be the closest I have come to knowing feminine delights in a very long time. I do not think privacy is too much to ask for that.'

The guards weren't happy about it, but they finally agreed. Only Kitto stayed wound around my body, tangled in the sheets.

'That one, too,' Sage said, pointing at the goblin.

'He faded today, Sage,' I said.

'He looks well enough.'

'His king, Kurag, has informed me that my body, my blood, my flesh, my magic is what sustains Kitto

298

out here among the humans. He needs to stay in contact with my skin for a time longer.'

'You would kick him out of your bed for one of your sidhe warriors.'

'No.' Kitto spoke softly. 'I have been privileged to stay while they mate. I have seen their light cast shadows on the walls, so bright they glowed.'

Sage fluttered down to hover over Kitto's upturned face. 'Goblin, your kind eats mine in times of war.'

'The strong eat the weak. It is the way of the world,' Kitto said.

'The goblin world,' Sage said.

'It is all I know.'

'You are far from that world now.'

Kitto cuddled under the sheet so that only his eyes showed. 'Merry is my world now.'

'Do you like this new world, goblin?'

'I am warm, safe, and she bears my mark on her body. It is a good world.'

Sage hovered for a few moments more, then flew back up to my waiting hand. 'If the goblin gives his word of most solemn honor that nothing he sees, hears, feels, or senses in any way will he repeat to anyone, then he may stay.'

Kitto repeated the promise word for word.

'Very well,' Sage said. He gazed down my body; and though he was no taller than my forearm, I shivered and had the most uncomfortable desire to cover myself. A tiny red tongue like a drop of blood licked across his pale lips. ' First the blood-letting, then the cure.' The way he said *cure* made me half wish I hadn't agreed to all the guards leaving me alone. He was smaller than a Barbie doll, but in that instant, I was afraid of him.

Chapter 28

HE FLUTTERED DOWN OFF MY HAND TOWARDS MY breasts. I put my other arm between him and my body. He ended up on my other wrist, which I moved out from my body in order to see him more easily. I raised the sheet over my chest with my other hand.

He looked disgusted. 'Will you deny me heart blood?'

'I saw what your kind did to my knight. I would be foolish to let you near such tender flesh before I see exactly how gently you feed.'

He sat down on my wrist, ankles crossed, hands on either side to steady him. He seemed to weigh more sitting down; not much more, but it was noticeable.

'I would be ever so gentle, fair lady.' His voice was the sound of chimes in a warm summer breeze. Had his lips been like a tiny crimson flower but a moment ago? He touched that flower-soft mouth to my hand, his body reclined along my arm as I would have reclined upon a couch. He ran his tiny mouth and hands over the minute hairs on my arm. Where a larger lover would have smoothed them with his mouth or fingertips, Sage played with them as if he was making music along my skin – soundless music that only he could hear, but I could feel it. It played along my skin, my arm, as if it were all larger, more than was actually happening.

I flung him sharply into the air, where he buzzed at me like an angry bee. 'Why did you do that? We were having so much fun.'

'No glamour, remember,' I said, scowling up at him, clutching my sheet.

'Without glamour the feeding will not be nearly so pleasant for you.' He shrugged his thin shoulders, the movement making him dip in midair. 'For me it is much the same, for Niceven's purposes it is much the same, but for you, fair princess, it is not the same. Let me save you some pain and discomfort, and let this be a friendly sharing.'

If he'd caught me on another day when Kitto's bite didn't still ache, I might have told him no, just to take his queen's blood and be done with it. Goblins could not do glamour of any kind, so Kitto had had no choice; without the natural glamour of sex to soften his feeding, there was nothing he could do magically. Sage was offering me a choice.

I took a deep breath, let it out slowly, then nodded. 'Just enough glamour to make it pleasant, but that's all, Sage. If you try for more than that, I'll call for the guards and you won't like what they'll do to you.'

He made a sound that would have been rude, except that it came out like a tiny trumpet, as if a butterfly could make an ass's bray. 'Darkness has been waiting centuries for me to put a foot out of line, Princess. I know well, perhaps better than you, what he owes me.'

'I noticed it seemed personal between you, more than with the others.'

'Personal? You could say that.' He smiled, and it managed to be pleasant and evil at the same time, as if he was imagining terrible things that would be a great deal of fun to do.

I could have asked Sage what was so personal, but I didn't. Either Doyle would explain or I would never know. I didn't think Doyle would take kindly to me prying his secrets from a fey he hated. It was one thing to gain information from one friend about another friend, but you didn't talk to people's enemies about your friends, and you didn't let those enemies talk to you behind your friends' backs. It just wasn't kosher.

'You may feed, Sage, and you may use a little glamour to keep it from being so unpleasant. But mind your manners.'

'Do you need to look so far for protection? You have your goblin there beside you. Will he not reach up and snatch me from the air and grind my bones if I play you false?'

'Goblins have little chance against strong glamour, and well you know it.'

He put his hands on his chest, widened his eyes. 'But I am but a demi-fey. I cannot have the glamour of a sidhe lord. Why should any goblin fear the likes of me?'

'The demi-fey of every description have powerful glamour and well you know that. They have led travelers and the unwary astray for centuries.'

'A little swamp water never hurt anyone,'

Sage said, hovering closer toward me.

'Unless there happens to be quicksand or sucking mud under that water. You are Unseelie fey, which means if the traveler falls through the murk to his death, so much more the fun.'

He crossed his arms, which were thinner than a pencil was round, over his chest. 'And what happens when a Seelie will-o'-the-wisp guides travelers into marshy land, and they fall to quicksand? Do not tell me that they then run for help and grab a rope. They may weep pretty tears for a poor mortal, but as soon as his last breath bubbles up from the swamp, they're away, giggling to themselves, looking for another traveler to lead astray. They may avoid that particular patch of swamp, but they won't stop their game simply because it led to some unfortunate's death.'

He landed on my sheet-covered knee. 'And is it so unfair to lead some net-waving butterfly collector to his death, when if he caught me, he would throw me in a killing jar and mount me with a pin through my heart?'

'You have glamour enough to keep away from that fate,' I said.

'Yes, but my gentler brethren, the butterflies and insects that we demi-fey mimic, what of them? One fool with a net can devastate a summer meadow.'

Put that way, he had a point, or seemed to. 'Are you using glamour now?'

'A sidhe princess should know when she's being tricksied about with,' he said, arms still crossed.

I sighed. 'Fine, it's not glamour, but I can't agree that you're within your rights to lead an

303

entomologist to his death just because he's collecting butterflies.'

'Ah,' Sage said, gazing up at me, 'but you do agree a little at least, or you wouldn't have asked about the glamour.'

I sighed again. I had made the terrible mistake of taking entomology in college. I hadn't understood that you had to kill insects to pass the course. I remembered a carousel of butterflies trapped in a killing jar. It was one of the most lovely things I'd ever seen. Alive they were magical; dead they were like tissue paper and sticks. I'd finally asked how many insects I had to collect for a D, and I'd collected that many and no more. There had been no point to collecting the insects when the college had a complete collection of almost everything the class was killing. It was the last biology class I took where you had to collect anything.

I stared at the little butterfly-winged man on my knee and couldn't find an argument that didn't make me feel like a hypocrite. I wouldn't kill someone for collecting butterflies, but if I had butterfly wings on my back and spent most of my life out among them fluttering from flower to flower, maybe I'd see the death of one butterfly on a different scale. Maybe, if you were the size of a Barbie doll, killing the small creatures was every bit as horrible as killing people. Maybe. Maybe not. But I didn't feel sure enough of my ground to argue.

Chapter 29

I MOUNDED THE PILLOWS BEHIND ME, SO THAT I was propped to half-sitting. I'd had to make Kitto move before I could move the pillows. He clung to me with hands and arms, but his eyes were all for Sage. He watched the demi-fey as if he didn't trust him, or expected him to do something dangerous, or maybe he was just wondering what Sage would taste like. Whatever Kitto was thinking, it was not friendly.

Sage didn't seem to notice the goblin's less-than-friendly stare. He simply hovered, fluttering as I made myself comfortable.

I secured the sheet across my chest and held my hand out to him. I cupped my hand upward so Sage could reach my fingers, because that was where he would take the blood from. Niceven had taken blood from me there once, and if it was good enough for his queen, it was good enough for Sage. Besides, something about him unnerved me. It was ridiculous to be nervous of someone I could smash against the wall with one hand, but silly or not, I couldn't deny how I felt. I didn't question it, just covered most of my more vulnerable bits and gave him my hand.

Sage landed on my wrist. He knelt in my upturned palm and wrapped tiny hands around my middle finger. He stroked my finger, and the movement was both nice and disturbing.

I must have tensed up, because he said, 'You have given me permission to use glamour, have you not?'

I nodded, not quite trusting my voice.

He smiled, and his mouth was like a tiny red petal, his eyes warm, sincere. I felt myself relax as if a hand had simply stroked all my nervousness away. I didn't fight it, because I had agreed and the pain in my shoulder was gone. Nothing hurt.

Kitto curled around my waist, sliding his leg along mine. My hand fell away from the sheet and stroked his curls. His hair was unbelievably soft. He snuggled his face in against my waist, and the brush of his face against my skin made me shiver. I think anyone could have touched me then and I would have reacted to them.

I looked at Sage. 'You're very good.' My voice was husky.

'We have to be,' he said, as he ran his hands up and down my finger. It was no longer nice; it was erotic, as if there were nerves in that one finger that had never been there before. I knew it was glamour, the natural magic of faerie, but it still felt so good, so very good.

Surrendering to someone's glamour, if his glamour ran to the sensual, could be a wondrous experience. Sidhe did not do it with each other, because to practice glamour on another sidhe in an intimate situation was considered a grave insult. But the lesser fey practiced it often among themselves, and almost always when lying with a sidhe. Perhaps it was insecurity. Perhaps it was just a way of saying, look what we have to offer.

Sage had much to offer.

He wrapped his arms around my finger, and it was as if he touched larger things, so much more intimate things. He laid a kiss against my finger-tip that was like the brush of finest silk. I felt his lips part, and they felt larger than they were. I had to open my eye and look at him to make sure that he was still small, kneeling in my hand. I had sunk back upon the pillows, my arm resting in my lap, but Sage was still kneeling in my cupped palm.

Kitto entwined his leg over mine, and I felt him growing firm against my leg. For a moment I wondered what the glamour was doing to and for the goblin, when suddenly Sage bit into my flesh. He bit me like he was biting into an apple, sharp, but the pain floated away, and when he began to suck at the wound, it was like he had a thin, red thread from my fingertip to my groin. Every movement of his mouth pulled on things low in my body.

He fed, drawing faster, harder, and it was as if he stroked lower things, faster, harder. I felt that growing warm weight in my body that said I was on the edge, the edge of pleasure. It was as if Sage had coaxed me to the edge of a cliff I hadn't seen, and I had to choose whether to fall over it into the embrace beyond.

I couldn't think. I couldn't decide anything. I had become only sensation, the growing tug of pleasure, the weight of warmth building, building in my body. Then that warmth flooded out of me, over me, through me. I called out, but it wasn't

pain that burst from my lips. I cried out in pleasure and writhed on the sheets, caught between
Sage's mouth still locked on my body, and the
firmness of Kitto's body pressed against my leg.
Kitto's body rode mine as I writhed on the bed,
his hands sliding over my waist, upward to brush
the tip of one breast. It was a tentative touch, but
in my heightened state, it felt like so much more.

I cried out again, and when Kitto slid his body
over the edge of my thigh, pressed himself against
me, not entering but lying across me, both of us
nude, both of us eager, I didn't protest.

Kurag had said that I had to give Kitto true sex,
and for a goblin that meant only one thing: intercourse. But I also knew that goblins didn't have
sex without drawing blood. Now, nothing hurt,
nothing would hurt.

I looked up to find Sage hovering over us. He
was glowing, a soft honeyed light as if a candle
had lit within him. His eyes burned like black
jewels and the veins of his wings gleamed with
black fire; the yellow, blue, and orangey-red
glowed like stained glass in a fall of brightest
sunlight.

I had enough sense left to ball up a handful of
Kitto's hair, and jerk his face up to mine. 'Blood
only, Kitto. No flesh missing when we're done.'

He whispered, 'Yes, mistress.'

I released his hair abruptly, and he looked up at
me, his eyes a solid drowning blue with his pupils
like a thin black line within them. It was as if I
could have fallen into the blue of his eyes, and
I knew it was Sage's glamour still at work, and I
didn't care. I gave myself over to it, let the illusion
ride me.

Kitto slid inside me, and I was more than wet, more than ready. He seemed larger than I knew he was, filling me up, swelling inside me. He raised himself up on his arms, pressing our lower bodies together, frozen for a moment with his body sunk inside mine, with us joined. He gazed down at me spread underneath him, and a single tear welled up from one blue eye.

I knew what the goblins considered sex, and they didn't cry at the first joining. Through the glamour I saw Kitto – through all the magic, I truly saw him – and I raised a hand up, a hand that had already gone white and shining. I touched that one crystal tear and did what goblins do with precious body fluids; I touched it to my lips. I drank the salt of his tears, and he made a sound low in his throat and began to thrust himself inside me.

With every thrust he seemed to grow bigger, swelling wider, touching parts of me that had never been touched, that were not supposed to be touched. I watched him entering my body, and his skin had begun to glow, white and pearlescent. He thrust himself inside me, a glowing shaft as if he were made of light, and that was not glamour. I lay under him, my skin glowing like moonlight. Only for another sidhe would my body shine like this. Colors began to dance under his skin as if rainbows danced inside his body, coming to the surface of his skin like fireworks glimpsed through crystal water.

His eyes held nothing but blue flame behind glass. His short curls moved around his head as if an unseen wind played with them, and the wind was Kitto. He was sidhe. Goddess help us, he was sidhe.

He brought me in a wash of light and magic that blinded me for a moment. All I could see was white light and rainbow flashes across my vision. All I could feel was my body locked around his, as if the place of our joining was the only part of our bodies that was still solid. As if we had become light and air and magic and only the anchor point of our joined bodies held us, tied us, bound us. Then even that fell away as he came inside me, and we became nothing but light and magic and color and wave upon wave of pleasure. It was as if you could become laughter, become joy, become whatever most pleasured you.

I came to myself slowly. Kitto had collapsed on top of me. We were still joined, our bodies still glowing softly like two fires banked down for a long winter's night. A warmth that would keep the house, the family, everything safe through the long cold nights to come.

Flashes of color were still flitting through the room like stray rainbows from some crystal sun catcher. But there was no sun, no crystal, only us.

Well, not only us. The guards stood around the bed, hands held up, palms toward us. I concentrated and saw the nearly invisible barrier that they had thrown up around us. They had put up a sacred circle, a circle of power.

Doyle's deep voice came. 'The next time you decide to invoke enough energy to raise an island from the sea, Meredith, a little warning would be good.'

I blinked up at him, for he stood closest to me. 'Did we hurt anything?'

'We caught it in time, I think, but the news will probably be full of unusual tides. We will have to see if the ground itself holds still for such a release.'

Kitto hid his face between my breasts, and whispered, 'I'm sorry.'

'Do not be sorry, Kitto. It is we who owe you an apology. We thought of you as goblin because you are half theirs. We never thought what it might mean for you to be half ours.'

Kitto moved his head enough to look up at Doyle, then he hid his face again. 'I don't understand.' He spoke with his mouth against my skin, and even after all we'd done, the feel of him whispering against my chest made me shiver.

My voice was a little breathy, but I answered, 'You are sidhe, Kitto, truly sidhe. You have come into your power.'

He shook his head, his face still buried against my breasts. 'I have no powers.'

I put a hand on either side of his face and raised him gently to look upon me. 'You are sidhe, one of the shining ones. There will be power now.'

His eyes widened, and he looked frightened.

'We'll help you,' Galen said from the far side of the bed. 'We'll help you learn how to control your magic. It's not that hard; if I can do it, anyone can.' He smiled, made it a joke.

Kitto didn't look convinced.

Some small movement made me turn my head farther, and I saw Sage perched upon a stray mound of pillows. He was still glowing softly like a golden, bejeweled doll. His face was tear-streaked, the line of tears like silver glitter upon his tiny face. His face was enraptured.

'Damn you, Princess, and damn this newest prince. I have glimpsed heaven and found it fair, and now I stand on the shores of earth, abandoned. I did not understand until this moment what it meant that you were sidhe and I was not.' He laid his face in his hands and wept, curling on his side on a satin pillow, his wings held out behind him, stiff, almost forgotten.

Kitto touched my chest, and it hurt, a little. I realized that he'd bitten me between my breasts, a little to one side, so that some of the mark was in the mound of my left breast. It hadn't hurt until he touched it. It wasn't as deep as the mark on my shoulder, because it hadn't needed to be. The sex had made up for the lack of violence. It should have healed cleanly and quickly, but somehow I knew it would not. Somehow I knew I would bear his mark over my heart forever.

'I am sorry,' he whispered, as if he'd read my mind.

I shook my head, touching the silken skin of his cheek. 'I wear your mark with honor, Kitto. Never doubt that.'

He gave a shy smile, then raised up on his arms much as he had through the beginning of the love-making. I noticed first the spots of blood on my own white skin. He had hurt me more than I'd thought; then I looked up at Kitto and saw that from collarbone to waist my nails had marked him. Bloody furrows across the perfection of his skin, across the small mounds of his nipples. I'd sliced into the meat of one of his nipples and it bled there more than the rest.

It was my turn to say, 'I'm sorry.'

He shook his head, and the smile wasn't shy now. 'You have marked me, and there is no higher compliment among my kind. May the marks never fade.'

I traced the edge of one of the nail marks, and he shivered above me. 'You are among your kind now, Kitto. Right now.'

Doyle seemed to know what I wanted, because he pulled his black T-shirt up enough to show Kitto the nail marks on his black skin.

'You are Unseelie sidhe,' I said.

He moved off me, his body grown softer with all the talking. He lay beside me, one arm over my waist. He gazed at the men around the bed. 'My mother's people were Seelie. They left me for dead outside the goblin mound.' His voice was matter-of-fact, as if it was just truth, something he'd always known.

Doyle lowered his shirt and turned to face the bed. 'We are not Seelie.' He did not lower the circle around the bed, but stepped inside it. He raised Kitto up with a hand on his shoulder. Kitto seemed frightened but didn't struggle.

Doyle laid a chaste kiss on the smaller man's forehead. 'You have already tasted the blood of our court and been tasted in return. Now receive our kiss and be welcome among us.'

One by one the other guards bent and laid lips upon Kitto's forehead. He was crying and shaking by the time they had finished. And when the last of my knights had kissed Kitto's forehead, Sage rose up into the air, his wings humming, a blur of color. It made an angry whirring sound.

'I hate you all.' The venom in those words was thick enough to choke on. 'Now let me out of this accursed circle.'

Doyle made an opening in the circle big enough for the demi-fey. The tiny figure flew through it, and Doyle closed the circle behind him.

Sage hovered in front of the closed bedroom door. I thought one of us would have to get up to open it, but the door opened of its own accord, and Sage hurried through the opening. He turned in the darkness of the living room, still glowing faintly from all the magic.

'The queen has had her price, but you have not had your cure. The cure lies within my body where the queen didst place it. I meant to share you with the goblin to ensure his silence, not be displaced by him.' He hissed like an angry cat. 'Who knew goblin could be sidhe? Would that it were me in thy arms and not he. What could have been done in pleasant glamour will nidst be done in unpleasant bargain.' He hissed again, and vanished into the darkness beyond. The door slammed shut behind him.

We all stared at the door. 'Did he mean what I think he meant?' Galen asked.

'It would amuse Niceven to force a sidhe princess to pleasure one of her tiny men,' Doyle said.

I raised eyebrows at that. 'How?'

'Best not to ask,' he said, and he looked down at Kitto, 'for tonight we will worry over nothing. We have found new blood of our blood, kin of our kin. We will sorrow over nothing tonight.'

As celebration of the faerie court went it was modest. We ordered out, Kitto's choice, bought some very fine wine, and partied until dawn.

It was a little after dawn when the earthquake hit, a 4.4 on the Richter scale, centered in El Segundo. There is no major fault underneath El Segundo. It's probably all that saved us from demolishing the entire city. It lasted for only about a minute, really not that much damage overall; no one was killed, though there were injuries. But it added an entirely new twist on the idea of safe sex.

Chapter 30

ON THE FIRST DAY OF MY BEING RESTRICTED TO the apartment, hiding behind our wards, Taranis's main social secretary, Dame Rosmerta, had called. She'd been dressed in pink and gold cloth that complemented her gold-tinted skin and dark gold hair to perfection. She'd been the soul of polite and proper decorum, more than making up for Hedwick's rudeness. She also made it clear that the ball in question was the Yule ball. I had to decline. If I attended any Yule ball, it had to be the Unseelie ball. Rosmerta had made noises that she, of course, understood that.

We weren't missed in helping with the murders, because Peterson had forbidden anyone from the Grey Detective Agency from interfering with the case. Jeremy had been pissed enough that he told Teresa not to tell them what she'd seen, but Teresa is all about helping her fellow man. She went dutifully from the hospital to the police station and finally found a detective who would take her report.

Teresa had felt the people suffocate, felt them die, and she'd seen the ghosts – white shapes, she said, sucking the life from them. The police had informed her that everyone knew ghosts didn't do shit like this. Peterson had come in about then and thrown the report in the trash can in front of Teresa. Usually the police wait until someone's left the room before doing that.

Teresa had managed to drag her husband out before he got himself arrested for assaulting a police officer. Teresa's husband used to play for the Rams back when they were the football team in L.A. Ray's like a nicely maintained mountain, with a winning smile and a very firm handshake.

We ended up with a lot of time on our hands. No, we did not just have sex all day. We pestered Sage. I had paid the price that Queen Niceven asked, but we had no cure. Why hadn't Sage given us the cure last night? Why did Kitto becoming sidhe change everything for Sage? Did he really mean to imply that he needed to have sex with me to effect the cure? Sage didn't want to answer any questions.

He had flown around the apartment trying to escape our questions, but it was a small apartment, even if you were the size of a Barbie doll. Late in the day he launched himself from the windowsill and got a little too near Galen, who batted at him like you'd swat a mosquito. I don't think he meant to strike him.

Sage fell heavily on the floor. He lay very still, a tiny butter-colored thing with his bright wings like a fragile shield. He raised slowly onto one arm before I could finish kneeling by him. 'Are you all right?' I asked.

He looked at me with such hatred in those tiny doll eyes that I flinched. He stumbled a little in rising to his feet, but he fanned his wings and caught his balance. He refused the hand I offered him. He stood there, hands on hips, and stared up at us as we towered over him.

'If I die, green knight, the cure dies with me. Best remember that, when you're being careless.'

'I didn't intend to hurt you,' Galen said, but there was something in his eyes that was not kind, not gentle, not Galen. Perhaps, more than just his manhood had been damaged by the demi-fey.

'Too close to a lie, that,' Sage said, rising into the air, his butterfly wings a blur. Butterfly wings just didn't work like that. It was more the way a dragonfly moved. When he'd gained height enough to meet Galen's gaze, the wing beats slowed and he hovered, the large wings fanning more slowly but still with enough force to stir the curls around Galen's face.

'I didn't intend to strike you that hard.' Galen's voice was low and warm with anger. There was a hardness there that I'd never heard before. Part of me mourned that tone; part of me felt a flare of hope. Perhaps even Galen could learn those harsh lessons that would be needed if he ever became king. Or perhaps he was just learning how to hate. That lesson I would have spared him if I could.

I watched the two men glare at each other, both hating. Sage was still the size of a Barbie doll, but his anger wasn't amusing anymore. That he could elicit such negativity from my smiling Galen was a little frightening.

'All right, boys, play nice now.' They both turned and glared at me. So much for breaking the tension. 'Fine, be that way, but what did you

318

mean that if you die, the cure dies with you?'

Sage rotated in midair, arms half crossed on his tiny chest as if he couldn't quite cross them and fly at the same time. 'I mean, Princess, that Queen Niceven left a present in my body. The healing for your man here is trapped in this tiny package.' He spread his arms wide as he said it, almost bowing as he hung, fluttering.

'What does that mean, Sage?' Doyle said. 'Exactly what it means, no prevaricating, just the truth, all of it.'

He gave another turn in midair so he could look directly at Doyle. Sage could have simply glanced over his shoulder, but I think he wanted Doyle to know he was being looked at. 'You want truth, Darkness, all of it?'

'Yes,' Doyle said, his thick voice, lower, deeper, not angry, but a tone that had made many a sidhe pale.

Sage laughed, a joyous tinkling sound that nearly drew a smile from me. He was very good at glamour, better than I thought any demi-fey could be. 'Oh, you'll be angrier than that when you hear what my dear queen has done.'

'Just tell us, Sage,' I said. 'Quit drawing out the story.'

He turned to me, hovered close enough for the breath of his wings to caress my face. 'Say please.' His tone made it an insult.

Galen tensed, and Rhys laid a hand on his shoulder. I think I wasn't the only one who didn't quite trust Galen around the demi-fey.

'Please,' I said. I had a lot of faults, but false pride wasn't one of them. It cost me nothing to say please to the tiny man.

He smiled, obviously happy. 'Since you asked nicely.' He grabbed his tiny crotch through the filmy skirt he wore. 'The cure is trapped here, where Queen Niceven laid it.'

I felt my eyes widen.

'How does Meredith retrieve the cure?' Doyle asked. His voice held emptiness, no tone at all.

Sage smiled, and even on a face not much bigger than my thumb, I recognized a leer when I saw it. 'The same way the queen gave it to me.'

'Niceven is not allowed intercourse with anyone but her husband,' Doyle said.

'Ah, but there are exceptions to every rule. You should know that, Darkness, better than most.'

Doyle seemed to blush, though through the pure night of his skin, it was hard to be sure. 'If Queen Andais knows she has broken her marriage vows, it will go badly for your queen.'

'The demi-fey never held to such rules until Andais grew jealous of Niceven's children. Three children she has, three pure-blood demi-fey. Only one belonged to Pol, but Andais chose that match to be permanent. Andais envies Niceven her babes, and all the court knows it.'

'I would be careful who I told that to,' Rhys said. There was no teasing in his voice, just truth.

Sage brushed it away with his tiny hands. 'You requested a cure for your green knight, and there is only one cure for it. She had to lay with me to lay the spell within me. Andais agreed that the green knight must be cured at all costs. She didn't seem too concerned what those costs might be.'

I shook my head. 'No, no intercourse, not with you.'

320

Sage rose into the air. 'Then your green knight stays unmanned.'

I shook my head again. 'We'll see about that.' I felt the first stirrings of anger. I didn't let myself get angry often. In the courts it was an indulgence that only the most powerful could afford. I had never been that powerful. Maybe I still wasn't, but we'd see.

'Doyle, call Queen Niceven. We need to talk.' The anger had leaked out into my voice.

Sage came hovering close enough that the wind from his wings fanned my face. 'There is no other way, Princess. The cure has been given for this curse, and cannot be given twice.'

I glared at him. 'I am not every man's meat to feast upon, little man. I am Princess of Flesh, and heir to the Unseelie throne. I do not whore for Niceven.'

'Only for Andais,' Sage said.

I came very close to swatting him, but I wasn't sure how hard I would have hit, and I didn't want to hurt him that badly, not by accident. No, if I hurt Sage that badly, I wanted it to be on purpose.

'Doyle, contact Niceven, now.'

He didn't argue, just went for the bedroom door. I followed him with the others trailing behind. Sage kept talking as we went. 'What do you plan to do, Princess? What can you do? Is one night with me such a high price to pay for your green knight's manhood?'

I ignored him.

Niceven was already in the mirror when I entered the bedroom. She wore a black dress today, utterly sheer so that her pale body seemed to gleam through the dark cloth. Discreet touches

321

of black sequins sparkled at neck and sleeve. Her white hair fell loose around her body. The hair fell almost to her tiny ankles, but it was thin, thin and strange looking, almost like it wasn't hair at all. All I could think of was a spiderweb blowing in the breeze. Her pale wings framed her like a white curtain. Her three ladies-in-waiting stood behind her chair, but each was clad only in a tiny silken robe, as if they'd been roused from bed. Each robe still matched each set of wings, rose-red, daffodil-yellow, and iris-purple. The hair that flowed loose around their faces was sleep-tousled the way real hair should be.

The white mouse was back at her side complete with bejeweled collar. For Niceven to wear no crown, no jewels, meant she had been in true haste to answer our call.

'Princess Meredith, to what do I owe this unexpected honor?' Her voice held just a trace of peevishness. Apparently, we had awakened her entire court from their beds.

'Queen Niceven, you promised me the cure for Galen if I fed your servant. I have lived up to my bargain, but you have not lived up to yours.'

She sat up a little straighter, hands folded in her lap, ankles crossed. 'Sage has not given you the cure?' She sounded truly puzzled.

'No,' I said.

Her gaze left my face and found the tiny man who had alit upon the edge of the dresser so he could be easily seen from the mirror. 'Sage, what is this about?'

'She refused the cure,' he said, spreading his hands out as if to say *not my fault*.

Niceven looked back at me. 'Is this true?'

322

'Did you truly think I would accept him in my bed?'

'He is a wonderful lover, Princess.'

'To one of your height perhaps, but to one of mine, it grows a little ridiculous.'

'Or rather doesn't grow enough,' Rhys said, from the back of the bedroom.

I shot him a hard look. He shrugged, almost an apology, then turned back to the mirror.

'If size is the only problem, that can be remedied,' Niceven said.

'Your majesty,' Sage said, 'I do not think this is wise. Only Meredith swore a solemn oath not to reveal our secret.'

'Then let them all swear,' she said.

I shook my head. 'We swear nothing,' I said. 'If you do not give the cure for my knight now, then I call you oath breaker. Oath breakers do not have long political careers among the fey.'

'The cure is there for the taking, Princess. It is not my fault if you will not partake.'

I stepped closer to the mirror. 'Sex is a greater boon than sharing blood, and well you know it, Niceven.'

Her face seemed to become even thinner, her pale eyes glittering with anger. 'You overstep yourself, Meredith, forgetting my title.'

'No, it is you who overstep yourself, Niceven. You retain your title as queen at Andais's sufference, and well you know that. I will have you up before my aunt as an oath breaker if Galen's cure is not forthcoming immediately.'

'I will not be turned from my course by anger, no matter how much you taunt me, Meredith,' Niceven said. 'Reveal yourself, Sage.'

'My queen, I think this unwise.'

'I did not ask what you thought, I said only to do it.' She leaned forward in her chair. 'Now, Sage.' You didn't need a translator to hear the threat in those two words.

Sage's wings slicked tight together, then he flung himself off the edge of the dresser, not flying, as if he meant to plunge to his death, but he didn't fall. He grew. He was suddenly tall, taller. He was nearly as tall as I was, four feet eight, nine. The wings that had been lovely when tiny were like stained glass, artwork worn across the back of his body. Muscles showed under his butter yellow skin, and when he turned to look at me over his shoulder, the black eyes were the shape of almonds, and his red lips were moist and full. There was something terribly sensual as he stood there, his wings nearly filling one side of the room.

'Is he not lovely, Meredith?' Niceven said, her voice full of longing.

I sighed. 'He is lovely to the eye, but in his present size sex is an even greater boon, for whosoever gets me with child will be king.' I had to step to one side to see her clearly past Sage's wings. 'Is it a bid for the Unseelie throne, Niceven? Is that your goal? I wouldn't have thought you that ambitious.'

'I bid for no throne,' she said.

'Liar and oath breaker,' Doyle said. He had never moved out of the mirror's sight, as if he wanted her to remember, always, that he was by my side.

She turned a flat and very unfriendly gaze to him. 'Mind your manners, Darkness.'

'Give Meredith the cure as you swore you would.'

324

'Queen Andais said the green knight was to be cured at all costs.'

Doyle shook his head. 'She could not have dreamt this cost. There have always been rumors that some of the demi-fey could grow larger, but rumors, fables, no truth until now. The queen would think ill of a demi-fey king, especially one who is your puppet in all things.'

She hissed at him, and in that one movement she seemed very alien, as if I'd figure out what she truly was if I thought hard enough, and it wouldn't be human. The white mouse had crouched away from her as if it feared her temper.

'You have a choice here, Queen Niceven,' I said. 'You can either give me the cure for Galen as you swore you would, or I can tell Queen Andais about your plotting.'

Niceven looked at me, eyes narrow. 'If I give you the cure, you will not tell Andais about all this?'

'We are allies, Queen Niceven. Allies protect each other.'

'I have not fully agreed to an alliance merely for an offering of blood once a week. Have sex with Sage and I will be your ally.'

'Give me the cure for Galen, take your blood offering once a week, be my ally, or I tell Aunt Andais what you tried to do here.'

Niceven didn't look angry anymore, she looked frightened. 'If I had not had Sage show you his secret, then you would not have had anything to blackmail me with.'

'Perhaps, or perhaps even a little seed in the wrong place can cause a large problem.'

'What do you mean?'

'Galen's father was a pixie, and that's not much bigger than Sage in his true form. There have been odder mixes in the courts. I think Andais would see your demand that one of your men fuck me as a grave breach of trust.'

She spat, and the mouse scrambled out of sight; even her ladies-in-waiting backed up. 'Trust, what do the sidhe know of trust?'

'About as much as the demi-fey,' I said.

She gave me a truly evil look, but I was expecting it, or something like it. I smiled at her around the curve of Sage's wings. 'I'd asked for an alliance so you and yours could spy for me.' I looked at Sage, nearly as tall as I was. 'But here is proof that you have other talents. Your swords are not merely the pinpricks of bees but something much more.'

She shifted in her chair, a small movement, but she was nervous. 'I do not know what you mean, Princess Meredith.'

'I think you do. An alliance I still want, but your contribution to the alliance will go beyond spying.'

'To what? Sage is but one man. You have other and larger swords at your back.'

I touched Sage's shoulder. He jumped as if it had hurt, but I knew that it hadn't. I leaned in against the back of his body. He tensed. 'Is what the queen says true, Sage? Is your sword so small?' I looked at Niceven as I said it.

She gave me angry eyes. 'That is not what I meant and well you know it.'

'Do I?' I asked, running my fingertips down Sage's arm. He shivered under my touch. I watched jealousy flare across her face before she could catch it back. 'Niceven, Niceven, do not give up to others what you hold most precious.'

Her face was angry, blank. 'I don't know what you mean.'

I touched Sage's hair, and the hair was soft as spider silk, or downy feathers, softer than any hair I'd ever touched. 'Never offer to give up that which you cannot afford to lose.'

She shook her head. 'I don't understand you, Princess.'

'Be stubborn then, but know this. I offer you alliance, true alliance in exchange for a blood offering once a week. You cease to spy for Cel and his people.'

'Prince Cel may be locked away, Princess, but Siobhan is not, and she is more frightening to some than Cel will ever be.'

I noticed her phrasing. 'More frightening to some, but not to you.'

Niceven bowed her head. 'I find Cel's brand of madness more frightening than Siobhan's ruthlessness. You can plan around a ruthless man, but a madman throws all your plans to the wind.'

I nodded. 'Your wisdom does you credit, Queen Niceven.'

'For a chance for one of my men to be king of all the Unseelie, I would have risked all, but for mere blood, I will have to think upon it.'

'No, an alliance now, or the queen will know of your ambition.'

Niceven gave me a look of pure venom.

'I will do it, Niceven, do not mistake me on this. Alliance, or answer to Andais.'

'I have no choices left then,' she said.

'No,' I said.

'Alliance then, but I think both of us will regret it.'

'Perhaps,' I said, 'but now the cure for Galen and our business can be done for today.'

Niceven turned her attention to Sage. 'Give the princess the cure, Sage.'

He frowned. 'How, my queen, if I am not allowed to give it to her as you gave it to me?'

'Though I gave it to thee through more intimate contact, it only needs your body to enter hers to be given.'

'No sex,' I said.

She gave me a long-suffering look. 'A kiss, Meredith, a kiss and you are free to take no pleasure from it.'

I had to move to one side by Doyle so Sage could turn around. His wings seemed to fill all the space between the dresser and the bed. When Sage was turned around, I stepped back in front of him. His wings rose above his shoulders like the top of some golden bejeweled heart. His hair was only a shade more golden than the soft yellow of his skin. He looked almost unreal in his loveliness until you reached his eyes. Those glittering black eyes held not just anger, but malice. It made me remember that he was just a bigger version of the things that had taken bites out of Galen.

'No biting, no bloodletting,' I said.

He laughed, flashing teeth that were a little too pointy for comfort. 'Blunt negotiating for a sidhe princess.'

'I don't want you to have any room to say you misunderstood me, Sage. I want this to be very clear between us.'

Niceven spoke from the mirror. 'He will not harm you, Princess.'

Sage turned his head to gaze over his shoulder at her. 'A little blood is fine spice for a kiss,' he said.

'Perhaps to us, but you are to do exactly as the princess bids you. If she says no blood, then no blood.'

'Why should we heed a sidhe princess?' he asked.

'You are not heeding the princess, Sage, you are heeding me.' She gave him a look that leaked some of the malice from his eyes.

His shoulders slumped a little, his wings flexing until they touched the dresser. 'As my queen bids, so shall it be.' He didn't sound happy about it.

'My word that he will not harm you in this,' Niceven said.

I nodded. 'I will take the queen's word.'

Sage turned to glare at me. 'But not mine.'

'My word is your word,' Niceven said, and her voice had fallen to a low hiss.

The look on Sage's face was so unfriendly that I knew if Niceven saw it, she wouldn't have been happy. His back shielded her view, and for just an instant something traveled through his eyes that was almost sorrow, almost, dare I say, human. It was gone almost instantly, but that one brief glimpse gave me something to think about. Maybe Niceven's little court wasn't any happier than Andais's.

I slid my hands on either side of Sage's face, not for romance, but to control him. His skin was like a baby's, so soft, unbelievably fine under my fingertips. I'd never touched a demi-fey this much, because there had never been enough of them to touch. I leaned toward him, and he just stood there, hands at his sides. He waited for me to complete the act.

I turned my head slightly to the side and hesitated, my mouth hovering just above his. The lips looked redder than they should have. I wondered if they would feel different, like the texture of his skin, then my lips brushed his, and I had my answer. They were just lips but soft, soft like silk, satin, rich like tasting some ripe fruit.

It was interesting, but there was no magic to it. I leaned back from him, hands still on his face. I looked at Niceven in the mirror. 'There was no spell, no cure.'

'Did his body enter yours?' she asked.

'You mean tongue?'

'That is what I mean, since you seem so determined to have nothing else.'

'No,' I said.

'Kiss her, Sage, kiss her like you mean it, then this can all be done.'

He gave a heavy sigh, his body moving under my hands. 'As my queen bids.'

His hands slid around my body, pulling me against him. We were too close for my hands on his face, but as my hands slid down his back, I found wings and didn't know where to hold on.

'Underneath where the wings attach to my back,' he said, as if he understood the problem. Maybe he'd had the problem before with other non-demi-fey.

I moved my arms under his, sliding them along his back to where the wings attached to his body. His back felt normal other than the extra softness of the skin. Shouldn't he have had extra muscles under there to flex the wings?

His hands kneaded my back as he brought his face close, closer. We kissed, and this time he kissed me back, gentle at first, then his arms convulsed around my body and he thrust himself inside my mouth. It was as if his tongue, his mouth, were heat. Heat to fill my mouth, heat to spill down my throat, heat like a stream flowing through my body, spilling out, out to my fingertips, my toes, until I was full of it, until my skin ran hot with it.

It was Niceven's voice that brought me back. 'You have your cure, Princess. Give it to your green knight before it cools.'

Sage and I pulled away from each other, bodies reluctant to part. Our hands slid down each other's arms as I turned from him to find Galen. Galen had moved up closer to us.

I went to him, slid my hot, hot hands over his arms, and even through the sleeves of his shirt I could feel his skin, feel the heat gliding over him. His breathing was fast and hard by the time he bent down to receive his kiss.

Our lips touched and it was as if the heat were hungry for him. Our lips sealed together, so that no drop of heat would be lost. Lips, tongue, even teeth fed at each other's mouths. The heat filled my mouth almost like liquid. I could feel the warm, sweet thickness of it like warm honey, warm syrup that filled my mouth and spilled into Galen. He drank at my mouth, drank the magic down.

He drew the heat out of me, pulled the magic from me with his mouth and his hands and his body. The magical heat fed on heat of a different kind, and with a small cry I climbed his body to wrap my legs around his waist. He cried out when my body touched his groin, and it wasn't pleasure.

He set me down quickly, not quite pushing me away. In a breathless voice, he said, 'I don't feel healed.'

'You will be healed two days hence by nightfall, or earlier,' Niceven said.

I was still standing, half swaying, breath coming in ragged gasps. I could barely hear over the pounding of my own pulse in my ears. So it was left to Doyle to be sensible. 'I want your word, Queen Niceven, that Galen will be healed two days from now.'

'You have it,' she said.

He nodded. 'We thank you.'

'Don't thank me, Darkness, don't thank me.' Then she was gone, the mirror just a mirror once again.

Galen sat down heavily on the edge of the bed. He was still gasping, struggling to breathe, but he smiled up at me. 'In two days.'

I tried to touch his face, but my hand was shaking so badly I missed. He grabbed my hand and put it against his cheek. 'Two days,' I said.

He nodded, still smiling, my hand still pressed against his face. But I couldn't smile back at him; I could see Frost's face. Arrogant, angry, jealous. He seemed to notice me noticing him, and looked away. He hid his face because I don't think he could control his expression. Frost was jealous of Galen. It was not a good sign.

Chapter 31

THAT NIGHT WAS FROST'S NIGHT, AND HE SEEMED determined to make me forget everyone else. I was licking down his stomach when Andais's voice came like an evil dream out of the empty mirror. 'I will not be blocked from the sight I wish to see, not by my own Darkness. You have one minute, then I will clear my own way.'

We froze, then rolled to our feet, got tangled in the sheets, and nearly fell. Frost said, 'My queen, Doyle is not here. We will fetch him for you, if you but wait.'

She made a low sound, almost a growl. 'My patience is low tonight, my Killing Frost. I will give you two minutes to find him and free this mirror, or I will do it for you.'

'We will make haste, my queen.'

I was already in the doorway. 'Doyle, the queen on the mirror, now. She wants to see you.' My voice must have carried the urgency I was feeling, because Doyle rolled off the couch, shirtless, wearing just his jeans. He was inside the bedroom, one hand outstretched, as Frost pleaded for just one more minute.

I climbed on the bed as the fastest way to make room for both of the men to stand in front of the mirror. Doyle touched the side of the mirror, and the glass flashed once with light, then cleared. Then there was something in the mirror. I couldn't see much of it around the two broad backs of the men, and what I could see made me half-glad my view was obstructed.

There was torchlight flickering, dark stone walls, and soft, hopeless moaning, as if whoever was making the sound had gone beyond the need to scream, beyond words, beyond anything but that utterly hopeless moaning. When I was little I'd always thought that the wailing of ghosts must be like the sounds in the Hallway of Mortality. Strangely, ghosts don't make noises like that. Or at least none that I've ever met.

'How dare you lock me out, Doyle, how dare you!'

'I asked Doyle to block the viewing on the mirror,' I said, speaking to the backs of both of the men.

'I hear our little princess, but I do not see her. If we are going to fight, then I wish to see her face-to-face.' Her voice held anger like a cup filled to the brim with something hot and scalding.

The men parted so that I was suddenly visible, kneeling on the bed, in the tangle of sheets and pillows. Andais was suddenly visible, as well. She was standing in the middle of the Hallway of Mortality, where I'd known she was. The viewing mirror in the torture area was set so that you couldn't see any of the devices, but Andais had made sure that she was horrible enough.

She was covered in blood as if someone had

thrown a bucket of it over her. Her face was speckled with little drying bits, and one side of her hair was caked with blood and thicker things. It took a minute of staring to realize that she was gore soaked and wore nothing else. She was actually so covered in blood and bits that I hadn't realized she was nude at first.

I took air in through my nose, out through my mouth for a few breaths while Doyle filled the silence.

'We have had many callers, my queen. The princess grew tired of being caught unprepared for visitors.'

'Who else has been calling you, niece?'

I swallowed hard, let out the breath I'd been half holding, and my voice came out just fine, not a tremble. Good for me. 'Taranis's secretaries mostly.'

'What does he want?' She nearly spit the word *he*.

'I was invited to the Yule ball, but declined.' I added the last hastily. I did not want her to think I'd snub her court.

'How terribly high-handed, and how terribly typical of Taranis.'

'If one may be so bold, my queen,' Doyle said softly, 'you are in an exceptional mood, despite the fact that you have obviously been indulging yourself heartily. What has so displeased you?'

Doyle was right. I'd seen Andais come back from a torture session humming, covered in gore and humming. She should have been having a very good time by her standards, but she wasn't.

'I have taken those who I deemed capable of either releasing the Nameless or calling the old ones. I have questioned them all most thoroughly. If any of them had done these things, they would have talked by now.' She sounded tired, the anger beginning to leak away.

'I am sure, my queen, that you have been most thorough,' Doyle said.

She looked at him, and it was a hard look. 'Are you making fun of me?'

Doyle bowed as far as the mirror would allow. 'Never, my queen.'

She rubbed her hand across her forehead, smearing blood across her white skin. 'No sidhe in our court did this, my Darkness.'

'Then who, if not our people?' Doyle asked. He did not rise from his bow.

'We are not the only sidhe, Doyle.'

'You mean Taranis's court,' Frost said.

Her eyes flicked to him, and they narrowed in a very unfriendly manner. 'Yes, that's what I mean.'

Frost bowed, mirroring Doyle. 'I meant no disrespect, Your Majesty.'

Doyle said, from his awkward position, 'Have you informed the king of his peril?'

'He refuses to believe that anyone in his beautiful shining court could do such a thing. He says that none of his people would know how to raise the old dead gods, and that none would touch the Nameless, for it has nothing to do with them. The Nameless is an Unseelie problem, and the old gods are ghosts, and that is an Unseelie problem, as well.'

'What exactly would be a Seelie problem?' I asked. I almost hated to have her attention back on me, but I wanted to know. If none of this was Seelie business, then what exactly was their business?

'That, niece, is an excellent question. Of late, Taranis seems unwilling to dirty his hands with anything of importance. I don't know what's wrong with him, but he seems to be living more and more in his own little dream haven, built of pretty illusions and his own magic.' She crossed her stained arms, looking thoughtful. 'It has to be one of his court. It has to be.'

'What can we do to get him to see that?' I asked.

'I don't know. I wish I did.' She waved her hands. 'Oh, for pity's sake, get up, both of you. Go sit on the bed. Look comfortable.'

Frost and Doyle stood and came to sit, one on either side of me. Frost was still nude, but his lovely body was no longer at the excited pitch it had been before the queen called. He sat with his hands in his lap, half hiding himself. Doyle sat on the other side of me, very still, like a prey animal trying not to draw the eye of the predator. I didn't often think of Doyle as a prey animal – he was so assuredly a predator – but tonight, the only predator was staring at us from the mirror.

'Move your hands, Frost. Let me see all of you.'

Frost hesitated, the briefest of seconds, and then let his hands drop away to either side of his lap. He sat there nude, eyes downcast, no longer comfortable in his nudity.

'You are truly beautiful, Frost. I had forgotten that.' She frowned. 'I seem to be forgetting a lot of things lately.' She sounded almost sad; then her voice became brisk again, hers again. Just the tone made all three of us stiffen, almost shiver, and it was a shiver of anticipation, but not of pleasure.

'I have not enjoyed myself this day. These were

people whom I respected, or liked, or valued, and now they will never again be my allies. They will fear me, but they feared me before, and fear is not truly the same as respect. I'm learning that, at last. Give me something pleasant to remember this night by. Let me watch the three of you together. Let me see the lights from your skin brighten the night like fireworks.'

The three of us sat there for a second, then Doyle said, 'I have had my night with the princess. Frost has made it clear that he does not wish to share her tonight.'

'He will share if I say that he will share,' Andais said. It was hard to argue with her, blood soaked and nude, looking like some terrible primal thing; but we tried.

'I would ask that Your Majesty not do this,' Frost said. He wasn't looking arrogant. He was looking almost frightened.

'You would ask? You would ask? What is it you are asking of me?'

'Nothing,' he said, head hanging so that the shine of his hair hid his face. 'Absolutely nothing.' He sounded bitter and sorrowful when he said it.

'Aunt Andais,' I said, keeping my voice level, soft, like I was trying to talk a crazy person out of setting off the bomb strapped to her body. 'Please, we have done nothing to displease you. We have done everything we can to please you. Why would you punish us for that?'

'Were you going to have sex tonight?'

'Yes, but—'

'You are going to fuck Frost tonight, are you not?'

'Yes.'

338

'You fucked Doyle last night, correct?'

'Well, yes, but—'

'Then what difference does it make if you fuck them both right now, tonight?' Her voice was rising again, losing its calm edge.

My voice went lower, more even as hers began to unravel. 'I have not been with both of them at once before, Your Majesty, and a ménage à trois must be done carefully or you spoil the game. I think that Doyle and Frost are both too dominant to share me comfortably.'

She nodded. 'Very well.'

I think we all relaxed, let a breath out.

'Then replace one of them with one of the others. Give me a show, niece of mine, give me something to enjoy this night.'

I'd done my best reasoning, she'd even agreed with it, and it hadn't helped us. I looked from one man to the other. 'At this point, I'm open to suggestions.' I hoped Andais thought I meant suggestions on who to invite in or who to replace. But I hoped that the men understood that I was still wanting a way out of all this.

'Nicca is less dominant,' Frost said slowly.

Had he understood what I meant?

'Or Kitto,' Doyle said.

'Kitto had his turn today, and Nicca isn't due for two more nights. I think everyone would agree on Nicca being moved ahead before they would agree to Kitto being allowed two turns back-to-back.'

'Agree?' the queen said. 'Why do the men have to agree to anything? Don't you just pick among them, Meredith?'

'Not really. We've got a schedule and we usually stick to it.'

'A schedule, a schedule?' She began to smile, then to grin. 'And how did you arrive at this schedule?'

'It was alphabetical,' I said, trying not to sound as puzzled as I felt.

'She has an alphabetical schedule, alphabetical.' She began to laugh, a low trickle of sound at first, then it grew into a huge genuine belly laugh. She half doubled over, clutching at her sides, laughing until tears trailed out of her eyes to trickle through the blood.

Belly laughs are usually infectious; strangely, this one was not. Or rather, it wasn't to us. I could hear others behind her joining in. Ezekiel and his assistants probably thought it was a hoot. Torturers have such an odd sense of humor.

The laughter slowed, and finally Andais stood up again, wiping at her eyes. I think we were all holding our breaths, wondering what she'd say. She managed to gasp, laughter still thick in her voice, 'You have given me the first true pleasure of the day, and for that I will give you all a reprieve. Though I fail to see what is so wrong with doing in front of me what you will do when I leave you. I do not see the difference.'

Wisely, we kept our opinions to ourselves. I think we all knew that if she didn't already understand the difference, there was no way to explain it to her.

The queen went away, leaving the three of us to stare into the mirror. I looked shell-shocked, stunned by our near miss. Doyle's face showed almost nothing. Frost got to his feet and screamed, a sound of such rage that it reverberated through the room and brought

340

the others to the door with guns drawn.

Rhys looked around the room, puzzled. 'What's happened?'

Frost wheeled toward him, naked, unarmed, but there was something fearsome in him. 'We are not animals to be paraded for her amusement!'

Doyle stood up, motioning the others back. Rhys looked at me, and I nodded. They left, closing the door softly behind them.

Doyle spoke softly to Frost. Some of it was simple soothing talk, but some was more insistent. 'We are safe now, Frost,' I heard Doyle tell him. 'She cannot hurt us here.'

Frost raised his head and grabbed Doyle by the shoulders. The pressure of his pale hands mottled Doyle's dark skin. 'Don't you understand yet, Doyle? If we are not the one who fathers Merry's child, then we are back to being Andais's playthings, her neglected playthings. I don't think I could bear it again, Doyle.' He shook him, just a little. 'I can't go back to that, Doyle, I can't!' He shook the other man, back and forth, back and forth.

I kept expecting Doyle to break his grip, to force him away, but he didn't. He'd raised his forearms to grip Frost's arms. Other than that he'd remained immobile.

I caught the shine of tears through the silver of Frost's hair. He slowly fell to his knees, his hands sliding down Doyle's arms, but never losing contact. He pressed the top of his head against the other man, his hands holding on. 'I can't do it, Doyle. I cannot do it. I'd rather die. I'll let myself fade first.'

With that last choked word he began to cry in

earnest, great racking sobs that seemed to come from deep, deep inside him. Frost cried as if it would break him in two.

Doyle let him cry, and when he had quieted, Doyle helped me get Frost into bed. We laid him between us, Doyle spooning from the back, and me entwined from the front. There was nothing sexual about it. We held him while he cried himself to sleep. Doyle and I gazed at each other over Frost's curled body. The look in Doyle's eyes, his face, was more frightening than the sight of Andais covered in gore.

I watched a fearful purpose be born that night. Maybe it had been born a long time ago, and I just hadn't noticed. Doyle wouldn't go back, either. I saw it in his eyes. We held Frost; and finally we both slept, as well.

Sometime during the night Doyle got up and left us. I woke up when he moved, but Frost did not. Doyle kissed me gently on the forehead, then laid his hand against the soft glimmer of Frost's hair.

He spoke softly, his deep voice like a purr, more than a whisper. 'I promise.'

I raised up enough to ask, 'Promise what?'

He just smiled, shook his head, and left, closing the door softly behind him.

I snuggled down beside Frost, but sleep eluded me. My thoughts weren't friendly enough for sleep. Dawn's light had greyed the window before I drifted into a fitful rest.

I dreamed that I stood beside Andais in the Hallway of Mortality. All the men were chained to the torture devices, untouched, unharmed, the only shining clean things in all that dark place.

Andais kept trying to get me to join her in torturing them. I refused, and I wouldn't let her touch them. She threatened me and them, and I kept refusing her, and my refusal somehow made it so she couldn't touch them. I refused until Frost's small whimpering woke me. He was twitching in his sleep, struggling. I woke him as gently as I could, stroking down his arm. He woke with a scream half-choked in his throat, eyes wild.

The scream had brought the other men to the door. I waved them away as I hugged Frost to me. 'It's all right, Frost, it's all right. It was just a dream.'

He choked on that and spoke fiercely, his face buried against my body, his arms hugging me so tight it hurt. 'Not a dream, real. I remember it. I will always remember it.'

Doyle was the last one in the doorway, closing it slowly. I met his dark eyes, and I knew what he'd promised.

'I'll keep you safe, Frost,' I said.

'You can't,' he said.

'I promise I'll keep you safe, all of you.'

He raised his hand, covered my mouth with his fingers. 'Don't promise, Merry, don't promise that. Don't be forsworn for something you have no hope of doing. No one else heard. I forgive it. You never said it.'

Doyle's face was just a dark shape in the nearly closed door. 'But I did say it, Frost, and I meant it. I will make the Summerlands into a wasteland before I let her have you back,' I said. The moment the words left my mouth, there was a slight sound, though not a sound, it was almost as if the very air held its breath. It was as if in that moment reality itself froze, and then remade itself just a little bit different than it had been.

Frost crawled out of bed and wouldn't look at me. 'You're going to get yourself killed, Merry.' He walked into the bathroom without looking back. I heard the shower a few moments later.

Doyle opened the door enough to salute me with his gun, as if it had been a sword, touching the side of the weapon to his forehead, then bringing it out and down. I nodded my acknowledgment of the gesture. Then he blew me a kiss with his other hand and closed the door.

I didn't understand completely what had just happened. I knew what it meant, though. I was now sworn to protect the men from Andais. But I had felt the world shift, as if fate itself had shivered. Something had changed in the well-orchestrated run of the universe. It had changed because I vowed to protect the men. That one statement had changed things. I had made the fates blink, but I wouldn't know if I'd bettered myself or worsened until it was far, far too late.

Chapter 32

WE WERE TALKING ABOUT THE FERTILITY RITE FOR Maeve Reed when the mirror sounded again; but this time it was the clear ringing of a bell, a clarion call, almost like a trumpet.

Doyle had gotten up saying, 'Someone new.' He came back a few minutes later with an odd look on his face.

'Who is it?' Rhys asked.

'Meredith's mother.' He sounded puzzled.

'My mother.' I stood up, letting the notes I was making fall to the floor. I started to bend down and pick them up, but Galen took my hand. 'Do you want company?'

I think of all the men, he alone knew how I truly felt about my mother. I started to say no, then changed my mind. 'Yes, I would very much like company.'

He offered me his arm, and I laid my hand across his in a very formal way.

'Would you like more company?' Doyle asked.

I looked around the room and tried to decide if I wanted to impress my mother, or insult her.

With the men in my living room I could do either, or maybe even both.

There really wasn't room for everybody to troop in, so I settled for Galen and Doyle. I didn't really need protection from my own mother. At least, not the kind of protection that bodyguards could supply.

Doyle went first, to tell her that the princess would be a moment. Galen and I waited outside the door for a little bit, then we walked in. He escorted me in front of the mirror, then sat down on the dark burgundy bedspread, trying to be unobtrusive.

Doyle stayed standing, though he moved to the far side of the mirror. He wasn't as concerned with being unobtrusive.

I faced the mirror. I knew her hair fell in thick, perfect waves past her waist, but you couldn't tell that from her image in the mirror. Her elaborate hairdo was piled upon her head in layers. She had used leaves made of hammered gold to encircle the hairdo. They almost hid the very ordinary brown of her hair. It wasn't as if no one of pure sidhe blood had brown hair, because some did. I think she hid her hair because it was exactly like her mother's, my half-brownie, half-human grandmother. Besaba, my mother, hated to be reminded of her origins.

Her eyes were merely brown, a nice solid chocolate brown with long, long lashes. Her skin was lovely. She'd always spent hours on her skin – milk baths, creams, lotions – but nothing she could do would ever give her the pure white of moonlit skin, or the soft gold tint of sunlight skin. She would never have sidhe skin, never. Her older twin sister, Eluned, had that glowing skin. But it was my mother's skin, more than the hair or eyes, that set her apart, at a glance, as not pure sidhe.

Her cream-colored dress was stiff with gold and copper thread. The square neckline made much of her bust, creamy mounds, but there was a reason why the sidhe are so fond of bust-improving styles: they don't have a great deal to work with.

Her makeup was artful, and she was, as always, beautiful. She'd never gone a single visit without reminding me that she was lovely, a Seelie princess, and I was not. I was too short, too human shaped, and my hair, dear Goddess, my hair was blood auburn, a color that was found only in the Unseelie Court.

I looked at her, her beauty, and realized that she could have been human. There were humans who were tall and slender, and that was all she had to prove she was more sidhe than I.

She was far too overdressed to pay a call upon her own daughter. The care with which she'd arranged herself made me wonder if she knew just how much I disliked her. Then I realized she was almost always this arranged, this carefully constructed.

I was wearing a pair of shorts and a tank top that showed off my stomach. The shorts were black, the top was a bloodred, and my skin gleamed between the two colors. My shoulder-length hair was beginning to catch some of the wave it had when I let it grow long, not the profuse waves of my mother's and grandmother's hair, but waves nonetheless. The hair was only two shades darker than the bloodred of the tank top.

I wore no jewelry, but my body itself was jewelry. My skin shone like polished ivory; my hair gleamed like garnets; and my eyes, I had tricolored eyes. I looked at my beautiful, but all-too-human-looking mother and had a moment of revelation. It was only as I'd grown older that she complained about my looks. Oh, the hair, she'd always hated the hair, and she'd always been unkind, but the worst insults had begun when I was ten or eleven years old. She'd felt threatened. I'd never realized until this moment – as she sat there in her Seelie finery, and I stood in casual street clothes – that I was prettier than my mother.

I stared at her, just stared for a time, because it was like rewriting a part of my childhood in a space of heartbeats.

I couldn't remember the last time I'd seen my mother. Perhaps she couldn't either, because for a moment she stared, seemed surprised, even shocked. I think she'd somehow convinced herself I didn't look like this shining thing. She recovered quickly, because she is, beyond all else, the ultimate court politician. She can school her face to whatever whim of the king without mussing an eyelash.

'Daughter, how good to see you.'

'Princess Besaba, the Bride of Peace, greetings.' I had deliberately omitted our blood ties. The only mother I'd ever truly had was Gran, my mother's mother. She, I would have welcomed; the woman sitting in the silk-draped chair was a stranger to me, and always had been.

She look startled and didn't quite recover her expression, but her words were pleasant enough.

'Princess Meredith NicEssus, greetings from the Seelie Court.'

I had to smile. She'd insulted me in turn. NicEssus meant daughter of Essus. Most sidhe lost such a last name at puberty, or at least in their twenties, when their magical powers manifested. Since mine had not manifested in my twenties, I'd been NicEssus into my thirties. But the courts knew that my powers had come at long last. They knew I had a new title. She'd forgotten on purpose.

Fine. Besides, I'd been rude first. 'I will always be my father's daughter, but I am no longer NicEssus.' I put a pensive look on my face. 'Has the king, my uncle, not told you that my hand of power has manifested?'

'Of course he told me,' she said, sounding defensive and contrite all at the same time.

'Oh, I'm sorry. Since you did not use my new title, I assumed you did not know.'

She let the anger show on that lovely, careful face for an instant, then smiled, a smile as sincere as her love for me. 'I know that you are now Princess of Flesh. Congratulations.'

'Why, thank you, Mother.'

She shifted in the small chair, as if I'd surprised her again. 'Well, daughter, we should not let it be so long between talks.'

'Of course not,' I said, and kept my face pleasant and unreadable.

'I have heard that you are invited to this year's Yule ball.'

'Yes.'

'I look forward to seeing you there, and renewing our acquaintance.'

349

'I am surprised that you have not also heard that I had to decline the invitation.'

'I had heard and find it hard to credit.' Her hands stayed gracefully poised on the arms of the chair, but her body leaned forward just a bit, spoiling that perfect posture. 'There are many who would do much to be so honored with an invitation.'

'Yes, but you do know that I am now heir of the Unseelie Court, do you not, Mother?'

She sat up straight again and shook her head. I wondered if all that gold leaf on her hair was heavy. 'You are coheir, not true heir. Your cousin is still true heir to that throne.'

I sighed and stopped trying to look pleasant, settling for neutral. 'I'm surprised, Mother. You are usually better informed.'

'I don't know what you mean,' she said.

'Queen Andais has made Prince Cel and me equals. It remains only to see which of us produces a child first. If I take after you, Mother, it will surely be me.'

'The king is most eager that you attend our ball.'

'Are you listening to me, Mother? I am heir to the Unseelie throne. If I travel home for any Yule celebrations, it must be the Unseelie ball.'

She made a small movement with her hands, then seemed to remember her poise, and placed them carefully back on the arms of the chair. 'You could be back in the king's good graces if you but come to our ball, Meredith. You could be welcome at court again.'

'I am already welcome at court, Mother. And how can I be back in the king's good graces, when to my knowledge I've never been in his good graces to begin with?'

She again waved that away, and even forgot to place her hands back on the chair. She was more agitated than she appeared, to forget and talk with her hands. She'd always hated the fact that she spoke with her hands; she thought it was a common thing to do.

'You could come back to the Seelie Court, Meredith. Think about it, truly a Seelie princess at last.'

'I am heir to a throne, Mother. Why should I want to rejoin a court where I am fifth from the throne, when I can rule another?'

She waved it away. 'You cannot compare being part of the Seelie Court to anything having to do with the Unseelie Court, Meredith.'

I looked at her, so carefully beautiful, so stubbornly biased. 'Are you saying it would be better to be the least of all the royals at the Seelie Court, instead of ruler of the Unseelie Court?'

'Are you implying that it is better to rule in hell than be in heaven?' she asked, almost laughing.

'I have spent time at both courts, Mother. There is not a great deal to choose between the two.'

'How can you say that to me, Meredith? I have done my time at the dark court, and I know how hideous it is.'

'I have spent my time in the shining court, and I know that my blood is just as red on shining gold-laced marble as it is on black.'

She frowned, looked confused. 'I don't know what you mean.'

'If Gran had not interceded for me, would you really have let Taranis beat me to death? Beat your own daughter to death in front of your eyes?'

'That is a hateful thing to say, Meredith.'

'Just answer the question, Mother.'

'You had asked a very impertinent question of the king, and that is not a wise thing to do.'

I had my answer, the answer I'd always known. I moved on. 'Why is it so important to you that I attend this ball?'

'The king wishes it,' she said. And she, like me, moved on from the earlier, more painful questions.

'I will not insult Queen Andais and all my people by snubbing their Yule celebration. If I come home, it will be for their Yule ball. Surely you see that that is the way it has to be.'

'I see nothing but that you have not changed. You are still as willful and determined to be difficult as always.'

'And you have not changed either, Mother. What did the king offer you to persuade me to come to his ball?'

'I don't know what you mean.'

'Yes, you do. It's not enough for you to have the title of princess. You want what goes with the title, power. What did the king offer you?'

'That is between him and me, unless you come to the ball. Come, and I will tell you.'

I shook my head. 'Poor bait that, Mother, very poor bait.'

'What is that supposed to mean?' She was very angry and made no attempt to hide it, which, from a social climber of her stature, was the supreme insult. I wasn't worth hiding her anger from. I was perhaps one of the very few sidhe whom she would have so insulted. Her own sister was someone she tiptoed around.

'It means, dear Mother, that I will not be attending the Seelie Yule ball.' I motioned to Doyle, and he cut the transmission abruptly, leaving my mother in midword as she faded.

The mirror rang almost immediately with that bell sound, that clarion of trumpets, but we knew who it was now, and we weren't home to her.

Chapter 33

DAME ROSMERTA CALLED EARLY THE NEXT morning, early enough that we were still abed. The sound of tiny bells woke me, tinkling into the still shadowed room. The smell of roses was almost overwhelming, and that was Rosmerta's calling card. Apparently she'd been trying to wake us for some time and finally resorted to the tiny bells and the scent of roses.

I tried to sit up, but was so tangled in Nicca's long hair and Rhys's arms that I couldn't manage it. Rhys opened his good eye and blinked blearily at me. 'What time is it?'

'Early,' I said.

'How early?'

'If you'd move your arm, I'd be able to see the clock and tell you.'

'Oh, sorry,' he muttered into the deep purple sheets. He moved his arm.

I sat up and looked at the clock. 'Eight.'

'Sweet Consort, what could be so important?'

Nicca propped himself up on his elbow, trying to sweep his hair behind his back and failing because Rhys and I were still sitting on it. I loved the feel of all that hair draping over my body, but I was beginning to remember why I never let mine grow quite so long.

Rhys and I moved around enough for Nicca to retrieve his hair. He didn't so much sweep it behind his back as lay it down the side of his body like a slightly tangled cloak.

Rhys turned onto his back – not to flaunt himself, though he accomplished that, but because he wanted to be able to see the mirror with his good eye.

Nicca stayed propped on his elbow behind me. I sat up in the middle of the two of them. I managed to tug enough sheets out from under everyone so that I was fairly covered. Nudity was casual in the Unseelie Court, but not always in the Seelie Court. Human vanity had been more contagious there. The three of us were placed to receive when Rhys and I realized at the same time that someone had to touch the mirror.

'Shit,' he said, then he rolled off the bed touched the mirror, and rolled back into bed very fast, as if we had posed for a picture with the camera set on automatic. When he rolled back onto the sheets, the weight of his body tore the sheet out of my hand and down to my lap. Rhys realized that he now was on top of the covers, not underneath them. We both had a second to choose whether we were going to be struggling with the sheets when the mirror flashed to life, or be calmly posed. We both chose to look comfortable, not harried. Rhys lay full length in front of me, one arm behind his head, the picture of muscular ease. I leaned back against Nicca as if he were a chair back. He curled himself around me from the back, so that his body both cupped and framed me. He had managed to keep just enough cover over his groin so that he was covered.

Dame Rosmerta appeared in the mirror. She was dressed in silk and stiff embroidery, a slightly darker shade of pink today, almost fuchsia. Her dark yellow braids were entwined with pink ribbon that matched her dress exactly. She was all pink and gold and perfect like a doll. Her tricolored gold eyes were bright and clear, as if she'd been up for hours.

Her smile slipped a fraction as she got a good look at us. She opened her mouth, said nothing.

I helped her. 'Is there something you wanted, Dame Rosmerta?'

'Ah, yes, yes.' She gathered herself visibly, remembering her duty. It seemed to steady her. 'King Taranis would like to invite you to a feast in your honor a few days before Yule. We are very sorry for the misunderstanding about the Yule ball. We understand completely that you must, of course, attend the festivities at your own court.' She smiled and it was just the right amount of *silly ol' us, but we've fixed it now*. It might even have been sincere.

I was tired. Nicca and Rhys had begun to routinely share their nights with me. I think it was purely so that they both got two nights in a row, rather than one having any preference over the other; but it meant that my night had been very busy. Since we didn't have to go to work we hadn't worried about the late hours. Now here was Rosmerta looking daisy fresh at eight in the morning. It was discouraging.

Why was the king so insistent on seeing me

before Yule? Was it about Maeve? Something else? Why did he want to see me now? He'd never given a damn about seeing me before.

'Dame Rosmerta,' I said, and tried not to sound as tired as I felt, 'I need to be blunt here, which I know isn't polite, but I need some questions answered before I say yes or no to the feast.'

'Of course, Princess,' she said, making a slight bow as she said my title.

'Why is my presence so important to the king that he would give a feast in my honor days before Yule? The entire court has been working and planning for the ball for months. The servants and the functionaries must be frantic at the thought of a feast only days before the great event. Why would the king need to see me so badly before Yule?'

Her smile never changed, never wavered. 'For that you would have to ask the king himself.'

'That would be lovely,' I said, 'if you would be so kind as to put him on.'

That threw her; confusion chased across her pretty face. I think most people would have just accepted that you didn't get to talk directly to the king, but too many important things were afoot to be that polite.

Rosmerta recovered, not as quickly as you'd have thought, but finally said, 'I will ask His Majesty if he could speak with you. His schedule is very full, though, so I can make no promises.'

'I wouldn't ask you to make a promise on Taranis's part, Dame Rosmerta. And I'm sure his schedule is very full; but I really do need the question answered. I cannot possibly agree to the feast without an answer, and I think getting the answer directly from the king should speed things up considerably.' I smiled as I spoke, mirroring her own pleasant, nearly professional smile.

'I will give him the message. He may contact you rather quickly, so may I humbly suggest that you take this time to dress and present yourself in a manner more befitting your station.' She smiled while she said it, but there was a tightness around her eyes that said she wasn't sure she should have said anything. Or maybe my thoughts were showing on my face while she was speaking.

'I think that I will present myself to the king as I see fit, Rosmerta.' I'd left off the *Dame* deliberately. She was a minor noblewoman, and I outranked her. That I gave her the courtesy of her title was just that, a courtesy. I didn't have to do it.

'I meant no disrespect, Princess Meredith.' She wasn't smiling now. Her face had closed down into that icy beauty that the sidhe are so capable of.

I ignored it, because to say almost anything was to accuse her of lying. Maybe she hadn't meant to be disrespectful; maybe she just couldn't help herself. 'As that may be, Dame Rosmerta, as that may be. I look forward to hearing from the king. Do you think he will call back before we have time to rise for the day?'

'I did not realize that I had woken you, Princess, I am most humbly sorry.' She looked it. 'I will make sure that you are given time to rise and do your morning . . . duties.' She actually blushed a little, and I wondered what word she'd thought of before *duties* or exactly what she thought my morning duties were.

I realized suddenly that Rosmerta had thought

we were having sex, not waking up. Andais did answer the Seelie in flagrante delicto more often than not, or nearly so. Maybe they expected the same of me.

'I thank you for the time, Dame Rosmerta. It is most unseemly to be roused from your early morning bed to speak with a king.'

She smiled and gave me a very pretty curtsy, almost disappearing below the mirror's edge. Rosmerta was the picture of absolute propriety. A deep curtsy from her was high praise indeed, for it meant she understood I was but a step away from the throne. It was nice to know that someone in the Seelie Court understood that.

She didn't rise, and I realized, a little late, why. 'You may rise, Dame Rosmerta, and I thank you.'

She came to her feet, a little unsteady, but I'd left her in a deep curtsy for too long. I hadn't meant to, I just had forgotten that the Seelie Court was a lot like the English court; once you curtsied you really couldn't rise until acknowledged by the royal before you. It had been a very long time since I was among the Seelie. I was going to be a little rusty on court protocol. The Unseelie Court was much less formal.

'I will speak with His Majesty on your behalf, Princess Meredith. Good day to you.'

'And good day to you, as well, Dame Rosmerta.'

The mirror went blank. I felt all three of us relax, let out a breath.

Rhys put both his hands behind his head, crossed his ankles, and said, 'What do you think? Maybe a little jewelry so we'll be more formal?'

I gazed down the length of his body, remembering the feel of my tongue running over his firm stomach, sliding lower. I had to close my eyes and evict the thought before I could answer.

'No, Rhys, I think clothes first. We'll worry about accessorizing later.'

He grinned up at me. 'Oh, I don't know, Merry. Aren't you the least bit tempted to have all of us on the bed when he calls? You, draped in bodies.'

I started to say no. Then realized it was a lie. 'A little tempted, yes, but we're going to behave ourselves, Rhys.'

His grin widened. 'If you insist.'

'You're the one that's always going on about, *ooh, the King of Light and Illusion*. Why the change of heart now?'

'He's still scary, Merry, but he's also a terrible stuffed shirt. He wasn't always like that, but somewhere over the centuries he became more ... human, in the worst sense of the word.' The grin faded around the edges.

'What's wrong?' I asked.

'Just thinking about what might have been. Taranis used to be good for a few laughs, and a drunken brawl or two.'

I raised eyebrows. 'Taranis? Having a boys' night out on the town? I can't picture it.'

'You've known him for only thirty years. He hasn't been at his best.' He sat up, got to his feet. 'Dibs on the shower.'

'If you get it first this morning, I get it first tomorrow,' Nicca said.

'Only if you're fast enough,' Rhys said, heading for the bathroom.

Nicca's arms slid around my waist, turned me to

him. 'Let him have his shower.' He raised a slender brown hand to trace the waves near my face. He rolled over on his back, drawing me with his hands at my neck and waist. The sheet had rolled off him, and I saw that he was firm and ripe again.

I half laughed. 'Don't you ever grow tired?'

'Of this, never.' His face grew more serious, a little less tender. 'This with you is the first time I have ever been with a woman and not been afraid.'

'What do you mean?'

'The queen is a fearsome thing, Meredith, and she likes her men submissive. I'm not dominant, but I don't enjoy her idea of sex.'

I leaned in and gave him a very gentle kiss. 'We do some rough stuff.'

He suddenly hugged me to him. 'No, Meredith, no, you don't. You never scare me.' He held me, and I relaxed against him, let him hold me. Almost too tight. It almost hurt.

I stroked his sides and what I could reach of his back, until he began to relax. His arms were not quite so crushing. I'd thought only days ago about sending Nicca back home, because I did not want him to be king. He wasn't able to be king, and it had nothing to do with whether or not he could breed.

I held him, stroked him gently, until the sudden panic in him eased. When he was calm, he reached for me again, and I went to his arms, his mouth, his body. I hoped King Taranis wouldn't call while we were in the midst of things, but the love-making took the last wounded look from his eyes. I needed to see those brown eyes turned to me with nothing but smiles in them.

361

When Rhys stepped out of the bathroom with his towels, we were just finishing. He cursed under his breath. 'Is it too late to join in?'

'Yes,' I said, and gave Nicca a last parting kiss. 'Besides, I get the shower next.' I scrambled out of bed and went for the bathroom before Nicca could protest. I left them laughing, and I left the room laughing myself. What better way is there to begin a day?

Chapter 34

THAT AFTERNOON MAEVE AND GORDON REED
showed up at our door. It had been only days, but
Gordon looked like it had been years. His skin
had gone from sallow to grey. He seemed to have
lost weight, so that the strong bones that had once
made him a tall, commanding figure now made
him look like a large-boned skeleton, covered in
paper-thin greyness. His eyes looked larger in his
face, and the pain in them looked constant. It was
as if the cancer were sucking him dry, eating him
from the inside out.

Maeve had said on the phone that Gordon was
worse, much worse, but she hadn't prepared us for
this. No mere words could prepare you for watching a man die.

Frost and Rhys had met their car on the
street so they could help her husband up the short
flight of steps to our apartment. Maeve had
followed them up with huge sunglasses hiding
most of her face, and a silk scarf around all that
blond hair. She held an ankle-length fur coat
tight at her throat as if it were cold. She looked
like a Hollywood imitation of a great movie star.

363

Of course, who had a better right to the look?

The men helped Gordon into the bedroom so he could rest while we did the first part of the fertility rite. Maeve was apparently going to pace the living room while she waited. She'd almost lit up a cigarette before I could tell her no smoking in my home.

'Meredith, please, I need it.'

'Then you can do it outside.'

She lowered her sunglasses enough to show me those famous blue eyes. She was wearing her human glamour again, trying to look as un-sidhe as possible. She kept that blue stare on me as she flung open the coat to frame that long golden body. She was nude except for her boots.

'Do I look dressed for your neighbors' viewing?'

I shook my head. 'Your glamour is good enough to hide you buck naked in the middle of a highway, so close the coat, and take your nerves and your cigarettes outside.'

She let the coat fall closed, leaving a thin line of her body showing between the soft mounds of fur. 'How can you be so cruel?'

'This isn't cruel, Maeve, and well you know it. You spent too many centuries around the courts to think I'm being cruel just because I don't want your cigarettes stinking up my apartment.'

She actually pouted at me. I'd had enough. 'When I come back inside heavy with magic, I want to find Conchenn, goddess of beauty and spring, not some spoiled star. No glamour either. I want to see those lightning-kissed eyes.'

She opened her mouth – to protest, I think. I stopped it with a wave of my hand. 'Save it, Maeve, and do what you need to do to help this work.'

She pushed her sunglasses back over her eyes and said in a much smaller voice, 'You've changed, Meredith. There's a hardness in you that wasn't there before.'

'Not hardness,' Doyle said, 'command. She will be queen and she understands that now.'

Maeve glanced from him to me. Fine, what's with the bikini? I thought you were going to fuck, not go to the beach.'

'I know you're angry and scared about your husband, and that cuts you some slack, but there's a limit to that slack, Maeve. Don't push it.'

She lowered her head, still fingering the unlit cigarette and unused lighter. 'I don't mean to be such a fucking prima donna, but I am desperately worried about Gordon. Can't you understand that?'

'I understand, but if I wasn't having to sit here and argue with you, I could already be at the ritual site preparing myself.'

I turned my back very deliberately on her, hoping she'd take the hint. 'Doyle, you've extended the wards to include the little garden area in the house behind us, as I requested?'

'Yes, Princess, I have.'

I took a deep breath. Here was the moment that I had been dreading. I had to choose one of the men to act as my consort for the ritual, but who? I don't know what I would have decided, because Galen said, voice clear but uncertain, 'I'm whole again, Merry.'

Everyone but Maeve turned to stare at him. He looked a little uncomfortable under the scrutiny, but there was also a pleased smile on his face, and a look in his eyes that I hadn't seen in a long time.

'I don't mean to dampen the mood,' Rhys said, 'but how do we know he's cured? Maeve and Gordon may not get another shot at this.'

Doyle interrupted. 'If Galen says that he is healed enough for this ritual, I for one believe him.'

I looked at Doyle. His face was its usual dark mask, unreadable. He rarely spoke unless he was certain of something.

'How can you be certain?' Frost asked.

'Meredith needs a consort to her goddess. Who better than the green man whose life has only recently returned to him?'

I knew that the green man was sometimes a nickname for the Goddess's Consort, sometimes a name for the generic forest god. I looked at Galen. He certainly was the green man.

'If Doyle thinks it's all right, then let it be Galen.'

I don't think Frost was happy with the choice, but everyone else took it in their stride, and Frost kept his mouth shut. Sometimes that's all you can ask of a man, or anyone else.

Chapter 35

I NEEDED TO BE ALONE TO PREPARE MYSELF FOR the ritual. Doyle hadn't liked me being on my own for even a little while, but we'd extended the house wards across the back wall to the small neglected garden of the house behind us. Neglected was good in this case because it meant that no pesticides or herbicides had been used in a very long time. We'd put up a ritual circle earlier in the day. I opened a doorway in that circle, stepped through, and closed it behind me. Now I stood not just in the wards of the house but in a circle of protection. Nothing magical could cross this circle, nothing less than a deity or the Nameless itself. The hungry ones that were slaughtering people would have been stopped by it; they weren't deities yet.

The yard had been planted within an inch of its life like most yards in Southern California. It was an abandoned lemon tree grove, now. The small trees were covered in dark green leaves. It was too late in the season for blossoms. I mourned that. But the moment I walked between the close crowding trees and the dry, crumbling grass and leaves underfoot, I knew this was it. The trees whispered among themselves like elderly ladies talking of the past softly with their heads close together in the warm, warm sun. The eucalyptus that lined the street just outside the garden wall was a heavy spicy scent that rode the air to mingle with the smell of the warm lemon trees.

A large cotton blanket lay on the ground, waiting. Maeve had offered to bring silk sheets, but all we needed was something of the earth, animal or vegetable. Something thick enough to cover the unyielding ground but not thick enough to separate us from it. We still needed to be able to feel the earth under our bodies.

I lay down on the blanket as if I was going to sunbathe. I pressed myself to the blanket, arms and legs wide, letting myself sink into the soft fuzz of the blanket, then past it to the coverings of the grass, leaves, and sticks, a covering of small sharp things, and farther still to the hard-packed earth beneath. There was water here or the lemon trees would have withered and died, but the ground seemed bone dry as if it never felt the touch of rain.

Wind caressed my body, drew me back. The wind played against my skin, rustled the dry leaves and weeds outside the edge of the blanket. The leaves whispered and shushed together. The smell of eucalyptus coated everything with its warm, pine-wood scent.

I rolled onto my back so I could watch the trees moving in the wind, feel the heat of the sun on the front of my body. I don't know if I heard a noise or just felt him standing there. I turned my head, my cheek lying on a bed of my own hair, and there he was.

Galen stood lost in the tossing green of the leaves and the small whispering trees. His hair lifted in a halo of green curls around his face. That one thin braid that was all that was left of his long, long hair trailed over his bare chest.

As he stepped out of the trees I could see that he wore nothing. His skin was a flawless white with a shade of green to it like the gleaming underside of a seashell. His waist looked longer without clothes, a slender expanse of flesh and bone leading up to the swell of his shoulders, and down to the slenderness of his hips. He was bigger than I'd thought he would be, longer, thick, growing as I watched, as if he felt my gaze travel down his body. His legs were long and muscled as he moved toward me.

I think I stopped breathing for a second or two. I hadn't really believed that he would come. I had grown tired of hoping. Now, here he was.

I raised my eyes to his face and found his smile. Galen's smile, the one that had made my heart skip a beat since I was old enough to care. I sat up on the blanket, holding my hand out to him. I wanted to run to him, but I was afraid to move out of the circle of trees and wind and ground. Afraid almost to look away from him because if I blinked, he would seep away into the trees like a summer dream.

He stood at the blanket's edge just out of reach and slowly lifted his hand toward mine until our fingers brushed, and that small touch sent a fluttering like a cloud of butterflies inside my body. It drew a sigh from my lips. Galen dropped to his knees on the blanket, hands at his sides, making no effort to touch me again.

I came up on my knees to mirror him. We knelt staring at each other, so close that we almost didn't need hands to touch. His hand raised slowly and hovered over the bare skin of my shoulder. I could feel his aura, his power, like a warm breath coming from his body. His hand skated across the trembling energy of my own aura, and those two separate warmths flared, reaching for each other. I'd feared that it would be hard to raise the magic, but I'd forgotten. I'd forgotten what it truly meant to be fey, to be sidhe. We were magic, as the earth and the trees were magic. We burned with the same invisible flame that bound the world together. That warm flame swelled between us, filled the air around us with a shimmering, beating energy like the sound of wings.

We kissed through that rising energy. It flowed between our mouths as he bent over me, and I raised my face to meet his lips. He was velvet warmth against my mouth, inside my mouth as his power spilled down my throat inside my body. When we'd shared Niceven's power it had been sharp, hot, almost painful. This was so much more, gentle warmth, the first breath of spring after a long winter.

His hands found my body, spilling my breasts bare to the wind. He drew his lips back from mine and lowered his face to my breasts, taking first one then the other into his mouth, rolling the nipples in the warmth, spilling power. His hands cupped my breasts, fingers tightening, until I cried out. His hands slid down my back to my hips, fingers catching the edge of the bikini bottoms, sliding them down my thighs, stopped at my knees, trapped. He rolled me onto my back and slid the last bit of clothing away.

I lay naked before him for the first time with the wind spilling over my body, spilling over his body. He was propped up on one arm, the long naked line of his body so close to mine. I ran my hand down his chest, down his stomach, his waist, and finally touched the warmth of him. I cupped him in my hands, holding him solid and warm, and he shuddered, eyes closing. When he opened them his green eyes were full of a dark light, a dark knowledge that stopped my breath and made things low in my body tighten. I squeezed gently, caressed him, and his spine bowed with it, head thrown back so far I couldn't tell if his eyes were open or closed.

I moved down while he was staring up at the sky, as my hand fondled him. I rolled him into my mouth in a sudden complete movement that brought a deep sound from his throat. I rolled my eyes so I could see his face when he turned from the sky and looked down at me. His lips half parted, his face almost wild. His breath came in quick gasps that started in his stomach, spilled to his chest, and came out his lips in a word. He breathed my name like a prayer and touched my shoulders. He shook his head. 'I won't last long.'

I lifted my mouth from his body, pushed him onto his back. I knelt over his legs and stared down at him. I'd wanted this for so long. I caressed his body with just my gaze, memorizing the way the color of his skin went from white to a pale spring green, the darkness of his nipples, tight against his chest. I rubbed my hand down the front of his body, feeling the skin like brushed velvet or suede, and still there was no word for

371

how soft the skin, how hard and firm the flesh. But it wasn't just his flesh I'd been wanting all these years. It was his magic.

I called my power like a breathing warmth from my skin, and his aura raised like a warm sea and spilled into my power. Our magic flowed together like two currents of an ocean, mingling, drowning together.

I moved my body over his, taking him slowly inside me a tight inch at a time, until he was sheathed inside me. He whispered my name, and I bent over him until we kissed, kissed with the feel of him inside me, our bodies pressed in the most intimate of embraces.

The wind blew against my back like a cool hand. It raised me up, until I was sitting looking down at him. I could feel the trees again. Hear them whispering to one another, whispering to me of dark secrets locked deep underground, and I could feel the ground underneath us. I could feel the earth turning in a ponderous dance under Galen's body.

We became a part of that dance. Our bodies locked together, my hips moving back and forth, his hips raising up and down so that we formed a double rhythm that fed on each movement until I felt his body swell tight and firm and I squeezed him tight inside my body, holding him, holding him with hands, mouth, every part of me, as if he would vanish if I did not hold on tight. The warmth swelled between my legs rising up in a wave of heat that spilled up my body until it felt as if my skin let loose, and I flowed away into the wind and the whispering trees. The only thing that kept me anchored to the earth was the hard, hot point of Galen's body. I felt him slip his skin, felt his power spill outward, and for one shining moment we were neither flesh nor blood nor real. We were the wind, the trees as they tugged at their roots like anchored kites, thinking both of deep earth and sunlight. We were the sweet evergreen smell of eucalyptus, and the thick warm scent of sunburned grass. When I could no longer feel my body and could barely remember who I'd been, I began to spill back into myself My body re-formed and Galen was still inside me. His body re-formed underneath me, and we were left gasping for air, laughing into each other's arms. I slid off his body to lie beside him in the circle of his arms, my cheek pressed to his chest so that I could hear the fast, sure beat of his heart.

When we could walk, we got to our feet and walked back the way we had come to find Maeve Reed and her husband and give them the magic that we had found.

Chapter 36

IT WAS CONCHENN IN ALL HER GLORY WHO WAITED
in my bedroom for her magic kiss. Gordon Reed
seemed even more like a grey skeleton beside her
glowing presence. The pain in his face as he gazed
upon her was horrible to see. Even through the
pulsing glow of the magic we held inside us,
Gordon's pain was visible. I could not heal his illness, but I hoped to ease his pain.

'You smell of wilderness,' Conchenn said. 'The
heart of the earth beats through you, Meredith. I
can see it like a green glow behind my eyelids.' She
began to cry crystal tears, as if her tears should
have been able to be held and set in silver and
gold. 'Your green man smells of sky and wind
and sunlight. He glows yellow inside my head.'
She sat on the edge of the bed as if her legs
couldn't hold her anymore. 'Earth and sky you
bring us, mother and father you bring us, goddess
and god you bring us.'

I wanted to say, *don't thank us yet; we haven't
given you a child yet*. But I didn't say it, because I
could feel the magic inside my body, could feel it
in Galen as he held my hand. It was the raw

power of life itself, the age-old dance of earth planted with seed bringing forth fruit. It could not be truly stopped, this cycle, because if it stopped, life itself would stop.

Maeve moved to sit beside Gordon and held one of his thin hands in both her shining ones. Galen and I stood in front of them. I moved to kneel by Gordon, as Galen moved closer to Maeve. We kissed them at the same time, our lips touching theirs like the last movement to some perfect dance. The power jumped from us to them in a rush that raised the hairs on our bodies and filled the room with that close hush like a lightning bolt ready to strike. The room was suddenly so full of magic that it was hard to breathe.

Galen and I moved back, and now I could see behind my own eyes that they both glowed, filled with earth fire and the gold of the sun. Maeve was already moving to kiss her husband's thin lips when we left them to it, closing the door quietly behind us. We felt the moment of release like a wind that poured from under the door and touched us all.

Doyle spoke into the sudden silence of us all. 'You have succeeded, Meredith.'

'You don't know that for certain,' I said.

He looked at me, just looked at me as if what I'd said had been ridiculous.

'Doyle is right,' Frost said. 'Such power will not fail.'

'If I have such fertility power, then why aren't I pregnant yet?'

There was a second silence, not awestruck this time, but awkward. 'I do not know,' Doyle said at last.

'We have to try harder, that's all,' Rhys said.

Galen nodded solemnly. 'More sex, we must have more sex.'

I frowned at both of them, but couldn't keep it up. Finally I laughed. 'We have more sex and I won't be able to walk.'

'We'll carry you everywhere,' Rhys said.

'Yes,' Frost said.

I looked at all of them slowly. I was pretty sure they were kidding, pretty sure.

Chapter 37

WE WERE FINISHING LUNCH THE NEXT DAY WHEN Taranis called back. I bolted the last of my fruit salad and fresh bread while Doyle spoke with him. Maeve was pregnant; the magic had quickened inside her. Taranis couldn't know that yet, but I feared what he would do when he found out. It added one more little stress to dealing with the king.

I'd chosen a royal purple sundress with a scoop neck and one of those little ties in back. It was very feminine, very nonthreatening, and a style that had been in vogue for a very long time. The only thing that had changed was the hem length. Sometimes when dealing with the Seelie Court, you wanted to go slow into the twenty-first century.

I sat on the freshly made bed, and it wasn't accidental that the purple of my dress complemented the burgundy bedspread and matched the purple pillows scattered among the burgundy and black ones.

I had refreshed the red lipstick and left the rest alone. We were going for dramatic natural. I had my ankles crossed, even though he couldn't see them, and my hands folded in my lap. It wasn't formal, but it was about the best I could do without a formal answering room.

Doyle stood on one side and Frost on the other. Doyle wore his usual black jeans, black T-shirt. He'd added black boots that reached to his thighs, then folded them down to just above his knees. He'd even pulled the spider necklace out of his shirt so that it gleamed in plain sight on his black shirt. The spider was part of his livery, his crest, and I'd once seen him cause the skin of a human magician's body to split as the spiders depicted in the jewels poured out of the man until he'd become nothing but a writhing mass of them. The unfortunate victim had been the man Lieutenant Peterson thought I had killed.

Frost had gone more traditional, dressed in a thigh-length tunic of white, edged with silver, white, and gold embroidery. Tiny flowers and vines were sewn in such detail that you could tell the vines were ivy and roses, with some harebells and violas embroidered around them. A broad belt of white leather, with a silver buckle, fastened at the tunic's waist. His sword, Winter Kiss, Geamhradh Pòg, hung at his side. He left the enchanted blade at home most days because it couldn't stop modern bullets; it didn't possess that kind of magic. But for an audience with the king, the sword was perfect. Its handle was carved bone, inset with silver. The bone had a patina like old ivory, rich and warm, like pale wood polished from all the centuries of being handled.

They both did their best to stand to one side and not overwhelm me physically, but it was hard work. Even if I'd been standing up, it would have been hard work; sitting down it was nearly impossible, but we were trying to have me seem friendly. They would do the unfriendly parts if it needed doing. It was a sort of good cop, bad cop, but for politics.

Taranis, King of Light and Illusion, sat on a golden throne. He was clothed in light. His undertunic was the movement of sunlight through leaves, soft dappled light, with pinpoints of bright yellow sunlight, like tiny starbursts appearing through the light and shadow. The overtunic was the bright, almost blinding yellow of full summer sunlight on bright leaves. It was both green and gold, and neither. It was light, not cloth, and the color changed and moved as he moved. Even the rise and fall of his breathing made it dance and flow.

His hair fell in waves of golden light around a face that was so bright with light that only his eyes shone out of the dazzlement. Those eyes were three circles of brilliant, livid blue, like three circles of three different oceans, each drowning in sunlight, each a different shade of blue; but like the water they were borrowed from, they changed and shifted as if unseen currents boiled within.

So much of him moved, and not in complementary ways. It was like looking at different kinds of light on different days in different parts of the world but having them be forced together. Taranis was a collage of illumination that flashed and flowed and fluttered, and never in the same direction. I had to close my eyes. It was dizzying. I felt I'd grow sick if I looked at it long enough. I wondered if Doyle or Frost were feeling a little motion sick, or if it was just me.

But that wasn't something I could ask aloud in front of the king. Aloud I said, 'King Taranis, my part-mortal eyes cannot behold your splendor without feeling quite overwhelmed. I would beg you lessen your glory so that I might look upon you without growing faint.'

His voice came in a rush of music, as if he was singing some wondrous song, but he was only speaking. In my head, I knew it wasn't the most beautiful sound I'd ever heard, but my ears heard something beyond beguiling. 'Whatever you need to make this conversation pleasant will be given to you. Behold, I am more easy upon mortal eyes.'

I opened my eyes cautiously. He was still as bright, but the light didn't move and flow so rapidly. It was as if he'd slowed down the play of light, and his face was not quite as dazzling. I could see more of the outline of his jaw, but there was still no hint of the beard that I knew he wore. His golden waves were more solid, less radiant. I knew what color his hair was, and this wasn't it. But at least it didn't make my head spin to look at him anymore.

Well, except for the eyes. He'd kept his eyes that swimming blue play of light and water. I smiled, and asked, 'Where are those beautiful green eyes that I remember from childhood? I had looked forward to seeing them again. Or has my memory deceived me and it is some other sidhe's eyes that I thought were yours? These eyes were the green of emeralds, the green of summer leaves, the green of deep, still water in a shaded pool.'

The men had given me tips on dealing with

Taranis, from centuries of doing it themselves and seeing the queen do it. Tip number one had been: You never went wrong flattering Taranis; if it was sweet to the ears, he tended to believe it. Especially if a woman said it.

He gave a musical chuckle, and his eyes were suddenly just as lovely as I remembered them from childhood. It was as if the huge iris of his eye was a flower with many, many petals, each one green, but different shades of green, some edged with white, some with black. Until I'd seen Maeve Reed's true eyes, I'd thought that Taranis's eyes were the prettiest sidhe eyes I'd ever seen.

I was able to give him a true smile. 'Yes, your eyes are as beautiful as I remember them.'

He finally appeared as a being formed of golden light with brighter gold hair in waves around his shoulders. His green eyes seemed almost to float atop that golden light like flowers riding on water. The eyes were real, as extraordinary as they were, but the rest was not. If you had tried to take a photo of him now, you'd have gotten those eyes and just a blur. Modern cameras don't like that much magic being pointed in their direction.

'Greetings, Princess Meredith, Princess of Flesh, or so I hear. Congratulations. It is a truly frightening power. It will make the sidhe of the Unseelie Court think more than twice about challenging you to a duel.' His voice had calmed to an almost normal, though lovely sound.

'It is good to be protected at last.'

I think he frowned. It was difficult to tell through all the glory in his face. 'I sorrow that you had such a dangerous time of it in the dark court.

I assure you that at the Seelie Court you would not find life so difficult.'

I blinked, and fought to keep my face pleasant. I remembered what life at the Seelie Court had been for me, and difficult didn't begin to sum it up. I had been quiet too long, because the king said, 'If you would come to our feast in your honor, I can guarantee that you will find it pleasant and most fair.'

I took a deep breath, let it out, smiled. 'I am most honored at the invitation, King Taranis. A feast in my honor at the Seelie Court is a most unexpected surprise.'

'A pleasant one, I hope,' and he laughed, and the laugh was again that ringing joyous sound. I had to smile when I heard it. The sound even pulled a laugh from my own lips.

'Oh, most pleasant, Your Highness.' I meant it when I said it. Of course it was pleasant to be invited by this glowing man with the extraordinary eyes to a feast in my honor among the beautiful, shining court. Nothing could be better than that.

I closed my eyes and took in a deep breath, then held it for a few heartbeats, while Taranis kept talking in a progressively more beautiful voice. I concentrated on my breathing, not his voice. I felt my breath, the ebb and flow of my body. I concentrated on just drawing air in and letting it out, on controlling it, feeling my body pull it inside me, then holding it until it was almost painful not to exhale, finally letting the air trickle slowly out.

I heard Doyle's voice moving smoothly into the silence I'd left. I caught pieces of it as I performed the breathing exercise and began to be aware of what was outside my own body again.

'The princess is overawed by your presence, King Taranis. She is, after all, a relative child. It is difficult to face such power unaffected.'

Doyle had been the one who warned me that Taranis was so good at personal glamour that he used it routinely against other sidhe. And no one told him it was illegal, because he was the king and most feared him. Feared him too much to point out that he was cheating. It had been Doyle's warning that had prepared me to do the breathing exercise rather than try to be brave and tough it out. I'd spend most of my life around beings that had better persuading glamour than I did, so I'd learned how to break free of it. Sometimes it required me to do things that were noticeable, like the breathing. Most sidhe would rather have been bespelled than show just how hard they found it to withstand another sidhe's power. I had never been able to afford that kind of pride.

I opened my eyes slowly, blinking until I felt myself slide more firmly into the here and now. I smiled. 'My apologies, King Taranis, but Doyle is correct. I am a touch overwhelmed by your glowing presence'.

He smiled. 'My most sincere apologies, Meredith. I do not mean to cause you discomfort.'

He probably didn't, but he wanted me to come to his little party. He wanted that badly enough to try to 'persuade' me magically.

I wanted so badly to simply ask why it was so important that I come to his little soiree. But Taranis knew exactly who had raised me, and no one ever accused my father of being less than polite. Direct sometimes, but always polite. I couldn't pretend to be an ignorant human, as I had with Maeve Reed. He'd know better. The problem was, without direct questions, I wasn't sure how to learn what I needed to know.

But it didn't matter. The king was far too busy trying to bewitch me to worry about anything else.

I didn't try to match glamour with one of the greatest illusionists the courts have ever birthed. I tried truth first. 'I remember your hair like a sunset woven into waves. So many sidhe have golden-yellow hair, but only you have the colors of the setting sun.' I did a pretty little frown, an expression that women have been using for centuries to good effect. 'Or do I misremember? Most of my memories of you when you were not clothed in glamour are from a child's memory. Perhaps I only dreamed of such color, such beauty.'

I wouldn't have fallen for it; none of my guards would have believed it; Andais would have slapped me for such obvious manipulation. But none of us had known the social coddling that Taranis had grown accustomed to. He'd had centuries of people speaking to him just like that, or even sweeter. If all you ever hear is how wondrous you are, how lovely, how perfect, is it really anyone's fault that you begin to believe it? If you believe it, then it no longer seems silly or manipulative. It seems like the truth. The true secret was that I did think that his honest form was more attractive than the light show. I was being honest, and flattering. It could be a powerful combination.

It was as if the golden waves were twisted, carved into individual locks of hair, so that his true hair didn't simply appear all at once but was brought slowly into view, like a striptease. His true color was that crimson that sunsets can have, as if the entire sky is filled with neon blood. But woven through were locks of that red-orange that sometimes happens when the sun is just sinking below the horizon, as if the sun itself had been crushed across the sky. A few strands of hair played throughout, like the yellow of the sun drawn down to threads that winked and shimmered through the more solid waves of his hair.

I let out a breath I hadn't realized I'd been holding. I had not lied when I'd said his natural color was more spectacular than the illusion had been.

'Does this suit you better, Meredith?' His voice was rich enough to touch, as if I could have grabbed handfuls of it and clutched it to my body. I couldn't quite figure out what it would feel like in my arms, but something thick, sweet, maybe. Like covering yourself in cotton candy, all air and spun sugar, something to melt and grow sticky.

I jerked back to myself when Doyle touched my shoulder. Taranis had been using more than simple glamour. Glamour changes the appearance of something, but you still have the choice of accepting it or not. Glamour might make a dry leaf appear to be a sweet bit of cake, and you are more likely to eat the cake illusion than the dry leaf of fact; but you must still choose to eat it. The glamour changes only the experience. It doesn't make your choice to accept it.

What Taranis had just done would try to make my choice for me. 'Did you just ask me something, Your Highness?'

'He did,' Doyle said, and his voice reminded me of dark, thick, sweet things, like honeyed mead done nearly black. I realized that a touch of glamour made me think that. But Doyle wasn't trying to control me; he was trying to help me fight against the king's power.

'I asked if you would do me the honor of attending a feast in your honor.'

'I am honored that you would go to such trouble, Your Highness. I would be more than happy to attend such a function in a month or so. Things are so busy right now, Yule preparations and all, you know. I do not have a cadre of servants to make my plans go as smoothly as yours.' I smiled, but inside I was screaming at him. How dare he try to manipulate me like I was some befuddled human or lesser fey. This was not the way you treated an equal. I shouldn't have been surprised. All along his treatment of me had been shabby, at best. He didn't see me as an equal. Why should he treat me as one?

I could turn my hair a different color, tan my skin, make small changes to my appearance. I was a master of that kind of glamour. But I had nothing that would keep me safe from the immense power Taranis was so casually throwing at me.

What did I do better than Taranis? I had the hand of flesh, and he didn't, but that was something that could only kill, and only by touch. I didn't want to kill him, just keep him at bay.

His sweet voice continued. 'I would very much enjoy your company before Yule.'

Doyle's hand tightened on my shoulder. I reached up to touch his hand, and the feel of his skin helped steady me. What did I do better than Taranis?

I moved my hand so that Doyle wrapped his fingers around mine. His hand was very real, very solid. It was as if the touch of his hand helped push back that heavy voice and shining beauty.

'I would hate to say no to Your Highness, but surely the visit could wait until after Yule.'

His power pushed at me in a nearly raw wave. If it had been fire, I would have burst into flames; if it had been water, I would have drowned; but it was persuasion, almost a type of seduction, and I could no longer remember why I didn't want to go to the Seelie Court. Of course I would go.

A sudden movement stopped me from saying yes. Doyle had sat down behind me, putting his legs on either side of my body so that I was cradled against him. His hand stayed pressed against mine. It stopped me from saying yes, but it wasn't enough. The press of his skin against my hand was still more precious to me than his entire clothed body against me.

I reached out blindly, and Frost found my hand. He squeezed it, and that helped, too.

I looked back at the mirror. Taranis was still a shining thing, beautiful like a work of art, but he was not the kind of beauty that made my pulse race. It was almost as if he was trying too hard for me to take him seriously. He looked a little ridiculous in his shining mask and his clothes made of sunlight.

His power surged again, like a warm slap in my face. 'Come to me, Meredith. Come to me in three days, and I will show you a feast the likes of which you have never seen.'

The opening door saved me that time. It was Galen. He stared at Doyle on the bed and Frost holding my hand. 'You called, Doyle?'

I hadn't heard Doyle say anything. I think I couldn't hear anything but the king's voice for a moment or two.

I found my voice; it was thin and breathy. 'Send in Kitto. Just as he is, please.'

Galen raised his eyebrows at that but gave a quick bow, unseen from the mirror, and fetched the goblin. I'd worded my request purposefully. Kitto wore very few clothes when he curled in his hidey-hole. I wanted skin touching mine, and I didn't want to ask the guards to strip.

Kitto came into the room wearing nothing but his short-shorts; from Taranis's view he would probably look nude. Let him think what he wished.

Kitto shot a questioning look at Doyle and me. He was careful not to look in the mirror. I placed Doyle's hand against the side of my neck and held out my free hand to Kitto. He came to me without question. His small hand wrapped around mine, and I pulled him to the floor so that he sat at my feet. I pulled him in against my bare legs. I had worn no hose, only purple open-toed sandals to match my dress.

Kitto curled his body around my legs, and the warm brush of his skin on mine, the feel of his hands, his arms around my bare legs underneath the skirt steadied me.

I began to realize a method behind the madness when Andais spoke to the Seelie Court covered in naked bodies. I'd always assumed she did it as a sly insult to Taranis, but now I wasn't so sure.

Maybe the insult began with the king, and not the queen.

'I thank you for the honor you do me, Taranis, but I cannot in good conscience agree to a feast before Yule. I would be most honored to attend once the busy season of Yule is past.' My voice came out very clear, very steady, almost clipped.

Doyle finally figured out that I was after skin, because he kept his hands busy on my neck, caressing the parts of my shoulders and arms that showed. Normally, the feel of his hands running over my skin would have been seductive; now it was just something to keep me anchored.

The king lashed at me with his power, fashioning it into a whip that hurt even as it felt good. It tore a gasp from my throat, and I would have flung myself at the mirror, even cried yes, if I could have spoken, if I could have moved. In that one desperate moment, three things happened: Doyle laid a gentle kiss on my neck, Kitto licked the back of my knee, and Frost sat down on the bed to raise my hand to his mouth.

The touch of their mouths were three anchors that kept me from slipping away. Frost slipped to the floor on the other side from Kitto and slid my finger into his mouth, perhaps to hide his actions from Taranis. I wasn't sure, and I did not care. The feel of his mouth was like a velvet glove around my flesh.

I let out a shaking breath – and I could think again, a little. Doyle ran his fingers from the base of my skull to the top of my head, kneading along my scalp under my hair. What should have been terribly distracting cleared my mind.

'I have tried to be polite, Taranis, but you have

been as blunt with your magic as I am about to be with my words. Why is it so important that you see me at all, let alone before Yule?'

'You are my kinswoman. I wish to renew our acquaintance. Yule is a time of coming together.'

'You have barely acknowledged my existence most of my life. Why do you care to renew our relationship now?'

His power seemed to fill the room, as if I were trying to breathe something more solid than air. I couldn't breathe. I couldn't see. The world was narrowing down to light; light was everywhere.

A sharp pain brought me back so abruptly that I screamed. Kitto had bitten my leg like a dog trying to get my attention, but it had worked. I reached down and stroked his face. 'This interview is over, Taranis. You are being unaccountably rude. No sidhe does this to another sidhe, only to the lesser fey.'

Frost rose to his feet to blank the mirror, but Taranis said, 'I have heard many rumors about you, Meredith. I wish to see for myself what you have become.'

'What do you see, Taranis?' I asked.

'I see a woman where once there was a girl. I see a sidhe where once there was a lesser fey. I see many things, but some things will go unanswered until I see you in person. Come to me, Meredith, come and let us know one another.'

'Truth between us, Taranis, I can barely function in the face of your power. You know it, and I know it. This is from a distance. I would be a fool to let you try this in person.'

'I give you my word that I will not vex you in

390

this manner if you will but come to my court before Yule.'

'Why before Yule?'

'Why after Yule?' he countered.

'Because you seem to want it so badly, and that makes me suspicious of your motives.'

'So, because I want a thing too much, you would deny me, just for the wanting of it.'

'No. It is because you want a thing too much and seem willing to do anything within your power to get it that I fear your wanting of it.'

Even through the golden mask I saw him frown. He wasn't following my logic, though it seemed clear enough to me. 'You have frightened me, Taranis. It is as simple as that. I will not put myself in your grasp, not until you take some very serious oaths . . . that you will behave yourself around me and mine.'

'If you will come before Yule, I will promise whatever you like.'

'I will not come before Yule, and you will still promise whatever I like. Or I will not come at all.'

He began to shine, his red hair glinting like hard blood. 'You would defy me?'

'I cannot defy you because you have no power over me.'

'I am Ard-Ri, the high king.'

'No, Taranis, you are high king of the Seelie Court, as Andais is high queen of the Unseelie. But you are not my Ard-Ri. I am not of your court. You made that clear to me when I was younger.'

'You would hold old grudges, Meredith, when I extend my hand in peace.'

'I will not be swayed by pretty words, Taranis,

or pretty sights. You nearly beat me to death once when I was a child. You cannot blame me for fearing you now, not when you went to such trouble to train me to fear you.'

'That is not what I meant for you to learn,' he said, without denying that he'd beaten me. At least that part was honest.

'What did you mean for me to learn, then?'

'Not to question your king.'

I sank into the feel of Doyle's hands and mouth on the back of my neck, on Frost's tongue licking across my palm, on Kitto's teeth biting gently along my leg. 'You are not my king, Taranis. Andais is my queen, and I have no king.'

'You seek a king, Meredith, or so rumor says.'

'I seek a father for my children, and he will be king of the Unseelie Court.'

'I have told Andais long that what is ill with her is lack of a king, a true king.'

'And are you such a king, Taranis?'

'Yes,' he said, and I think he believed it.

I didn't know what to say to that. Finally I said, 'I seek a different kind of king then, one who understands that a true queen is worth any amount of kings.'

'You insult me,' he said, and the light that had been friendly before became harsh, and I wished for sunglasses to shield from the unfriendly glare.

'No, Taranis, you insult me, and my queen, and my court. If you have no better words for me than this, then we have nothing to discuss.' I nodded at Frost, and he blanked the mirror before Taranis could do it himself.

We remained in silence for a second or so, then

Doyle said, 'He's always thought himself quite the ladies' man.'

'Do you mean that was some sort of seduction?'

I felt Doyle shrug, then his arms encircled me, hugging me to him. 'For Taranis, anyone who isn't impressed with him is a thorn in his side. He must scratch at anyone who does not worship him. He must pluck at it, like a small piece of grit in the eye, always there, always hurting.'

'Is this why Andais talks to him nude and covered in men?'

'Yes,' Frost answered.

I looked up at him, still standing by the mirror. 'Surely it's an insult to do such to another ruler?'

He shrugged. 'They have been trying to seduce one another, or kill one another, for centuries.'

'Killing or seduction – is there a third choice?'

'They have found their third choice,' Doyle said against my ear. 'An uneasy peace. I think Taranis seeks to control you – and through you, eventually the Unseelie Court.'

'Why is he so pressing about Yule?' I asked.

'Once there were sacrifices at Yule,' Kitto said softly. 'To ensure the light would return, they slew the Holly King to make way for the rebirth of the Oak King, the rebirth of the light.'

We all looked at one another. It was Frost who said, 'Do you think the nobles at his court are finally getting suspicious of his lack of children?'

'I have not heard even the breath of that rumor,' Doyle said. Which meant that he had his own spies in that court.

'It was always a king to be sacrificed for a king,' Kitto said. 'Never a queen.'

'Perhaps Taranis wants to change custom,' Doyle said, holding me close. 'You will not be going to the Seelie Court before Yule. There is no reason good enough.'

I sank back against his body, let the solid circle of his arms be my comfort. 'I agree,' I said softly. 'Whatever Taranis is planning, I want no part of it.'

'We are all agreed then,' said Frost.

'Yes,' Kitto said.

It was unanimous decision, but somehow not very comforting.

Chapter 38

WE CAME OUT INTO THE LIVING ROOM TO FIND Detective Lucy Tate sitting in the pink wing chair, sipping tea, and looking less than happy.

Galen was sitting on the couch and trying to be charming, which he was actually pretty good at. Lucy was having none of it. Everything from the set of her shoulders to the way she crossed her long legs to the way her foot bobbed said she was angry, or nervous, or both.

'About damn time,' she said, when I came out of the bedroom. She looked the three of us over, rather critically. 'Aren't you a little overdressed for a little afternoon delight?'

I looked from Galen on the couch to Rhys and Nicca lounging about the room. Kitto went into his 'dog house' without a word. I didn't see Sage, and wondered if he was outside on the growing force of potted flowers by the door. Galen had bought several in a bid to keep the little fey happy. It hadn't worked, but Sage did spend a lot of time lounging in the plants. The three visible men gave me very innocent faces. Too innocent.

'What have you been telling her?'

Rhys shrugged, then pushed away from the wall where he'd been leaning. 'Telling her you were having sex with both Doyle and Frost was about the only way to keep her from storming the castle walls while you finished your little business meeting.'

Lucy Tate stood up and shoved the cup of tea in Galen's direction. He grabbed it, barely in time. Her face had taken on a flush of unhealthy color. 'Are you telling me that I've been out here for nearly an hour and they've been on a business call?' Her voice was dangerously low, each word very calm, very clear.

Galen got up and walked the dripping cup into the kitchen, one hand held underneath it to keep from leaving a trail of tea behind.

'Business call to the faerie courts,' I said. 'Trust me when I say that I'd rather you'd have walked in on a full-blown ménage à trois than the call I just finished.'

She seemed to see me clearly for the first time. 'You look shaken.'

I shrugged. 'My family . . . gotta love 'em.'

She looked at me a long time, almost a minute, as if she was making up her mind about something. Finally, she shook her head. 'Rhys is right. Only the threat of seeing you in flagrante delicto would have kept me out here this long. But family business isn't police business, so screw it.'

'Are you here on police business?' Doyle asked as he moved smoothly past me into the larger room.

'Yes,' she said, and stepped around the couch to face him.

He kept moving into the dining area so it wasn't

so confrontational, but Lucy wanted a confrontation. She stood with her arms crossed under her breasts, looking belligerent like she wanted to pick a fight with someone.

'What's wrong, Lucy?' I asked, moving into the room to sit down on the far edge of the couch. If she wanted to keep eye contact with me, she'd have to walk around the couch and face me. She did, settling uneasily into the pink chair again.

She leaned forward, hands clasped together, fingers entwined as she fought with herself.

I asked again, 'What's wrong, Lucy?'

'There was another mass killing last night.' Lucy usually gave good eye contact, but not today. Today her eyes roved over the apartment, restless, not looking at anything too long.

'Was it like the one we saw?' I asked.

She nodded, resting a momentary gaze on me, then turned away to look at the television, the line of herbs that Galen had growing in the window. 'Exactly the same except for location.'

Doyle came to kneel behind the couch, arms touching my shoulders lightly. I think he'd knelt so he wouldn't loom over us. 'Jeremy has informed us that everyone at his agency has been forbidden from this case. Your Lieutenant Peterson doesn't seem too happy with us.'

'I don't know what's gotten up Peterson's craw, and I'm sitting here trying to decide if I care. If I talk to you about this case, it could mean my job.' She pushed to her feet and began to pace in the small space of the living room; picture window to pink chair, caught between the couch and the white painted wood of the entertainment center.

'All I've ever wanted was to be a cop.' She

shook her head, running fingers through her thick brunette hair. 'But I'd rather lose my job than see another one of these scenes.'

She sat down in the pink chair abruptly, and now she looked at me, those wide eyes, that earnest face. She'd made her decision. It was there in her face. 'Have you been following the case in the papers or the news?'

'The news called the club incident a mysterious gas leak.' Doyle rested his chin on my shoulder as he spoke. His deep voice vibrated down my skin, along my spine.

I had to fight to keep how it affected me from showing on my face. I don't think it showed.

'The second was one of those traveling clubs, raves, I believe, bad drugs.'

She nodded. 'A bad batch of ecstasy, yeah. At least, that's the story we leaked. We made sure the press had something to chase so they wouldn't put two and two together and start a citywide panic. But the rave was exactly like the first two scenes.'

'First two?' I asked.

She nodded. 'The very first scene probably wouldn't even have come up on anybody's radar if it hadn't been in a ritzy area of town. Just six adults that time, a small dinner party gone very bad. It'd still be floating around on someone's weird shit pile as unsolved. But the vics were high profile, so when the club got hit, it rang bells downtown, and suddenly we had a task force. We needed one, but we never would have gotten it this quickly if one of the first vics hadn't been friends with several mayors and a chief of police or two.' She sounded bitter and tired.

'The first murders were at a private residence?' I asked.

Lucy nodded, hands just clasped now, not wringing tight. She was tired and depressed, but calmer. 'Yes, and it was the first related scene, as far as we've been able to find. I keep dreaming that there's some crack house or sweat shop that was really the first hit, and we're going to find dozens of dead bodies rotting in the December heat. The only thing worse than one of these scenes fresh would be a really old one.' She shook her head again, running her hands through her hair, then she shook her head, fluffing out the hair she'd just smoothed. 'Anyway, the first one was a private residence, yeah. We found the couple that lived there, two guests, two servants.'

'How far was that house from the club that we saw?' I asked.

'Holmby Hills is about an hour away.'

I felt Doyle go very still behind me. The silence seemed to widen out from us like circles in a pool. We all stared at her and, I think, fought not to look at one another.

'Did you say Holmby Hills?' I asked.

She was looking back at us. 'Yes. Why does that ring everyone's bell?'

I looked at Doyle. He looked at me. Rhys settled in to lean against the wall as if it meant nothing, but his face couldn't quite hide the shine of excitement. The mystery was deepening, or maybe shallowing, if that was a word. Rhys couldn't help but enjoy it.

Galen went into the kitchen and hid, fetching a cloth to dry the teacup. Frost came and sat on the couch beside me, giving enough room so Doyle wasn't crowded. Frost's face gave nothing away. Nicca looked genuinely puzzled, and I realized that he'd been out of the loop on exactly where Maeve Reed lived. He'd helped with the planning for the fertility rite, but he didn't know her address.

'No,' Lucy said. 'No, you are not all going to just sit there and look innocent. When I said Holmby Hills you all looked like I'd stepped in something, something nasty. You can't give me innocent faces now and not say what's going on.'

'We can do anything we wish, Detective,' Doyle said.

She looked at me. 'Are you going to stonewall me on this? I risked my career to come down here and talk to you all.'

'We are a little curious about that,' Doyle said. 'Why would it be worth your career to come and speak with us? You have Teresa's information, and Jeremy's assurance it was a spell. What more can we tell you?'

She glared at him. 'I'm not stupid, Doyle. There are fey everywhere I look on this case. Peterson just doesn't want to see it. The first incident is in Holmby Hills almost right next door to Maeve Reed's house. She's a sidhe royal. Exiled, or not, she's still fey. We put out calls to all the local hospitals, looking for anyone exhibiting symptoms similar to our victims. We got one bite on a live person. No new dead have come in.'

'You have a survivor?' Rhys asked.

Her gaze flicked to him, then back to Doyle and me. 'We're not sure. He's alive, and getting better every day.' She stared at the two of us. 'Would it make you share information with me if I told you our possible survivor is fey?'

I don't know about the rest of them, but I didn't even try to keep the puzzlement off my face.

Lucy smiled at us, an almost mean smile, as if she knew she had us. 'This fey doesn't want to contact the Bureau of Human and Fey Affairs. Seems real eager to avoid it. Lieutenant Peterson says the fey have nothing to do with the case, says it's a coincidence that Maeve Reed lives close to the first incident. He had the fey interviewed, but insists you can never really tell what's wrong with the faeries; insists that if it had been the same sort of events the fey would be dead.' She looked around the room at all of us. 'I don't believe that. I've seen fey heal injuries that would have killed any human being. I've seen one of you fall off a high-rise and walk away.'

She shook her head again. 'No, this has something to do with your world, doesn't it?'

I fought not to look at anyone around me.

'Would you talk to me, tell me the whole truth, if I let you interview the injured fey? Lieutenant Peterson has declared the fey noninvolved. So, technically, even if he finds out, he can't fire me. Or even discipline me for it. In fact, the injured fey is my cover story. Since the fey won't speak to the fey authorities, I'm looking for a few fey faces to try to talk to him, help him adjust to the big city.'

'You think he's from out of town?' I asked.

'Oh, yeah, he's got *never been to the big city* written all over him. He screamed when his heart rate monitor beeped at him the first time.' She shook her thick hair all around her face. 'He's from somewhere where they've never seen modern equipment. The nurses say they had to take the television out of his room because he had some sort of seizure after he saw it work.'

She looked at all of us in turn, and finally came back to me, Doyle, and Frost. 'Talk to me, Merry, please. Talk to me. I won't tell the lieutenant. I can't. Please help me stop this, whatever it is.'

I looked at Doyle, Frost, Rhys. Galen came back out of the kitchen, but he spread his hands wide and shrugged. 'I haven't been doing much of the detective stuff lately, so I don't feel like I should get a vote.'

Nicca spoke up, which surprised us all. 'The queen won't like it.' His voice was clear, filling the room, but somehow soft, like a child whispering in the dark, afraid to be overheard.

'She didn't tell us not to share with the human police,' Doyle said.

'She didn't?' Nicca's voice seemed so small, so much younger than that tall, strong body.

I turned on the couch so Nicca could see full into my face. 'No, Nicca, the queen didn't tell us not to talk to the police.'

He let out a large breath. 'Okay.' Again it was a child's answer. The grownups had told him he wouldn't get in trouble, and he believed us.

We all exchanged looks one more time, then I said, 'Rhys, tell her about the spell.'

He did. We emphasized that we weren't sure anyone left in the courts could still do the spell, and that it might possibly be a human magician or witch. It wasn't anyone at the Unseelie Courts, that we were sure of.

'How can you be so sure?' Lucy asked.

We exchanged another series of looks. 'Trust me, Lucy, the queen doesn't have to sweat civil rights or review boards. She's very thorough.'

402

She studied our faces. 'How thorough can you guys be?'

I frowned at her. 'What do you mean?'

'I've heard rumors about what your queen does to people. Can you do anything that effective without leaving marks?'

I raised my eyebrows at that. 'Are you asking us to do what I think you're asking us to do?'

'I'm asking you to stop this from happening again. The fey in the hospital won't talk to the police; he won't talk to the social worker that the Bureau of Human and Fey Affairs sent over. The fey went wild when I suggested we could contact the ambassador personally if he wasn't comfortable with a human social worker. Seeing how scared he was to talk to the ambassador made me think he might be even more scared of you guys.'

'Why?' I asked.

'The ambassador isn't sidhe.'

'What do you expect us to do to this fey?' Doyle asked.

'I expect you to do whatever it takes to get him to talk. We've got over five hundred dead, Doyle, almost six hundred. Besides, from what Rhys says, if these things aren't stopped, if we just keep letting them feed, they'll regenerate or something. I don't want a pack of newly born ancient deities with a taste for killing running around loose in my town. It's got to be stopped now, before it's too late.'

We agreed to go with her, but first we made a phone call. We called Maeve Reed and let her know that the ghosts of dead gods had been resurrected to kill her. Which meant it was somebody in the Seelie Court, and moreover they had the king's permission to do it.

Chapter 39

LUCY FLASHED HER BADGE A LOT TO GET US through the metal detectors with our guns and blades intact. The men even had to show the cards identifying them as queen's guardsmen before the nurse in charge would let us on the floor. But finally we stood at the bedside of a man . . . well, of a male. He was a tiny, misshapen thing. Sage was tiny, too, but he was perfectly proportioned. He was meant to be the size he was; clearly, the man who lay in the bed with the sheets tucked up under his arms was, even at a glance, wrong.

I am Unseelie Court and I call many shapes right, pleasant, but something about this one made the hair on the back of my neck crawl. It made me want to look away, as if he was hideous, though he wasn't.

I wasn't the only one having trouble. Rhys and Frost had looked away, turned their backs. Their reaction said that they either knew him or knew what had happened. It was a turning away like a shunning. Had he broken some age-old taboo? Doyle did not look away, but then he almost never did. Galen exchanged a look with me that said he was as puzzled and disturbed as I was. Kitto stayed near my side, where he'd insisted on being, one hand in mine like a child seeking comfort.

I forced myself to keep looking, to try to figure out what it was about this small man that made me want to cringe. He was a little over two feet tall, his tiny feet making small bumps in the sheet. Something about his body seemed foreshortened, even though everything was there. His head was a little big for the thin torso. His eyes were large and liquid, far too large for the face. It was as if the eyes were left over from some other face. His nose matched the eyes, but because the rest of the face had receded, the nose looked too large, as well. That was what it looked like, as if his eyes and nose had been left stranded while the rest of his face had grown smaller, meaner, pinched, and wasted.

Nicca moved through the rest of us and held his hand out. 'Oh, Bucca, what has become of thee?'

The tiny figure on the bed remained immobile at first. Then, slowly, he raised one small hand on an arm so thin it was like thick string. He laid that tiny pale brown hand against Nicca's strong brown one.

Kitto turned a face shining with tears up to the lights. 'Bucca-Dhu, Bucca-Dhu, what are you here?'

I thought at first Kitto had left out a word or two; then I realized he hadn't. He'd asked exactly what he wished to know.

'The two of you know him,' Doyle said, making it more statement than question.

Nicca nodded, patting the tiny hand ever so

gently. He spoke rapidly in the strangely musical tones of one of the old Celtic tongues. It was too rapid for me to follow, but it wasn't Welsh and it wasn't Scots, Gaelic, or Irish, which still left several dialects, not to mention countries to go.

Kitto joined in, speaking something close to what Nicca spoke, but not exactly – a different dialect or maybe from a different century, like the difference between Middle English and modern English.

I watched Kitto's face, the eagerness, the sorrow. I knew he was very sad to find this man here in this condition, but that was all I could follow.

Doyle spoke in modern English at last. Maybe everyone else had been following just fine, but I had not. 'Nicca knew him in a form not so different from this one, but Kitto remembers him as we are now, a sidhe. Bucca was once worshipped as a god.'

I looked down at the wizened shape and knew what had made my skin crawl. Those huge brown eyes, that strong, straight nose – they were very like Nicca's. I'd always assumed that Nicca's brown skin and eyes had come from the demi-fey in his heritage; but now, staring down at the tiny figure, I knew I'd been wrong.

I looked at the man with a renewed fit of horror, for now I could suddenly see it. It was as if someone had taken one of the sidhe and compressed him down into something the size of a large rabbit. I had no words for the horror that lay nearly lost in that hospital bed. And no thought to how he could have come to that form.

'How?' I asked softly, and wished instantly that

I hadn't, because the small figure on the bed looked at me with those eyes, that shrunken face.

He spoke in clear though accented English. 'I have brought myself to this, girl. Me and me alone.'

'No,' Nicca said. 'That isn't true, Bucca.'

The small figure shook his head, his dark hair cut short, but resting thick upon his pillow, bunching as he moved. 'There are faces here I know, Nicca, beyond yours and the goblin's. There are others who were once worshipped and eventually lost their followers. They did not waste away like this. I refused to give up my power, because I thought it would diminish me.' He laughed, and the sound was bitter enough to choke on. 'Now look at me, Nicca, what my pride and my fear have done to me.'

I was confused, to put it lightly, but, like is so often the case in fey society, the very questions I needed to ask were considered rudely direct.

The man in the bed turned his oddly heavy head to look at Kitto. 'The last time we met, I thought you tiny.' Those strangely compelling eyes looked up at the goblin. 'You have changed, goblin.'

'He is sidhe,' Nicca said.

Bucca looked surprised, then laughed. 'You see, I fought so hard for so many centuries to keep our blood pure, to mix with no one. I considered you an unclean thing once, Nicca.'

Nicca kept patting the other man's hand. 'That was long ago, Bucca.'

'I would not let any of our pure Bucca-Dhu line go out among the other sidhe. Now all that is left of my line is those like you who were not pure.' He turned his head and it looked like it took effort.

'And all that is left of all the Bucca-Gwidden is you, goblin.'

'There are others among the goblins, Bucca-Dhu. And you see the moonlight skin on these sidhe? The Bucca-Gwidden are remembered.'

'They may share the skin, but not the hair or eyes. No, goblin, they are lost, and it is my doing. I would not let any of our people join with the others. We would stay the hidden people and keep to the old ways. There are no old ways left, goblin.'

'He is sidhe,' Doyle said, 'acknowledged by the Unseelie Court as such.'

Bucca smiled, but not like he was happy. 'And even now all I can think is that I did not know the Unseelie sidhe had sunk so low as to accept goblins into their ranks. Even dying as I am, having seen the last of my people die before me, and I cannot see him as sidhe. I cannot.' He took his hand out of Nicca's grasp and closed his eyes, but not like he'd fallen asleep, more like he was trying not to see.

Detective Lucy had been very patient through all of this. 'Could someone explain to me what's going on?'

Doyle exchanged glances with Frost and Rhys, but none of them spoke. I shrugged. 'Don't look at me. I'm almost as confused as you are.'

'Me, too,' Galen said. 'I recognized either Cornish or Breton, but the accent was too archaic for me.'

'Cornish,' Doyle said, 'They were speaking Cornish.'

'I thought there weren't any goblins in Cornwall,' Galen said.

Kitto turned from the bed and looked at the tall

knight. 'Goblins were not all one people any more than the sidhe were merely two separate courts. We were all more than this once. I was a Cornish goblin, because my sidhe mother was a Bucca-Gwidden, a Cornish sidhe, before she joined the Seelie Court. When she saw the form her babe had taken, she knew where to lay her burden down and left me among the snakes of Cornwall.'

'There are nests of snakes everywhere in the Isles,' Bucca said in a thick voice. 'Even in Ireland, no matter what the followers of Padrig want you to believe.'

'Most of the goblins are in America now,' Kitto said.

'Aye,' Bucca said, 'because no other country would have them.'

'Aye,' Kitto said.

'Okay,' Lucy said, 'whatever's happening, old home week, family feud, I don't care. I want to know how this Bucca, who lists his name as Nick Bottom, which I looked up – a character from *A Midsummer Night's Dream*, very cute – ended up here nearly sucked dry of life.'

'Bucca,' Nicca said softly.

The small figure opened his eyes. They were full of such aching tiredness that I had to look away. It was like looking down a tunnel into something worse than oblivion, so much worse than death.

His accent thickened with his emotions. 'I cannae die, you understand that, Nicca, I cannae die. I was the king of my people and I cannae even fade like some did. But I am fadin'.' He raised one piteously thin arm. 'I am fadin' like this, like some giant hand is squeezin me down.'

'Bucca, please, tell us how you came to be

attacked by the hungry ghosts,' Nicca said in his soft voice.

'When this flesh I am still clingin' to fades, I'll be one of 'em. I'll be one of the Starvin' Ones.'

'No, Bucca.'

He held out that thin, thin arm. 'No, Nicca, that is what happened to most of the others who were strong. We cannae die, but we cannae live, so we be betwixt and between.'

'Not good enough for heaven,' Doyle said, 'nor bad enough for hell.'

Bucca looked at him. 'Yes.'

'I always love getting insight into fey culture, but let's get back to the attacks,' Lucy said. 'Tell me about the attack on you, Mr Bottom, or Mr Bucca, or whatever.'

He blinked up at her almost owlishly. 'They attacked me at the first sign of weakness.'

'Could you expand on that a little?' Lucy said. She had her notebook open, pen poised.

'You raised them,' Rhys said. It was the first time he'd turned around, the first time he'd really looked at Bucca since we'd entered the room.

'Aye,' Bucca said.

'Why?' I asked.

'It was part of the price I had to pay to rejoin the faerie courts.'

That stopped us all. For a second, it seemed to make sense. Andais had done it, or had it done. That was why no one could track it back to her. It explained why none of her people had known about it. She hadn't used any of her people.

'Pay to whom?' Doyle asked.

I looked at him, almost saying aloud, *we all know*. Then Bucca spoke. 'Taranis, o' course.'

410

Chapter 40

WE ALL TURNED TO THE BED LIKE A SLOW-MOTION scene from a movie. 'Did you say Taranis?' I asked.

'Are ya deaf girl?'

'No,' I said, 'just surprised.'

Bucca frowned up at me. 'Why?'

I blinked down at him, thought about it. 'I didn't think Taranis was this crazy.'

'Then ya ha' not been payin' attention.'

'She hasn't seen Taranis since she was a child, Bucca,' Doyle said.

'I apologize then.' He looked at me critically. 'She looks like Seelie sidhe.'

I wasn't sure what to do with the compliment. I wasn't even sure if, under the circumstances, it was a compliment.

Lucy walked around to the far side of the bed. 'Are you saying the king of the Seelie Court had you raise these hungry ghosts?'

'Aye.'

'Why?' she asked. We seemed to all be asking that question a lot today.

'He wanted them to kill Maeve Reed.'

411

Lucy just stared at him. 'Okay, I'm lost. Why should the king want the golden goddess of Hollywood dead?'

'I don't know why,' Bucca said, 'and I didna care. Taranis promised to give me enough power to recover some of what I'd lost. I was finally willing to join the Seelie Court. But he promised it to me on condition of Maeve's death, and that I could control the Starving Ones. Many o' them were friends of old. I thought they were like me and would welcome a chance to return, but they are no longer Bucca, or sidhe, or even fey. They are dead things, dead monsters.' He closed his eyes and took a deep shaking breath.

'The first time I faltered, they attacked me, and now they feed, not to return to the old ways, but because they are hungry. They feed for the same reason that a wolf feeds. Because it hungers. If they gain enough lives to return to something close to sidhe, it will be so awful that not even the Unseelie Court will be able to match the horror of them.'

'Not to complain,' Lucy said, 'but why didn't you tell all this to the social worker or the ambassador?'

'It was when I saw Nicca, and even the goblin, that I knew I'd been a fool. My time is past, but my people live on. As long as me blood is walkin' around, then the Bucca are not dead.' Tears glittered in his eyes. 'I tried to save meself, even if it meant destroying what was left of me people. I was wrong, terrible wrong.'

He reached out for Nicca's hand this time, and Nicca took his with a smile.

'How do we stop them?' Doyle asked.

'I raised them, but I cannae lay them. I have not the strength.'

'Can you tell us the spell?' Doyle asked.

'Aye, but that da' na mean you can do it.'

'Let us worry about that,' Doyle said.

Bucca told us how he'd planned to lay the ghosts. Lucy actually took notes. The rest of us just listened. It wasn't a matter of magic words, more of magical intent and just knowing how to think it through.

When he'd finished telling us everything he knew about the Starving Ones, I asked, 'Have you been hiding the Nameless from the Unseelie Court?'

'Girl, have ya not been payin' attention? Taranis is hidin' it.'

'You raised that for him, too?' I couldn't keep the surprise out of my voice.

'I raised the Starvin' Ones with a little help from Taranis, but Taranis raised the Nameless with only a little help from me.'

'He was one of the main powers behind its casting,' Doyle said.

'Why would Taranis do that?' I asked.

'I thought he meant to take some of his power back from the thing,' Bucca said, 'and mayhap he did, but it didn't work out like he'd planned.'

'So Taranis is controlling the Nameless,' Galen said.

'Nay, lad, do not ya un'erstand yet? Taranis freed it, gave it orders to kill this Maeve, but he no more controls it than I do the Starvin' Ones. He hid what he had done, but it is the thing itself that is hiding it now. Taranis was not half-panicked when he realized that, I tell you. He was scared, and he should be.'

413

'What do you mean?' I asked.

'When I tried to send the Starvin' Ones through Maeve's wards, they couldna reach her. They turned on me, and found other prey. I saw the thing that you call the Nameless. It will breach her wards, and once it has killed her, then what will it do?'

'I don't know,' I said softly.

'Anything it damn well pleases,' Bucca said.

'What he means,' Rhys said, 'is that once the Nameless kills Maeve Reed it won't have a purpose anymore. It will just be this huge powerful thing, and it will destroy everything around it.'

'Now there is a smart boy,' Bucca said.

I looked at Rhys. 'How do you know that for certain?'

'I gave most of my magic to that thing. I know what it will do, Merry. We have to keep it from killing Maeve. As long as she's alive, it will keep trying to kill her, and it will keep trying to hide its presence until it's done that. Once she's dead it'll just explode all over the city. The most alien energy the fey had to offer will be let loose in Southern California. The thing will stomp through L.A. like Godzilla through Tokyo.'

'How am I supposed to convince Peterson that some ancient fey magic is about to stomp the city?' Lucy asked.

'You aren't,' I said. 'He won't believe it anyway.'

'Then what are we going to do?' she asked.

'We're going to go keep Maeve Reed alive. Maybe convince her that Europe would be good this time of year. Maybe just keep her moving ahead of it until we can figure out something else.'

'Not a bad idea,' Rhys said.

'I take it back,' said Bucca. 'You're a smart one, too.'

'Glad to hear that,' I said. 'Does someone have a cell phone?'

Lucy had one. I took it from her, and she gave me Maeve Reed's number out of her little notebook. I dialed, and Marie, the personal assistant, answered. She was hysterical. She began to scream, 'It's the princess, it's the princess!' Julian took the phone from her. 'Meredith, is that you?'

'Yeah, Julian, what's wrong?'

'Something's here, something so psychically big I can't even begin to sense all of it. It's trying to get through the wards, and I think it's going to do it.'

I started for the door. 'We're on our way, Julian We'll send the police on ahead of us.'

'You don't sound surprised, Meredith. Do you know what this thing is?'

'Yes,' and I told him as we ran through the hospital toward the cars. I told him what it was, but I didn't know if anything I told him was going to help at all.

Chapter 41

BY THE TIME WE ARRIVED MAEVE REED'S PLACE was surrounded by police everything. Marked cars, plain cars, special forces armed vehicles, ambulances waited at a sort of hopeful safe distance. Guns were everywhere. They were even trained on the wall in front of Maeve's house. The trouble was, there was nothing to shoot at.

A woman in full police battle armor with S.W.A.T. written across it was standing behind a barrier of cars in a pentagram and circle that she'd drawn in chalk on the road. L.A. had been one of the first police departments to attach witches or magicians to all special units.

The moment the car engine died I felt her spell. It made the air hard to breathe. Doyle, Frost, and I had ridden with Lucy. Doyle in particular had not enjoyed the wild ride. He half staggered over to a line of planted shrubbery and knelt. The humans would think he was praying – and he was, in a way. He was renewing his touch with the earth. Doyle was quite frightened of almost all man-made transportation. He could travel through mystical pathways that would have made me scream forever, but driving fast through L.A. traffic had nearly done him in. Frost was fine.

The other guards, including Sage, poured out of the van. At Doyle's urging we had gone back to the apartment for some more blades. Lucy had been against it, until he pointed out that until the Nameless's glamour was broken, bullets wouldn't hurt it. He assured her that they had things at the apartment that would break its glamour if anything could.

Lucy had decided it was worth a side trip. She had radioed ahead that without some magical aid, the police might not be able to see the thing, let alone shoot it.

Apparently they'd taken our word for it. The witch had probably tried something simple, and when that didn't work, she'd begun to work on the chalk drawing, complete with runes and the whole nine yards. It worked in a skin-ruffling, throat-closing rush of power like an unfelt wind.

The spell rolled out and hit its target. The air wavered like heat rolling off summer asphalt. Except this heat wavered up and up, towering over twenty feet into the air.

I wasn't sure that the police without psychic talent were going to be able to see anything, but the wave of gasps and curses let me know I was wrong.

Lucy stared up at the shimmer. 'Do we just start shooting it?' she asked.

'Yes,' Frost said.

It didn't really matter what we did. Whoever was in charge gave the order, and suddenly the sound of gunfire was everywhere, bursting open like one huge explosion.

The bullets passed through the shimmering almost-form like it wasn't there. I began to wonder where all those bullets would end up, because they'd keep going until they found some target. Then men were yelling, 'Stop firing, cease fire,' all up and down the line.

The sudden silence rang in my ears. The shimmering form just kept pushing at the wall, or rather the wardings in the wall. It didn't seem to have noticed the bullets or the police.

'What just happened?' Lucy asked.

'It is in a time between this time and the next,' Doyle said. He had walked back to us while we were watching them throw bullets at the thing. 'It is a type of glamoury that allows the fey to hide themselves from mortal eyes.'

Lucy looked at me. 'Can you do that?'

'No,' I said.

'Nor can the rest of the sidhe,' Doyle said. 'We gave up that ability when we made the Nameless.'

'I've never been able to do anything like that,' I said.

'You were born after we'd done two castings like the Nameless,' Doyle said. 'How could anyone have blamed you for being less than we once were?'

'The witch has broken some of the glamoury,' Frost said.

'But not enough,' Doyle said.

The two of them looked at each other.

'No,' I said. 'No to whatever you're thinking.'

They looked at me. 'Meredith, we must stop it here.'

'No,' I said. 'No, we must keep Maeve Reed alive. That's what we talked about. No one talked about killing the Nameless. I mean, it can't die, can it?'

They looked at each other again. Rhys joined us. 'No, it can't die.'

'Is it real?' Lucy asked.

He looked at her. 'What do you mean?'

'Is it solid enough to be hurt by our weapons?'

He nodded. 'Oh, yes, it's real enough for that. Once it's stripped of the magic that keeps it safe.'

'We must strip that magic away,' Doyle said.

'How?' I asked, and my stomach was tight at the idea of what it might take.

'It must be wounded,' Frost said.

I looked at his arrogant face and knew that he was hiding something from me. I grabbed his arm. 'How can you wound it?'

His eyes softened as he looked down at me; the grey went from the color of storm clouds to sky just after the rain when the sun is about to break through. I watched the color swirl like clouds itself across his eyes.

'A weapon of power would be able to wound it, if the warrior were skilled enough.'

I held on to his arm tighter. 'What do you mean, skilled enough?'

'Skilled enough not to get killed doing it,' Rhys said.

Both Frost and Doyle gave him unfriendly looks. 'Look, we don't have time to play around here. One of us with a weapon of power and enough skill to do it has to draw blood,' Rhys said.

I kept my grip on Frost's arm but looked at Doyle. 'Who's on the list of skilled enough?'

'Now that's just insulting,' Rhys said. 'Doyle

and Frost aren't the only people standing here.'

They gave him another unfriendly look.

'I was never the queen's favorite guard, but once I was favored in battle.'

Galen said, 'I'm like Merry. I came along after all the old times. I've got good blades, but none of them are weapons of power.'

'Because we lost the knack of making such things,' Frost said.

'We have become more flesh and less pure spirit with every casting. It has allowed us to survive, even to thrive, but it has not been without cost.'

I slid in against Frost's body and found his sword, Winter Kiss, in our way. How apt. I looked at the other men. Frost was the only one in a tunic. Everyone else was wearing street clothes, T-shirts, jeans, boots, except for Kitto, who had thrown a shirt on over his shorts. The clothes were wrong, but the weapons were right.

Frost had a second sword strapped to his back, a sword almost longer than I was tall. I knew the tunic covered more blades. He always carried some blade somewhere on him, unless the queen had forbidden it.

Doyle had kept his gun in its shoulder holster, but he'd added a sword at his hip and wrist sheaths on both arms. The knives glinted silver against his dark skin, but the sword was as black as he was. The blade was iron, not steel. I'd never known what the black handle was made of; it was metal, but what kind of metal I did not know. The sword was called Black Madness, Báinidhe Dub. If anyone other than Doyle tried to wield it, they would be struck permanently mad. The daggers on his wrists were twins, formed together at one making. These legendary blades were thought to hit any target once thrown. Their nicknames at court had been Snick and Snack. I knew they had true names, but I'd never heard them referred to as anything else.

Galen had a sword belted at his side, and it was a good sword but not magical, not in the way of the great weapons. He had a dagger on the other side of his belt to balance the sword. He'd added a shoulder holster and gun over his button-down shirt, and a second gun tucked in the small of his back.

I had put a belt around the middle of the sundress and threaded a side holster through it to hold my own gun. It ruined the line of the dress, but if things went really wrong, I'd rather survive looking a little silly than die looking perfect. I had two folding knives in thigh sheaths under the dress, and a smaller gun in an ankle holster. I'd been deemed unworthy even of a nonmagical blade by both courts.

Rhys had his sword on his back, the one he'd used of old, Uamhas, Dread Death. He had his axe belted at his side, because with only one eye his depth perception just wasn't up to a sword. He had daggers on him, but I wasn't sure I'd want to be standing to the side of whatever he was throwing at. When you're missing an eye, there's only so much you can compensate for.

Nicca had a sword that was almost identical to Galen's, standard knight ware, beautiful, deadly, but not powerful. Nicca had two guns on either side of his shoulder holster. I had reason to know that he used either hand equally well. He had added a third gun to the small of his back, and a dagger on the opposite side from his sword. Maybe it was standard issue, too, like the sword.

Kitto didn't know enough about guns to be trusted not to shoot his foot off, but he had a short sword belted across the back of his Wile E. Coyote T-shirt.

Sage had a tiny sword that gleamed bright silver in the sunlight. He would not give us the name of it. 'To know the name of something is to have power over it,' he said.

There was a rumbling sound, and the ground seemed to swell up as a portion of Maeve's wall fell inward. The Nameless had cheated. It hadn't gotten past her wards; it had destroyed what she attached them to.

The shimmering thing moved through the hole while a few shots rang out, and officers in charge yelled, 'Don't shoot, don't shoot!'

Doyle was striding forward. 'I will use the daggers. They must strike true, as is their nature.'

'Can you get close enough and still stay out of reach?' Frost asked.

Doyle gave a small glance back. 'I think so.' He kept walking.

Frost moved me away from him, his hands gentle on my arms. 'I must go with him. If he falls, I must be there.'

'Kiss me first,' I said.

He shook his head. 'If I touch your lips, I will never leave your side.' He kissed my forehead quickly, then jogged after Doyle.

Rhys swept me up into his arms while I was still too surprised to react. He kissed me, thoroughly and completely, and ended up wearing most of my red lipstick on his lips. He sat me back on my feet a little breathless.

'You can't steal my courage with a kiss, Merry. You don't love me enough for that.' He ran after the other two before I could think of anything to say.

The police rounded up an armored group of S.W.A.T. officers to back up the men; then they moved forward, through the hole in the wall, and vanished from sight.

Strangely, the Nameless had vanished, as well, as if once inside the wall the shimmer was lost, even though it should have towered above it.

'What if we go in the back and get Maeve out?' Galen said into the heavy silence.

We all looked at him.

'We can't fight the Nameless, but we might be able to do that.'

Lucy slapped her forehead. 'Dumb. *Really* dumb, we should have evacuated Ms Reed before this.'

'It will follow her,' I said. 'Unless you can get a helicopter in here, we won't be able to get her away fast enough.'

Lucy seemed to think about that for a moment. 'I might be able to swing it. The Reeds have a lot of clout in this town.'

'Do it, if you can,' I said.

'In the meantime give us a few men and let us go in the back,' Galen said.

'I'm going with you,' I said.

He shook his head, looking so serious. 'No, Merry, you're not.'

'Yes, Galen, I am. I was raised to know that a

leader never asks of her people what she isn't willing to do herself.'

'Your father was a good man ... but you're mortal, Merry. The rest of us aren't.'

'The police are, all of them, and they're still here.'

He shook his head. 'No.'

We argued, but in the end I got my way because all the men that could have argued me down were inside the broken wall facing off against the thing we'd come to destroy.

Chapter 42

GETTING OVER THE WALL WAS SURPRISINGLY EASY. It was tall, but not that tall, and setting off the silent alarm was no longer a problem. The police were already here. I was helped down into a narrow lane that was planted so thickly with dark green camellias that they formed a second wall to nearly hide the house in front of us. It wasn't the right time of year for blooming, so they were just tall bushes with thick, waxy leaves. I knew exactly how the leaves felt because Lucy and Galen both made me stand in the damn shrubs. I could come along, but they were both going to make sure I didn't get to do anything.

A uniformed officer ducked around the corner and came back with whispered news that there was a sliding glass door: easy access. We were about to slip around that corner and enter the door to search for Maeve Reed, when something awful happened.

The Nameless became visible.

Its glamour went down with a magical back-wash that staggered every fey in the area. Still pressed into the camellia bushes, I couldn't see anything, but two of the policemen opened their mouths wide and started to scream. The other policemen paled, but tried to calm the other two down, until one of the screamers dropped to his knees and tried to claw out his own eyes. One of the calm ones fought to hold the screamer's hands away from his body. Another older officer slapped the other screamer over and over, cursing under his own breath with each blow. 'Son of a bitch,' slap, 'son of a bitch,' slap . . . until the screaming officer sat down on the grass and hid his face, whimpering.

The remaining two policemen and Lucy, pale but ready, had their guns out.

Galen had moved out from the wall when the glamour crashed down, and all the fey with us were staring fascinated at what lay up ahead. I almost didn't look. I was part human; maybe my mind would break like the two policemen. But in the end, I couldn't not look.

How do you describe the indescribable? There were tentacles, and eyes, and arms, and mouths, and teeth, and too many of all of it. But every time I thought I understood its shape, that shape changed. I'd blink my eyes, and it wouldn't be the way I remembered it. Maybe I couldn't see what the Nameless looked like. Maybe my mind just couldn't hold it all, and this was the best my poor mind could come up with. All I could think was if that shambling mountain of horror was the protective version that my mind would allow me to see, I did not want to see anything worse.

Lucy looked down at the ground, pain crossing

426

her face as if it hurt her to simply look at the thing. 'We're going to kill that?'

'Contain it,' Galen said. 'You can't kill magic.'

She shook her head, took a tighter grip on her gun, and turned resolutely back to look at the very large target.

The radios on the uniforms crackled to life. The message was, if you can see it, you can kill it. Fire.

I had a second to think, *where's Maeve*, when Galen threw himself on top of me and forced me flat on the ground. A heartbeat later bullets flew overhead. One of the screaming policemen got loose of the two trying to wrestle him down, and when he stood up, his body did a jerking dance and he fell dead beside us. In that one moment bullets were more dangerous than the Nameless.

Lucy yelled into her hand radio. 'We're taking friendly fire in here! We haven't secured the civilians yet! Cease fire unless you fucking know what you're hitting.' The shooting continued. Lucy screamed again, 'Officer down, officer down, hit by friendly fire, repeat, hit by friendly fire!'

The shooting slowed, then stopped altogether. We all stayed plastered to the ground for a few moments, waiting. It seemed very important to breathe, as if I'd never done it quite right before. Or maybe it was the bleeding body of the dead policeman that made breathing such a treat, as if we all had to make up for him being dead somehow.

When everything stayed quiet, Lucy carefully got to her knees. The rest of the police began to get to their knees, until finally one of the younger uniforms stood up. He didn't fall back down dead, so the rest of us stood up cautiously.

'Look,' one of the policemen said.

We looked. The Nameless was bleeding. Blood trickled like crimson string down its 'head'.

'Shit,' Lucy said. 'We're going to need antitank weapons to blow that thing up.'

I agreed with her. 'How long will it take to get some sort of National Guard stuff here?'

'Too long,' she said. Her radio squawked again. She listened to the unintelligible talk, then said, 'Helicopter's en route. We need to find Ms Reed and get her over the wall.'

We didn't have to find Ms Reed; she found us. She and Gordon Reed came running around the edge of the house at as fast a pace as he could manage. Julian was behind them. The greatest danger in that first second was shooting each other out of sheer nerves. We all managed not to be that stupid, but my pulse was thudding in my throat, and everyone looked big-eyed, like they were ready to get back over the wall.

Maeve Reed grabbed my hand in both of hers. 'Is it Taranis? Does he know?'

'He doesn't know about the baby.'

She frowned. 'Then . . '

'He found out we saw you.'

'Ms Reed—' An officer was holding out his hand. '— we need to get you over the wall.'

She kissed me on the cheek and let the nice officer hand her to another nice officer waiting on top of the wall.

Gordon Reed was next. He didn't say anything. He seemed to be struggling just to breathe and stay upright between Julian and the same nice officer who had helped Maeve over the wall.

When they were safely over, I asked Julian, 'Where are your other people?'

He shook his head. 'Everyone but Max is dead. He's too hurt to walk. I made him hide in the house so I could get the Reeds out.'

I didn't know what to say, but a policeman said, 'You're next' to Julian, and I didn't have to say anything, just watch him climb to safety.

Most of the cops that could still walk were already over, when Lucy's soft 'Oh, my god' turned me around to look at the Nameless.

Rhys's white hair shone out against the darker colors of the monster. Something between an arm and a tentacle wrapped around his chest. The blade of his axe sparked in the sun as he drove it into an eye the size of a Volkswagen. The eye bled, the monster screamed, and so did Rhys.

'Get Merry out of here,' said Galen. Then he was gone at a run toward the fight.

Chapter 43

I DIDN'T WAIT FOR NICCA OR LUCY TO GRAB ME, I just started running after Galen. My sandals weren't meant for running full out, and I threw them off as I rounded the corner. Kitto was at my heels, and Nicca, with Sage on his shoulder, wasn't far behind. Lucy and the last uniform had come with us, too.

But what we saw froze us all for a few seconds. The Nameless had no legs, yet it did. It was a writhing mass of a thing, and my eyes could not hold it. I felt a scream clawing at my throat, but I knew if I let that sound come out of me, I'd never stop – like the policeman still huddled by the wall. Sometimes the only thing that keeps you from going mad is stubbornness and need.

Rhys was still wrapped in its flesh, but he'd stopped moving. His arms hung pale and empty, and I knew that to have let all his weapons fall away, he was at best not conscious, at worst . . . I refused to finish the thought. There'd be time to think the unthinkable later.

The armored cops who had come in with the other guards lay scattered about the thing like discarded toys. The swimming pool lay just behind the thing, and its trail of destruction had taken out the pool house.

Frost's silver hair blew in a shining curtain. One arm hung limp at his side, but he'd won his way to the creature's base. He plunged Winter Kiss into one moving piece, and a tentacle came swinging out of the mass and smashed into him, tossing him back to bounce against the wall. He lay in a broken heap where he landed. Only Galen's hand on my arm kept me from running to him.

'Look,' Galen said.

Where the sword still stood in the thing's flesh, a white spot was growing. When it was the size of a large table I realized it was frost and ice. Winter Kiss was exactly that. But the Nameless struck at the blade and sent it spinning off behind itself. The growing spot of cold remained, but ceased to grow.

I looked for Doyle, and found him like a pool of blackness beside the turquoise of the water. Blood spread like a drowning puddle from underneath him. He raised himself on one arm, and the thing hit him casually, knocking him into the water. He vanished from sight without so much as his hand surfacing. He just fell into the blue water and was gone.

Galen jerked me around to face him, hands grabbing my arms so hard that it hurt. 'Swear to me that you won't go within its reach.'

'Galen . . .'

He shook me. 'Swear to me, swear it!'

I'd never seen him so fierce, and I knew he wouldn't let me go to help them, and he wouldn't help them himself until I'd promised.

'I swear it.'

He drew me in and gave me a fierce, almost bruising kiss, then handed me to Kitto. 'Stay with her, keep her alive.'

Then he and Nicca exchanged a look and drew their guns. Lucy and the officer did the same thing, and they fanned out in a line and started shooting. It was easy not to hit Rhys; there was so much monster to aim at.

They fired until their guns clicked empty. The creature waded into them, and Lucy managed to dodge for the house, but the older uniform was picked up by things that looked like giant taloned hands but were not quite that. Those huge claws ripped into him, sending blood through the air in a bright arch of crimson. The man's scream was sharp, pain filled, horror filled; then came silence, abrupt silence, and I swear I could hear the sound of tearing cloth, the thicker sound of tearing flesh, the wet pop of bone as the thing ripped the dead man in half and flung him in our direction.

Kitto flung himself on top of me and pressed me under his smaller bulk as the body parts flew overhead, spraying blood so that it pattered his clothes like rain.

When I could raise my head enough to see the fight again, Nicca and Galen had each drawn sword and dagger, one for each hand. They began to circle it, each to one side – but how do you circle something that has multiple eyes and multiple limbs?

I don't know if the other blades had hurt it badly enough that it didn't want to chance more, or if it was simply tired of being pricked, but it struck not with limbs, but with magic. Nicca was suddenly covered in a white mist. When the mist cleared he was motionless on the ground. I didn't have time to see if he was still breathing because the Nameless rushed Galen, who stood his ground. No one had ever accused Galen of cowardice.

I yelled his name, but he never turned, and I didn't want to distract him from the fight; I just wanted to keep him safe.

I started struggling to get up off the ground, and Kitto finally stopped hindering and started helping me. Galen didn't have a magic weapon of any kind; I had to do something. I walked forward and Kitto grabbed me back. I tried to jerk free, turning in my bare feet to order him to let me go, but I slipped on the bloody ground, falling butt first onto the slick grass. My hands came away covered in blood — fresh, crimson blood like rain on the grass that hadn't soaked in yet. My left palm began to itch, then to burn. It was the blood of the Nameless, and it was as poisonous as the rest of it.

I got to my feet, trying to scrape the blood off my hand with my dress, but it didn't help. The burning had sunk into my hand, my skin, and it was flowing through my veins, feeling as if all the blood in my body had turned to molten metal, solid and burning hot, as though my own blood was boiling its way out of my skin.

I shrieked in pain, and Kitto touched me, tried to help. He yelled and let go of me, staggered back. The front of his T-shirt bloomed red, fresh blood. He clawed at his shirt, raised enough for me to see the marks of my nails spilling blood everywhere, worse, so much worse than the original injury.

433

My cousin Cel was Prince of Old Blood. He could call any injury to life no matter how ancient. But it was only ever as bad as the original hurt. This was something different. Doyle had told me once that I would have a second hand of power, but there was no way of knowing when it would manifest or what it would be. The pain in my own body was receding as Kitto bled. But I didn't want Kitto to bleed. I wanted the Nameless to bleed.

If I had to touch the Nameless for this new hand of power to work, I was going to die, but I was going to try with magic like you'd try with a gun. Shoot from far away before you're forced to shoot up close. And as long as you have the ammunition, keep shooting.

I pointed my left hand toward the creature, palm out, and thought, not the word *blood* but *of* blood. I thought about the taste of it, salty, metallic; the feel of it fresh and almost scalding hot in large doses, the way it thickened when it cooled. I thought of the smell of blood – that neck-ruffling scent – and the way enough of it freshly spilled always smelled like meat, like raw hamburger.

I thought of blood and began to walk toward the Nameless.

Chapter 44

I'D TAKEN ONLY A FEW STEPS WHEN THE PAIN returned, my blood boiled in my veins, and I stumbled to my knees, hand still out toward the creature – but I was betting that Kitto had stopped bleeding. I screamed and watched one huge eye swivel to look at me, to truly look at me for the first time. The pain clouded my vision and finally stole my voice, my air. I was suffocating on pain. Then it eased, just a bit, then a bit more. When my vision cleared, blood was trickling out of the wounds in the mountain of flesh, trickling out not like blood should flow, but like water, faster, thinner. The last of my pain vanished as blood began to pour out of every wound the creature had sustained that day. Every bullet hole, every blade mark burst scarlet. The blood began to rain down the sides of the thing.

The Nameless began to move toward me, ponderous, and unnerving like watching a mountain roll toward you. I knew if it reached me, it would kill me, so I had to stop that from happening.

I thought not of blood alone, but of wounds; I thought not *bleed* but *die*. I wanted it to die.

A wound opened like a new mouth, slashing down its side, then another, and another. It was as if some giant invisible blade was hacking at it. The blood flowed faster, until the Nameless was covered in a slick red coat from top to bottom, covered in a dress of its own blood. Then blood gushed out of it in a nearly black wave, like a lake being dumped out upon the grass. It spilled and flowed and billowed toward me, until I knelt in a hot pool of blood, and still it bled.

The more it bled, the calmer I became. A stillness filled my body, almost a peacefulness. I knelt in the growing spread of blood, watching the thing quiver toward me, and I had no fear. I felt nothing, was nothing, but the magic. In that one instant I lived, breathed, and was one spell. The hand of blood rode me, used me, as surely as I had tried to use it. With the old magicks, who is master and who is slave is never sure.

The Nameless rose above me like a great bloody mountain, one curl of its body reaching out, out toward me, and only a few yards away, I heard it take a breath, a sharp sound, almost a sound of fear, then it exploded, not its body, but as if every last ounce of blood in that vast shape had burst forth at one time. The air became blood, and it was like trying to breathe underwater. For a second I thought I would drown, then I was choking in air and trying to spit out blood at the same time.

Something large hit the side of my head, and I fell to the bloody ground. Even in its death throes it had tried to take me with it. Kitto's crimson-washed face with a blood-soaked Sage on his shoulder was the last thing I saw before darkness swallowed the world.

Chapter 45

I WOKE TO FLOATING. I WAS FLOATING IN MIDAIR, and at first I thought it was a dream. Then I saw Galen floating just out of reach. I woke to find that all the fey in the yard were floating. Magic was everywhere, streaming through the air like multicolored fireworks, flying around us in flocks of fantastic birds that never knew mortal sky. Entire forests rose and fell before our eyes. The dead rose and walked and faded. It was like watching someone else's dreams and nightmares march through the bright California sunshine. It was raw enchantment with no hand to contain it or order it about; it was simply magic, everywhere.

And that magic was spilling into Rhys, Frost, Doyle, Kitto, Nicca, even Sage. I watched a phantom tree float over Nicca's body and vanish inside him. Sage was covered by a flowering vine. The dead men all went to Rhys and marched into him while he screamed. Frost was hidden by what looked like snow. He hit at it with his good arm, but he couldn't stop it. I caught a glimpse of Doyle half-hidden behind something black and serpentine; then the magic finally found Galen and me as we hung there only a few feet from each other. We were hit by scents and bursts of color. I smelled roses, and blood appeared on my wrist as if by the prick of thorns. I think the others were regaining what they'd given up to the Nameless, but neither Galen nor I had given anything to it. I thought it would pass us by because of that, but it turned out I was wrong. Wild magic had been freed, and it wanted to be somewhere in someone again.

Something white like a great bird rose from the bloody mess and came for me like it had a purpose. Galen yelled, 'Merry!' and the glowing shape smashed into me, through me, but not out the other side. For an instant I saw the world through crystal and mist. I smelled something burning, then darkness again.

By the time Galen and I were conscious again, the others had bound the Nameless into the soil, into the water, into the very air. They had bound it as it was meant to be bound. It couldn't be killed, but it couldn't be allowed to heal and go free either.

Maeve Reed had graciously allowed us to use some of her plentiful estate as the burial place, though that wasn't exactly what we did. It was both buried on her land and not buried in any land. It was trapped in a place betwixt and between.

Maeve offered us permanent use of her guest house, which was bigger than most people's entire homes. It solved the problem of a bigger apartment, and kept us within reach in case Taranis thought up some new way to attack Maeve.

I'd always thought that Andais was the crazy

one, but I've changed my mind. Taranis is willing to do anything to save himself, anything. That's not the way a good king thinks. Bucca-Dhu is in Unseelie protective custody. We've had to tell Andais everything. We have a witness to what Taranis did, but that's not enough to overthrow a thousand-year reign. It will be a political nightmare to tiptoe around. But he cannot be allowed to remain in power.

Taranis is still insisting I come for a visit to his court. I don't think so.

Rhys laid the hungry ghosts easily. He's regained the powers that the Nameless had taken from him, and so have all the others. But what does that mean?

It means that Rhys talks to empty rooms . . but if they are empty, why do voices answer him from the empty air? Frost can put a tracery of his namesake on my summer window, a spread of icy lace he uses to draw pictures for me. Doyle can vanish in plain sight, and none of us can find him. I am assured he is not invisible, but he might as well be. Nicca caused a tree to explode into blossom months off schedule . . . just by leaning against it. Kitto talks to snakes now. They slither out of the grass to greet him like you'd greet a king. It is positively unnerving how many snakes there are that you never see unless they wish you to see them. Sage has kept a single jasmine blossom alive and fragrant for two weeks with no water. The flower just sits tucked behind his ear and shows no sign of fading.

As for Galen and me – touched by so much wild magic, none of it our own – we don't know yet. Doyle thinks the new powers will come a little at a time. My second hand of power has well and truly come. All I need is a small wound and I can call all the blood from a being's body. I am Princess of Flesh and Blood. The hand of blood hasn't been seen as a power since the days of Balor of the Evil Eye. For those of you not up on pre-Celtic history, that's thousands of years before the birth of Christ.

The queen is pleased with me. She was in such a good mood that I got her to give me the men. Prince Cel has his own private guard; she has hers. Shouldn't I have mine? Andais agreed, so everyone who comes my way is mine. I'm keeping them all.

I promised Frost that I would keep him safe, that I would keep them all safe. A princess should always keep her promises.

Andais is sending more guards to help ensure my safety. I asked to be allowed to choose who they will be, but she wasn't that happy with me. I asked that Doyle be allowed to choose, and she refused that, as well. I think the Queen of Air and Darkness has her own agenda, and she will send who she wishes. I can do nothing about it but wait and see who shows up at my door.

There are gentle nights with my green knight, Galen mine at last. My Darkness is still as dangerous as he ever was, but underneath I get glimpses of his pain and his resolution to better things for us all. Rhys has changed and is no longer my laughing lover, nor does he wish to share me with Nicca. It's as if with Rhys's returned powers he's grown more serious, more compelling. There is simply more to him now, more magic, more desire, more force.

Nicca is still just Nicca. Lovely, gentle, but not strong enough.

Kitto, too, has grown and changed. He is more. I watch him grow into his power with something like awe.

Then there is Frost. What can you say of love, for love it is, but I am still without a child.

I performed a fertility rite that brought life to another sidhe's womb, but my own remains empty. Why? If I was truly infertile, the spell would have failed, but it did not.

I must be with child soon or none of the rest matters. Yule has come and gone, and we have only two months left of Cel's imprisonment. Will he be insane when he is released? Will he throw all caution away and try to kill me? Best to be pregnant before Cel gets out. Rhys has suggested we hire an assassin to slay Cel the moment he gets free. If it weren't for the queen's anger and grief I might almost agree. Almost.

I kneel at my altar and I pray. I pray for guidance, and I pray for luck, good luck. Some people will wish someone luck, but they don't say which kind. Always be careful when you pray, because deity is listening and will usually give you what you ask for, not what you *meant* to ask for. Goddess grant us good luck and a fertile winter.

THE END

Laurell K. Hamilton is the *New York Times* best-selling author of the first novel starring Meredith Gentry, *A Kiss of Shadows*, which is also published by Bantam Books, and the acclaimed Anita Blake Vampire Hunter novels. She lives in St. Louis, Missouri, with her family.

A KISS OF SHADOWS
By Laurell K. Hamilton

My name is Meredith Gentry, but of course it's not my real name. I dare not even whisper my true name after dark for fear that one hushed word will travel over the night winds to the soft ear of my aunt, the Queen of Air and Darkness. She wants me dead. I don't even know why . . .

I fled the high court of Faerie three years ago and have been in hiding ever since. As Merry Gentry, I am a private investigator for the Grey Detective Agency: Supernatural Problems, Magical Solutions. My magical skills, scorned at the courts of Faerie, are valued in the human world. Even by human standards, my magic isn't flashy, which is fine by me. Flashy attracts attention and I can't afford that.

Rumour has it that I am dead. Not quite. I am Princess Meredith NicEssus. To speak that name after dark is to call down a knock upon your door from a hand that can kill you with a touch. I have been careful, but not careful enough. The shadows have found me, and they are going to take me back home, one way or another.

So the running is over. But the fighting has just begun . . .

Rich, sensual, brimming with dangerous magic, *A Kiss of Shadows* is a dazzling tour-de-force where folklore, fantasy and erotically charged aventure collide.

'Relentless high-paced trashiness – it's good fun'
SFX

'A glorious erotic, funny and horrific novel . . . but it's probably not one for your granny'
Shivers

A Bantam Paperback

0 553 81383 8

THE DRAGON QUEEN
by Alice Borchardt

You must understand, my name was not written down. Those who say and sometimes write it use what form they care to. So the spellings sometimes differ greatly. So much so that it might seem as though I had many different names; but in reality, I still have only one. And, like all true names, it was a word of power . . .

It is that time known as the Dark Ages. The Romans have abandoned Britain's shores, leaving behind a country riven by terrible strife, warfare, superstition and wild magic. Born into this cruel world, Guinevere, daughter of a mighty pagan queen, is both a threat to her people and a prize to the dread, power-crazed sorcerer Merlin.

Sent into hiding, Guinevere grows up under the protection of a shape-shfting man-wolf and a cantankerous druid, watched over by dragons. Yet through his dark arts, the malign, all-seeing Merlin tracks her down. For he knows her extraordinary destiny and will stop at nothing to prevent what has been foretold. He knows that should Guinevere become queen and Arthur king, they will bring a peace to this ravaged land that will leave him powerless, a shrivelled husk of a man in a weary cloak.

But Guinevere is no mere mortal. She has inherited dazzling powers of her own – powers she must learn to control, yet strong enough to rival Merlin's own. With Arthur trapped in a netherworld from which the only escape is seemingly death, Guinevere must face the sorcerer's wrath alone. Summoning a magic she barely understands and ancient spirits who walked upon this earth when it was still young, she, who will one day sit upon the dragon throne, confronts her destiny . . .

Interlacing a keenly felt sense of history with soul-stirring fantasy, *The Dragon Queen* – the first book in a magnificent trilogy – is an exciting, richly told and wonderfully subversive reworking of a legendary tale.

'A fully fledged work of the fantastic that is wildly imaginative and astonishinly exhilirating'
Interzone

0 593 05062 2

NOW AVAILABLE FROM BANTAM PRESS

THE FIFTH SORCERESS
By Robert Newcomb

'Only the four Mistresses remained from the hundreds she had loved, lost and left behind. Soon, my dear Sisters, she thought. So many shall pay. Pay for the sins of their ancestors . . .'

It is three centuries since the devastating war that all but destroyed the kingdom of Eutracia. Those who masterminded the bloodshed – four powerful, conquest-hungry sorceresses – were banished and sent into exile beyond the feared Sea of Whispers, with return all but impossible, death all but inevitable. Since those dark days, Eutracia has flourished, protected and guided by its council of wizards. Now a land of peace and plenty, it is about to crown a new king and the spirit of celebration fills every heart. Except one.

Prince Tristan is a reluctant monarch-to-be. Though born with the endowed blood that will enable him to master magic, and destined to succeed his father as ruler of this land and its people, he is a rebel soul.

But more than tradition compels Tristan to ascend the throne. The very survival of Eutracia depends upon it. For after these long years of peace, dreadful omens have begun to appear, heralding something too unspeakable to ponder. It seems an ancient evil, nurtured over centuries of darkness, has returned and is thirsting for blood, for domination and, above all, for revenge. Tristan's fate is to fulfil a role chosen for him by an ages-old prophecy – to face an adversary whose hatred knows no bounds and whose greatest weapon is the person he loves most . . .

Not since Terry Goodkind unsheathed the *Sword of Truth* has such a tale of heroism and magic so captured the imagination. Brimming with excitement and wonder, dark intrigue and dread enchantments, *The Fifth Sorceress* marks the beginning of a magnificent fantasy adventure by a remarkable new storyteller.

0 593 04961 6

AMERICAN EXORCISM
Expelling demons in the land of plenty
by Michael W. Cuneo

There is perhaps no other religious ritual more fascinating, or more disturbing, than exorcism.

This is particularly true in America today, where the ancient rite has a surprisingly strong hold on the popular imagination. Whether conducted by officially appointed exorcists, maverick priests or Episcopal charismatics, it seems exorcism is alive and well in this new millennium. The archdiocese of Chicago recently appointed its first full-time exorcist in its 160 year history, while in New York four priests have officially investigated forty cases of suspected demonic possession every year since 1995.

Having attended more than fifty exorcisms and interviewed those who took part, Michael Cuneo brings this fascinating phenomenon vividly to life, conjuring up memories of the infamous film and other bizarre (and occasionally stomach-churning) images.

Exploring this strange netherworld of American life, including such provocative topics as the 'Satanic Panics' of the 1980s, repressed memory and ritual abuse, Cuneo reflects on the meaning of exorcism today and the relationship between religious ritual and popular culture. The result is a remarkably revealing, occasionally disconcerting but always entertaining work of cultural commentary.

'A pioneering work of extraordinary depth and insight'
Father Andrew M. Greeley

A Bantam Paperback

0553 81419 2

A SELECTED LIST OF FINE WRITING
AVAILABLE FROM TRANSWORLD

40488 1	FORWARD THE FOUNDATION	Isaac Asimov	£6.99
81244 0	DARKNESS PEERING	Alice Blanchard	£5.99
14775 3	THE EXORCIST	William Peter Blatty	£6.99
05062 2	THE DRAGON QUEEN	Alice Borchardt	£10.99
14871 7	ANGELS & DEMONS	Dan Brown	£5.99
81419 2	AMERICAN EXORCISM	Michael Cuneo	£6.99
14807 5	BELGARIAD 1: PAWN OF PROPHECY	David Eddings	£6.99
81217 3	GARDENS OF THE MOON	Steven Erikson	£5.99
81311 0	DEADHOUSE GATES	Steven Erikson	£6.99
81312 9	MEMORIES OF ICE	Steven Erikson	£6.99
14675 7	RAVENHEART	David Gemmell	£6.99
14877 6	DYING TO TELL	Robert Goddard	£6.99
77080 9	FINDING HELEN	Colin Greenland	£6.99
81383 8	A KISS OF SHADOWS	Laurell K. Hamilton	£5.99
14623 4	THE RETURN	Andrea Hart	£5.99
81272 6	THE TREATMENT	Mo Hayder	£5.99
14986 1	UNTO THE WICKED	Dylan Jones	£5.99
14584 X	THE COLD CALLING	Will Kingdom	£5.99
14585 8	MEAN SPIRIT	Will Kingdom	£5.99
81222 X	MYSTIC RIVER	Dennis Lehane	£6.99
14870 9	DANGEROUS DATA	Adam Lury & Simon Gibson	£6.99
50588 2	TO HOLD INFINITY	John Meaney	£5.99
50589 0	PARADOX	John Meaney	£6.99
81284 X	LET THERE BE LITE	Rupert Morgan	£6.99
04961 6	THE FIFTH SORCERESS	Robert Newcomb	£10.99
81258 0	WALKING ON WATER	Gemma O'Connor	£5.99
50581 5	STONE DANCE OF THE CHEMELEON 1: THE CHOSEN	Ricardo Pinto	£6.99
81216 5	GATES OF FIRE	Steven Pressfield	£6.99
99777 3	THE SPARROW	Mary Doria Russell	£7.99
14766 4	NIGHT VISITOR	Gillian White	£5.99